PLEASE DIAL AGAIN

Over three minutes later, Mission Control gave the crew of the space laboratory their recommendation to go ahead with the contact attempt. Salwi looked across at Sheilagh.

"Ready," she called calmly.

Salwi pressed the button once again.

At that instant, the whole craft shook with a terrible violence. The screens on the console shattered, and a great arc of electricity shot out of the accelerator as it burst open. Moments later the laboratory was in darkness. Sheilagh and Salwi, their feet still under the bar beneath the console, swayed gently, their bent arms floating up in front of them. Droplets of blood were scattered over the remains of the shattered console.

THE VOICE OF CEPHEUS

Ken Appleby

A Del Rey Book
BALLANTINE BOOKS • NEW YORK

A Del Rey Book
Published by Ballantine Books

Library of Congress Catalog Card Number: 89-91793

ISBN 0-345-36269-1

Printed in Canada

First Edition: December 1989

Cover Art by David B. Mattingly

PART ONE

11 1010 1100 1101 0110 0010 1010 1001 1111 0100 1100 1110 0100
11 0110 0011 0011 0100 0001 1010 1010 1110 0101 0011 0010 1000

3ACD62A9F4CE4
363341AAE5328

1034460768193764
0953500367213352

CHAPTER 1

WITH THE BARE SILHOUETTES OF CHESTNUT TREES sliding over its sleek surface, a gray Jaguar saloon quietly approached an old mansion in southwest England. Professor Adrian Holdsworth looked up at the graceful white radio dish facing the sky from behind the fake battlements and noticed with concern the spreading rust stains disfiguring its sides. He turned the car into a reserved parking space at the front of the building and got out stiffly.

Passing the desk in the entrance hall, he was hailed by the porter from the office within.

"Happy anniversary, Professor Holdsworth."

He turned toward his uniformed greeter, who had emerged from the back room and stood grinning behind the desk.

"Good afternoon, Jack. What anniversary might that be?"

"Thirty years to the day, sir."

The professor's smoothly shaved chin jerked forward, and his bushy eyebrows came closer together in a wordless expression. "What the devil do you mean?"

Jack straightened his back. "Thirty years to the day, sir, since your telescope was started. It don't seem like it, do it?"

"Good grief! Is it really?"

Jack had unwittingly reminded the professor that in all that time, the Springley Castle radio telescope had produced precisely nothing in the way of positive results.

Springley Castle was a Victorian manor built in ostentatious

3

imitation of a medieval fortified house and was currently the property of the University of Avon. Its extensive grounds were used for agricultural research programs, and its rooms had been turned into echoing laboratories. Professor Holdsworth, as head of the department of radio astronomy, had been responsible for the construction of an eighty-foot-diameter radio telescope there in 1963, taking advantage of the site's relative isolation from built-up areas.

In 1981 the telescope had been the first in Europe to be dedicated to the search for signals from extraterrestrial civilizations. The professor had used his own substantial resources, gained from the royalties on two of his patents, to finance the telescope's much-needed restoration and consequently had persuaded the Science and Engineering Research Council to fund his new project. In 1991—being seventy at the time, with an independent income, and wishing to make room for younger people—he had retired from the chair of radio astronomy, but he remained associated with the department in order to continue his project. Under his tutorship, four successful doctoral theses had been produced. The fifth was the task of Sheilagh Matthews, who was just beginning her three-year course.

After rather absently taking his leave of the security guard, Professor Holdsworth headed toward the two rooms allocated to his project at the far end of the south wing. He was used to the discomfort caused by reminders of the passing of the decades and normally never let such thoughts trouble him for long. This time, however, he allowed himself a rare few seconds of indulgent reminiscence as he passed through the dark and familiar corridors. He was grateful to his old friend Jack for reminding him that it was time to put his new student to a little test.

As he entered the tiny office, Sheilagh was deep in study over a computer printout.

"I've just been informed that today marks the beginning of my thirty-first year at this place. Feels more like thirty days sometimes."

"Well, congratulations, Professor," Sheilagh said in her gentle Scottish accent. "May the next thirty be just as fruitful." In the brief three weeks they had worked together she and the professor had adopted an easy familiarity that made light of the half century that separated their ages.

He moved over to the high window and gazed out across the leaf-strewn lawn to the telescope building, his hands clasped behind his back.

"Fruitful, you say? Actually, I was just pondering that on my way in. I suppose four fully fledged doctors of philosophy sent forth to spread the good word of science could be regarded, if you don't mind your metaphors mixed, as fruits. Unripe fruits, of course. But this project—what is it now?—eleven, no, twelve years and not a single positive result." He turned and shot an inquiring look at her. "What do you make of that?"

Sheilagh looked up confidently at her tutor. "To me it's not a negative result to have shown that the galaxy probably contains no advanced civilization that is trying to make contact with others. It's a positive result of great significance to the world."

The professor was greatly pleased though not surprised by her response. It was a question he put to all his students early in their studies. Sheilagh had already thought through the significance of what they were doing, and he marveled that such a young person could embrace with such ease ideas that encompassed whole galaxies and civilizations. What a shame she would be his last student, now that the project was almost obsolete.

Her predecessors had completed the original task, that of searching the whole sky visible to the Springley antenna at a broad range of frequencies in the microwave spectrum. There remained only this one last effort to squeeze the last drop of performance out of the aging hardware. The first stage of her three-part project was to improve the sensitivity of the detector by designing and building a new microwave amplifier very finely attuned to the antenna's imperfect physical shape.

The second stage would be to extend and improve the signal-processing computer. Looking for very narrow-band, or monochromatic, signals in a broad radio frequency band required huge amounts of processing power if it was to be done in real time. The professor's computer did that by using thousands of transputers all working in parallel. The transputer was a multiprocessing element that could be connected into huge arrays to attack the problem at high speed. By replacing the existing ones with the latest version, they could quadruple the number of frequencies to be searched.

Those changes would greatly increase the telescope's power, and Sheilagh would be repeating the sky survey at all frequencies in stage three, during her final year.

He walked around the desk and peered over her right shoulder at the printout. Funny, he thought, how after all these years of high-resolution graphics workstations, people still can't work without paper printouts!

"Have you made any progress with the signal-processing software?"

"Yes. It's fairly straightforward, I think. It does look as if it's been written by several different people at separate times. There are some strong contrasts of style here."

"Quite right, though only two people actually." He leaned forward and peered at the thick stack of pages. "It was first started by Colin Rudge in, let me see, 1987. Then Bill Tomlinson took over. I think they were both unfamiliar with the transputer and multiprocessing. Their styles probably evolved a bit as they learned."

"I suppose I've got an advantage over them, having had my hands on transputers as an undergraduate. I think I may be able to make some improvements to speed it up once I get to know all its nooks and crannies."

He straightened up. "Every microsecond helps."

Speed of processing was vitally important because of the vast quantities of data that would be pouring out of the telescope receiver. The telescope was scanned across the sky by the Earth's rotation. In twenty-four hours it covered one complete narrow band, and every day at the same time it was moved up or down in declination to point at the next one. The computers received and analyzed the signals as they came in. With a more sensitive receiver, there would be a large increase in the number of signals to analyze, and so the computers would have to work harder. The analysis routines were very sophisticated and would alert an operator whenever anything interesting was found. The original idea had been to divert the telescope from its static scan and track the target of interest as it moved across the sky with the Earth's rotation. However, because the telescope's old and worn bearings no longer permitted it to move outside one particular narrow azimuth band, that had become impossible.

"Incidentally, Professor," Sheilagh said, twisting in her chair to meet his eyes, "how many targets do you normally expect to get in one twenty-four-hour scan?"

He looked down at her, mildly surprised. "None. That's been the average recently. Since Colin's day the system has been very predictable. Why? Have you been running the system?"

"I did run it for a couple of nights. I wanted to see the processing software run in real time, so I just turned on the system to get some live signals."

"And you got a target?" Professor Holdsworth's surprise increased both at her initiative and at the implication that the system had found something.

"Oh, I was probably using it incorrectly. But there was one target that passed all stages of analysis. All versions of the software that I ran gave it the *meep-meep* status, which I take it is Bill Tomlinson language for possible little green persons."

"Did they, by Jove?" The professor was amazed to feel an unfamiliar surge of adrenaline, but his natural caution prevailed over his brief excitement. "I fear, however, that it was probably just a new satellite up there. Although Colin's software gets the satellite information automatically from the Admiralty's data base, there are always lots of unannounced military launches that no one admits to."

Sheilagh was frowning.

"What did the target summary say?" he asked.

She pulled another printout from under a pile. "I just left the channel selections and antenna position where they were. The frequencies centered on the zero Doppler hydrogen line, and the declination was at sixty degrees. The target showed up at, let's see, 21 hours 55 minutes right ascension."

The professor found a place for the target in the sky model he had built up over the years in his mind's eye while Sheilagh continued to read from the summary.

"It started in channel 4104389, so it was very close to the central frequency, and passed through the next 1,205 higher channels in about twenty minutes. The Doppler rate was equivalent to an average of 5.3 centimeters per second squared and decreased a few points during the traverse."

"Signal width?"

"Less than one channel; less than one hertz. There was no significant modulation or pulsing."

In the latter days of the project the extra processing power available had made it possible for the analyzer to eliminate most interference sources. Known sources were added to a data base that was used to filter out likely false alarms. The analyzer could handle over 8 million channels simultaneously—at the same rate that the antenna was providing the signals—in "real time." Any target that the computer came up with was always very significant and needed to be followed up. The "Doppler rate" Sheilagh had mentioned was a measure of how quickly the speed of the source was changing. If the source was in orbit around a star, the signal would be expected to show a changing frequency as it moved alternately toward the Earth and then away. Unless, that is, the transmitter was designed to compensate for that.

The lines on the professor's forehead deepened, and he reached for the paper in Sheilagh's hands. "That's a textbook target. And, moreover, it is a target we've seen before, I think. If memory serves me correctly, that is very close to a target in Cepheus that was seen, oh, three years ago. We tracked it for a few days, then it disappeared."

Sheilagh nodded. "I thought it was surprising myself. It's appeared twice so far. The first time was two nights ago."

"What!"

She pulled out another piece of paper. "Last night it was still there, showing pretty much the same characteristics. The Doppler rate is down to 5.1 centimeters per second squared. It has perfect sidereal timing, so it's unlikely to be man-made noise unless it's a distant planetary probe. But that declination is way out of the ecliptic, so it's unlikely."

Sidereal timing was important if a target was to be classed as possibly alien. It referred to the fact that because the Earth orbits the sun in 365 days, the time it takes to rotate on its axis with respect to the stars, rather than the sun, is four minutes short of twenty-four hours. That was the so-called sidereal day.

"It may be Cepheus 8 resurrected, in which case we could be in for an interesting few days," the professor said, looking proudly at his student. But inwardly he expected that there would be a perfectly normal explanation. There always was.

"It's most likely to be a new satellite that some uncivil so-and-so has plonked in our sky. You just left the antenna pointing straight up, you say?"

"Well, it's parked a few degrees north of the zenith. Like I said, the declination is sixty degrees, so we could check it again right now, perhaps?"

The professor shook his head slowly. "Sadly, no. Our venerable polar bearings groaned their last many years ago. We must rely upon the angular momentum of our good Earth to bring it once more into view, which in my experience we can safely do. The only question is, will the target still be there? The good ones have a damned annoying habit of disappearing just as you get a good fix on them. But if it is still there and it still looks real, then I'll get our friends in Massachusetts to take a good look at it. Mind you, they're about to close their project down any day now."

"That's the Denning telescope, you mean?"

"Yes."

"Why are they closing it down?"

"Principally because they have finished what they set out to do. They've reached the limit of their 'scope's abilities. Dr. Feinberg—he's in charge of the project—thinks they should move on to bigger things. Orbital telescopes or something of the sort."

"I suppose from Massachusetts they cover pretty much the same part of the sky as we do. Doesn't their failure to find anything rather bode ill for our chances?"

"Oh, now, don't be so pessimistic. If you can design a receiver that meets my specifications, then our 'scope will have four times the sensitivity of Feinberg's, and with the same size dish, that gives us an eight times bigger chunk of the galaxy for our search. Now, that doesn't sound too bad, does it? And in any case you may well have found us an alien signal already."

Sheilagh knew very well that it would be the professor's genius that would go into the new receiver design. Her only responsibility would be to build and test it. But his enthusiasm was encouraging.

"Shall we come in this evening?" she said.

"Yes, I think we should. If this chappie is still there, we'll get Feinberg onto it straight away."

Professor Holdsworth was certain that Sheilagh had come up with a false alarm, but he had seen in the past how the careful checking of a potential target was a wonderful lesson in technique. It also made the students realize that they were lucky to be working on a project that might make their names famous around the world. They all dreamed of being the first person to detect a signal from an alien civilization.

When he had started his project twelve years previously, the professor had never contemplated transmitting signals with the telescope even though that would have been easy to do. There was enough radio energy being beamed into space by radio and television stations, not to mention the military, to completely swamp anything that they might do at Springley, except possibly the beaming of signals to very specific stars. In any case, even if a response was going to come from somewhere, it would most likely not arrive for several centuries. He belonged to the school of thought that argued that humans were new to the galactic club and should play it quietly and learn the rules by listening in on the established members.

The strategy, then, was to scan the sky for likely signals. But what kind of signals? Back in 1959 Cocconi and Morrison, both then at Cornell University, had answered that question. They had decided that microwaves were the obvious choice. If one looked at the amount of energy that reached the Earth in all the forms of electromagnetic radiation—radio, microwave, infrared, visible light, ultraviolet light, x-rays, and gamma rays—it was apparent that nature was much better than man at making all of them, except microwaves. The sky was quiet at microwave frequencies. On the other hand, microwaves were easily generated artificially, and mankind had been doing just that ever since the war. So if other beings in the galaxy wanted to make themselves known, a microwave beacon would be easier to make and more easily seen against the background of natural sources than, for instance, a visible light beacon. Seen from afar, the simultaneous explosion of all the world's nuclear weapons once every minute would be like a firefly in a searchlight beam, whereas a very modest microwave transmitter could outshine the sun.

For the same reason that nature was not good at producing microwaves, it was also not good at stopping them, and so any signal would travel large distances across the galaxy before being completely absorbed or scattered.

There were a few natural producers of microwaves in the galaxy. Clouds of atomic hydrogen transmitted faint signals at a very precise wavelength—21.1 centimeters. Within those clouds, another signal at 18.0 centimeters was produced by the hydroxyl radical, OH, a molecule containing one atom of oxygen and one of hydrogen. Atomic hydrogen and OH together made H_2O—water. Their wavelengths sat on either side of the microwave energy minimum from the night sky, which had therefore become known as the "water hole." The cosmic water hole was expected to be the meeting place where intelligent civilizations would introduce themselves.

One of the problems was that for a beacon transmitting in all directions to be noticeable at great distances, it would have to be phenomenally powerful. The problem was lessened if the transmitter was made directional, broadcasting its power only in the directions most likely to bring a response, for example, the plane of the galaxy or the directions of individual stars.

Since the late eighties, several searches had been carried out around the world with telescopes sensitive enough to detect modestly powerful omnidirectional beacons out to a few thousand light-years. The volume of space covered contained billions of stars and represented about one percent of all the stars in the galaxy.

Despite the odds against discovering such a beacon, Professor Holdsworth privately admitted to being disappointed that alien signals had not been detected.

The professor returned to his car and set off for home. As he turned onto the main Bath-to-Wells road and engaged the autodrive, he reflected on the conclusions to be drawn from the negative results repeated many times all over the world.

One could only say that within a few thousand light-years of the sun, no civilizations were making themselves known with microwave beacons. Anything beyond that had to be speculation. One such speculation would have been that the Earth hosted the only intelligent life to have evolved in the galaxy. Or maybe others *had* developed but had not reached mankind's level yet. That was a sobering idea, he thought, especially as mankind had made such a bloody mess of it so far. Perhaps civilizations typically spent only a brief time at mankind's level before passing on to some state that was beyond detection and possibly beyond comprehension.

It was increasingly probable that the human race was destined to remain alone in the galactic wilderness, and that was a disturbing and deeply dissatisfying thought. He felt that mankind needed, subconsciously at least, to know that it was not alone. Prior to the sky surveys, it had always been possible to believe that we were not alone, because no one had seriously looked. Now, however, people had looked and failed to find.

The optimist, on the other hand, he thought, would say that the search has barely begun. We may have been searching the wrong frequencies or the wrong kind of radiation altogether. What about gravity waves or neutrinos? What were those strange x- and gamma-ray "bursters" all about? Maybe there were dozens of civilizations out there all busily listening but not one of them daring to advertise its presence.

But the question to be faced was where to look next. After Sheilagh's final survey perhaps it would be time to cease looking from the Earth's surface. Feinberg might be right, he thought. Perhaps we should wait until we have permanent bases on the Moon's far side, away from the noise of Earth. Perhaps we should think about using completely different kinds of detectors based on some of the implications of Russell Voss's new geonics theories.

The recollection of Russell Voss sent the professor's thoughts back to his only meeting with the man. He had seen Voss a year before, delivering a paper to a small conference of fellow scientists, and had been struck by the incredible intensity of the young man. A subsequent attempt to converse with him had resulted in an absurd and embarrassing disagreement, and the professor had come away with the impression of a man wholly obsessed by his very singular theories to the exclusion of all else, in particular the value of social interaction. The disagreement had arisen when the professor had carelessly hinted at his own view—that Voss's theories, because they were so mathematical and removed from experimental verification, were essentially untestable and therefore, by implication, of dubious actual value. He had immediately regretted that slip and had been rewarded with a display of ill-mannered, unconcealed contempt from Voss. That had of course only strengthened the professor's opinion. Nevertheless, Voss's theories were widely accepted as being immensely significant, and there was no doubt that the young man possessed by far the ablest mind seen in science for many decades.

The professor had been affected by his extraordinary brush with Voss, and the young man had never been far from his thoughts ever since. He wondered, not for the first time, what Voss's real opinion of the search for extraterrestrial signals was.

In the meantime he had a responsibility toward a young and very promising mind. Sheilagh could be the last student he ever tutored, and she might turn out to be the best. He could look forward to this, the last of his tutorships, with great pleasure. One day, perhaps Sheilagh would be among those brave and lucky people who would spend some of their lives on the Moon, pushing humanity's frontiers to the edge of the universe.

CHAPTER 2

AT SEVEN O'CLOCK THAT EVENING SHEILAGH WAS joined by the professor in the cramped and chilly control room next to the telescope tower, about a hundred feet past the south wall of Springley Castle's west wing.

Sheilagh had configured the software so that a graphic display of the energy being received on all channels was continuously displayed on the screen. There were four rows of narrow vertical bars, 2,048 of them in total. When all the data coming in were displayed, each bar represented the combined energy in 4,096 adjacent channels of the receiver. With a few moves of the cursor she could change the scale and zoom in on any part of the spectrum, right down to one channel per bar. At the top of the screen a wide window showed the coordinates of the center of the telescope's beam. Next to it was a small box displaying the results of the analysis.

"Now," the professor said, "I'd like to try something here. I'm going to look for polarization changes. If it really is an alien beacon, then it's not likely to be devoid of information. I've always favored the idea that they'd use circular polarization of the signal and change its direction from left to right as a way of encoding zeros and ones."

"Why?"

"Because circular polarization doesn't get scrambled by the interstellar medium so much, and it can be used without modulating the signal's amplitude, which would decrease its detection probability. Then there's something else we should do, and that is to waggle the antenna a bit to make sure the target's in the main lobe. We should be logging both the spectrum and the analysis results.''

"I've put a blank disk in the recorder's drive.''

"Good. Now, what time did the target first appear last night?''

"1916.''

"Well, that will be 1912 tonight if it really is sidereal. Let's start the data logging at 1910 just to be certain we don't miss anything.''

Moving the command cursor over the screen, he called up menus in swift sequence. He selected the start time and a data-recording interval of thirty seconds, which was the integration time of the analyzers.

"Hey, this is great,'' Sheilagh exclaimed, admiring the software. "I've not seen those before.''

"Bill Tomlinson's handiwork.''

"Clever lad!''

"Yes. I hope you get a chance to meet him some day.''

Using a well-known radio galaxy as a source, they practiced moving the antenna through a few degrees of declination so that Sheilagh could see the effect of the beam shape on the signal. To do that, they had temporarily switched the display inputs to a point before the analysis routines had subtracted known sources from the signal. The bars showed a very broad peak on the second row that rose and fell three times as the telescope's circular main beam and surrounding side lobe moved to and fro across the target. Then they returned the antenna back to its old position.

At 1910 they heard the faint scratchings of the disk as the incoming signals were logged. The four rows of bars showed a normal, low level of noise, each bar moving slightly up and down in a smooth motion unrelated to that of its neighbors.

A few seconds after 1912 the status box at the top of the screen changed from NO TARGET to CHANNEL 4278905 CLASS 1. Within a second, the class number displayed had jumped to 4 and a red mark appeared bracketing one of the bars.

Sheilagh felt her heart racing. Thank heavens, she thought. He's seen it now. It's no longer just me.

He zoomed in on the highlighted bar. In the expanded display there was nothing obvious to see.

The professor was unperturbed. "Not surprising. The signal's still very weak. It may have passed undetected through the side lobe. We'll have to wait until we can see it before we move the antenna. Don't want to lose it now.''

Again he moved swiftly through control menus. The display changed so that all the bars except one were motionless and at their minimum level. The one bar alternated slowly between maximum and minimum height for a while, then it became steady. He zoomed in again. There was still nothing to distinguish it.

''Computers can at last outperform the human eye at pattern recognition,'' the professor said. ''At least at the very specialized stuff.''

It was another fifteen minutes before they were able to discern anything special about the marked channel. The mark had been moving to the right as they watched.

''Right. Let's try a few degrees north.''

Above them the antenna, driven by electric motors, tilted imperceptibly toward the north polestar. Almost immediately the signal disappeared.

He reversed the motion of the antenna, and the bar began to show again distinctly above its neighbors. About once every two seconds the bar moved to the right. Occasionally it would broaden out to two, sometimes ten bars. Sometimes it all but disappeared for several seconds. He carefully tuned the antenna position until they both felt the signal was at a maximum.

''Fifty-five degrees, thirty-two minutes,'' Sheilagh said breathlessly.

The status box flashed up the message *meep-meep* a few times, and a little caricature of a green alien with tiny antennas appeared in the top right-hand corner of the screen. The terminal beeped twice. Sheilagh noticed that the alien's comic face bore more than a faint resemblance to the professor's, especially the eyebrows.

The signal held for about ten minutes before beginning to fade. After another fifteen minutes it disappeared altogether.

Professor Holdsworth stopped the recorder and sat back to look at Sheilagh.

''I'd be willing to bet my eyebrows that that little chappie is Cepheus 8 back from the depths. I can hardly believe it!''

He requested the computer to display the summaries for Cepheus 8 and the new target together on the screen. After a few seconds studying them he said, ''Well, Sheilagh, what do you think? Is that or is that not a match?''

''It certainly looks like it.''

The professor was beaming. "Sheilagh, my dear, you may or may not be the most promising student I have ever had, but you certainly appear to be blessed with the most amazing fortune."

"Just beginner's luck."

"My dear, have you ever been to the races?"

"Do you really think this is an alien signal, then?"

"Too early to tell that yet. It may be artificial. All I can say is that it is the first time a good-looking transient signal has returned. I must get Feinberg onto this right away."

He jumped up with an agility that surprised Sheilagh and, target summary in hand, made for the door.

Sheilagh turned off the power to the telescope, leaving just the computers running. She was investigating the data analysis menus when the professor returned.

"Miss Matthews, you are enough to make a hard-boiled skeptic turn to religion. Not only was Dr. Feinberg in his office, but the Denning 'scope is running and within a few minutes will be moved to our little target."

They spent the next hour running various signal-processing algorithms over the recorded data. The signal was very narrow band, practically monochromatic. About every two seconds it hopped to the next channel. They calculated from this that the source was accelerating at 4.8 centimeters per second squared. That figure, together with the base frequency, correlated perfectly with the previous two nights' results. They also found some tantalizing indications that the signal was circularly polarized.

"Okay, Sheilagh. Let's shut down and celebrate your luck at my home. Feinberg may be calling me any moment."

Twenty-five minutes later they were in the professor's study in his modern bungalow ten miles from the castle, sharing a decanter of claret with his wife, Doreen.

The telephone rang, and the professor put the call through the speaker.

"Walter, I've got Doreen here, and Sheilagh Matthews, who's my latest postgrad. She discovered the target a couple of nights ago."

After a brief exchange of greetings, Dr. Feinberg gave them the news in a strong American voice. "Well, Professor, we found your target almost immediately. It's Cepheus 8, all right. The guys here are climbing the walls with excitement. It's definitely extraterrestrial and definitely sidereal. The coordinates match the ones we got from Cepheus 8 three and a half years ago. We're getting a real good signal from it. Well done, you guys!''

Sheilagh's excitement grew, fed by the wine.

The professor directed his voice toward the speaker. "Is there any chance of getting some help over there? We would really like to get a good position for it. We found indications of circular polarization that may be modulated. We should move quickly; it's very likely to disappear again.''

"I'll call the NASA group. Their antenna is capable of monitoring polarization changes. For an accurate fix we really need Arecibo or the VLA to help. I'll get on that right away, Professor. In the meantime maybe you could try Shipston Grange.''

"I was planning to do that, Walter. I'll call Sir Maurice tonight.''

Afterward, Sheilagh again asked the professor what the chances were that they had found an alien signal.

Doreen interrupted before he could answer. "Fifty percent, I'll bet! He never says anything else when asked a question like that. Anything he's not absolutely sure of is fifty percent.''

The professor laughed. "Yes, you're quite right. We've got a lot of work to do before we can be sure of what we've found. Remember that this has happened before, and every time we've been able to prove nothing. This time, though, we have a chance of getting a really close look. But don't raise your hopes too high.''

"But what else could it be?'' Sheilagh asked.

"If it's not alien, it's most likely a military satellite. Feinberg will check that with the Pentagon. It may even be a natural astronomical source. At the moment we can only speculate. Now I must telephone Sir Maurice.''

The two women left the professor to make his call and walked into the living room.

"Does he mean Sir Maurice Preston?'' Sheilagh asked.

"I expect so, Sheilagh. They were at Cambridge together, you know.''

Sir Maurice Preston had the most respected name in radio astronomy in Britain. He was the director of the Radio Astronomy Institute at Shipston Grange, run by the University of York, which boasted 250-foot, 100-foot, and several smaller telescopes. Sheilagh was beginning to realize just how important her find might turn out to be.

The professor reappeared about thirty minutes later.

"They'll have the 250-foot onto it by tomorrow lunchtime.

They have to switch receivers for the new frequency. I fear, Sheilagh, that this is going to interrupt your work quite seriously at least for a few days. But I think it's important that we stay on top of events. I have arranged with Sir Maurice for you to help them up at Shipston tomorrow. You'd better go by train, judging by the noise your car makes. I'll have to stay here and hold the fort in case the US chaps call.''

''What? Me? Up at Shipston Grange? With Sir Maurice Preston?''

''Well, I don't suppose he'll be working on it himself, but I'm sure you'll meet him. Why, don't you want to go?''

''Oh, yes. I want to go.'' She looked slightly panicky. ''It's just a bit sudden, that's all. I'm not used to scientific progress being this rapid.''

''Only on very rare occasions is it. But this might just be the signal we've been searching for all these years. Like Doreen says, I'd give it a fifty percent chance. I'd prepare for a two- or three-day stay if I were you.''

Sheilagh drove home an hour later. She felt she had caught hold of a tiny thread that had suddenly grabbed her and dragged her off under its own will. Her intuition told her that her future had just changed, transformed by a chain of events that had started two nights previously.

She could not know then, and would not dare think, that those events were also going to change the future of the whole human race.

CHAPTER 3

THE LECTURE THEATER AT THE MASSACHUSETTS
Institute of Astronomy contained about a hundred members of
the Interplanetary Society, who slowly quieted as the speaker
approached the podium.

Dr. Walter Feinberg waited patiently for their attention. He
had given talks to the society in that room many times before,
and this, on October 16, 1993, was scheduled to be the final
report on his SETI project.

At the back of the room a video camera operator quietly started
recording and received a few puzzled looks from nearby members.

"Good morning, everyone."

The room was hushed.

"Eight years ago this society generously began sponsorship
of an exciting new research program, called Project Beta, that
set out to survey the sky for microwave signals coming from
galactic civilizations. The project was originally to have run for
just two years, but because of advances in electronic technology,
it proved possible to repeat the survey many times at ever greater
sensitivities. It has been my privilege to be the director of that
project for those eight years. I am here tonight to deliver the
final report on Project Beta, for last month the final sweep of
the sky was completed and Project Beta came to an end."

He pressed a button on the small controller in his left hand.
The room lights dimmed, and a picture appeared behind him of

the Denning telescope dish, thrusting out above the tree-covered slopes of a Massachusetts hillside. He moved away from the lectern toward the side of the screen.

"The project was set up to answer the question, Are there any civilizations nearby in the galaxy transmitting microwave signals to us specifically? This was soon changed, because of the increase in sensitivity of the equipment, to the following."

On the lower quarter of the screen appeared a sentence.

ARE THERE ANY CIVILIZATIONS IN THE GALAXY ATTEMPTING TO ATTRACT THE ATTENTION OF OTHERS BY USING MICROWAVE BEACONS?

He turned to the audience again and paused, timing his next statement carefully. "We now believe the answer to be yes."

He waited for the audience to appreciate what he had said. They were all expecting the same negative answer they had heard repeatedly and predictably over the preceding years. Murmurs of amazement ran through the audience. Heads turned left and right, and then everyone sat transfixed, ready for Feinberg to elaborate on his astounding statement.

"Just two days ago, in the very last scheduled week of Project Beta, I received a call from my friend Professor Adrian Holdsworth, who many of you will know has been performing a similar sky survey in England for many years. He gave me the approximate coordinates of a target that Sheilagh Matthews, one of his postgrads, picked up four days ago. He was fairly sure that it was the reappearance of an interesting target we last detected in 1990 and tracked for a few hours before it faded.

"I immediately had our telescope turned to look for Professor Holdsworth's target. In less than an hour we had detected it, and we successfully tracked it for another twenty hours as it moved at an exact sidereal rate across the sky.

"The signal fits all our criteria of alien origin." He paused, counting out several seconds to himself, as he had rehearsed earlier. "The human race is not alone!"

Someone in the audience whooped with excitement, and a lengthy and noisy burst of applause followed. At the back of the room someone picked up a telephone.

"However—" He held up a hand to quiet them. "—however," the signal has since disappeared."

This news was received with shocked but eager silence.

"It may be that we will recover it again one day. It has disappeared before, of course, so this may be a pattern."

He held up his notes. "I was scheduled to give you this, the final report on Project Beta, but I know you will forgive me if I concentrate on this exciting news. I have been able to prepare a few slides in the last hour that will help me explain what we have found so far.

"We have managed to do some detailed observations from the Arecibo telescope in Puerto Rico. You will appreciate that larger antennas mean narrower beams for pinpointing targets. The 1,000-foot Arecibo antenna was able to place our signal within three milliradians, or an area roughly one-tenth the size of the moon. Its position is this."

He turned as a new slide appeared on the screen, a photograph of a page from a sky atlas. It contained hundreds of different-sized black dots on a white background representing stars of various brightnesses. Two swirling bands of blue shading, one darker than the other, filled the lower left corner. Scattered around the slide were small, irregular blobs of color representing clouds of gas and dust. Just left of center, near the bottom of the screen and within the darker blue band, was a small, empty red circle. At the bottom of the screen appeared the coordinates of its center:

$$RA\ 21\ 07\ \pm\ 2\ Dec\ 56°\ 50'\ \pm\ 10'$$

"It's in Cepheus, near the junction with Cygnus and Lacerta. As you can see, this location is within one degree of the galactic equator. Its galactic longitude is 102 degrees, which is about 11 degrees east of the direction in which the sun is traveling in its motion around the galaxy. We don't know yet how far away the source is, except that it's definitely beyond the solar system. There are no bright or nearby stars in this direction, but there are thousands of very distant ones. The signal's wavelength was very close to the twenty-one-centimeter hydrogen line that we have been monitoring all these years, but it changed over the four days we were receiving it in a way consistent with the source being in an elliptical, possibly circular orbit around a star.

"The most convincing evidence that this truly was an alien signal is that it seems to have contained a message, which, I hasten to add, we have not deciphered yet. The signal was not modulated, but it was circularly polarized. This polarization reversed direction in a regular kind of way at an approximate rate of 0.1 hertz, or about once every ten seconds.

"This latest information I received from Puerto Rico only a couple of hours ago while I was preparing these slides, and I have not had time myself to study it. So you are getting a chance to look at this just as soon as I am."

Another slide appeared on the screen. At the top it showed a thin line rising and falling between two stationary levels in a nearly regular way. Underneath was a long row of the numbers, "0s" and "1s," at first glance in a random order, though with a preponderance of ones. Everyone in the audience stared at it intently.

"Is this the actual signal?" someone asked.

"Yes, it is. This is the polarization pattern. Where the line is high, it represents a period of right-handed polarization, or a "one," and where it is low, it represents a period of left-handed polarization, a "zero." Someone suggested that this sequence of alternating ones and zeros, three of each, may mark the beginning of the message. It may set up the timing for the rest of the signal. That would indicate a kind of binary encoding. But that's as far as we've gotten. There are three consecutive zeros exactly halfway along the string. I've counted the ones and zeros, and there are a total of 309—255 ones and 54 zeros. The only other feature immediately apparent is that you can divide the message into groups of three bits, and in every one, except those special groups, the first and last bit is a one.

"But whatever it means, there's not a lot of information here. Anyone expecting a flood of wonderful revelations is going to be disappointed."

"You mean that this is the entire message?" asked an incredulous voice.

"Er, yes. I'm sorry, I thought I'd mentioned that. Yes, this is the entire message. It was repeated over and over. Every fifty minutes or so."

The audience had started breaking up into small groups gesturing at the screen and arguing among themselves.

Dr. Feinberg moved back to the lectern and pressed a button that raised the lighting.

"Ladies and gentlemen. If you will bear with me for just a moment longer."

Slowly the audience became quiet.

"You will all be interested, I know, in the press conference that will be held jointly with Professor Holdsworth in England

and from this building in about forty-five minutes. The World News Network is carrying it live.

"As our society has been partly responsible for this historic achievement, I thought it appropriate that you should be informed first. You, ladies and gentlemen, are the first people outside the research teams to hear the news."

At Shipston Grange in Yorkshire, Bill Tomlinson was tapping his pencil on a copy of the alien message spread out on the table. Sheilagh was sitting on the edge of the table gazing down at the paper.

"You know what it looks like to me?" Bill said. "It's a navigation beacon, and this is its identification code. Or maybe it's a commercial: 'Drink Coke,' or 'Last Antimatter before Blackhole Freeway.'" He looked up at her expectantly through his steel-rimmed glasses.

Sheilagh laughed but was not inclined to continue his joking. "Come on, Bill, be serious. You heard Prof Preston. 'The most significant event in history,' he called it. You could show it a bit more respect."

He tugged at a forelock. "All right. What does Miss Matthews make of it?"

"It's quite simple." Sheilagh had made up her mind what the signal meant almost immediately after seeing it. "We received the signal at a frequency very close to the 'magic' frequency that most people in SETI have been saying is the best one to use. If they're right, that indicates it's almost certainly being transmitted at *exactly* the magic frequency by a slow-moving source; when we receive it, the slight variation is caused by Doppler shift."

"I'll buy that."

"Then we find that its polarization changes at a very slow rate. It must be intended as an attention grabber, a kind of lighthouse beacon."

"You still haven't told me what it means."

"Yes, I have. It's a lighthouse beacon, except that this beacon is flashing in a particular way that does more than just identify it. You see, it's in two parts. The first part is saying, 'This is how we represent the frequency, or wavelength, on which we are transmitting this signal.' The second part is saying, 'And this is the way we represent the frequency, or wavelength, of the other signal we are transmitting that contains our real message.'"

"But why not put the real message in this signal? Why go to the trouble of transmitting two signals?"

"That's easy. The first signal is probably transmitted by a directional antenna in order to concentrate more power in one direction at a time. That's why it keeps disappearing; they're sweeping the antenna across the sky just like a lighthouse and for the same reason. It's better to attract attention with a bright signal appearing at intervals than with a permanent weak one that may go unnoticed."

"Like the second signal?"

"Yes. The other signal is probably transmitted by an omni-directional antenna, because that's the only way a long message can be received without constant interruptions."

"Hey, yeah! Once they've picked up the first signal, the eager listener knows where to look for more!"

"And the first signal should therefore contain a pointer to the frequency. The Doppler shift of the first signal tells us the exact motion of the source, so we can work out the frequency of the second. Where's your calculator?"

He reached under a sheet of paper. "Here. This first signal tells us one more thing at least: the units they use to represent time or distance depending on whether this"—he indicated the first half of the message—"is a frequency or a wavelength."

Sheilagh stood up, dragged a chair over to the table, and sat down, pulling over a pad of paper.

"Okay, then if this is a frequency, how do we decipher it?" she asked.

"I would say," Bill said slowly, "that the leading group is there to set the timing, and the middle one is just a divider. It's a lot like asynchronous serial communications in computers. Without a common clock signal and no way to handshake, you'd need to know when each word starts and ends. It's my guess that the ones that start and end each group of three are your start and stop bits. So, let's see what we get if we just look at the middle bit of each group. You do the second half of the message and I'll do the first."

They each wrote down a series of ones and zeros that was composed of the middle bits of the groups of three.

"All right," Bill said, "let's suppose they are numbers. They each have fifty bits, which means they've got fifty binary significant figures." He picked up the calculator and hit a few keys. "That's about fifteen decimal figures."

"Just the accuracy to which we know the hydrogen line frequency," Sheilagh said. "If my idea is right, then the two numbers won't be very different. We would expect the other frequency to be near the first."

Bill scratched his scalp with the pencil. "The question is, how do we know that we've got the ones and zeros the right way around? Maybe right polarization means zero, and left means one?"

"And what order are the bits in?" Sheilagh said. "Is the most significant bit sent first or last?" She studied the sequences closely. "Let's rewrite them using R and L instead of one and zero."

They quickly rewrote the numbers using the two letters to avoid any unjustifiable connection between the polarization direction and the binary values.

"Okay," Sheilagh said, scrutinizing the new sequences. "They both begin with R and end with L. Now again, if my idea is right, they wouldn't send numbers with leading zeros at the most significant ends; that would make no sense. So either it's R equals zero and least significant first, or it's R equals one and most significant first."

"But look," Bill said, dropping his pencil and stabbing a finger at each of the sequences, "they're symmetrical! It doesn't matter which alternative you use. See? The sequences can be read front to back using Rs as ones *or* back to front using Ls—you get the same sequence. We've found it!"

Sheilagh saw with delight that he was right. Each number was transformed into the other when the meanings of the Rs and Ls were switched and the numbers were read in the opposite direction.

Bill hurriedly divided each string of fifty digits into groups of four, starting from the right. He then jotted down a number or letter beneath each group. Each number was then represented in hexadecimal, or to the base sixteen, assuming R represented one. The hexadecimal numbering system was a favorite of computer programmers because the conversion between it and binary was much simpler than was the case with base ten. Each hex digit covered four binary digits. The letters zero to nine had the same meaning as in decimal notation. The digits ten to fifteen were represented by the letters A to F.

Bill then used the calculator to convert the two numbers he had written down to decimal. Next he calculated their ratio and computed from that two possible frequencies for the second signal. He passed the calculator to Sheilagh.

"One point five four one gigahertz," Sheilagh read. "Well, that's very reasonable, slap bang in the middle of the water hole. And one point three zero nine gigahertz. Outside the water hole, of course. I like the first one, don't you?"

"It's a beauty," he answered, mimicking her accent. "Especially in a *heel*and accent! It certainly gives your idea a bit of weight. I wonder what the profs will think." He looked at his watch. "Nearly time for the press conference. Do you want to watch it? There's a television in the common room. Incidentally, why aren't you there? It's your discovery."

"Well, Professor Preston did ask me to be there. But, well, I didn't think I should, really. Not with television cameras and everything."

"It's being broadcast live all over the world, would you believe?"

"Yes, I know. And I'd really rather watch it somewhere more private and comfortable if possible."

"We could see it at my place. Cindy'll be home by now, and we can pick up some nosh on the way. How about it, then?"

"Okay."

Twenty minutes later they sat with Bill's wife, Cindy, in the tiny living room of the Tomlinsons' Edwardian terraced house in the city, picking fish and chips out of paper wrappers while they watched the news conference.

Bill's research post at the university—which he was immensely and rightly proud of landing—provided him and his new wife with only a fraction of the income needed to buy a property, and so they had been forced into renting. Cindy, who had her own small graphic design business, usually contributed more to the household economy, a fact that bothered Bill not at all. Cindy had left the education system as soon as she had been allowed and had never looked back; she was as close to being the ideal partner for Bill as could be.

The three sat on a settee cast off by Cindy's parents and concentrated their attention on the small, blurry screen of the TV in front of them, which had been lately saved from the scrap heap by Bill.

Professors Holdsworth and Preston described the discovery process and the contributions made by teams in the USA and Britain. In the day since the modulated signal had been recorded they had not produced any convincing explanations for it. That would probably take many weeks of work.

Most of the questions put to the two professors were quite sensible. Some were less so.

"How far away is the source?"

"We don't know," Preston answered. "It is certainly beyond the edge of the solar system and possibly hundreds or even thousands of light-years away."

"Why hasn't anyone detected it before?"

"The signal only lasts for a day or so before disappearing— no one was looking in the right direction at the right time. Of course, it has been detected once before, but if it's been there at other times, then we have missed it simply because we were not looking in that direction. If it does repeat at a regular interval, we have no idea as yet how long that interval is. It could be three and a half years."

"What do you plan to do next?"

"Keep looking for it to return. We're also trying to find a good explanation for the message's contents. It may be telling us about another transmission from the same source. We are, of course, looking at other frequencies."

"Does this mean that soon we will be inviting these aliens to visit us?"

"No," Professor Holdsworth answered patiently. "There is no possibility of that, I'm sure. If the source of the signal is hundreds of light-years away, as is most likely, then it will take centuries for us to make responses to each other's transmissions. And we have no evidence that interstellar travel over such distances is possible at all."

"If that's the case, Professor Holdsworth, what is the significance of this event to the world, if nothing is going to come of it as a result?"

Professor Holdsworth sighed. He detested the press and had been determined to make his first and probably only news conference a dignified and sensible affair. "I'm not going to attempt to answer that question. We must each answer that for ourselves." He gave the questioner a withering stare. "If it is insignificant to you that we have proved the existence of intelligent beings other than ourselves in our galaxy, then your best contribution to this press conference would be to leave it. Let someone else who understands take your seat!"

"Have you spoken to the government about this? Surely this is a matter of such importance that the information should have been coordinated, sent through official channels, to avoid public panic and so on."

"Oh, rubbish," Professor Holdsworth said. The previous question had warmed him up. "How the hell are a few millionths of a microwatt of radio energy filtering down on the Earth going to cause public panic? Especially when there's hardly any information in them. And who the devil are a bunch of . . . of hormonally imbalanced egomaniacs to have control over an alien signal? This news is the property of every human being on this planet. And so is every other piece of progress made by science. Anyone who thinks otherwise is a dangerous fool."

He smiled mischievously. "Haven't you lot got any *good* questions?"

CHAPTER 4

PROFESSOR HOLDSWORTH ADVISED SHEILAGH TO JOIN
the group being organized by Professor Preston at York. The
work at Springley Castle would be abandoned; after all, one alien
signal was enough for the time being.

Preston appointed Professor Holdsworth as the director of the
group, which was formally christened the Center for Extraterrestrial Studies, and they installed themselves in Shipston
Grange. Funds were skillfully and speedily obtained by Professor Preston from the Science and Engineering Research Council, which was responsible for allocating government funding.
SERC insisted rather apologetically that a condition of the funding was that a civil service science administrator called Protheroe be stationed with them. The government had demanded it.

Despite the paucity of information in the received signal, there
was much optimism that more would be discovered before long.
Professor Preston was organizing a search for another signal at
the frequency predicted by Sheilagh's theory, using a special
linkup between seven radio telescopes in England, one in Holland, and one in Spain. The combination was known as EMERI,
for European Multiple-Element Radio Interferometer. The technique they used was called long-baseline interferometry and had
been practiced for a couple of decades. The idea was to simultaneously record the signal from the region of Cepheus 8 at each
telescope, together with timing signals from an atomic clock,
and then use computer processing to combine the recordings.

The result was like using a telescope the same size as the entire array, hundreds or even thousands of kilometers in diameter. The larger the telescope, the narrower its beam, and so a source could be pinpointed more accurately. Also, with less of the noisy background in the beam, compared with the point source, the signal looked relatively stronger.

The technique, however, was not wholly reliable because the radio waves were bent and deflected by the "weather" in the ionosphere, high above the Earth. That weather was stirred up by many natural and artificial processes. Most recently a particularly disruptive influence had come from huge radars used by the Soviet Union in its antiballistic missile defenses.

On November 3rd Professor Preston announced that the predicted signal had been detected. It was very narrow band and linearly polarized, and its Doppler shift exactly matched the first signal. The American group confirmed it two days later. The signal was extremely weak, too weak for continued, reliable detection, but it did show a hint of modulation.

There was great excitement around the world. To most people the knowledge that a message from an alien civilization, possibly millions of years more advanced than Earth's, was passing them by because mankind was not quite able to grasp it, was tantalizing and frustrating. To others it was the threat of doom. A debate raged across the world between the proponents of continuing or accelerating the progress toward reception of the message, if any existed, and those who would prohibit such "dangerous experiments."

On November 11th the "lighthouse" signal returned and was tracked for five days. Its overall strength was reduced, and its content was unchanged.

By then the work at the center had begun in earnest. Part of the plan was to equip the EMERI telescopes with the new receivers originally conceived by Professor Holdsworth for Springley Castle. The aim was to make it possible to monitor the signal from Cepheus 8 for longer periods of time with all or parts of the EMERI array. The trouble was that uninterrupted operation of any telescope for very long periods could not be guaranteed. Another, more basic problem was that Cepheus 8 was not visible at all times of the day from the Spanish telescope. Arranging for enough of the telescopes to be running all the time would be a difficult logistical problem.

One group was working on bringing other telescopes around

the world into the array, the so-called Big Link, in order to get a better positional fix on Cepheus 8 and to improve the strength of the received signal.

Another small group, which included Bill Tomlinson, was responsible for putting together all the available data and gleaning everything possible about the nature of the alien transmitter. They were the ones at the head of the information pyramid. Without having to worry about the technical problems of getting the information, they could concentrate all their efforts on the purely intellectual task of making sense of the data that the other groups provided.

The British government was showing no overt signs of wanting to take control of the center's activities, but in the USSR and USA it was becoming clear that some senior politicians regarded the aliens' signal as a potential threat to world stability and peace. Cynics suggested that the threat to the politicians' jobs was greater.

By early January, a total of seventeen research scientists and twenty administrators were occupying Shipston Grange. Once or twice a week Professor Holdsworth would call all the researchers together in the main hall for a brief informal meeting during which information and ideas could be shared. One of these meetings was held on Thursday, January 6th.

Twenty people were seated around the immense oak table that occupied the room, most of them wrapped in several layers of clothing in an attempt to keep out the cold that the ancient hot-water radiators failed to repel. A bright, cold light shone through the tall limestone-framed windows along one side of the room, telling of the thin layer of snow lying on the ground outside.

Professor Holdsworth sat at the head of the table. Sheilagh and Bill occupied adjacent chairs on his left, their faces illuminated by the white glare.

"Morning, everyone," the professor said, his voice echoing faintly from the walls of the room. "This morning I have asked Bill Tomlinson to give us a rundown on our current knowledge of Cepheus 8."

Bill cleared his throat. "Thank you, Professor." He dumped a pile of thin blue booklets in the center of the table. "These contain the essential facts about Cepheus 8," he said as they all reached for a copy. "As you can see, it's not a lot. They've been prepared for release to the great unwashed, and if there are no objections, I propose that our PR man over here publish them today."

"Good idea," the professor murmured.

Bill continued. "The first important fact is that Cepheus 8 seems to be associated with a star. This first photograph is from the Hubble Space Telescope and was obtained last week. The exposure was made based upon the rough position given by the Arecibo results last year. Since then our interferometer results have reduced the error box to a region of the sky that contains just one unnamed and unnumbered twenty-second magnitude star of spectral class M0. There is a twenty-fourth magnitude star on the edge of the box and several hundred fainter stars all over the frame, but we believe that this one in the center is our fellow. There's a good agreement between the Doppler shift in the star's spectrum and the lighthouse signal. The spectrum indicates a star just over one percent as bright as the sun; not very bright. This is a low-luminosity star but quite typical nevertheless. The huge majority of stars in the galaxy are dimmer than the sun.

"The distance, as you have no doubt already spotted, comes out at 2,947 parsecs, or 9,607 light-years, plus or minus ten percent. That puts it on the nearer edge of the Perseus arm of the galaxy, the one outside our own.

"The spectrum also shows that it is moving at 15.3 kilometers per second toward us. Assuming Sheilagh's theory that the lighthouse signal was transmitted at exactly the 'magic' frequency of neutral hydrogen, then the Doppler shifts indicate that the source is orbiting the star once every 21.6 days. Now, that ties in beautifully with the lighthouse signal's reappearance period. The radius of its orbit works out at 16 million kilometers—about one-ninth of the Earth's about the sun. If the orbit is circular or nearly so, then it is tilted at thirty degrees to the line between it and us."

Those facts were illustrated by line diagrams in Bill's booklet.

"The star has a radius about three-tenths of the sun's, which means its average density is thirteen times. It is a perfectly average, stable, main-sequence, garden-variety star. In fact, stars of that mass are stable for much longer periods of time than the sun is going to be. The star could be any age, up to the age of the universe. And one more suggestive result is that the amount of energy received by a planet orbiting at that distance from such a star is about the same as the Earth receives from the sun. Just a little more, in fact.

"That's about all we can say so far. I hasten to add that there are many uncertainties in all this. We're not even certain that we've got the right star. The source may be orbiting a much dimmer star that we are not able to detect even with the space telescope. We are certain that it's orbiting something, however.''

He looked at the expectant faces around the table. "So, these are the most likely set of consistent facts that we can produce concerning Cepheus 8. The fact that we can tie together so many results into a self-consistent bundle like this is very encouraging.''

"Yes, I agree, Bill," the professor said. "Your team is to be congratulated. One thing I would like to know is, have you worked out the power that is being pushed out by the aliens' transmitter? That would give us some idea of their capabilities."

"I have, indeed. Roughly one thousand megawatts. No big deal, really. Especially considering they might have had not millions but *billions* of years start on us."

"What sort of power would impress you, Bill?" the professor asked with a chuckle.

"Oh, maybe a thousand times that much. That would be something. One thousand megawatts is your typical nuclear power station. That doesn't impress me much."

"Don't forget that in converting power to microwaves there are bound to be losses. The process may only be a few percent efficient. Then there are losses in propagation."

"Yes, I know. But I'm still not impressed."

Bill sat down, meeting the general amusement with a broad grin.

"Question, Bill." The speaker was Dr. Bernard Protheroe, the civil-service scientist. "What do you make of the fact that the lighthouse signal, as you call it, only reappeared once since its original discovery in October?"

"I think that it fits in exactly with Sheilagh's idea that it's a lighthouse beacon," Bill replied. "The beam is probably being broadcast as a kind of fan shape ahead of the source as it orbits the star. Each revolution, the fan is moved up or down a bit to cover the next band of sky, but with a sizable overlap. The Doppler shifts suggest that. There would be no Doppler shift at all if the beam was being broadcast out, away from the direction of the star. If it was being broadcast back from the source, we'd see a Doppler shift of the opposite sign. It means that each part of their sky is in the beam for a few days at a time whenever the beam sweeps past. That makes it a lot more likely to be seen, of course. At the same time they're concentrating all its power into a small area. They are probably repeating this process over and over, though we don't know the period because we can't guess at the thinness of the fan. That would depend on the physical size of their antenna. I suppose we don't really know whether they use a conventional antenna at all.''

After a short pause the professor indicated that the meeting was over by placing his palms flat on the tabletop.

"Well, thank you, Bill. Most interesting. As regards that star, we should have a better fix on the position of the source very soon. The Big Link is about to be completed. That's twenty-seven telescopes throughout the northern hemisphere, including Russia. Quite an achievement! I expect we'll be getting some news in the next day or so.''

That evening Sheilagh and Cindy were in the Tomlinsons' living room attempting to finish the sky in a particularly difficult jigsaw puzzle while Bill was in the cellar bottling his home-brewed beer. Cindy was obviously troubled by something.

"Sheilagh, do *you* think there's anything dangerous about this alien signal business?''

Sheilagh thought for a moment. "I can't see any danger arising from the signal itself.''

"But if these Cepheans are more advanced than us, even by a hundred years or so, isn't it likely that the new signal will contain knowledge that may be harmful to us?''

Cindy used the current popular name for the aliens. Scholars of Greek mythology cringed whenever they heard it; the soft "C" and the erroneous ending hurt their ears.

"That's what some of the media people are saying," Sheilagh said. "And a lot of others who ought to know better, like the prime minister, for example.''

"Well, isn't it possible?''

Sheilagh turned a featureless blue jigsaw piece between her fingers. "Do you think a piece of knowledge could be dangerous?''

"Of course! If it showed how to make a weapon or something. One that was very dangerous.'' She leaned forward on her elbows and looked about for inspiration. "Like telling the world all about nuclear bombs before the first world war.''

"It *is* possible that that kind of knowledge could be found in the signals. But it's not the knowledge itself that's dangerous.''

"Oh, you're not going to give me that old 'It's the way it's used' line, are you?''

"Yes, I am. Well, it's true, isn't it? If the world is given that level of knowledge all in one great lump, it still would take years and years for it to get digested. No one could use it to build a superweapon to threaten his enemies without many years of work. In any case, we've had the means to destroy the planet for decades. What difference does it make what color the bomb is? The important thing is to ensure everyone gets hold of the knowledge. If one of the big developed nations grabs it for themselves, then we would really have trouble. Actually, with the signal flooding the whole of the Earth, even the whole galaxy, it's hardly likely to be stolen by anyone. The UN have made the right kind of noises on the subject, so there's some hope it may be done properly."

Cindy was not convinced, especially as Sheilagh looked uncertain herself. "Look," Cindy continued, "say the signal shows how to make a machine that can eavesdrop on anyone, anywhere. And it was easy to make. Wouldn't that be bad for the world? Police states and all that?"

"But something like that would *not* be easy to make. You see, my point is that the human race has already discovered nuclear bombs. Something as big and as dangerous as a nuclear weapon has always been and always will be difficult to make. It's not the sort of thing you can build in your cellar. Anything even more deadly will be correspondingly more difficult to make and will need huge resources, not the least of which will be people who understand the new knowledge, and they won't come along for years. I think the whole point about progress is that it keeps getting more difficult to achieve. The rate of progress goes up, but the amount of investment needed to maintain it goes up even faster. We have already discovered all the easy things to do with technology. Anything beyond what we can do now would probably require national-sized budgets and international cooperation. No one would be able to do it in secret. There's no way that any alien is going to be able to show us how to make a black hole out of stuff you can get in your local hobby electronics shop."

"You never heard of the black-hole diode?" Bill said, arriving with a bottle in each hand. "Two inputs and no outputs. Zero impedance."

"Do you agree with her, then?" Cindy asked, the joke lost on her.

"I always agree with Sheilagh. She has a profound grasp of the sensible. Even Professor Preston listens to her. Trouble is, she hardly ever says anything. Have a beer.'' He thrust a bottle into Sheilagh's hands.

"I'll get you a glass," Cindy said, making for the kitchen.

"What's your opinion, then?" Sheilagh asked.

"My opinion about what?"

"About the chance that the aliens' signal contains dangerous knowledge for the world."

He sat down and took a deep breath. "From what I heard of the conversation, I agree with you. But there are some other aspects that I'm not so sure about."

"Such as?"

Bill wiped the sticky beer from his hands on the legs of his jeans. "What if the aliens show us in quick easy steps how to cure biological aging? A cure for death. We're almost there ourselves now, and I'm certain the world isn't ready for that yet. And it won't be the day after tomorrow, either. If everyone wanted vaccinations for their children against aging, who would assume the right to tell them they can't have them?"

"You said we're close to that already. Whatever we may learn from the Cepheans, it can't be worse or more dangerous than the things we're doing now. You can only destroy the world once. Can't you?"

"You may be right. You may not be. What about the ubiquitous terrorist who provides governments even less respectable than ours with the perfect excuse for repression? I don't know. But if we ignore the signals, I'm sure we'll be in deeper shit than if we don't." He beamed brightly at her. "Do you realize what you've started here, young lady? You've put a ferret down the world's trousers. Everybody's in a tizz!"

It was, in fact, the next day when the teams met to hear the news about the Big Link.

"Morning everyone," Professor Holdsworth said, slowly rubbing his dry, cold hands together. "I think that Dr. Registre has something interesting to report today."

Doctor Wayne Registre, an Oxford-educated West Indian, rose from his chair and looked around for everyone's attention. He was very tall, and when he spoke, his deep, resonant voice echoed from the oak panels and reverberated around the room.

"You will all be pleased to hear that the 1.541 gigahertz signal *is* modulated." The excitement around the table was immediate. "We finally managed to operate the Big Link for just over six hours yesterday, and we have detected a strong modulation at 10.6 megahertz. The modulation is switched at a rate of roughly one and a half times a second, and whatever message it contains, it seems to be encoded in the same way as the lighthouse signal. Unfortunately, while the modulation is strong enough to be detectable, it is not strong enough for us to reliably detect every bit of the message over long periods of time."

He passed around a set of single-page computer printouts on which the new signal was represented as a string of hexadecimal digits.

"These contain the entire signal that we received during the six-hour run. Each hex character has a code above it that represents its reliability. On the average we can rely on nineteen out of twenty. That's not very good, I know, but that's the best possible even with the smallest ionospheric disturbances. Unfortunately, again, that's about the longest we'll ever be able to run the Big Link due to alignment and some logistical difficulties, especially at the Soviet 'scopes, where they insist on limiting our time slots.

"These copies don't make enlightening reading, I know, but I thought some of you would appreciate full dumps of the raw data. It is of course available on the file server; the file ID is on the top of the page."

He then went on to give details of the experiment.

After Dr. Registre was seated again, Professor Holdsworth spoke.

"Those are very exciting results. I'm sure that Alicia's group have enough to go on for a while." He was referring to Bill's group, which was headed by Alicia Cartwright, a short, energetic woman in her sixties who in her youth had built a reputation as a leading mathematician. "Dr. Registre," he continued, "you have a better idea of the nature of this new signal than anyone here. Could you tell us your opinion of the kind of system we will need to reliably capture all of the messages."

Dr. Registre turned a pencil end over end on the desk. "The signal is very weak," he said. "The biggest limiting factor is the ionospheric weather. As you know, this is stirred up by cosmic rays and sunspot activity, which is actually quite low at the moment. There are some complaints that the Soviet military radars are pumping megawatts into the ionosphere, so we cannot guarantee reliable reception with any large-scale multiple telescope link. I'm afraid that the only way to get round these problems is to build a large-aperture telescope and fly it above the atmosphere."

The professor leaned back in his chair. "Hm, that's what I was expecting," he said. "How big an aperture?"

"Above the atmosphere? We could probably do it with a couple of twenty-five-meter antennas."

"I see. Dr. Registre, I'd like you to work with me on a preliminary study of this, just to get some numbers that we can push under some noses."

Dr. Registre looked surprised. "Of course," he said. "But you don't seriously think we could get the government to sponsor such a project?"

The professor looked pleased with himself. "No," he said. "We may not need to build them at all."

Several of the people at the table had their faces buried in Dr. Registre's data dumps and were paying little attention to the conversation. The rest wore puzzled expressions.

Then Sheilagh exclaimed, "The orbital microwave stations! The ones the Mars Mission is building in orbit."

"Precisely. Actually, it was not my idea. I received a call yesterday from Konstantin Lebovsky, who's the biggest wig in the Mars program. It appears they're feeling left out of all the excitement and want in. He suggested that their OMSs would be suitable for such a job. I think I'll agree with him. Apparently they're building them now because they won't have the shuttle capacity once they start building the Mars Transfer Vehicles. They'll be ready in five months. So there'll be nearly a year before the Mars project wants them."

"But are they equipped with the right kind of receivers?" Sheilagh asked.

"They are intended for transmission and reception of UHF, which is what we need. The antennas will be suitable, but I don't know about the receivers. It may be necessary to modify those. Lebovsky did imply they were amenable to such things."

The meeting had broken up into an excited and informal discussion group, with most attempting to make sense of the new data. Professor Holdsworth led Sheilagh out toward his office. As they were walking along the corridor, he said: "How would you like a trip to Fort Worth, Texas? I think the two of us should go and talk to the Mars Mission chaps about their OMSs. Just for a few days. It may be that their orbital microwave stations are the only way of squeezing the information out of that signal."

They entered his office.

"I'd love to go with you," Sheilagh said. "But am I really the best person to go? And what about my work?"

"You're our receiver expert, aren't you? And I thought you had completed the prototype receiver design. The technicians can get on with the construction on their own. You'll not be missed for a few days. We may not actually be needing those receivers for this job."

Sheilagh spread out her arms and let them drop. "Okay. Great! When do we leave?"

CHAPTER 5

THREE DAYS LATER, ON MONDAY, JANUARY 10TH,
Sheilagh and the professor were sitting opposite Konstantin Lebovsky in his enormous sunlit office in the Multinational Mars Mission headquarters in Fort Worth.

Sheilagh thought that Lebovsky could not have looked less like a Russian. He was slightly built, with a handsome face that advertised tremendous confidence in his own abilities. He was dressed immaculately in a three-piece light-gray suit and spoke with charm and only a hint of an eastern European rather than Russian accent.

"I'm greatly honored by your visit, Professor Holdsworth and Miss Matthews. You are both very famous people now. Have the press been bothering you since your arrival? I hope not too much."

"Bloody rabble," the professor muttered.

"Er, yes, we did have a bit of a problem at the airport. The professor got a little upset," Sheilagh said, smiling toward Professor Holdsworth.

"Damned ruffians! Seemed to think they've the right to assault people, poking their bloody microphones in your face and getting under your feet."

The others laughed. The professor's eyebrows, which had merged at the top of his nose, found their separate identity again and resumed less unusual positions. He broke into a laugh.

"Let's not dwell on them, then," Lebovsky said. "How was the trip otherwise?"

Through the open door of his office a woman appeared carrying a tray of coffee. She set it down on a low table and proceeded to pour. Their coffee was set before them, and the woman left the room, closing the door behind her.

The personal conversation continued for a long time, and Sheilagh was beginning to wonder if they were ever going to get on to the important things. Eventually it was Lebovsky who brought up the reason for their visit.

"Well, now, about our OMSs. I can tell you that the idea of using them to receive the Cephean signal came from some of our engineers. After they become operational in July it seems that we will have about twelve months during which they're scheduled to be loaned to NASA and used as part of their deep space network. Now, NASA has said openly that they don't really need these new transceivers for communicating with their satellites and planetary probes, so I thought that as we are a multinational organization here and your group is the most international among its kind, it might be an idea to offer them to you during that time."

"It's a splendid idea, Mr. Lebovsky," the professor said. "In fact, it may well be the only way that we can get at the signal with sufficiently reliable coverage to extract the message from it. We are fairly certain it's going to need beyond-the-atmosphere antennae." He frowned slightly. "But we're not an international organization at Shipston Grange. I have merely set up some contacts with the groups in your country and the USA."

It had suddenly struck him that there might be an ulterior motive in Lebovsky's suggestion. "What do your European and American counterparts have to say about this?"

"I don't have any counterparts, as you call them, Professor Holdsworth. I am the sole chief administrator of the Mars program. I have, of course, many staff members from all countries in the consortium, but I have not asked their opinion of this. There is no need." He smiled innocently.

"Professor Holdsworth," he continued, "I think I detect perhaps a little, er, puzzlement in your voice." It was actually suspicion written plainly in the professor's face. "I can assure you the idea came from our engineers, not from the administrators." He sighed. "But between you and me, the people at the Soviet embassy were rather interested in the idea. I think they have some silly notion that the Americans are going to get their hands on the Cephean signal before they do. The Soviet Union is rather poorly equipped with suitable radio telescopes to make an interferometric array. I think they saw this idea of using the Mars Mission hardware as a way to get a piece of the action, as it is phrased here. But I can promise you that the embassy had nothing to do with it. There aren't any technical people there. They merely reacted to my suggestion. There, have I satisfied you? There is no intermember rivalry in this organization. I do not permit it. We are committed to establishing permanent manned stations on Mars, regardless of political ideologies.''

The professor's expression softened. ''I'm sorry,'' he said. ''I did not mean to imply there were any sinister motives in your suggestion. I was merely inquiring if the multinational flavor of this place will be carried through to our project, if we proceed with it. It's very important that no single party get control over this, as I'm sure you'll agree.''

''Yes, of course,'' Lebovsky said smoothly. ''But if you are right about the signal, then for a time at least, we at the Mars Mission will effectively have a monopoly. We are the only ones equipped to receive the signal. Now, one day someone is going to realize that and want to start taking control of our facilities. I would be very upset about that. So what I am suggesting is that we proceed with this idea immediately and stay one jump ahead.''

''Yes, I wouldn't blame you for being upset about that,'' the professor said. ''But I can see that it's going to be difficult. Perhaps we ought to start talking to these people right away. Who knows what they're cooking up behind our backs. Politicians, I mean.'' The professor made it clear that he held politicians in about as much regard as he did the press.

''In my opinion,'' Lebovsky said, ''the politicians are caught, I think you say 'on a sticky wicket' in your country. If any of them begins to show any inclination to claim rights of ownership to or censor the Cephean messages, then their rivals will immediately denounce them. And for once, their favorite ploy of using physical force to seize or obliterate anything that embarrasses them is useless. They can hardly put a microwave shield around the planet! I also believe that the leading politicians dare not expose themselves to the chance of ridicule if this whole affair turns out to be an elaborate hoax. I suspect that they cannot quite believe what they hear about all this.''

''Yes, you're probably right,'' the professor said. ''But I'm rather worried that our independence is about to disappear. I believe this business was an embarrassment to the politicians at first. It was making all their antics look rather puerile. But now that we've detected a definite message and are on the verge of unscrambling it, they're probably going to start taking it seriously. I shouldn't be surprised if we start feeling some pressure from them soon."

"But we must be thankful for one thing at least," Lebovsky said. "The foresight with which this organization was set up. We must be generous in our praise to the politicians who wrote the Multinational Mars Mission charter. We are completely free of political interference for the duration of the program. Our budget is guaranteed, and our individual tenure is also secure provided we meet the predetermined milestones. It means in effect that it would require a change of international law to interfere with our work here."

"But surely, using the OMSs to monitor the Cepheans' signal is not part of the contract," the professor suggested.

"No, of course not. But we are at liberty to do whatever we please with our hardware, provided we meet our milestones. If we choose to use our OMSs to monitor the Cepheans, then no one can stop us. I admit that if someone objects to such a thing and can persuade all the other countries in the consortium likewise, then we may be directed to cease. But that would take months to achieve and would almost certainly fail because if I read my Russian friends correctly, they would veto any such attempt. In the meantime we are free to do as we please."

Sheilagh spoke up. "How do these microwave stations work, Mr. Lebovsky?"

Lebovsky smiled at her and replied, speaking in a careful slow manner and using his hands to shape the objects he described. "They are receiving dishes, forty meters across, made of the new, specially developed, metalized Nylar fabric. We make two sheets of this extremely light and strong fabric and stretch them across a circular frame. The material is normally totally transparent to microwave radiation, but one of the sheets is coated with aluminum to make it reflective. The space between the two sheets is kept inflated so that the Nylar sheets are stretched out into paraboloids—dish-shaped. This is much less massive than using rigid metal dishes, and, of course, in orbit there's no gravity to deform them. The reflective sheet focuses the microwaves to a point behind the other sheet, where they are converted to an electronic signal by the receivers. The receivers are supported by a light framework that extends outside both sheets."

"Don't you get problems with ripples running across the Nylar and ruining the flatness?" the professor asked.

"We handle that by putting stress sensors and actuators around the edge of the sheets. They're actively controlled to dampen out the oscillations. The whole structure is mounted on a platform that contains the attitude control and propulsion systems and secondary dishes for communicating with the ground and the comsats. There will be two of them placed 180 degrees apart on polar ecliptic orbits. Their propulsion and guidance systems will keep them positioned so that at all times they are both able to point at Mars. If you can visualize it, their orbits will be kept nearly perpendicular to the line joining the Earth and Mars throughout the mission. We have two for redundancy's sake. The Mars Mission will be very long—two and a half years—so the possibility of failure in one is quite high. Also, we are able to use them for parallactic fixes on the spacecraft during the trips to and from Mars. We use such big dishes so that we can directly communicate with low-power transmitters on the surface of Mars."

"How will you communicate with them?" Sheilagh asked.

"Via the existing space communications satellites. These are in geosynchronous orbits, and there will always be at least two of them visible to each OMS. There are also telemetry channels direct from the vehicles to the ground that can also be used to command the spacecraft should communication via the satellite be lost for some reason."

"I take it 'polar ecliptic' means they're going to orbit in a plane perpendicular to the plane of the planets," Sheilagh said.

"That is correct."

She looked at the professor. "Isn't it going to be a problem with the OMSs having polar orbits? Cepheus is about sixty degrees from the ecliptic. They're going to keep getting eclipsed by the Earth."

"That is not a problem, Miss Matthews," Lebovsky said. "They were launched so that their orbits were as close as possible to the final orbits during construction while also being accessible to the shuttles. As it happens, that orbit is only a couple of degrees away from being ideal for Cepheus. It is a trivial problem to align them just so for this project. They were built for just such maneuvers so that they can follow the position of Mars during the missions."

Sheilagh thought for a moment. "I think that the answer to these political problems you're both anticipating is to get the

OMSs to transmit the raw received signal to the space comsats, which should then transmit it in a broad beam down to the ground—unencrypted data, just as it arrives. That way anyone with a small receiving dish could pick up the signal and do what they like with it. These communications satellites are visible to your ground stations, I take it, so they are also always visible to anywhere else on the same half of the Earth.''

"Not quite, but nearly so. The beams are fairly tight, but that can be altered. Actually, the two satellites are 180 degrees apart, one over the eastern Pacific and the other over the Indian Ocean.''

"Well, I must confess I like the idea," the professor said. "The problem of having to go into space to get the signal turns to our advantage when we come to spreading the good word.''

"Yes. It is the kind of thing I had in mind," Lebovsky said. "Of course, the signal from our space comms vehicles has always been available to anyone on the ground, and they are not equipped with encrypting circuits.''

"Well, now we're getting somewhere," the professor said. "The big question is about the OMS receivers. We need to know if they're suitable for the job.''

"Quite so, Professor. Let's proceed to the OMS engineering department, where we will talk with the people who can answer your questions.''

The trip to the OMS engineering department turned into a full tour of the facility. As there were eight years to go before the first manned vehicle was due to leave Earth orbit, much of the detailed design had not been started. The OMS design was, however, just about sewn up.

The work carried out by the Copernicus Center, as the institution was named, was basically administrative. The engineering was all done at other centers in the USA, Europe, and the Soviet Union, where the spacecraft's systems were being built and tested. The Copernicus Center had organized the whole project and had a sizable staff of engineers to provide the liaison with the hard engineering plants.

The professor and Sheilagh spent the rest of that day and the next with the engineers responsible for the OMS receivers. They discovered that to use the OMSs for detection of the Cepheans' signal and not jeopardize their usefulness to the Mars Mission, some hardware would have to be added. The receivers had been designed specifically to exclude the twenty-one centimeter and other nearby wavelengths because the natural sources might interfere with the reception of spacecraft signals. The additional hardware put a small extra demand on the power supplies and also exceeded the available circuit board space. The increased power consumption would alter the thermal conditions inside the box such that the failure rate of certain critical components would creep over the acceptable limit given by the failure analyses. It was obvious that some expensive redesign was going to be necessary, which raised the question of who should pay for it.

When the discussion got to that level, Professor Holdsworth and Sheilagh decided to end their visit, disappointed but undaunted. They spent an hour with Lebovsky and agreed on the next stages of the project, then returned to their hotel.

The next afternoon, while returning over the Atlantic, the professor seemed to Sheilagh to be rather subdued and thoughtful. Guessing at what was troubling him, she asked him about the possibility of the British government wanting to get involved in the work.

He sighed quietly. "I think we'll probably be hearing from them soon."

Sheilagh peered through the window at the blue curve of the Earth. She imagined the nearly infinitesimal flow of microwave photons that had started life in some alien machine nearly ten thousand years ago and were currently faintly percolating down over the planet before her eyes after their lonely journey through the stars. How long had they been coming? And what was their message?

Unchanged in all those years, the gray sea, whipped by strong gales, churned and spouted seven miles beneath her.

CHAPTER 6

WHEN SHEILAGH RETURNED TO YORK AT SEVEN-THIRTY on Thursday evening, she was welcomed by a note from Bill.

"DOWN THE LION. COULDN'T HOLD OUT ANY LONGER."

She washed her face and, without unpacking, walked the hundred yards to the pub.

Pushing open the door, she had no difficulty spotting Bill and Cindy in their usual seats around one of the small, elaborately formed cast-iron tables in the far right corner. Bill stood up, and, having taken her order, went to the bar.

She sat down close to Cindy. After asking Sheilagh about her trip, Cindy gestured with her head toward the bar.

"He's been rather excited the last couple of days," she confided. "Apparently they've discovered something important up at the Grange."

Bill returned with two pints of beer in his hands.

"Cindy says there have been some developments," Sheilagh said.

"Oh, there have indeed!" he said, placing the beers in the center of the table next to a half-full glass.

"Oh, Bill! Not another one already!" Cindy complained. "You're going to stink of beer all night, I can tell."

"Silence, wench. We have things of great moment to discuss."

"Is it about Wayne's data?" Sheilagh asked.

"It's a message, all right," Bill said. "But we haven't the foggiest what it means."

"But you must have made some sense of it by now?"

"All we know is that it is made up of blocks. Each block is a nice round 2,048 bits and is preceded by a number," Bill said.

"The blocks are numbered!" Sheilagh cried with amazement.

"That's right. There's a thirteen-bit number encoded in binary, would you believe, at the start of each block. The number goes up by one every block. We got five complete blocks in the six hours."

"What are the block numbers?" Sheilagh asked, intrigued.

"They start just over the two thousand mark."

Sheilagh tried to think. She was tired and jet-lagged, having forgotten to take the melatonin pills at the correct time.

"What's two to the power thirteen?" she asked.

"What!" Bill exclaimed. "Do my ears deceive me?"

"Oh, come on. I'm tired."

"Eight thousand one hundred and ninety two," Cindy said. "I heard him say it several times."

"Eight thousand," Sheilagh mused. "That means there's something like six thousand to go before they run out of bits." In spite of her tiredness, or perhaps because of it, she felt oddly disturbed by that. There was something wrong, but she could not quite see what.

"That's right," Bill said. "It also means that they must have started with block number one sometime last September."

"When will they come to the eight thousand mark?" Sheilagh asked.

"Well, it works out at sometime early next August," he said.

Again Sheilagh felt certain there was something wrong. "How do we know that they don't just keep adding one bit on to the length of the block numbers every time they need another one? The message might be of any length."

"Well, because the numbers we have at the moment, two thousand or so, need only eleven bits. The first two bits are zero."

Sheilagh drank her beer, relishing its smooth, dark sweetness. "Did they manage to get any more data?" she asked.

"Nope. The bloody ionosphere is not behaving, apparently." Bill picked up his beer.

"Have you really no idea about the data? The stuff that's actually in the blocks?"

"Nope." He sucked a line of beer froth from his mustache. "It's not a picture of any sort that we can work out. We've tried dividing it up into rectangular pieces of all sizes, and it still makes no sense. Alicia has managed to find some evidence that it is made up of nine-bit pieces, rather like characters. But it's only a statistical clue. And of course we don't know what such symbols mean. The consensus is that the first blocks that were transmitted last September contain the key to the rest. We'll just have to wait until August for when they come again. What did the Mars-bar people have to say?"

Sheilagh told them all about the OMSs and Lebovsky's plans. Bill was enthralled, but Cindy could only display polite interest.

"Well, that's grand," Bill said. "If they pull it off, then all we'll have to do is tune into their comsats and tap off the goodies. We might as well stop trying by ourselves."

"I hope they do manage it," Sheilagh said. "Mr. Lebovsky seemed to think that there was a danger of the politicians stepping in if he didn't hurry. The prof agreed, I think."

"A pox on all politicians," Bill said, raising his glass. "I've a nasty feeling something is afoot at the Grange. There were a couple of troglodytes in government-issue raincoats there last night, accompanied by a very senior looking policeman. When they found that the prof was away and expected back tomorrow morning, they went away apparently content. No doubt they'll show up tomorrow."

"Oh, no!" Sheilagh said. "I hope the government's not going to start messing us about now. The prof was talking about it on the plane. I think he's expecting it."

"He'll be a match for any civil servant wallies," Bill said.

They finished their beers and returned home.

Sheilagh showered and fell into bed and was on the very brink of sleep when she suddenly realized what had been puzzling her at the pub. For a few moments her head was totally clear. She quickly did some rough mental arithmetic. She had been right; there was something very odd about the new signal.

Then sleep descended on her heavily, and she did not resist.

The next morning Professor Holdsworth called a meeting of all available researchers and told them about Lebovsky's plans. The news was met with enthusiastic approval. Bill Tomlinson reported on the latest ideas about the message's contents, then Dr. Registre reported that the Soviet team had abruptly cut off communications. Their chief scientist had made some embarrassed comment about the ionospheric disturbances and had stated bluntly that there was nothing more they could usefully get from further collaboration.

Back in his office after the meeting with Alicia, Sheilagh, and Bill, the professor received a call from Walter Feinberg. He put the call through the speaker.

After the introductions Feinberg said, "I hear you were over in Texas talking to Lebovsky."

"Yes, that's right. I'm sorry we didn't get over to Massachusetts to see you. I tried calling, but I couldn't find you," the professor said, speaking loudly into the set.

"What happened?" Feinberg asked.

The professor explained briefly about Lebovsky's proposal.

"I guessed as much. Professor, I'm at NASA Ames in California at the moment. I must have been traveling when you called. Listen, the NASA team here have kinda been taken over by some spooks from the Pentagon or somewhere. They have their own plans for the Mars Mission's OMSs and got very upset when they heard that Lebovsky was not going to loan them to NASA after all."

"What do you mean 'was'?" the professor asked.

"Lebovsky is no longer the chief administrator. In fact, no one knows where he is. He just failed to show this morning, er, I mean yesterday morning; it's after one A.M. here. There was a very confused announcement from the Copernicus Center saying that Lebovsky had been recalled by the Soviets and that some guy called Janssen had taken over as acting chief. I don't think that the Mars Mission people know what happened really. It's not made big news over here yet because no one realizes the importance of the OMSs to the Cephean business."

The professor groaned while the others exchanged puzzled and worried looks. "But Lebovsky told us that the Soviets were in favor of using the OMSs," he said. "They would hardly recall him if that was the case."

"Hmm. Did Lebovsky know the OMSs were the only way of getting at the signal?" the American asked.

"Yes, Dr. Feinberg," Sheilagh replied. "Mr. Lebovsky said that quite clearly. He also said the Soviets were looking for a way to ensure that the Americans didn't hog the Cepheans' signal for themselves."

"Listen, Professor, I can't talk any further. I'm at a pay phone, and I have to go now. I'll call again later today. Good-bye."

There was a brief burst of static, and then the buzz of the

trans-Atlantic connection issued from the speaker as Dr. Feinberg hung up.

"What's going on over there, Professor?" Alicia asked. Her face was wrinkled with concern.

"God only knows." He sighed deeply. "Well, it has started. It seemed too good to be true that we should be able to proceed in the most sensible way."

He looked up as his secretary came in the office. "Excuse me, Professor Holdsworth. There are three gentlemen here to see you," she said.

The professor sat up and looked at the others with a sardonic smile. "Now it's our turn," he said. "Okay, Mrs. Fairclough. Show them in."

She went out and returned, leading the visitors. The first was dressed in the uniform of a chief constable, the others in dust-colored raincoats.

"Good morning, gentlemen. What may we do for you?" the professor said charmingly.

"Good morning, Professor Holdsworth," the policeman replied. "I am Chief Constable Elliot of the Yorkshire Constabulary. These two gentlemen are from the Office of Strategic Studies in London, Mr. DuPont and Dr. Redmane."

The professor introduced the others and bade the visitors sit down. Alicia moved to a seat beside the professor's desk while Sheilagh and Bill vacated theirs and arranged them for their guests. They then seated themselves on a table beneath the window.

DuPont spoke first. "Professor Holdsworth, we are here on a matter of some sensitivity. We would be grateful if we could speak to you alone."

"Sensitivity? I'm not a medical doctor, you know. Astronomy, that's what I'm qualified at," the professor said. Bill and Sheilagh lowered their faces to hide their smiles.

"A matter of national security, Professor," DuPont said loudly in a commanding tone.

"These people are all citizens. I'm sure they can be trusted, Mr. DuPont. Now, tell me what you want. You're in Yorkshire now. You can speak plainly," the professor replied genially.

The three guests looked at each other. Then DuPont continued. "Professor Holdsworth, the minister of defence, to whom we are responsible, has directed us to take a close interest in the work at Shipston Grange as a matter of national security. Now—"

"National security!" the professor interrupted. "You jest,

surely? This is a university department doing legitimate research. We're not building weapons or developing new military technology. Radio astronomy, that's all.''

"This center," DuPont persisted, "is concerned with receiving alien signals that are believed to contain information that might be of great importance to the country. Now the government"—his voice rose to smother any objections—"is insistent that adequate precautions are taken to prevent any such information getting into the wrong hands or being made available to the wrong parties. The minister has accordingly used his authority as granted by the Defence of the Realm, Special Powers Act, 1991, to assume responsibility for the work of this center.''

"Just how is he going to do that?" the professor asked, still smiling despite his intense dislike for men like DuPont. Here was one of the faceless, imagination-bereft failures who preferred carrying out other people's orders and mouthing rote dogma to thinking for themselves.

"Dr. Redmane here, as I'm sure you know, is a physicist with some reputation in this country. The minister has appointed him as chief administrator of this establishment. You, as director, will in future report directly to him.''

Redmane continued in a more conciliatory tone. "I'm sure you will appreciate, Professor, that in no way do we wish to interfere with your work here. We don't want you to think that your position is being usurped. We merely wish to ensure the security of the output from your researches.''

"How?" the professor asked bluntly. He was no longer smiling. Anyone calling himself a scientist and capable of participating in that kind of chicanery was beneath contempt.

"Dr. Redmane will simply be stationed with you here and will take charge of all security arrangements," DuPont said smoothly.

"That includes censoring all our publications, I take it?" the Professor asked.

"All information issued by the center will be screened by Dr. Redmane. Just to ensure that nothing that might be against the nation's interests is fool—er, accidentally disclosed.''

Just then the professor's intercom beeped.

"Yes, Mrs. Fairclough?"

"Sir Maurice, Professor.''

"Put him through, please.''

He picked up the telephone and greeted Professor Preston.

"Look, Adrian," Preston said, "I'm sorry I couldn't get to warn you in time. I expect you've had a visitation by now."

"Yes, they're with me now."

"Well, I'm afraid there's nothing we can do about it. The chief constable has got an order that apparently obliges him to enforce this action. We don't have any option; we can't defy the law. That's just not sensible in our position. I suggest you agree to their requests. We'll work out some way of dealing with them later."

Professor Holdsworth replaced the receiver.

"Well, gentlemen," he said, smiling once more at his visitors. "It's very encouraging to see that our elected representatives have our interests at heart. Why don't you let me call our staff together so that you can address them yourselves. Let them hear the good news from the horse's mouth, so to speak. No, no, I insist." He stood up and walked out of the office, calling to Mrs. Fairclough. Bill and Sheilagh followed him out, and he gave them a quick look that said, "Leave this to me."

Redmane was looking apprehensively at DuPont. DuPont stood and followed the professor. "Er, Professor. That won't be necessary, I'm sure. In fact, Professor . . ."

But he was too late to stop the professor, who was passing along the corridor putting his head into each office and calling the occupants to the meeting. Sheilagh and Bill busied themselves spreading the word around the building, while Mrs. Fairclough was quickly on the telephone to the more distant laboratories.

In five minutes all of the research staff members who were at the center that morning and most of the technicians and administrative staff members were assembled in the main hall.

Dupont, Redmane, and Chief Constable Elliot stood behind the professor against the wall at the front of the room, looking very uncertain of themselves. It was not the way they had wanted it. The less openness, the better, Benson, DuPont's chief, had said.

The professor stood and addressed the room in a loud voice. "I must apologize to you all for the short notice, but I knew you would all be very pleased to hear the news. These two gentlemen are from the ministry of defence. Mr. Dupont and Dr. Redmane."

The two men self-consciously suffered the stares from the staff.

"And this," the professor went on, "is Chief Constable Elliot. You will be delighted to hear that our dutiful government have at last decided to take an interest in our work.''

This was greeted by a stony silence and more distrustful stares were directed at the two MOD men. They in turn looked at each other, uncertain of the professor's intentions.

"Dr. Redmane," the professor continued, "has been appointed as official chief administrator of this place, and I'm sure I speak on behalf of you all when I say how delighted we are to have him here.''

Puzzled and concerned looks were exchanged all around the room.

"On the other hand," the professor went on, "some of you may feel that the government should not be concerned with our work here. If you feel like that, then let me remind you of your responsibilities as scientists. One day soon we may well have our hands on the most important knowledge ever possessed by the human race. As responsible citizens we must make sure that such knowledge remains the property of those in government who have been elected to protect our interests, even from ourselves.''

Someone in the room hissed.

"We wouldn't want this knowledge getting into the hands of just anyone, now, would we?'' the professor added.

DuPont stepped forward. "Er, Professor, I think—''

"Ah," the professor said quickly. "Mr. DuPont wants to explain this point himself.''

DuPont was abruptly left holding the floor.

His surprise, compounded by a lusty cry of "Bastards" loudly and clearly delivered by an anonymous voice at the back of the room, caused him to hesitate for a couple of seconds.

Judging the duration of Dupont's hesitation perfectly, Professor Holdsworth stepped in. "Poor fellow's lost his tongue.''

DuPont finally found angry speech. "This meeting is completely unnecessary.''

"You mean you didn't want these people to know about this?'' the professor asked with mock incredulity.

DuPont lost his composure altogether. "Look, we have an order signed by the minister himself. There's nothing you sods can do about it. From now on you work for us.''

It became obvious from his face that as soon as the words were out, they were regretted. Elliot stepped forward and was about to attempt to fill the embarrassed pause, but the professor again timed it perfectly and spoke a moment before him.

"Oh, dear," he said, addressing his staff with amusement, "I think they mean to press-gang us."

Dupont attempted to make amends. He took control of himself and said, "Professor Holdsworth, this is being blown out of all proportion. We are here merely to advise you about the interests of national security that you must agree have to be addressed. We do not wish to interfere in any way with your day-to-day work. We simply want to be party to your results. I assure you that in a day or so you will forget that we are here."

"Sounds to me like you want to take over the place," said a male voice from the room.

That met with loud concurrence from the others.

"*I'll* certainly forget that you're here—because *I* won't be," said someone else.

Many more people echoed that sentiment.

DuPont became heated again. "I'm afraid it makes little difference whether you choose to cooperate or not. There are plenty of civil-service scientists who can be stationed here to take your places. It really would be best to cooperate with us."

"Well, here's my cooperation," said a woman researcher strongly. She was wearing a white lab coat that, as she walked past DuPont, she took off and flung at his feet. She then walked out of the hall.

Five other research and technical staff members who were dressed the same way followed her example. The others, including Bill and Sheilagh, were close behind.

"Well, Mr. DuPont," the professor said. "It looks like you have got a mutiny on your hands before you start. I would love to stay and see how you handle it, but unfortunately I have more pressing and interesting things to attend to. Doesn't look like you'll have much trouble censoring our results, does it, Dr. Redmane? There aren't going to be any! Good-bye."

He followed his staff out of the door. A few minutes later the entire group had gathered in his office. They were talking loudly together when he entered. He sat down behind his desk while the others found seats or squatted on the floor.

"Well, I must say I was delighted by your support," the professor said. "I think they got the message, all right. Thank you, everyone."

There were some gentle cheers, and a technician raised her fist in the sign of solidarity. Someone by the window called out, "There they go. 'Please, Mr. Minister, sir, what do we do now?' " as the three visitors hurried back to their car.

"What's this all about, then, Professor?" asked one of the senior members.

The professor spread his hands. "Who knows, Dave? There have been some similar things going on in the US and Russia, apparently. It seems the politicians have finally started taking this business seriously. I note that Dr. Protheroe is not with us."

"But what can we do about it?" asked another.

"I can only speak for myself, of course. If we really are being forced to accept these people over us, then I for one will resign. I could not go against all my principles and help them in their efforts to steal whatever knowledge we may learn from the Cepheans."

They spent three-quarters of an hour discussing the ramifications of the morning's events. Professor Holdsworth then advised them to go back to their work. He promised he would inform them immediately of any further news.

After the room had cleared, Sheilagh came back to speak to him alone.

"I know, Sheilagh," he said. "You're worried about your doctorate. Well, don't worry. You are officially a member of the astronomy department—"

Sheilagh interrupted him. She was not thinking of herself. "But what about the Cepheans? Here we are with the prospect of the center being closed down, the OMSs in the hands of goodness knows who, the Russians not speaking to us. Who's going to pick up the Cephean signal when it starts back at block one in August?"

The professor gave a heavy sigh. He rubbed his chin and gazed absently out of the window. Then suddenly he turned and banged his fist on the desk.

"Oh, to hell with all confounded politicians! Damn and blast the lot of them!"

CHAPTER 7

BILL AND SHEILAGH WALKED HOME. FOR THE MOMENT the rain had abated and a beautiful sunset was spread before them, so they decided to take a long detour by walking around the city walls, which formed a nearly unbroken elevated footpath around most of the medieval city.

"It don't make sense," Bill said gloomily.

"No, it doesn't," Sheilagh agreed. "Lebovsky was the one who suggested using the OMSs. When we spoke to him, he seemed genuinely concerned about the signal being made freely available. So why would the Russians remove him from his post? And why did he contact our group? Why didn't he approach the American group at NASA Ames? Or his own countrymen? Those OMSs belong to the consortium; they're at the disposal of all the countries."

"We don't know that he didn't. But he obviously knew that the NASA folks were either about to be or had already been put under the thumb of the US Defense Department. Same kind of thing for his own people. In fact, it does make some sense if you assume that he also knew that he was about to get the chop himself."

"How does it?"

"He wanted to let the world know of the idea before it got suppressed, let our group know he was in favor of it. The prof's group was independent then. The Soviets and Americans may not have been."

Sheilagh looked down at the ancient city streets that incongruously echoed with the sounds of the modern world, rumbling engines and squealing brakes. The great cathedral of York Minster towered over the scene, its craglike tower eerily highlighted by a flood of sodium light. She felt very small and powerless. What a sordid turn the most important development in history had taken. After an open and hopeful start, it looked as if governments were going to turn it into one of their usual contests for power. What conceit there was in the minds of the older ruling generation.

An orange glow in the western sky faded behind the yellow streetlight haze that was scattered by the damp air. Between the low, broken gray clouds appeared a crystal-clear patch of deep turquoise through which the brilliant sparkle of a star shone remotely. It was difficult to tell what the isolated star was. Was it Vega?

At that moment she became certain of the role she had to play in future events. The professor would be channeling his efforts toward confounding any plans of the British government to suppress the aliens' messages, "doing a spot of agitating," as he put it, and he would need all the help he could get. She did not have the faintest idea how she could be of any use in such matters, but she was not going to back out. Contrary to her natural inclinations, she would have to start using whatever fame she had achieved to its best effect. But she knew so little about the devious motives of ministers and generals. Why, for instance, should Lebovsky, a Russian, want the professor to know about his plans for the OMSs? It still did not make sense.

"But to what effect?" she asked. "Whose interest was he supporting? The Americans stood to gain by his removal from the chief's position because they would then get the OMSs on loan, as already agreed. But they had no way to get rid of him. Only the Soviets could do that. And they are the ones that suffer most, because they now have no hope of being party to the OMSs data."

Bill brought his gloved hands out of his coat pockets and gesticulated as he spoke. "Given that he was about to be chucked—for whatever reason—then he was serving the Soviets' interest by letting us know of his plans. He was maybe hoping that the prof would be able to publicize the facts and embarrass the Americans into freeing up the OMSs again. Maybe the Yanks had some leverage with the Soviets. Or with him. Perhaps he was forced by them to quit because they've got the finger on him. 'Quit now or we'll publish these 'ere pictures we've got.' Or 'Quit now or we'll tell the Ruskies that you were one of our best double agents when you were back in Volgograd.' There are endless possibilities."

He sighed. "But none of them very likely, I admit. Then there's the British, Italians, and Germans. They may be party to the Americans' game, if there is one. They probably would be. But it's not always correct to assume that they all share the same purpose against the Ruskies."

"Wait a minute," Sheilagh said. "How do we know that there aren't other microwave receivers in orbit? There's the NASA-European space station and a Russian one. Maybe one of them is equipped with a big enough antenna."

"But two or more are needed to work together to get enough resolution," Bill objected. He thrust his hands back in his coat pockets.

"Hmm, that's right," she conceded.

"You were right the first time," he said.

"How was I?"

"It don't make sense."

When they reached the front door to Bill's house, they heard the telephone ringing in the hall. Bill hurriedly opened the door and grabbed for the receiver. Sheilagh took off her coat and went through to the kitchen.

"That was the prof," Bill said, entering shortly afterward. "He wanted to know 'where the devil' we've been and would we be interested in coming round to his place for dinner."

"And you said?"

"And I said okay."

"What about Cindy?"

"I'll leave a note. Come on, let's go."

"What are your plans, Professor?" Bill asked as they relaxed after their meal.

"That's what I invited you here to discuss," the professor said. "Have either of you any idea about what's happening in this Lebovsky affair?"

"We've tried making sense of it but failed, I'm afraid," Sheilagh said.

Professor Holdsworth sat up and looked around at his guests.

"When I got home this afternoon," he said, "I decided to contact Walter Feinberg via his home computer. He'd given me the number years ago when we routinely exchanged data. I don't know what prompted me to do it, but I'm glad I did. He had left a message for me there. It was put there about two hours after he made that call this morning, so he had been up all night by the looks of it. It contained some information about Lebovsky that he had obtained somehow, maybe from the man himself. Apparently Lebovsky had been approached by the Five Nations Committee on Space, who are effectively his superiors, or sole customers, I suppose. This was the day after Sheilagh and I spoke to him. They wanted him to abandon his plan to use the OMSs as a sort of public service and to promise them to NASA as originally planned. He told them more or less to bugger off. It seems that our friend Lebovsky is a true fighter for the cause."

"Oh, I knew it!" Sheilagh said.

"He fought valiantly for the plan of broadcasting whatever the Cepheans have to say to all the world, only to be told that if he wasn't a good boy, then he'd be looking for a new job. He then threatened them in turn with the MMM charter. Their response to that was to get the Soviet Embassy to arrange for his sudden transportation to Siberia or wherever he's got to."

"Oh, no! I hope he's all right," said Sheilagh, who suddenly felt a strong feeling of warmth toward the man who had so impressed her in his sunlit office in Texas.

"We just don't know where he is. He's vanished in a way that only the Russians know," the professor said.

"Are you saying," Bill asked incredulously, "that this Five Nations Committee, or whatever they're called, have control over the OMSs now? Who are those people?"

"They are effectively the governments of the five consortium nations," the professor replied.

"So they are all in cahoots together?" Sheilagh asked.

"It certainly looks that way."

Doreen gave a little snort. "The Russians and Americans in league? That'll be the day."

"If we can believe Walter, then I'm afraid that's about the size of it," the professor said.

"Maybe those 'spooks' he was mentioning planted the message to you on his machine," Sheilagh suggested.

The professor shook his head. "It was in a directory accessible only via a password. And I'm sure they haven't gone that far, tapping phones and planting fake messages and things. In any case the message incriminates them as much as anyone else. No, I think it's true, all right."

Bill spelled it out slowly. "So you think the evidence points to the USA, Britain, West Germany, Italy, and the USSR scheming to keep the OMS results, if there are any, to themselves?"

"But what for?" Cindy asked.

The professor turned to Cindy with a gentle smile. "So that the other countries of the world who don't have the resources to pick up the signal themselves will be left out of the game." He shook his head. "Please don't ask me to explain the motives, because I have difficulty getting into the mind of that kind of person. Probably afraid that some popular tyrant in some part of the world will use the knowledge against them. Disturb the status quo."

"Rather like the nuclear test ban treaties of the sixties," Doreen suggested, understanding her husband's point.

"How's that?" Bill asked.

"Well," she replied, "the countries that had already developed the bomb—Britain, America, and Russia—got the other countries of the world to sign treaties banning any further testing and therefore preventing development. The intention was purely to prevent those other countries from ever getting the bomb themselves. And it worked, too, until the French thumbed their noses at the treaty."

"That makes a sort of precedent for this, then," Bill said.

"It could be, I suppose," Doreen said. "It may be the case that the five nations have got together on this. They probably see it as a chance to gain back some of the ground they lost to the so-called developing nations over the last twenty years. If there is valuable knowledge in these signals, then it would rather put the clock back to when only the richest nations were party to scientific advances. We'd have another empire-building period where the poorer nations get exploited by the developed ones."

There was a pause. Everyone at the table was contemplating the truth in Doreen's words. The whole affair was becoming far more serious.

They left the table and settled in the Holdsworths' living room. The Victorian house was drafty, and Sheilagh sat on the floor near the open coal fire. She was looking into the dreamlike landscape of incandescent caverns and canyons when she suddenly recalled the previous night.

"Professor!" she called.

"Please, we are no longer colleagues but friends. Call me Adrian."

"Good grief, no thank you," she said. "I couldn't do that. If you don't mind, I'll continue to call you Professor. It would be like, well, like calling Einstein 'Bert.' "

They all laughed.

"Never have I been compared in any way, shape, or form to the great man before," the professor commented. "What were you about to say, Sheilagh?"

"Last night, when Bill was telling me about the progress they'd made with the messages, I had this funny feeling that there was something wrong about them. Something important we were missing. It came to me just before I fell asleep. It's quite obvious, really. Bill said that the messages were numbered starting at about two thousand."

"That's right," Bill said.

"And that the total was going to be two to the power of thirteen, or roughly eight thousand."

"Right again," Bill said.

"Well, doesn't that strike you as odd?" she asked all of them.

"I see what you mean, Sheilagh," the professor said. "It had occurred to me as well."

"Well tell us, then," Cindy demanded.

"Eight thousand blocks, each of two thousand bits, is not enough!" Sheilagh declared. "It's hardly anything at all! We've been expecting a great flood of information—the complete knowledge of thousands of years of civilization. But eight thousand blocks is what? 16 million bits altogether."

"Sounds a lot to me," Cindy said.

"Not if you compare it to, say, a book," the professor said. "Let's work it out. If a typical physics book is, say, two hundred thousand words, and each word is, say, an average of five letters, that's 1 million letters. Assuming we can represent all the letters with all the sixty-four permutations of 6 bits—that leaves room for graphics and symbols—that's a total of 6 million bits per book.

"Now, Sheilagh's point," he went on, "is that the Cepheans are sending us about two and a half average-sized books in the signals. That's not very much in anyone's book, if you'll pardon the pun."

"How do you know that they will stop at eight thousand?" Cindy asked.

"The messages are numbered using binary numbers, like I've told you about before," Bill explained. "Well, there are only thirteen bits available, so they can't be numbered above two to the power of thirteen minus one—eight thousand-odd. Also, the fact that they must have started at block one sometime last September is pretty convincing evidence that they repeat over a short cycle. The probability of us picking up the first signals that close to the beginning of a hundred-year-long cycle is just too low to believe.''

"So what does it mean if you're right, Sheilagh?" Cindy asked.

"My guess is that it's another message like the lighthouse message. They are 'bootstrapping' us, as the computer people say."

Cindy screwed her face up at the unfamiliar term. "What on Earth does that mean?"

"It's an old-fashioned term coined in the early days of computers," Sheilagh said. "In those days, when you turned on a computer, there was nothing in its memory, no programs for it to run. In order to load a program into the memory you had to run a program to do it, a kind of a chicken and egg problem. So what you did was to introduce a very simple piece of program, using some special circuits that fooled the computer into thinking it had something in a tiny part of its memory. This very simple program loaded another, less simple one from a disk drive, or even from punched cards, which I believe they used. This second one would then load another even more complicated one and so on until the operating system program had been loaded. They called it 'bootstrapping' because it was rather like pulling oneself up by the bootstraps, or laces. But I suppose 'bootlacing' doesn't have the right ring."

"So, back to the meaning of the shortness of the messages . . ." Cindy prompted.

"This new message is like the second bootstrap program. It's telling us what to do to get the next one. The next one is almost certainly the real thing. It may well be a very high bandwidth system with vast quantities of information coming in very short periods."

"I see," Doreen said. "If that's the case, then the Five will be the only ones able to pick up this final signal, the important one?"

Sheilagh nodded and turned her eyes back to the flames.

"But Sheilagh," Bill said, "I can't really see why the Cepheans would do it that way. I know I asked this question about the first signal, but why could they not put the final message, this ultimate communication, in the current signal, the one the OMSs will pick up?''

Sheilagh turned around to face him and collected her thoughts. "The first time you asked the question, the answer was, 'Because this first lighthouse signal is an attention grabber.' Well, now I think the answer might be something like, 'Okay, you've found us. Now here's the next clue.' Like a cosmic treasure hunt.''

Her remarks were met with scornful looks from Bill and Cindy.

"The Cepheans are teasing us?" Cindy said with a laugh.

"Look at it from their point of view," Sheilagh said. "We must assume they desire contact with other civilizations or they wouldn't be transmitting at all. Agreed? We know that their transmitter is not powerful enough to impress Bill here, so what can we conclude from that?''

"That Bill's a real cool guy?" Cindy suggested.

"That they chose the power very carefully," the professor said quietly.

"That either they don't want just anyone to hear them or they are incapable of transmitting with greater power," Sheilagh said firmly.

"Yes and no, respectively, Sheilagh," the professor said. "I admire your logic, but you've forgotten your boundary conditions. All we can say is that when we detect their signals, they appear to have a certain power. Just insufficient, and modulated in a particular way, I may add, to prevent us from detecting them on the surface. We have to go into space to get the message from them.''

"That's right. That's my first point, really," Sheilagh said.

"But," Bill protested, "if we just happened to be five thousand light-years closer to them, then the signal would be four times as strong. More than enough to be picked up on the ground, isn't it?''

"No, it's not, Bill," the professor said. "Wayne said that normal ionospheric disturbances would prevent any multiple telescope from seeing the signal and that it would take a single telescope about a hundred kilometers in diameter to pick up enough energy to decipher it. Even then it would need special real-time monitoring of the ionosphere to be absolutely reliable. Well, a hundred kilometers, that's three hundred or so times the diameter of the Arecibo antenna. So to receive the signal with the Arecibo dish we'd have to be three hundred times nearer to the Cepheans, if Wayne's numbers are correct. That would make the distance about, let's see, thirty light-years. That's on the cosmic doorstep.''

"All right," Bill said. "What if the Earth just happened to be twice as far away . . ." He did not complete the sentence.

"The signal would be one-quarter as strong," the professor continued, "and we'd be in exactly the same position we are in here. Your logic is correct, Sheilagh, and I think that your conclusion that the intensity of the signal is carefully judged is sound. But your alternative conclusion that the Cepheans are incapable of transmitting at higher powers is not sound. We can't make assumptions like that about aliens. They may be capable of generating an electromagnetic field of uniform intensity all over the galaxy. That *would* take a lot of power.''

Sheilagh nodded her agreement. "I intended the improbability of the second conclusion to reinforce the first one, if you follow me.''

"I don't understand about these OMSs you talk about," Doreen said. "They're not very big, I presume. Then how come you're talking about needing a hundred-kilometer telescope on the ground?''

Bill explained. "It's possible to make two small telescopes look like one big one. The effective size of the single one is the same as the distance between the two, not in terms of how much energy it receives, which is proportional to the sum of the areas of the two, but in terms of how small an area of the sky it is looking at. The bigger the diameter, the smaller the area of the sky—or the narrower the beam, if you like.''

Doreen nodded.

"Now, if you're trying to get a signal from a point source in the sky, like we are, then the smaller the area of the sky around that point, the better. You get less of the background. That makes the signal from the point source stronger relative to interference from the background.''

"Then, are you saying, Adrian," Doreen said, "that the Cepheans are deliberately transmitting the signal at a power carefully calculated to be difficult to receive?''

"They are transmitting at least two signals," the professor said. "With constant surveillance going, the 'lighthouse' signal that Sheilagh discovered last year is, with all due respect to her abundant talents, quite easy to detect. It is strong enough to be detectable by very modest receivers. All that is needed is perseverance.''

"The second," he continued, "is more difficult, and because we suffer from a cantankerous ionosphere, probably like all inhabited planets with substantial atmospheres, I may add, it can only be detected by a huge antenna with sophisticated electronics or by orbiting telescopes. Both of which require a high level of technology."

There was a pause.

"Now," he continued, "a high level of technology implies a well-advanced science." He paused again, as if waiting for someone else to finish the chain of deduction.

Doreen was first with an offering. "The Cepheans are being careful not to transmit knowledge that is beyond the recipients' capabilities to understand."

"If the recipients can't understand the knowledge, why should the Cepheans be careful about sending it?" the professor said, gently placing his hand on Doreen's.

"The Cepheans," Cindy suggested, "are being careful not to send information that may be understood but is not *safe* for the recipient?"

"Exactly," Sheilagh said.

"So the Five are quite justified in trying to control access to the messages," Cindy said, as if dissatisfied with where the logic led.

"No, no," Bill said. "It's perfectly safe for consumption by anyone."

"I'm confused." Cindy said, shaking her head.

The professor explained. "We accept the argument up to the point where the Cepheans are being careful not to send potentially harmful information to civilizations that are unready. Then we have said that their measure of a civilization that is ready is the fact that they can detect and decipher the signal."

Cindy was still looking lost.

"In other words," the professor continued, "they don't put information into any of their signals that might harm any civilization whose science has developed sufficiently far to detect them. We're capable of detecting the new signal, so we are therefore sufficiently mature to be given the knowledge."

"That's a compelling idea, Professor," Bill said, "but how could the Cepheans possibly make judgments like that? They'd first need to know what kind of knowledge is harmful at what level of civilization."

"Easy enough," Doreen said. "We've enough test cases here on Earth to tell us that. The story has been repeated hundreds of times all over the world where so-called primitive cultures have come up against the so-called advanced ones. Think of the societies that have disappeared or been transformed beyond recognition: the American Indians and Eskimos, Australian aborigines, New Guinea, Amazonia . . .''

''Sheffield?'' Bill said.

''It almost certainly happened in Britain two thousand years ago. Either it's the knowledge of guns, or alcohol, or money, or fire, or denim jeans, or computer games, or nuclear physics. Any of those things could destroy a culture that is unprepared. The Cepheans have probably had thousands of years of direct observation of cultures all over their world. Or even the galaxy. They can probably simulate the effect on their computers.''

Bill was not wholly convinced. ''Secondly, they'd need to know what level of scientific advancement accompanies a particular stage of civilization.''

''Like Doreen says,'' the professor said, ''they probably simulated it. There may well be predictable patterns of development followed by all civilizations. There are obviously some things you can say immediately. You can set some limits. A race that is still using stone tools, one that has not discovered metals, will be unlikely to have invented the equivalent of printing—a generally available nonoral store of knowledge. There are clearly many other such relationships of much more sweeping consequences.''

''But surely,'' Bill objected, ''you're making too many assumptions. It's as if you already think of them as having two arms and legs and thinking like us.''

''We *are* making a lot of assumptions, I grant you, Bill,'' the professor said. ''But many may be valid. We can assume, for instance, that they developed on the surface of, or in the atmosphere of, a planet orbiting a star. We know that almost all stars have planets, so that's not unlikely. So there would be an up and a down, and probably a day and a night in their world. We assume that they are made of the atoms familiar to us, because we know the same atoms exist out to the edges of the universe. We know that for any physical or chemical reactions to take place, temperatures must be above a certain minimum. For meaningful individual entities to remain stable long enough to evolve, temperatures must not be too high. For evolution to take place at all, the entities must be above a certain minimum size or, in other words, above a certain potential for complexity.''

He presented his open palms. "There, we've come a long way already."

Bill sat back thoughtfully.

"It's pure speculation, of course," the professor continued, "and a sensible person does not spend too much time on speculation. It is useful only as an aid to thought, a dynamo for ideas. But now we may be more justified in attempting to predict the form an alien being might take, because we are on the verge of hearing from one. Providing we can get our hands on their signals. We do know that such beings exist. So it is worthwhile trying to make a sensible theory out of what was once conjecture. The predictions of our theory can be tested at last."

He sighed. "But we jump the gun. We should be addressing the question of what to do next."

"What we do next," Sheilagh stated boldly, changing to a cross-legged position on the floor, "is make sure that Comrade Lebovsky's dream is not lost."

"Well said, but do you have any suggestions?" Bill asked.

"Not just at the moment," she replied, "but let's think about it."

"Fact number one," Bill said, marking it off on his fingers. "The only way currently available to pick up the new signal is with the OMSs. Agreed?"

"Agreed," Sheilagh said.

"Fact number two: The Mars Mission owns the OMSs."

"Right."

"Fact number three: The Mars Mission is now controlled by some puppet of the Gang of Five."

"Correct."

"Fact number four: We're stymied."

Sheilagh was more optimistic. "Only temporarily. It seems to me that our only hope is to get closer to the action. We can safely assume that the OMSs will be used to detect the Cepheans' signals, right? I mean, they'd not be stupid enough over there to let the opportunity slip, whoever's in control."

"I think we can safely assume that," the professor said.

"Right," she continued, thinking rapidly as she spoke. "Then the signals are going to be coming down from the OMSs in some scrambled form. They will not run the risk of letting others pick them up. And we know that the comms satellites that are already in orbit to relay the data don't carry scrambling circuits. So they will need to put scramblers into the OMSs. We also happen to know that there is not enough room to put more circuitry in the receivers without major modifications. But assuming they get around that problem, it means that the Mars Mission ground stations are going to be picking up the scrambled signal and sending it somehow to the American ET team who are now under the boot. We have to get our hands on the data stream, either directly from the satellites, whose signal is freely available, in which case we'd need only the encryption key, or from someone in their team after it has been decrypted.''

''We should therefore attempt both ways,'' the professor said. ''We've got one thing to help us. We know that in order to put encryption circuitry on the OMSs they are going to have to rely on the MMM engineers at the Copernicus Center. Now, Sheilagh and I met most of those engineers a few days ago. We also saw all the details of the receiver design.''

Sheilagh looked up at the professor and grinned.

''That's right,'' she said. ''It's my bet that some of those engineers are just as unhappy about these latest events as we are.''

''How do you know that those engineers won't just be replaced with ones who will do as they're told?'' Doreen asked.

''None of us are engineers, dear,'' the professor said, ''but I can't see them making such large changes in such a short period of time without relying on the existing engineers. From what we saw, it's going to be very difficult for them—technically, I mean.''

''And,'' Sheilagh added, ''those engineers are going to know that it's a scrambling capability they're putting in. One thing in our favor is that the Copernicus Center was set up as a multinational place. There's no security there, beyond the usual physical-threat kind. It should be easy to get information in and out of the place.''

''What we have to do, then,'' Bill suggested, ''is to let those engineers know that we're still here, and independent. If any of them do listen to their consciences, then they'll surely think of you and the professor.''

''One would hope so,'' the professor said. He was looking at his young friends with admiration.

''If they wanted to contact you,'' Sheilagh said, ''they'd try the Grange first.''

Doreen was not altogether happy about the implications of their conversation. She folded her arms and looked slightly disapprovingly at her guests.

''Yes, and get a stony reply that I don't work there anymore,'' the professor said, "that I'm persona non grata. Then they'll get the wind up and cease trying."

"Then we must advertise our independence and willingness to fight the buggers as soon as possible," Bill said. "Let them know where we are and what we stand for."

"But if we do that by denouncing the MOD's takeover of the Grange publicly," the professor warned, "we'll then have the security people on our backs for certain. MI5 or whatever those clowns call themselves. Telephones tapped, mail intercepted."

"Oh, Adrian, surely not!" Doreen said, laughing nervously. Things were getting worse.

"I think it's extremely likely, dear," the professor said sadly.

"My goodness," his wife said, definitely alarmed. "I'd never thought I'd see the day that you got involved in cloak and dagger stuff. You are much too old for that now. I forbid you to do anything that might provoke such things. I'll bonk you on the head and shut you in the cellar until this blows over if you try anything!"

"I am greatly touched by your concern, my darling," he replied. His smile faded. "But we are personally involved in the most important development in human history, certainly in my lifetime. And we, of all the people on this planet, are the ones best equipped to ensure that the results are made available to all mankind, not just the dangerous, egocentric fools whose evil we have just been touched by."

Doreen was undaunted. "I have not lived with you these last forty-five years," she said spiritedly, "just to see you spend the rest of your days imprisoned as a traitor, however just your cause is. You are not getting involved, Adrian, and that is final."

"But," he protested, "this is the event I have been working toward for the last forty years. You're not going to dash the cup from my lips now, are you?"

"Certainly I am if it saves you from a dungeon somewhere," his wife retorted.

The others did not dare interrupt the private debate.

"Let me put it another way," the professor said, setting down his glass. "For twelve years I have been searching the sky, at great expense, for signs that the human race is not alone in the galaxy. Now I've found such a sign, and as a result we are on the verge of hearing what they have to say to us. But we, and the rest of the world, are about to be deprived of those alien words by the idiotic mentality of selfishness and greed manifested by the politicians. We have here a golden opportunity to strike the greatest blow for science and freedom, and I'm damned if I'm going to pass it by!''

"I warned you, Adrian, and I meant it. If you start anything that might cause problems with the government or the police, I shall truss you up like a chicken and keep you in the cellar fed on bread and cheese until you come to your senses.''

She and her husband faced each other in a silent contest of wills that ended, after a moment's silence, in both of them exploding with laughter. The others joined in.

The professor feigned hurt. "How could you embarrass me by putting such images into the minds of our friends? Trussed up, indeed!''

Sheilagh found herself seeing Professor Holdsworth as if he were a young man again, in his thirties. The hair returned, the dry skin softened, the movements more fluid. Doreen, she thought, had been an extremely lucky woman for those forty-five years.

"Well, adjusting for Doreen's objections," said the professor, smiling, "how's this for an idea . . .''

CHAPTER 8

SHEILAGH GAZED AT THE HUNDREDS OF PEOPLE IN front of her and shivered with apprehension. They were with Dr. Walter Feinberg in a small conference room in a hotel in downtown Boston. The room was filling with researchers, supporters, and people just interested in the activity known by the name of SETI. Professor Holdsworth was the principal guest speaker at the "Symposium on Cepheus 8," subtitled "Extraterrestrial Update," which had been organized with commendable speed and efficiency by Feinberg.

It was Friday, February 18th. Feinberg had planned such a symposium earlier in January, but the events at Fort Worth and at the NASA SETI group had diverted him. When Professor Holdsworth had contacted him on January 15th, he had quickly drawn up some simple one-page fliers advertising Professor Holdsworth's prospective presence and sent copies to his contacts all over the country. He made sure to send one to his friend who worked at the Copernicus Center as a propulsion systems engineer.

"Do you recognize any OMS engineers, Sheilagh?" Bill asked quietly as they sat at the head table beside the professor. Feinberg was opening the meeting.

"No, and I hope I don't," she replied. "It could ruin everything if one of them actually approaches us."

Feinberg concluded the opening remarks and introduced one

72

of his colleagues from the institute, who gave a presentation on the design of the Denning telescope receivers.

The day was made up of a series of presentations given by Feinberg and his colleagues and certain invited specialist speakers. During the breaks Sheilagh, Bill, and the professor were forcibly split up and individually bombarded with questions about their discovery.

The professor made the final presentation, confining his remarks to purely scientific matters. Afterward there was a lengthy question and answer session during which all of the questions concerned the Cepheans and their signal—except one.

"Professor Holdsworth, is it true that the British Ministry of Defence has taken over Shipston Grange? And if so, was that the reason for your resignation?" The questioner was a young bearded man wearing a casual checked shirt and jeans.

"No, they haven't taken over Shipston Grange, as you put it. They have simply exercised their right to be involved. That was always expected, right from the start. The British government, like those of the USA, the Soviet Union, and the other European countries, seem to believe they have a responsibility to ensure that the Cepheans' signal is safely distributed across the world. Who am I to question that? But I resigned because my work at the Grange was complete. We had discovered the original signal, deciphered it, and then gone on to find the second, more important signal. There was nothing more we could do. It was natural that further progress should become the responsibility of governments. After all, this is very important for the whole world, and we now depend upon the utilization of very expensive space-based systems to make further progress."

After the symposium ended, the professor's group was invited by Feinberg to dine with him at an Italian restaurant in the city. The restaurant was so dark inside that they had to wait several seconds while their eyes adjusted. Feinberg rose from an alcove table set for four at the back of the long, narrow room and came over to them. Without waiting for the host, he led Sheilagh to the table and seated her opposite him while the others followed.

When they had all ordered from the massive menu and answered what to Sheilagh seemed like an unnecessarily long list of questions from the waiter, Feinberg leaned forward and asked in a conspiratorial tone, "So, did anyone make contact?"

"No," Sheilagh answered, "no one, which is just as well.

That's not what we wanted, Dr. Feinberg.'' She was glad Feinberg also had a discreet voice.

"Walter, Walter. We're not so formal over here," Feinberg said, smiling broadly at her. "So you just wanted to advertise your presence as free agents, eh?"

"That's right," the professor said. "I think it went very well. The press that found us last night at the airport were helpful as well."

"You were almost pleasant to them, Professor," Bill remarked.

"Oh, dear. I hope I didn't give the game away," the professor said with a grin. "We're very grateful to you, Walter," he went on. "You must have worked very hard to get the symposium organized. I'm sure we'll be approached by one of the Copernicus engineers in the next few days."

"It was all for a good cause," Feinberg answered. His smile faded from his face. "But let me tell you the news about the NASA extraterrestrial group." He sat back in his seat and looked around at his companions. "I'm afraid it's bad. Real bad. The place is crawling with security agents, and most of the original team has gone. It's in the hands of the Pentagon, I'm afraid. There's just no way into that place."

"You say most of the original team has gone?" Sheilagh asked.

"There are a couple of senior scientists left. The others have been replaced by about ten guys taken off secret projects at the other NASA research centers."

"How do you know all this?" Bill asked.

"From the four who got their pink slips. I know them all personally. They naturally objected strongly to the government barging its way into the project and got canned for their troubles."

"Where are they now?" Sheilagh asked.

"Looking for work, I expect," Feinberg answered. "The two turkeys who stayed on are the kind who'll believe anything told them by a guy with a shiny badge and a lump under his jacket."

"That is disappointing, but I suppose it was not unexpected." The professor sighed. "We were hoping for some kind of toehold in the place as a backup in case our main ploy fails."

"There's very little chance, I'm afraid," Feinberg said. "It's all locked up tight over there."

"What exactly are they planning? Do you know?" Sheilagh asked.

Feinberg sighed in turn and rested his elbows on the table. "It looks like they're modifying the OMSs to scramble the Cepheans' data. It's gonna come through the same path, the Mars Mission's space comsats, but in a language only they can speak."

"That means we'll need the encryption key, or keys," Sheilagh said.

"Forget it," Feinberg said with a shake of the head. "Not even the president will know that."

"Would he know what to do with it?" Bill said unhelpfully.

"I'm afraid I can't help you," Feinberg said. "You can bet that the encryption is gonna be foolproof—and genius-proof."

"Where will the data be picked up?" Bill asked.

"It will be coming down in the regular telemetry from a geostationary satellite, in a nice tight beam over the western US."

"So they're confident about the encryption," Sheilagh said.

"Oh, yes, they've good reason to be," Feinberg said. He wrinkled his brow and looked at the professor. "Doesn't look good, eh?"

"Not good at all, Walter," the professor said with a frown. "Not good at all. We can probably intercept the signal, but it will be just meaningless noise to us."

That night, in the early hours, Sheilagh was startled out of her sleep by the telephone ringing beside her bed.

"Sheilagh?" the caller said. "Adrian here. We've just had our contact."

"What! How?"

"Why don't you come down to my room and I'll explain."

She put on her dressing gown and headed down the corridor to the professor's room. She met Bill on the way.

"Two prime numbers," the professor said.

He was sitting at the table dressed in slacks and a cardigan, which had been hastily pulled on over blue pajamas.

They sat down under the dim yellow lamp and peered at the sheet of paper that had been folded into three parts. Handwritten in the middle of a page that bore the letterhead of the Copernicus Center were two very large integers, both with about twenty digits.

"I was just failing to get to sleep about ten minutes ago, when this was pushed under the door in an envelope."

"It's just two numbers. Is that all?" Sheilagh asked.

"That's all."

"You said they are prime numbers," Bill said.

"I haven't checked them. I don't happen to have a computer on me, but they almost certainly are," the professor replied.

"Why do you think that?" Bill asked.

"Data encryption keys," Sheilagh said.

"Exactly," the professor said. "One standard type of encryption scheme uses a pair of large prime numbers as a key. We can infer that these two large numbers pushed under my door in a Boston hotel in the small hours of the morning are prime and constitute an encryption key." His eyes were sparkling, and he was clearly very pleased with himself.

"Did you see who it was?" Bill asked.

"Good heavens, no! I didn't move a muscle for fully five minutes."

They all looked at the numbers as if they were about to spring to life and walk off the paper.

"This is the key to the OMS data encryption?" Sheilagh asked.

"I don't know," the professor said. "I have been thinking about that. It's highly unlikely that they'll use just one code of this kind. I believe they usually have a whole program of encryption that changes on the fly between many different codes."

"So what else could this be?" Bill asked.

"The only other possibility that springs to mind is that our mysterious friend will be sending me an encrypted message at some future date and this is the key that will decipher it."

"In which case," Sheilagh said, "this messenger wishes his or her identity and the contents of future messages to remain secret."

"Brilliant!" Bill said sarcastically.

"What I meant," Sheilagh said with infinite patience, "was that whoever our messenger is, he or she believes it likely that normal means of communication are being monitored." She smiled wryly. "In other words, the professor is running the risk of being knocked on the head and locked in the cellar by Doreen because his telephone is being tapped and his mail opened. It fits in perfectly with our friend being an engineer at the Copernicus Center, one who is involved with the mods to the OMSs and is likely to remain so. Soon he or she will be sending us information that may enable us to eavesdrop on the transmissions."

"The letterhead is pretty much proof of the messenger's origin," Bill said. "Our mission to Boston has been successful sooner than we thought."

To Doreen's great delight she and her husband had moved back to Somerset two weeks previously. The professor had set up a private research company based in his home and employed Bill and Sheilagh as consultants. Bill and Cindy had rented a house a mile and a half away, and Sheilagh had moved in with them.

The conservatory that had been added on to the rear of the professor's house many years before had been converted into a workshop, and the bulk of the equipment from the Springley Castle laboratory had been installed there.

On February 23rd, just three days after their return from Boston, Professor Holdsworth received the communication that they had been expecting. It was in the form of an electronic mail transfer from a mysterious sender called "Plutonca" in northern California. The first section was a letter pretending to reply to a previous correspondence, which the professor had no knowledge of. It contained a lengthy discussion of some quantized Hall-effect electronic devices for microwave circuits. Attached to it was an executable computer program that was supposed to be a simulation of the devices but was actually a large block of impenetrable binary code. Impenetrable, that is, until they applied a standard encryption algorithm using the two prime numbers that had been slipped beneath the professor's hotel room door. As if by magic, it turned into a long file of text.

Sheilagh, sitting across both arms of an armchair, finished reading first and flung her copy onto the table. She held up both arms and legs and waved them around in excitement.

"We did it! We bloody well did it," she cried.

The others laid down their copies, looked up at Sheilagh, and burst into laughter. Bill jumped up and grabbed Sheilagh for a brief but energetic and noisy dance around the room. When they had settled down in their chairs again and picked up their copies of the remarkable communication, Bill remarked, "More precisely, our friend Pluto has done it. What a risk that bloke must be taking!"

"He has a brilliant idea," the professor said.

"Do you think we could manage to pick up the telemetry?" Bill asked.

"I expect so," the professor replied. "We have five months or so, after all. We should manage something in that time."

"What a genius! I hope somehow we can give him a medal when all this is done," Bill said.

"Bill," the professor said, "go and erase that message, would you? No sense in leaving it lying around in the BT computers longer than necessary."

"Hey, I'm the junior member around here!" Sheilagh protested. "None of this antiquated chivalry rubbish, if you please." She jumped up and skipped over to the computer terminal.

She tapped a few keys, and in seconds the extraordinary document that had appeared in the professor's mailbox one hour and thirteen minutes earlier disappeared from the British Telecom computer's file system.

It had contained no indication of its originator, no introductions, no explanations, just a straight description of the OMSs' orbits and the vehicles' normal K-band radio telemetry transmissions. Those were continuous transmissions that contained routine information about the spacecrafts' state of health: condition of power supplies, internal temperatures, fuel quantities, operational mode changes, communications status, electronics self-test results, and the like. The telemetry information was packaged into discrete messages. The contents of some of those messages could be changed by command from the ground station personnel, while the remainder were fixed and unchangeable. The latter reported the health of the spacecraft's critical systems. One of the messages was a report of the output of a strain gauge mounted on the circular supporting frame for the Nylar sheets that made up the antenna. That strain gauge had two identical neighbors. They measured to great accuracy the moment-to-moment position of the edge of the sheet as it tried to pull away from the frame. This measurement was sampled two hundred times per second, and the resulting numbers were sent off to the control microcomputers. Within their high-speed programs they calculated the strength of the tug that the piezo-electric actuators on the frame should make in order to prevent ripples across the surface of the Nylar sheets. Any such movement would totally destroy the antenna's ability to focus the microwaves. So important was the role of the strain gauges that three were mounted at each location. Should one of them fail, there were two more to take over its function.

Sheilagh asked the professor to confirm her understanding of the message. "So what Pluto has done is to make it look as if one of the eighteen strain gauges on the antenna has gone haywire?"

"That's how I understand it."

"Then the numbers coming back in the telemetry will show just noise, where they should be showing sensible strain gauge outputs?"

"Correct."

"But it won't actually *be* noise, but the Cepheans' signal data, scrambled using the encryption key we used just now?"

"That's it."

"So the engineers monitoring the telemetry won't suspect a thing . . . other than a wonky strain gauge, that is?"

"No."

"And all the time," Sheilagh said, "the Cepheans' signal, which the Gang of Five's gorillas have scrambled, will be pouring out of one of the unscrambled channels."

"Well, that's the bit I didn't follow, actually," Bill said.

The professor explained. "This telemetry signal is sent out on a different channel from the Cepheans' data. It's just one of the normal telemetry channels they have not modified."

"And is being beamed to the west coast of the US?"

"That's right," Sheilagh said. "It's very convenient, really."

"What I'm amazed at," the professor said, "is how the heck this Pluto chap managed it. He must have made substantial changes to the telemetry computer's software. How did he smuggle it through?"

"Who cares how he did it!" Sheilagh said.

"If you think about it," Bill said, "all he had to do was to replace the number from the strain gauge with a number coming from the new circuits that detect the Cepheans' signal. Then that number would be stored in memory until the telemetry was transmitted. Oh, it would have to be encrypted on the way somewhere, I suppose."

"You see?" the professor said. "It's remarkable. I suppose he was helped by the fact that they were in such a tearing hurry. Whoever heard of a major modification being made to a spacecraft just weeks before launch? From what Pluto says, these systems are already built and in orbit."

"If this wheeze works," Bill said, "the guy should be knighted. Deified. I hope we find out who he is someday."

CHAPTER 9

PROFESSOR HOLDSWORTH SET HIS TEAM TO WORK ON the design of a portable receiving station tailored to the special requirements of eavesdropping on the telemetry from the OMSs. They were confident of achieving it in plenty of time before the crucial beginning of the Cepheans' message returned in August.

By May they had constructed a prototype in the professor's laboratory, and they tested it in his garden by picking up the signals from known geostationary commercial satellites. After a few minor modifications, they were in business and proceeded to construct three more. All four receivers, without the antennae, could fit into a single small suitcase and were powered by twenty-four volts obtained from batteries. Inside each case was a tiny optical disk device that could write over a half billion words of data onto a single shiny disk.

On May 21st, Bud Randall, a colleague of Feinberg's at the institute, moved into a rented house in Carpinteria on the Pacific coast just east of Santa Barbara, California. Within a few days he had installed a new satellite TV antenna on the roof, which made the house less conspicuous among its neighbors. On May 27th, a Federal Express van pulled up outside the house and delivered a package sporting COMPUTER EQUIPMENT labels and the international symbols signifying that the contents were fragile. Inside were two of the professor's OMS telemetry receivers.

One week later, in the yard of a house in Santa Paula, a town fifty miles farther east, another satellite TV antenna appeared.

Shortly afterward a package of electronic equipment was delivered to the house and into the hands of Jacob Klein, who by a strange coincidence had been one of Randall's closest buddies at the institute. Klein started running a mail-order business from his newly rented home.

No one noticed that the satellite TV antennae at both houses pointed in a slightly different direction from any others in southern California.

Seven hundred kilometers overhead, at 0207 Universal Time on July 12th, OMS 1 made a short, strong thruster burn, its Nylar-covered dish locked in the central position to align the center of gravity. It dropped away gently from its sister, white and gleaming in the sunrise.

At 0227, OMS 2 began its thruster burn to tilt its orbit northward by nine degrees.

OMS 1's burn had changed the shape of its orbit from a circle to an ellipse, the two ends of which extended out to the original circle. As it fell, OMS 1 picked up speed and, because of the shorter distance around one-half of the ellipse, made it back to altitude ahead of OMS 2 by ten minutes.

Five half orbits later OMS 1 performed another short, powerful thruster burn to circularize its orbit at the original altitude, its orbit having been simultaneously tilted southward by nine degrees. Exactly one half orbit apart, hidden from each other behind the Earth's massive globe, OMS 1 and OMS 2, like two tiny white ears, circled the Earth every 100 minutes.

After repeating systems checks and reestablishing the permanent telemetry and command data links, ground systems controllers issued the commands for the receiving antennas to be pointed with great accuracy at Cepheus 8.

In the Mars Mission Western Control Center in Ventura, California, a computer screen reported the malfunction of a strain gauge on the edge of OMS 2's dish. Onboard control processors were disregarding its data.

At 1237 UT on July 13, 1994, the encrypted Cephean signal was beamed from a Mars Mission geostationary satellite above the Galápagos Islands to the receiving station in the Santa Clara Valley in southern California. From there it passed between microwave relay stations along the California coastal mountains to the NASA Ames research station. Accompanying it to the ground station's antenna were four ordinary telemetry channels, streams of data reporting the health of the new spacecraft.

They were routed to the command center in Ventura, where the failure of the strain gauge was detected. Since they were part of the critical systems data, however, there was no way to remove the noise-filled messages from the telemetry. A failure report was generated by the systems analysis computers and included a large sample of the noisy signals. The report was marked for distribution to the overseeing engineers and managers at the Copernicus Center and also to the manufacturing company in Eindhoven, Holland.

On July 27th Professor Holdsworth received a small package airmailed from Los Angeles. Inside was a sturdy plastic container about thirteen centimeters square. Inside it was an iridescent silver disk that scattered the daylight into all colors of the rainbow.

"Batch number one has arrived," he announced, proudly holding up his prize as he entered the workroom. Sheilagh was busy typing at a terminal, and Bill was peering at a colorful diagram of a circuit board on a screen. "I think we may put aside our documentation efforts now."

"Sheilagh, would you do the honors?"

She took the disk, inserted the precious object into a drive on the professor's computer, and typed in a single command. A set of programs, written weeks before and tested with synthetic data, instantly began generating a file of neatly formatted messages extracted from the encrypted data on the disk. In a few seconds the conversion was complete, and a long dump of the messages began to pour quietly out of the printer. Bill tore off the first two pages and carried them over to the table.

They crowded around. There was a brief, tense pause, then Bill gasped in astonishment.

"Shit!" He banged the table with his fist. "I don't believe it. How stupid can you get?"

Sheilagh groaned. The professor was silent. The first message on the printout was numbered 279.

Bill placed his hands on his hips, turned around, and walked to the window, where rain was spattering against the glass.

"We've missed the first message again," he said, turning to face the others.

"Certainly looks like it," Sheilagh said. The shattering disappointment was evident in her voice.

"By how much, I wonder?" the professor said. He looked

up at the corner of the ceiling for a second and then said: "About thirteen days. That's a shame. What bad luck!"

"Bad luck! It was stupid. We should have guessed they might not use all the eight thousand available numbers. They must have stopped somewhere in the seven thousands."

"That must be what happened," Sheilagh said, "but we could not have done anything about it even had we known."

Bill dropped his hands to his side and sighed dejectedly. "Yes, I know. It was just that I never even thought of the possibility that we might not be getting the first messages. I'm angry at myself, I suppose."

"We've got the messages, and that's a major achievement," the professor said. "Let's celebrate with a glass of claret."

He went off toward his study as Bill and Sheilagh bent over the table to look at the messages again.

"Same format," Bill said, "and same incomprehensible contents."

Sheilagh agreed. "But with a continuous flow of these, we may be able to decipher some of them even without the first messages."

"Doubtful," Bill said glumly.

The professor returned with a full decanter in his hand. Doreen followed with four glasses and placed them on the table. The glasses were quickly filled.

"To Pluto and us," the professor proposed, raising his glass.

The others echoed the toast, and they all drank.

"What are we celebrating?" Doreen asked after sipping her wine.

"The success of our two young friends' labors," the professor said happily.

"We've received the first set of data from the Cepheans' second signal," Sheilagh explained. "Only they're not quite what we were hoping for. It seems the Mars Mission satellites were finished a couple of weeks too late, and we missed the first part of the messages."

"Oh, I see. It will be repeated, though, won't it?" Doreen asked.

"Yes, in ten months' time," Bill said with a grimace.

"Haven't you got enough to work on in the meantime?"

"The first messages hold the key to deciphering the rest," the professor said. "Sort of a basic introduction to the Cepheans' way of communicating. Without them we're probably not going to make any sense of the rest."

"I thought this was supposed to be a celebration," Doreen kidded. "You don't sound too happy, I must say. And what has Pluto got to do with it?"

"We're celebrating the arrival of the first batch of data. Pluto is the chap in America who is sending it to us," the professor explained, looking a little worried.

"What a funny name." Doreen turned slowly on her husband. "Sounds like a code name to me. You're not up to any tricks, are you, Adrian? Because if you are, I shall go and prepare the cellar. I'm warning you!"

"No, no, dear. Nothing like that. He uses the name Pluto as a sort of identification on his electronic mail. That's all. Funny chap. Er, let's see the rest of the messages." Replacing his glass on the table, he went over to the printer, flinching at the holes being bored in his back.

Each week that passed they received a new data disk from California. Each disk contained a copy of the previous three weeks' results as well as the latest week's in case any were lost or intercepted in the mail.

It soon became public knowledge that the signals were being received by the Mars Mission's antennas, but statements issued periodically from NASA Ames said only that nothing of significance had been found in them. No one outside the Five's research teams was allowed near the data. The Five had efficiently and effectively gained absolute control over the data. Or so they thought.

After two months they could no longer ignore the intense political pressure to publish the data and, to the professor and his team's amazement, released a large batch. In quantity it matched the amount of data so far received, but in a monumental piece of deception, the Five had subtly altered about five percent of the data to prevent anyone from successfully deciphering the whole signal.

In the real data that were being smuggled to Professor Holdsworth's team, the message numbers in the data followed the predictable numbering scheme, but without the key first blocks, the contents of the messages remained an impenetrable jumble of bits. The team wrote dozens of analysis programs on the professor's computers. They tried dividing the data into pieces of varying lengths, from two to thirty-two bits, and calculated how many of each type of the resulting pieces were contained in the data. The first clue they obtained was that when the data were divided into pieces nine bits long, some of the "symbols" thus created were much more common than others, some were much less, and others were absent altogether. For all lengths except multiples of nine, the result was an even spread of each type of symbol. The conclusion naturally reached was that the data were divided into pieces 9 bits long. There were 225 such symbols in each message and 13 bits for the message number. The 5 start and stop bits made up the 2,048 total bits in a message.

Because they had no idea what the Cepheans were trying to say, the team could attach no meaning to the symbols they had discovered. Sheilagh suggested looking for balanced pairs of symbols. Her reasoning was that the messages might be in the form of mathematical equations or symbolic logic or even in a language similar to a type of computer programming language, as those were the best known ways of expressing precisely defined ideas. All of them used balanced parentheses of some kind in their syntax. She found ten pairs of symbols that regularly occurred the same number of times in individual messages.

But that was as far as they got. They had exhausted their ideas, and their efforts seemed increasingly futile.

The professor, long a believer in the saying "When you find yourself in a hole, stop digging," ordered a complete break. He fought off their protests and sent his young companions away with instructions to not return for at least two weeks. He also made sure they carried nothing resembling work away with them, and not just because of the utmost secrecy of their activities.

Bill and Cindy returned to York, while Sheilagh, at first embarrassed by the professor's authoritative stance, caught a train to Glasgow, then a bus to her family's home in the town of Oban on the west coast of Scotland. She had always had great difficulty making the jump between the two worlds of home and work, and it was especially difficult this time as she could not tell her family what she was working on. However, she evaded their questions for the first two days of her stay, after which they lost interest and bothered her about it no longer.

Her two younger brothers were away, one at sea and the other at agricultural college in Edinburgh. Her father, who was a general practitioner, neglected his patients abominably, except in dire emergencies, and relied on the generosity and understanding of his partner in order to make time to spend with his daughter.

Sheilagh loved her father very much despite his several glaring failings, in particular his reliance on alcohol and neglect of his own health. She had never really talked to him, and in fact she doubted whether even her mother had. One did not talk about personal things to Duncan Matthews. But he was a great sharer of life. If you went with him in his boat, across to the island of Jura, to float silently among the seals and clamber over the ancient ragged cliffs, you might not speak more than ten words in the whole day, but you would fall into bed that night exhausted and exhilarated by the experiences you'd had.

When she was a young girl, he had talked much more, but always about the natural world, not about himself or the activities of people. He had shown her a rock as large as a house stuck deep in the sands of the shoreline and had told her how one night, when he was a boy, it had been moved by a storm more than a hundred feet along the beach. He had taken her to the top of Ben Cruachan and waited while the sun set behind the cusp-shaped hills of Uist, seemingly a thousand miles away over the glittering ocean, and explained how, as they were eroded by the elements, they rose gradually out of the Earth so that the beautiful deep-colored rocks now exposed on their crags were almost as old as the Earth itself. As the darkness deepened, they had silently watched the pale multitude of stars emerge and the sky take on its true nature: that of the interior of a galaxy.

If you were out in space, he had told her, a million miles from Earth, that was just what you would see.

After nine days Sheilagh was very much refreshed and felt a strong urge to return south. She telephoned a college friend who lived in London and invited herself to stay for a couple of nights. Her parents tried to make her promise to see them more often but were gently refused. She did not like to make promises that she could not keep. She caught the train to Edinburgh, presenting herself at her brother Robbie's doorstep, and spent a glorious evening regressing back to her undergraduate days. The next day, feeling slightly fragile, she got herself to the station and boarded an early train for London.

The train's only stop was at York, and while it was stopped at the wide curved platform, Sheilagh's attention flitted idly from face to face as several new passengers queued to board her carriage. She became conscious of having the silly notion that she might recognize one of the faces, and she smiled at her foolishness.

Moments later she did see a face she knew, but it took several moments to register, by which time the young man had marched earnestly past her window without so much as a glance in her direction. She knew Russell Voss's face, as did most people with even a vague interest in modern science, and she gradually became curious to know what had brought him to York. Had he been visiting Shipston Grange? Surely he was not involved in the Cephean signal business? He would certainly be interested in the recently released batch of data—who wouldn't?—and perhaps he had been invited by the British government to get involved and was party to their schemes. That was not difficult to believe. The government was highly likely to at least attempt to recruit him to their cause, and from what she had heard of his character, he was unlikely to be overly concerned about the ethics of the matter. It would be all too easy to lure him into their camp with the promise of access to the real data.

Dislike and distrust for the man rose spontaneously within her, but she caught herself quickly.

"Come on," she whispered to herself, "what's happened to your objectivity? At least give him the benefit of the doubt."

Thirty minutes after the train had resumed its journey south, Sheilagh left her seat and walked slowly toward the middle carriages, hoping to find out where Voss was sitting. She felt an obligation to her friends to make an attempt at discovering the extent of Voss's involvement, but it took a great effort to overcome her nervousness.

In the next carriage she saw him seated by the aisle, studying what looked like a computer manual. He did not look up. The seat opposite was vacant, but Sheilagh could not find sufficient courage to speak and feebly walked on. She reached the buffet in the next carriage and, scarcely knowing what she was doing, bought a coffee and carried it back toward her seat. As she passed Voss, she looked over his shoulder at the book he was reading and with a shock realized that inside the computer manual was hidden the summary report that accompanied the recently released corrupted data from the Cepheans' signal.

So he was involved! Her blood raced as she tried to steady her mind. She turned and spoke. "Dr. Voss?"

Voss looked up suddenly, as if taken by surprise. He made no reply.

"Er, I saw you getting on the train. I'm Sheilagh Matthews."

Again he made no reply, gave no hint of recognition. He was

unaffected by her obvious unease, appearing shocked and affronted at having been spoken to.

"Er, do you mind if I join you for a while?" Sheilagh asked, attempting to be as pleasant as she could.

At last he broke his silence. "I suppose I have no choice," he said with some indignity. He spoke quickly and impatiently.

Her heart sank. It was going to be hellishly difficult. She sat down and struggled to make conversation. Voss looked at her for a moment, resumed his reading, then thought better of it and closed his book.

"I hope I'm not disturbing you, Dr. Voss."

He looked up and gave a single sardonic laugh. Of course she was. Then he apologized, very unconvincingly, Sheilagh thought, and said he was pleased to meet her.

Sheilagh tried again to start the conversation. She was unusually flustered and could not gather her thoughts. "I noticed you got on at York . . ."

"So you mentioned."

"Have—have you been to Shipston Grange?"

He appeared greatly puzzled to know what his presence in York could have to do with her. "No. As a matter of fact, I had other business at the university."

He clearly was not going to be forthcoming. Sheilagh noticed that the man in the seat on the other side of the aisle had recognized one or both of them and was paying a great deal of attention to them. The situation was impossible, and she decided to end it as soon as possible. Coming as straight to the point as she dared, she said: "Perhaps you have had a chance to look at the new data from NASA?"

There was a pause, and Voss looked steadily at her. She was unable to discern his thoughts.

"No," he said at length. "I have little interest in such things, and even less time to get involved. If you will excuse me, Miss Matthews, I'm rather busy."

Sheilagh apologized and with a polite smile took her leave of him. She was convinced he was involved. He had lied directly to her, for she was certain she had recognized the pages of the summary report hidden in his book. The diagram on the left-hand page was unmistakable.

She was also convinced she did not like him and spent several minutes noting to herself the arrogance and contempt written all over his features. As she was never naturally inclined to such feelings, however, she soon resumed a more reasoned contemplation of the matter. Voss definitely *was* interested in the Cephean affair, for he was reading about it at that very moment. What other evidence was there? His presence in York and his desire to keep his interest unknown to her. Possible explanations? Either he was part of the government's scheme or—or what? Perhaps he had simply taken a personal interest and had been to Shipston Grange in order to find out more information. But why should he be so secretive about it? And why so bloody rude? If he was not involved with the Big Five's games, then he could not possibly know about the doctoring of the released data and could therefore have no reason to behave so to her.

The conclusion that Voss was involved with the five nations' plot to keep the Cepheans' signal to themselves grew to a certainty in her mind. The thought depressed her greatly not just because it shook her faith in the honesty and objectivity of such an important figure in the scientific world but also because he was such a valuable asset to the other side. How useful he would have been as one of their tiny team!

She recounted her remarkable meeting with Voss to the professor and Bill when they were all back in Somerset four days later. They both agreed with her conclusion. The arrival of Voss in the opposite camp was a bitter blow.

"Don't get too depressed about it," the professor said. "It's not actually going to change things very much, you know. After all, the fact that Voss may be helping the Shipston Grange people to decipher the signal is not going to affect our chances of doing the same, is it? I expect you're both absolutely bursting with new ideas and fresh insights after your little rest. Don't squander your energies thinking about Voss. The important thing is that we are still getting the real data, and we stand as good a chance as anyone of unlocking its secrets. Providing the data keeps coming in, we'll be able to take as long as we like in deciphering it."

They set to work and tried their best to follow the professor's advice. The next morning Professor Holdsworth received a letter that amazed and puzzled him. He waited for his two young friends to arrive, which they normally did together at about 9:30 each morning, and without comment placed the letter in front of them on the large table. It read:

Imperial College
19th. October 1994

Dear Professor Holdsworth,

I have recently discovered some very significant facts concerning the alien data and would appreciate your opinion of them. I understand you are no longer actively engaged in the project, but I would be very grateful if you could spare me a few hours of your time, and I feel sure that what I have to show you will be of some interest.

It would be easier for me to show you my results here on my computer system, but if it is inconvenient for you to travel to London, I will be happy to come to you in Somerset. If you can make it, please come tomorrow afternoon (the 20th) to my home. My address is 87a Clareville Grove, South Kensington (Gloucester Rd tube station).

Yours sincerely,
Russell Voss.

"It arrived this morning, Federal Express. What do you make of it?"

"Well, it looks genuine," Bill said.

"I wonder why he didn't use the phone," Sheilagh said. "And why he doesn't give his own number."

"Yes, I wondered that," the professor said. "But I think maybe we've not been entirely fair to Dr. Voss. Arrogant he may be, but this is at least an indication that he may not, after all, be the villain we imputed him to be."

Bill and Sheilagh thought in silence.

Bill eventually spoke. "It's possible this is entirely genuine, but it's also possible that the authorities are using Voss to probe into our activities. They're sure to be very curious as to what we've been up to over the last few months."

"What do you think, Sheilagh?" the professor asked.

Sheilagh sighed. "I just don't know. I fail to see how Voss cannot be involved with them, but I'm at a loss to explain his motive in sending this letter. Perhaps we should take him up on his invitation and go and see him. I've no desire to endure his disdain anymore, but I think we should follow this up."

The professor smiled. "My thoughts exactly. I'll reply straightaway, and we can go in the morning. Bill, you hold the fort here, and Sheilagh and I will take the earliest train from Bath. Sheilagh and I have both earned an apology from the man, so I think it best if we go."

Bill made no objection. "Why does he owe you an apology, Professor?"

"I met him briefly last year sometime. At a meeting. I accidentally let slip some comment about physics being a cyclical process of theory and observation in mutual support of each other, something which nobody in their right mind would disagree with, and he took umbrage for some reason. Gave me a telling off, apparently convinced, after less than two minutes' acquaintance, that I was completely incapable of reaching the intellectual heights he was used to. Perfectly accurate, I'm sure. But even so . . ."

It was clear that the professor was highly amused by his experience. "Poor chap was obviously very sensitive about his much-acclaimed theories being essentially untestable."

"So you disagree with his theories?" Sheilagh asked. "They're way beyond my capabilities, I'm afraid."

"Well," the professor said, frowning and scratching the back of his head, " 'disagree' isn't the right word, I suppose. I don't understand them either, but, well, they don't seem like good science to me. Science has always progressed with theory in close contact with experiment, with observation. These geonics theories have developed almost by accident, out of pure mathematics. They still don't make any firm predictions that can be used to test them, like the ratios of the masses of the fundamental particles, or the strengths of their couplings. And they also involve these 'internal dimensions' which don't have any justification from observation and never will, it seems. More importantly, there is not one single principle upon which they are built, like the principle of equivalence of gravitation and acceleration that Einstein's general relativity is based upon: a principle based purely on observation, I might add. Geonics, like its forebear superstring theory, is just a set of admittedly very interesting and rich equations, sitting in the middle of nowhere, with no principles and no experimental evidence to connect it with reality."

"But that is beside the point," he added. "I'm an old man, a simple old-fashioned astronomer, and no doubt my ideas are all out of date. His may be the finest mind in the country, possibly the world. If we could get him on our side, it would be marvelous."

"If you do find that he's not been recruited by the dark side of the Force," Bill said, "will you let him in on our little secret?"

"We would have to sound him out very carefully first, before we spill the beans," the professor said.

"It's a risk, though," Bill said.

"It is. But life is full of risks. I wonder what, if anything, he has discovered," the professor said.

CHAPTER 10

THE FOLLOWING DAY PROFESSOR HOLDSWORTH AND
Sheilagh met Russell Voss in the study in his Kensington flat.
He welcomed them very coolly and made no reference whatsoever to either previous meeting. He was especially cold toward Sheilagh, speaking almost without exception to the
professor. Sheilagh became more and more upset by it as the
meeting progressed.

Voss led them into his study. A large, cluttered desk, behind
which he seated himself, filled much of the floor space, while
to his right a ceiling-high rack of computer equipment hummed
with the whine of cooling fans. There were three large, very
high resolution monitor screens, all crammed with information.
He put on a small headset that supported several tiny pads that
made contact with the skin of his temples and scalp.

The professor had asked him some questions about the equipment that surrounded him and was being treated to a demon-
stration of the computer software that gave him access to the
university's library.

On a large screen before them an extensive menu appeared.

"This is the library's top-level index," Voss said. He spoke
and acted swiftly, as if impatient to get the enforced formalities
over with.

"I have access to the entire library from here. Most of the
books are in machine-readable graphic form."

Seemingly from nowhere, a quiet female voice announced: "Science library main index. Please choose a category."

"Biographies," Voss said. The screen was quickly overwritten with a new menu headed BIOGRAPHIES. "Living, male, astronomy," Voss intoned. A list of ten books appeared on the screen within a second.

"No one has written your biography yet," Voss said to the professor. "That's a serious omission. Someone should get on it right away."

The professor showed suitable modesty. Voss invited them to take a seat on the couch that lay along the wall on the other side of his desk.

"I'm grateful," Voss said, "that you should come to see me, Professor Holdsworth, especially at such short notice."

"We were intrigued by your letter, Dr. Voss," the professor said. He frowned as if to impart to Voss the importance of what they were to talk about. He then looked across at Voss and held his gaze for a few seconds.

"Dr. Voss, you mentioned that you have discovered something about the Cepheans' signal."

"No. I have discovered nothing at all about the Cepheans' signal, Professor Holdsworth," Voss replied. "What I said was that I have discovered something about the released data."

The professor outwardly showed none of the surprise that Sheilagh felt at that reply.

"Might I ask what that is?" the professor said.

"It is not entirely the genuine Cephean signal."

Sheilagh and the professor looked at each other. "What makes you think that?" the professor asked, this time showing exactly the correct degree of surprise.

"I ran some simple analyses of the data—I have it all on my machine here. You are no doubt aware that the six hours of data that you published from Shipston Grange have recently been repeated and have appeared again in the data released in the USA. Well, that segment of data of course contains some random errors due to the reception conditions. Nevertheless, I have some statistical evidence that it is qualitatively different from everything else that has been published."

"That's very interesting, Dr. Voss," the professor said. "Do you have the results at hand?"

"Yes, I do. I prepared them especially for your visit." Voss typed rapidly on a keyboard. In a few seconds the screen on the wall to his right, and their left, displayed four very straggly horizontal lines. A thin, gray vertical bar passed through the lines. Where it crossed them, the straggly lines all dipped markedly.

"These," Voss said, "are the results of just four of the tests I performed. One of the approaches I took was to analyze blocks individually and try to identify any categories that might exist. I found several characteristics that could be used to distinguish the messages. Sixty out of a hundred blocks have at least one of a particular set of features."

He waited for a sign that they were following him. "Like I said, sixty percent of the blocks contain certain features, which I therefore assumed were normal. That means that it is ninety-nine percent probable that there is least one block in the Shipston Grange data that contains one of the features. There are none." He indicated the screen.

"Not completely convincing, I know, but there is more. Each of these lines represents the correlation of each block of data to a particular characteristic. I obtained each characteristic by some lengthy analyses of the entire data set." A small dark arrow moved smoothly over the bright screen. It settled on the center of the top line. Sheilagh could not detect how Voss controlled it. He moved it so smoothly. "The central line depicts the six hours of data that you obtained in January. Now, the characteristic on the top line indicates the relative position within each message at which a particular pair of symbols appears." He broke off and turned toward them.

"I take it we all agree that the data is in nine-bit words?" he asked. They nodded, not taking their eyes off the screen.

"Okay," he continued. "Your six-hour section differs from the rest by a statistically significant amount—about ninety-five percent." The arrow moved down to the next line.

"Now, the second one," he continued, "shows also at the ninety-five percent level. It is also a relative position criterion, but of a different pair of symbols, this time separated by one variable symbol."

"This is remarkable," the professor said.

"It is, indeed," Voss agreed. "The next one is also very close to the ninety-five percent level. It is actually a negative correlation with prominent features in all other parts of the data. When I discovered these, I started looking for the reasons, and that is when I started categorizing the blocks. This bottom line represents an anomalous characteristic. As you can see, the correlation is completely absent in the Shipston Grange data. The combined probability that the six hours of data are actually different in all these respects is negligible. It is in fact different to some extent due to errors that have crept into the original Shipston Grange data, but those are of a purely random nature. These characteristics are not.''

There was a long pause while Voss's visitors pondered his presentation.

"That's an excellent piece of work, Dr. Voss,'' the professor said eventually. He was visibly impressed by Voss's skill. "May I ask you what your conclusion is, then?''

"I can speculate. But the only even slightly plausible explanation is that someone deliberately altered the data. Errors in reception would be random in nature; these anomalous characteristics are not. I estimate that about one in five data words have been altered. They have based their changes on some detailed analyses of frequencies of occurrence of symbols and suchlike, but they couldn't possibly hope to cover every feature, and as we have seen, they inadvertently introduced some new features that helped the altered blocks stand out when analyzed carefully. The delay in releasing the data supports this idea, of course. They needed time to perform the analyses in order to make the forgeries even remotely plausible.''

He paused and looked across the desk at them. "They could not, of course, alter the six hours of data you published in January in a way inconsistent with the error analyses. They had to appear just as they did originally within error bounds. It is that tiny fraction of the data that gives it away. I have no idea why they should do such a strange thing.''

There was a lengthy silence. The professor rubbed his chin with his left hand. "You're quite right,'' he said at last. "It *is* doctored. We have known it all along.''

Helped by Sheilagh, he recounted the story of the Shipston Grange takeover; Lebovsky, Feinberg, and the symposium; Pluto and his encrypted message; and how they were also privy to the real data. Voss was stunned.

"That's amazing. You are a lot more involved than I thought. If you really have the genuine data, then I would be greatly interested in getting a copy of it. I understand the need to be discreet, of course.''

Sheilagh spoke up. "Dr. Voss, we came here today hoping to persuade ourselves that you were not yourself involved in the deception. After our accidental meeting on that train last week, I felt sure you *were* involved. You see, before I spoke to you, I had seen the copy of the NASA summary report that you were actually reading inside that computer manual, so I knew you were lying to me when you denied any interest in the data."

Voss sighed and smiled the first genuine smile Sheilagh had seen from him.

"Yes, I'm sorry about that. I was very rude. You see, I was under the impression then that *you* were still working at Shipston Grange and had been involved in concocting the false data. Just the day before I had realized that the released data had been fixed, and I'd gone up to York to find out for myself what was going on. I didn't know at the time that you and the professor had left the organization. I don't pay much attention to such things, I'm afraid. Seeing you on the train at York sort of reinforced that idea. I realize now that I would almost certainly have seen you before if we had both boarded at York, though I'm sometimes not very aware of people around me, I'll admit. You probably were already in the train, weren't you?"

Sheilagh nodded, delighted by his admissions.

"Well, there we are. I'm sorry. Perhaps this is a good time for me to apologize to you, Professor Holdsworth. I have some recollection of behaving badly to you at some time."

"Really?" the professor said, feigning complete ignorance. "I can't remember any such occasion."

"I'm sure you do. But it's good of you to pretend otherwise. Anyway, let's get on with the important matters, shall we?"

Obviously apologies for his appalling behavior were not important matters to him, Sheilagh thought. She was greatly relieved that he was not after all a villain of the plot, but she remained unimpressed by his manners.

"Our first and most important goal," she said, "is to get hold of all of the real signal and to publish it to the world. We can't do that, of course, until we have it all, otherwise the signal would be cut off. Our second priority is to decipher the message and publish our results. It will be the only real proof we have that we are telling the truth. The story is a little hard to believe if you're not closely involved. People don't expect those countries to collaborate at such a level."

"I can see the reasons it might happen the way you described," Voss said. "None of the countries have the individual ability to get at the signal, so each has the choice of sabotaging the whole scheme or of cooperating. It is natural that they should all combine to detect the signal—even if they do distrust each other. From there it is a short step to withholding the real data.

Until, I suppose, they have got well ahead of everyone else in making use of any knowledge to be gained from it. No doubt they'll be racing against each other, but they will have the race to themselves.''

"That's about how we see it," Sheilagh said.

"However, that's not a stable situation," Voss went on. "Any one of them could have a change of heart and back out."

"Then they would be admitting that they have been defrauding the rest of the world," the professor said.

"True," Voss said. "I suppose it is sort of stable as long as they are all neck and neck in the race to understand the message. If one gets too big a lead, one of the others would be sure to threaten them. Or if one gets too far behind. But until the key messages at the beginning are repeated, that's unlikely to happen. Intriguing."

"I'm beginning to think that the Five will never disclose the real data if no one gives them a reason to," Sheilagh said dejectedly. "So we would like to ask you to help us on the second task. We've made some headway, with the real data, of course. It was the professor's idea. He said we needed a fresh mind."

"I'll do my best. I would, of course, like to get my hands on the real data. Do you think we might get some meaning out of it even without the first blocks?"

"We don't know, but we have been trying, and we have discovered a few things," Sheilagh said. She then described to Voss their recent discoveries about symbol combinations in the data. Voss was especially interested in her balanced parentheses theory.

"That's exciting," he said. "It sounds very plausible to me. But tell me, what confidence do you have that your friends in California will be able to continue picking up the signals? If the data runs for nine and a half months, well, that's a long time. A lot could happen."

The professor's face darkened a little. "Yes," he said, "that's my big worry. We have no viable backup. We've got two stations out there, but we've no control over the downlink. And it is possible that someone may suspect, with that sensor just producing noise like that."

He folded his arms with a sigh. "Either we just hang on and hope we can last until we get those first blocks, or we decipher what we have now. The first alternative we can do no more with. But the second, Dr. Voss, well, that is why we have come to you. We believe it is possible to make some sense of the data even without the key blocks. Especially, if I may say so, with the finest minds employed on the task. We would very much like you to help us.''

"I find it difficult to agree with you. It's clear, even from the corrupted data, that the message does not have a simple format. We couldn't hope to decipher it starting partway through without some idea of what it is trying to say. And we can hardly expect to be able to do that.''

"Actually, we do have an idea about that," the professor said. Sheilagh was impressed by the unpretentious charm he managed to put into his voice. "As you can imagine, we have spent a great deal of time debating this question, and, well, we think there are some pointers. But our idea, if we are right, is the only advantage we have over our adversaries. So we are very careful indeed about who we share it with. I'm sure you understand.''

"Naturally.''

"Well," the professor said, turning to Sheilagh, "perhaps I should let Sheilagh explain.''

"The most significant thing about the data, Dr. Voss,'' she said, "is its quantity. There are fewer than eight thousand blocks—we are certain of that—so there is not actually a lot of information in the message.''

Voss nodded, his face expressionless.

"The other thing is that we need to use space-based antennas to securely receive its content. Also, our calculations show that this would be true if the Earth was a factor of ten nearer to or farther away from the source than it is.''

She waited for Voss's nod of acknowledgment.

"So we think that the message is deliberately aimed at civilizations like us, who are in a certain stage of development, namely, the beginnings of space exploration.''

"And the use of electromagnetic waves for communication,'' Voss said.

"Yes," Sheilagh said. "So we think the message contains knowledge understandable only to such civilizations, or those that are more developed. We know it doesn't contain detailed descriptions of the originators and their world, the kind of stuff put on the Pioneer spacecraft, because it's too short. We think it probably contains scientific knowledge. Knowledge that would provide us with an understanding of the Cepheans rather than just a description like a painting or a video.''

"I see," Voss said. "Knowledge that would presumably be very valuable to us.''

"Certainly," Sheilagh said. "That's why it's so important that we beat the Five to it."

They discussed their idea with Voss for over an hour, trying to convince him. Throughout, he showed no indication of his reaction.

Eventually he smiled broadly at them. "I agree with you," he said bluntly. "I think you have a very convincing argument, and I would be most delighted to assist you in any way possible."

CHAPTER 11

DURING THE NEXT FOUR WEEKS SHEILAGH AND VOSS
worked together with great intensity on the Cepheans' signal,
making considerable progress. At first she visited Voss and
worked with him in his study. She did that several times, feeling
each time that she had melted further through the barrier between them.

Slowly, the person behind the icy front emerged.

She quickly gained a deep respect for the clarity and agility
of his mind. The way she described it was to imagine two points
on a plane representing where the mind was and where it was
trying to get. Her mind would wander and skip all over the place
until it finally stumbled across its destination by chance, if she
was lucky. Voss's mind would find the most direct path available, without straying. That did not mean that he was incapable
of fanciful thinking or of unconstrained open-mindedness. He
could switch at will between many states of mind in rapid succession or maintain a resolute concentration for hours on end.
It was that mental authority which she had sensed subconsciously when she had first met him. Once she understood those
things, she became more relaxed in his company, more so, she
thought, than with any person she had ever known.

What helped convince her of his extraordinary faculties was
the discovery that all the equipment in his little office was controlled with brain waves. But when she once attempted to talk
to him about it, he became irritable and refused to speak of it

beyond a cursory dismissal of it as a "trivial little trick not worth talking about."

Early in December there was a change in the incoming data received clandestinely from the OMSs. It seemed to mark a genuine change in the Cepheans' data and corresponded closely with the expected halfway point in their total message. One day, a week afterward, Voss was eagerly awaiting Sheilagh in his study.

"I think, Sheilagh, that last night I made a very important discovery," he said as she sat down opposite him. He was looking at some diagrams on his screen. These were in the form that he and Sheilagh had made up to depict the symbols in the Cepheans' message. To others they might have looked like very abstruse mathematical equations, but they were simply sequences of symbols arranged into groups. The 9 bits in every symbol allowed 512 different values. Sheilagh and Voss had come up with graphic signs to depict each value but so far had found it impossible to give them any definite meanings.

"You asked last time," Voss said, "if they weren't parentheses, then what were they? Well, I've been thinking about that. You notice how the relative abundance of the ten pairs changes gradually throughout the data?" He indicated a group of three pairs of symbols on the lower left of the screen. "These here appear much more often earlier in the messages than these." He indicated another three. "But later the situation is reversed."

"Yes, I'd noticed that," Sheilagh said.

"Well, I had an idea just after you left last time. I should have thought of it much sooner."

"What idea?"

"The balanced pairs may represent operators."

To a physicist involved in quantum mechanics, the notion of operators had a special meaning. Operators acted on mathematical quantities to create new entities. Arithmetic addition was an operator that acted on two numbers to produce a third. In quantum mechanics the operators were often very complicated, but the idea was essentially the same. Some symbologies had been developed that allowed the most sophisticated and far-reaching ideas to be expressed with an elegant ease using operators.

"That would explain why there are as many as ten of them, wouldn't it?"

"Well," Voss said warily, "I'd be happier if there were more. But ten may be enough. The changing abundances as one progresses through the messages seem to fall in with the notion of operators being expressed in terms of other, simpler ones.''

"But why are the pairs balanced? What kind of operators occur in balanced pairs?''

"There are examples throughout physics, but few of them in a truly fundamental sense. Except, however, in geonics.''

"Really? In your own theories?''

Voss turned to look at her and paused for a few seconds. "I once started to express the theory in a new notation I'd developed that looked promising. But I gave up in the end because a much more direct, if incomplete, way occurred to me. It's this direct way that I used in my publications. This new notation was a rather radical way of looking at things, I'm afraid, and I got myself into all kinds of difficulties.'' He laughed at the memory. "The interesting thing was that the notation always used pairs of operators. I ended up with something like forty-eight of them by the time I gave up.''

"So you think these messages might be expressing geonics in something like your own notation?''

"Well, geonics does show signs of being able to elegantly unify most of physics if only we could untangle the horrendous equations that it always seems to produce. If those signs are not misleading, then it is likely to be a very long-lasting theory, maybe even everlasting. And assuming the laws of physics are the same across the galaxy at the Cepheans' star, then it would be just as significant to them, even if they did discover it long ago. It's a bit of a wild speculation, but it could be that the Cepheans are trying to tell us about it in their own notation.''

"Hmm. I would have thought it unlikely that one race's scientific notation would have any universal qualities that would correspond to others'. Look at the English and Chinese languages. Two groups of almost identical human beings coming up with such utterly different languages.''

"Different when written, yes,'' he said, "but when spoken there are direct translations between English and Chinese sounds. Especially for the fundamental things like 'yes,' 'no,' 'mother,' 'son,' 'black,' 'white,' and so on. What I'm getting at is that the underlying structure, the symbol-less concepts involved in a theory, are indeed universal, and perhaps a notation can be generated that reflects those concepts best of all.''

Sheilagh was silent.

"That's the beauty of the way the Cepheans' message is encoded,'' he continued. "They are not trying to send us ideas in their own symbology. The basic symbols can be represented in any way we like. It is the sequence and arrangement of the symbols that we have to decipher, and that is where, perhaps, the fundamental or absolute nature of what they are saying is to be found. It's like having a crossword to do, but backward. We know all the answers, but we don't know how they fit together. We have to assemble all the words into a square symmetric grid in which all of the interconnections are valid.''

''Maybe I'm wrong,'' he confessed. ''It's basically only an intuition, I admit. But there is something about these messages that seems familiar to me. They give me a feeling when I look at them that they may be the geonic theory expressed, well, properly, so that all the equations suddenly drop out as simple expressions.''

Sheilagh could not help him. Only the simplest, most general ideas of geonics theory had penetrated her mind so far. The dense mathematics was completely beyond her. ''Sorry, Russell. You are going to be on your own on that path. The math that you use in your papers is several light-years above my head.''

''Yes, I know I'll be on my own. After all, the notation I invented was never published. It only exists inside my head, and my computer. In fact, it's largely been pushed out of my head by other things.''

Sheilagh looked up at him and saw that he was studying her face. ''What kind of other things?'' she asked.

He smiled. ''Oh, all these recent developments.''

She hesitated. During the previous weeks they had become close friends. The secret task they shared had bound them together with a personal bond. They discovered that Voss enjoyed the theater, to which Sheilagh had introduced him, and they spent many evenings relaxing in the West End of London, sharing the stimulus and energy of the place. So far, however, their relationship had not crossed the boundary into the realm of romance. Sheilagh felt it was about time it did.

Returning his smile and pretending to be unconcerned about the answer to her next question, she said, ''Is there room inside your head for the more normal things in life?''

Again he smiled. ''I can maybe make some room.''

''Good. You know, I thought you were a real sod when I first met you. You seemed to enjoy being rude to people. But you're not so bad, after all.''

''I'm sorry. I'm sorry if I was rude to you.''

''You're forgiven. But I don't understand why . . .''

"Sheilagh, you must have realized by now that I'm not like other people. For the last six or seven years I've become increasingly hermitlike. I no longer have a social center to my brain. But I could do better, given your help."

Sheilagh laughed and reached for his hand, which he nervously withdrew.

"I feel like I'm driven by an irresistible force, Sheilagh." He stood and paced around the room, using his arms in broad sweeps as if to signify the vastness of his thoughts. "Years ago I realized I was fortunate enough to be around at a time when mathematics contained tools of such fantastic elegance and power that the deepest, most profound secrets of the universe seemed to be within reach. And also fortunate to live in a place where those tools can be learned, taught by the best teachers. And I also knew I was bloody good at it! I became obsessed by the idea of finding the ultimate truths and spent my entire life to that end. I found it impossible to make new friends. I came to college here in London and completely immersed myself in mathematics. I read about all the current, amazing theories that looked so promising and found I could understand them easily and even develop them myself. This goal formed in my mind, the ultimate goal: to explain the origin of all fundamental particles and their interactions, the origin of the universe. I thought I could do it, be the first. I still do. I wanted no distractions.

"I'm also very obsessive by nature, a characteristic I actually consciously developed." He laughed. "You've probably noticed."

"Er, just a little."

"You won't believe me, but I didn't always used to be quite so intense and serious about things. I think I may even have a sense of humor packed away somewhere."

"Good. Is it me that's made you think about these things, then?" She knew perfectly well that it must have been, but it made her so happy to think about it that she could not resist making him tell her.

He nodded. "Just thought I'd tell you. I didn't want you to think . . . well, you know."

Sheilagh bubbled with joy. She went close up to him and stood looking into his face, inviting him to kiss her.

She did not travel home that evening.

Late the next morning they had great difficulty resuming their urgent work.

"There's something else that the professor thought of," Sheilagh said. "Some time ago we were talking about what we thought the Cepheans' idea was in sending out two signals. I'd been suggesting that apart from the obvious fact that the first signal was like a lighthouse beam, they were 'bootstrapping' us by giving us information that would lead to our detection of the next message in a series. Well, the professor said that if that idea is correct, then we might expect the data to contain not only the theory of such a detector but instructions on how to build one. He suggested that the change we saw early in the month was just where the theory stopped and instruction started."

"Forget the bloody Cepheans. Let's go back to bed."

"Now come on, Russell." She playfully wagged a finger at him. "We've already wasted a day. I can't believe anyone can change that much overnight. Where's that obsession of yours gone?"

"You're my obsession now."

Sheilagh did not show it, but she was uncomfortable about the way Russell had spoken. She did not want to change things that much.

"Do you think the professor may be right?" she asked.

He sighed. "All right, all right. It sounds very plausible to me. It's a good idea to look at the second part in that light. Why don't you do that while I tackle that rather wild idea of mine I told you about yesterday?"

"Good idea." Sheilagh went to the desk that she had taken over on the other side of the room. She had never been happier.

A week later that happiness was shattered. She telephoned Voss as usual prior to paying him a regular visit.

"Don't come," was the strange and startling reply she got. "We don't need to be together in order to work together. I get distracted with you here."

Sheilagh was too startled to reply. He gave her instructions to communicate via electronic mail and said bluntly that he had made no progress in deciphering the Cepheans' messages.

"I'm sorry, Sheilagh."

Then he rang off.

CHAPTER 12

TWO WEEKS EARLIER AN ENGINEER IN EINDHOVEN HAD signed his name to a line-item failure analysis report and attached two sheets of commentary. In the box labeled ACTION he had recommended that his report be sent to the OMS Systems Engineering Department at the Copernicus Center in Texas.

Five days later his report was on the desk of the leading OMS systems engineer. The report had implied that a software error might be the real cause of the spurious values coming from strain gauge 3B on OMS 2. The systems engineer knew that it was impossible that such a prominent and serious software error could have escaped their design reviews and tests. But the antenna systems engineer's report had convinced him that the sensor could not possibly generate the numbers they were getting in the telemetry, and so there had to be another cause, something they had not thought of.

He called an informal meeting of the responsible people in his group, and they rapidly came to the conclusion that what they were seeing was indeed impossible. When his engineers started accusing each other of being mistaken, of lying, and then of being incompetent, he decided that the issue should be taken seriously and followed up.

The problem was that if a memory fault had changed the program instructions in a way that caused such symptoms, it must have happened identically and simultaneously in all three redundant copies of the control computers aboard OMS 2. That was clearly to be discounted. On the other hand, the program itself was apparently incapable of singling out one strain gauge from all the others. All were treated identically by the same piece of program code. Moreover, no one could see any such error in the program listings.

The baffling problem soon became the favorite topic of discussion among the Copernicus Center engineers. There was nothing more interesting to the engineers than clearly visible but impossible behavior by one of their creations.

In the end someone had the idea of getting the spacecraft management computers to dump a copy of the programs down the data link to Earth. They then discovered that the impossible had indeed happened: The program in the spacecraft did not match the one in the software archive at the Copernicus Center. What was more puzzling was that it did not match any program that had ever existed, according to the configuration control system. Clearly someone had managed to smuggle a doctored program on board.

The OMS program manager made the decision to upload the correct version of the telemetry program immediately. The engineers worked out a way of doing that one channel at a time so that the Cephean data would not be interrupted.

Less than one second after the corrected programs were loaded, perfectly reasonable strain gauge readings were being packaged into the telemetry messages where once only noise had been seen. The numbers were dutifully written onto compact data disks in Professor Holdsworth's receivers secretly being operated in two houses in southern California.

The revelation that the OMSs were loaded with secretly altered control programs created quite a stir. When knowledge of the subterfuge reached the Five Nations Committee on Space headquarters in New York, they issued orders that the news should be treated as top secret and started an immediate emergency inquiry.

Who had been tapping the Cepheans' signal right under their noses?

"Here's a list of all his telephone contacts for the last six months, incoming and outgoing," Benson said, passing a sheet of paper across the desk.

DuPont struggled to contain his pleasure. What a stroke of luck! This was what he had dreamed of for years. Stupid old Benson had put him on the idiotic aliens case because nothing important could ever come of it. Now it had turned into one of the biggest things the department had ever had. Even Benson had not been party to the real issues. How Benson hated it!

"It's an important job, DuPont. Don't cock it up."

Squirm, Benson, squirm.

"You do understand, DuPont?"

"Of course."

"That means you don't make any mistakes. Use whatever means are necessary. If you're too slow or give them any hint of what's about to happen, they'll pass the data on, and we'll never recover it. So you've got to be damned quick. Get the teams out immediately. Personally I wouldn't trust you with the job, but the minister insists no one else be involved."

Say whatever you like, Benson, you can't stop me now, DuPont thought. After a job as important and as easy as this one, you can't possibly block my promotion any longer. We'll be on equal terms then.

So Holdsworth has been getting the alien data from the States! God knows how he managed it. But who cares? We've got him now. And all his contacts.

"It also means there are no restrictions. But keep it very tidy, DuPont. These people are well known."

And he could now do whatever he liked to that old idiot Holdsworth and his little band of boys and girls. Whatever means are necessary. Retrieve the real data and ensure no copies exist. Utmost urgency and secrecy. Perfect.

Earlier that day, in Santa Paula, California, two unmarked cars drew up outside Jacob Klein's home. Four men in plainclothes got out and went to the door. When it was opened, they identified themselves as special agents of the FBI and pushed their way into the house. The satellite receivers were confiscated. Klein was arrested and taken away.

The same events were played out an hour later in Carpinteria at the home of Bud Randall.

"They're still in the jug, I'm afraid," Feinberg said.

He was sitting with the professor, Doreen, Bill, Cindy, and Sheilagh in the Holdsworths' local pub. It was two days after Klein's and Randall's arrest. Feinberg had unexpectedly arrived on the professor's doorstep in Somerset, bringing the news of the collapse of their plans.

They sat around a large ancient table in one of the separate rooms in the rambling public house. A dusty and bedraggled stag's head adorned the wall above Feinberg, flanked by a small collection of antique objects whose original purpose mystified the modern mind. Nobody was really surprised at his news. It had been expected for weeks. Nor did it really depress them. They'd had over half the data tucked away, and it was impossible to believe that Randall and Klein would be kept for long. Nobody had broken any laws. But the way ahead was uncertain. They needed time to think.

"What have they been charged with?" the professor asked.

"Espionage. Bail was refused."

"Phew," Bill exclaimed, "they mean business over there!"

Doreen looked sternly at her husband. She had heard the full story of their activities. The professor had been aided by Sheilagh and Bill in a passionate plea for clemency and had, at least for the time being, been spared from the cellar.

"And our beautiful equipment being mauled by the FBI," Sheilagh moaned.

"That's the least of our concerns," the professor said.

"Then there's Pluto," Sheilagh said. "I hope he's not in trouble as well."

"He's all right." said Feinberg. "Without breaking my pledge of secrecy to him, I can assure you that Pluto is alive and well."

Nobody spoke for a while. Each was trying to adjust to the new situation.

"Perhaps we should break cover now and make the story public," the professor said. "Let the truth be known."

"We might fail," Feinberg said. "The government would just deny our allegations and make out we're a bunch of crazies with a grudge."

"Oh, I hardly think anyone would regard Adrian as crazy, Mr. Feinberg," Doreen said indignantly.

"I'm sorry, Mrs. Holdsworth," Feinberg said, "but I think it's highly probable that even the professor would find it difficult to oppose the wishes of the governments of five of the most powerful nations in the world. You've got to realize who we're fighting. I'm not kidding when I tell you that I didn't fly over here because I was desperate to see you guys again. I wanted to be difficult to find for a while. It won't be long before the FBI pays *me* a visit."

There were several alarmed gasps from his British friends. "There's absolutely nothing they can pin on me or anyone, except perhaps Pluto. Intercepting nonsecure telemetry signals is a dubious hobby, but it's not illegal. Still, I'd rather not give them the chance until we've had time to make some plans together.''

''Do Randall and Klein know about the connection with Adrian's group?'' Doreen asked. She was very alarmed.

''Er, no. Just me. And I'm the only one the feds might suspect. Bud and Jacob sent the disks to me every week by Federal Express, and I of course airmailed them here. They're certain to trace the shipments from California, but they couldn't trace them beyond the institute.''

''What do you suggest we do?'' Sheilagh asked.

''The way I see it, there are two possibilities,'' Feinberg said. ''Our aim is to get the real data published, right? From the entire message of course, including the stuff we haven't received yet. Well, number one is your suggestion of publicly denouncing the Five and trying to prove our case. But we run a hell of a risk of being made out as a bunch of jerks. I would be more hopeful if we could make some sort of sense of the messages so far. That might convince some important people. But we can't and we won't until we get the first blocks, and that is out of the question now. Or we could try a little blackmail.''

The others looked at him with a mixture of alarm and perplexity.

''It all depends on a judgment call. It's possible that just the threat of going public would be enough to persuade the Five to release the real data. They could do it with a story about some processing error in the OMSs that garbled the signal and say that their boys were getting the same garbage the rest of us were. Also, they could say that they'd been clever enough to send the data through two different channels for safety but had just chosen the wrong one to believe. See, maybe by giving them the chance to chew it over, we could scare them more than by hitting them with all our aces at once. You guys ever play poker?''

''What about the option they have of just putting us all in jail?'' Doreen asked with an angry tremor in her voice.

''Oh, now, Mrs. Holdsworth,'' Feinberg said soothingly, ''that card just isn't in their hand. Imagine what the rest of the world would say to that. All we have to do is make sure our story, backed up by evidence, is in the hands of some independent organization, like a national newspaper, with instructions to publish the dirt in the event of our arrest.''

''In the event of—'' Doreen fought for speech.

''It can't possibly come to that, Doreen,'' the professor said.

"But I must say I don't like the idea of playing games with politicians. I'm strongly in favor of just explaining the facts and relying on the persuasion of truth."

"I agree with the professor," Sheilagh said. "I think Walter is getting carried away with this espionage business. We're scientists, not spies."

"Walter doesn't know about Russell's ideas, either," Bill said.

Sheilagh explained Russell Voss's theory about the messages being a description of geonic theory. She did not bother to describe his odd behavior on the telephone. That was too private.

"Russell Voss!" Feinberg exclaimed. "You've got him in on this? Jeez! That makes a big difference. He's about the best guy we could call on. Why didn't you mention this before? And he's got an idea about the messages as well?"

He flung his arm over the back of his chair and laughed loudly. "Well, that means we can squeeze them for sure. In fact, we could do it either way. It's just a matter of whether you want to give the bastards a chance to cover their asses before we kick them."

"I'm afraid," the professor said, "that we've got to be very careful and clever from now on, and we've also got to act quickly." He looked around at his friends. "It's most likely that if we fail to decipher the data and make it widely known, then the Five will keep it to themselves forever. The Cepheans' message, which *we* discovered, will be kept secret, even from us. We've got to take this affair very seriously. Our only hope is to get more people involved—people we can trust. I suggest we start straightaway. In the meantime, let's hope Dr. Voss succeeds very soon. If he doesn't, then I'm afraid the world may never get to know what the Cepheans are telling us."

They left the pub and set off back to the Holdsworths' house. Sheilagh, sitting in the back of the professor's car, was suddenly very frightened, realizing how isolated the house was. She looked out the back window at the lights of Feinberg's rental car, in which her friends Bill and Cindy were traveling. Was it Feinberg's car? There was no way of telling.

She laughed a little at her wild thoughts. Perhaps her imagination was getting a little out of hand. In any case, it certainly was Feinberg driving the car behind them. His manner of driving down the middle of the road, at least down narrow English country lanes in an English car, was unmistakable.

The two cars pulled into the driveway. There was no light on in the house, and the darkness surrounding them was almost impenetrable. Sheilagh heard Bill's and Feinberg's voices loudly sharing a joke, suddenly released from the car's interior as the doors opened and the three occupants climbed out.

"Why isn't the outside light on, dear?" Doreen asked.

"The bulb—"

They were suddenly dazzled by an intense light, and a rough voice with an American accent called out, "That's the guy."

The light went out, and with their eyes blinded in the sudden darkness, they were rushed by about a dozen men. There was a single shout of despair from Feinberg. A momentary scuffle ended with the sickening sound of a blow being dealt to someone's head, followed by the sound of two vehicles racing away into the dark, wheels scrabbling over the gravelly road. They saw a closed van and a sedan, with what looked like five men in it, disappear behind the hedgerows and blast off into the dark.

They remained frozen in complete shock for several seconds. Doreen was the first to speak.

"What happened? What on earth is going on?"

Still unable to see, they groped for each other in the darkness.

"Walter. They got Walter." It was Bill speaking. "I saw four men drag him away. I think they hit him on the head."

"Oh, my God!" Doreen was sobbing.

"We must call the police," the professor said, hurrying her to the front door with the others close behind. They were all shaking and bewildered as they staggered through the hall to the living room. Bill wanted to jump into the professor's car and give chase, but he was quickly persuaded of the futility of such an effort. Whoever the kidnappers were, they were already far away. He stood beside the professor, whose trembling hands worked the telephone.

Professor Holdsworth spoke into the receiver as calmly as he could, stating his name and address. Then he removed the receiver from his ear and turned to Bill with utter bafflement written on his face.

"He hung up!"

"What? You mean you were cut off?"

"No. He definitely hung up." The professor pressed the switch hook, then the 9 button three times. From the doorway came a sharp command.

"Put down the phone, Professor Holdsworth."

A man stood just inside the door. Two more came in behind him and moved swiftly across the room. One planted himself in front of the patio doors; the other took the handset out of the professor's hand, replaced it in its cradle, then firmly shoved Bill and the professor into seats. Sheilagh and Cindy were sitting on either side of Doreen, whose face was gray with fear and shock. The three intruders were casually dressed in jeans and pullovers and looked unarmed. They were clearly well trained and daunted their victims simply by their hard appearance and movements.

The man by the door, the leader of the trio, spoke again, looking over their heads and avoiding eye contact. He gave the impression of being almost mechanical, a professional man of action carrying out orders with no concern for their reasons.

"Do not be alarmed. We are from the British security services. Stay calm and no one will get hurt."

Bill was breathing hard. "Who the hell do you think you are? This is a private home. We have already called the police. They're already on their way."

The man continued to look beyond them. "As far as you're concerned, chum, we *are* the police. Stay calm and be patient. In a few minutes a government official will be here to explain what is going on."

Bill was about to protest, when the professor, who had for the last few moments been concerned about Doreen, held up a hand to him and told him to be calm.

"Just what do you mean by 'security services'?" he demanded. "Police? Army? MI5? The SAS? I think you owe us some explanation."

"I'm sorry, I am not permitted to say any more. Like I said, a government official is on his way who will provide the explanations. You'll have to be patient."

The extreme tension of the last few moments subsided gradually. The two guards relaxed their postures.

"What has happened to our guest? The one you have just kidnapped," Sheilagh demanded.

"Look," the leader said, suddenly adopting a personal tone and giving Sheilagh a tired smile, "just hang on until the man arrives. Go and make yourselves a cup of tea while you wait."

The professor quickly recovered his composure and told his companions that as it seemed they were not in the hands of criminals, they could all guess what the absurd intrusion was concerned with. They might as well relax, but they should say nothing whatsoever.

A half hour passed. Nobody spoke. Sheilagh watched the

professor's expression slowly change during that time from one of alarm, like everyone else's, to one of despondency.

All their hopes seemed to be dashed. It was obvious to her that the Americans had taken the dramatic discovery of the altered control program in the OMSs very seriously indeed. They had traced the data to Walter and then to the professor. They must have followed Walter across the Atlantic to the professor's home. It had been silly of him to come here. But who could have expected such a violent overreaction? Presumably the British government wanted to get hold of all the copies of the smuggled data, and if they managed that, they would certainly have won.

Sheilagh's thoughts were racing. What about Russell? Let's hope they know nothing about him! He's got all the data and—Oh, God, maybe he told the government about us. Maybe this is his doing. No. No, that's unthinkable. He's on our side. Do they know about his involvement? Our conversation in the pub just now may have been overheard. Damn! How naive we've been. Russell hasn't phoned for days; it'll be just our luck if he phones tonight. Somehow we must keep his involvement secret. He's our only hope. If these people get to him before he deciphers the message, then we're finished. The Five will have firmly grabbed complete control over the Cepheans' message, and the world will never get to know it. Oh, please, Russell, dear Russell, don't phone tonight!

An hour later "the man" arrived. It was DuPont. Several other men arrived with him and straightaway started searching the house. There were some alarming sounds of breaking coming from the professor's workroom. DuPont paced up and down the room as he gloatingly lectured his captives.

"You have been caught red-handed in an international conspiracy. We know that you have managed to obtain the real data from the aliens' signal." He swept an imperious gaze around the room. "I must commend you on your ingenuity. But you've been caught."

"International conspiracy?" the professor scoffed. "Don't be a fool, DuPont. You know perfectly well that we've broken no laws. I suggest you stop this puerile behavior before you go too far."

DuPont leaned over the professor, stabbed a finger toward his face, and with a hate-filled voice said, "You're the one who has gone too far, Holdsworth. I didn't mention breaking any laws.

When it comes to national security we don't bother with laws in this country. And what's more, I've got the authority to use whatever methods I choose.'' His face contorted with contempt. ''So if I decided that it was necessary to do a little damage to this cozy little place of yours, or perhaps to you and your friends, there would be nothing to stop me.''

He scowled threateningly at the professor, rigid with hatred, while the professor looked calmly up at him, his expression completely neutral except for a hint of pity.

''Where do you store the data?'' DuPont snapped.

''In the workroom,'' the professor said. ''There's a rack of optical disks on one of the shelves. It sounds like your people have already found them.''

''Where do you keep backups?''

The professor sighed.

''Well?''

''I have them at my house,'' Bill said dejectedly.

''Good. Then we will have found them.'' DuPont sneered at them as they reacted to that news. Bill and Cindy exchanged looks of alarm.

''Who else have you passed the data on to?''

''No one,'' the professor said.

DuPont straightened up and turned away. ''There have been a lot of telephone calls between you and Dr. Voss recently,'' he said as he sat in an armchair by the door. ''You're not going to deny his involvement, surely.''

He got no reply. Sheilagh's heart raced. She found it impossible to hide her despair.

''Well, never mind,'' DuPont continued, ''we'll have found out by now.''

Russell Voss stared in wonder at the large monitor screen in front of him, its glow the only source of illumination in the room. His face was eerily lit by the smoke-blue radiance, and his shadow was cast huge and deformed on the wall behind. The cooling fans hummed steadily.

It was like looking at the birth of the universe. The mystery of the Cepheans' code had been revealed to him three days previously, and since then he had sustained an intense intellectual effort, building up in his mind the dazzlingly clear and profoundly beautiful description of the universe that constituted most of the Cepheans' message in his possession.

He was exhausted, having eaten almost nothing for three days.

His mind began to flicker, and the picture started to lose coherence. But he had seen it; it would never really be lost.

A few million bits of information stored in the memory of the machine in front of him had been transformed into the story of the universe, of the origin and history of time, space, and matter. And he had been the first on Earth to know it.

It was very late. Through his third-floor window, above the high roofs of nearby buildings, the sky was utterly dark. He wanted to see the stars, but they were hidden. He had just grasped the ultimate secret, the unifying theory of the universe, and it would have been wonderful to stretch his gaze light-years out into the galaxy.

He thought of Sheilagh. He had successfully kept her out of his mind since that agonizing minute when he had frozen his heart and his voice and falsely declared his indifference. He could never explain to her, or to anyone, what had driven him to that painful lie.

He was a uniquely lucky man. He had the mental powers to get closer to the ultimate secrets of nature than anyone before had ever been. He could get there, to the dark center of the universe where the answers lay hidden. But there was so little time in which to make the journey. He was twenty-six years old, at the peak of his mental powers, and he had maybe eight or ten productive years left. He was not going to jeopardize his goal, not for any reason.

There would be time later on for the ephemeral, the insignificant, the human.

His doorbell sounded. He detested its sound, the sound of the microscopic, trivial world of everyday living.

Who the hell? What's the time? One-thirty.

Without moving, he turned on the video intercom. On the screen he could see two men, their dark faces hidden.

"Who is it?"

"Police, Dr. Voss. Please let us in."

"Police? Let me see your identification. Put it up to the panel. There's a TV camera there."

The two men suddenly moved out of the camera's sight. He heard a quick discussion in the background. Then everything went quiet.

Obviously not police, he thought. But who, then? They knew my name. This is too much for coincidence. It must be government agents come to collect Holdsworth's data. Oh dear, how depressing. The professor's plot must have been discovered.

He pulled the keyboard over toward him and out of habit picked up his headset with the encephalographic controls. Hitting the keys heavily, he activated the mailer process. As he did so, he heard the sound of several heavy feet running up the fire escape steps at the rear of the building.

He constructed an electronic-mail message addressed to a colleague at the physics department and added a copy-to list that included eight destinations overseas, from Argentina to China. The binary data file containing the raw Cephean data was attached as an auxiliary file.

The men had reached the door, and he heard voices outside his front door as well.

Okay, *send*. If the department's mail-server computer is down, then we're in trouble.

His front door had opened almost without a sound. They must have skeleton keys. He heard voices and heavy feet in the next room.

Damn! It *is* down. Hell! Of course it is at this time of night! Okay, so send the file to the main file server and set up a command file.

The door burst open, and a voice shouted a command that failed to register in his mind. He jumped up out of his seat, and suddenly a jolt like a massive electric shock exploded in his senses. An agonizing pain pierced his chest as a bullet that had been intended for his computer screen hit him between the shoulder blades. He crashed onto the desk, unable to control his body.

Idiot, he thought. You can't stop a computer by smashing its screen. Who's the idiot?

A brilliant light shone in his face. Or was he imagining it?

Oh, no! Not this! Not now!

Send.

The word hammered in his rapidly fading consciousness. *Send.*

His headset was still on his head. Wasn't it? He couldn't tell. *SEND. S - E - N - D.*

PART TWO

PART TWO

CHAPTER 13

ON A LONG, PALE RUNWAY NEAR THE ATLANTIC COAST in South America, a slender white aircraft lined up for takeoff. Shimmering waves of heat from its idling engines liquefied its outline. Its nose pointed at the distant ocean.

The runway was one of two at the Guyana Space Terminal, 120 kilometers northwest of Georgetown. From there, the Mars Commission, originally the Multinational Mars Mission, conducted its principal flight operations. Completed in 1997, the space terminal was a complex of space-age structures surrounded on three sides by forest and plantations and on the east by the ocean.

Two huge rectangular hangers lay between the parallel, five-kilometer-long runways. Just inland from them was a sprawling three-story office building, colored to match the sands of Mars, and the slender pinnacle of the airport control tower. On the other side of the hangars a cloud of vapor issued from a giant cryogenic plant. North of the runways, next to another two-story building, like a Martian cliff, three sixty-meter radio antennas pointed skyward. A broad tunnel under the north runway connected those structures. On the south side of the terminal a tall concrete tower blossomed with microwave antennas.

So big and bright was the complex that it was visible from orbit, according to astronauts who had flown in the twenty-seven successful missions that had been launched there.

On the inshore end of the northern runway, pre-takeoff

checklists were being performed for mission twenty-eight. The vehicle was shaped like a narrow winged cylinder. Its long nose tapered downward uniformly from one-third of the total length to a strikingly small-angled point. The downward and inward taper produced the illusion that the nose drooped. Sharply angled double-delta wings extended along the central third of its length and flared out near their trailing edges to narrow, curved tips. There were no tail fins. Three circular exhaust nozzles, set in a triangle pattern, protruded past the broad, truncated rear. The underside of the wings, the fuselage, and the first few feet of the nose were colored a dark gray. On the sides the word MARSCOM was painted in red and gray. The only window was halfway up the rising surface of the tapered nose. The long sides of the vehicle were smooth and unbroken. Its overall appearance was that of a vehicle capable of immense speeds.

The vehicle was *Pegasus*, one of the three Trans-Atmospheric Vehicles operated by Marscom. These true spaceplanes were powered by a new kind of engine that operated both in and out of the atmosphere, obtaining liquid oxygen fuel in flight by liquefying it out of the air during ascent.

Pegasus was supported along its full length by a sturdy pedestal. As the engines were throttled up, the pedestal began to slide frictionlessly between the sunken twin rails that stretched the length of the runway. With a rush of power it gathered speed smoothly, free of any vibration from its magnetic support. In seventy seconds it lifted clear of the pedestal, which came almost instantly to a halt under inductive braking. In a fast and low trajectory the vehicle shot out over the ocean.

Suddenly the motion was less smooth as their weight was supported by the warm, damp air that churned up from the sea in the morning sun. The ship passed through a layer of clouds whose turbulence flung the passengers strongly against their seat restraints.

The acceleration began to ease slightly, and the noise lessened as they climbed into the thin middle stratosphere. At twenty-six kilometers the engines began to use liquid oxygen from onboard tanks, and the variable-geometry inlet beneath the rear of the fuselage was closed. *Pegasus* had become a rocket.

On board were six people. Two pilots occupied the cockpit. Behind them, where the fuselage broadened, sitting abreast, were four astronauts who were being transported to orbit three hundred kilometers up for a rendezvous with the Marscom space station, Mars Terminus. The leftmost seat was occupied by Dr.

Sheilagh Matthews, twenty-eight years old and about to experience spaceflight for the third time. From Mars Terminus they would embark on a yearlong journey of discovery, but their destination would not be Mars.

Acceleration increased sharply, and noise from the engines became dominant over all other sounds. The oblong of light ahead of them in the cabin became darker and darker as they arched out over the blue curve of the Earth, upward toward the silent sky.

The world they were speeding over had become a different place in the six years since the complete Cephean message had been received. Apart from the psychological effects of the discovery that the Earth was not alone as a haven of life and intelligence in the galaxy, there had been serious political scandals caused by the discovery of the five-nation plot to keep the aliens' knowledge from the general public as well as most of the scientific community. It marked one of the final episodes in the centuries of domination of the old developed nations over the majority of mankind.

The heads of all five governments had been replaced or forced to resign. In Britain, the scandal had reached its highest pitch. The failure, by a hair's breadth, of the security service to prevent Professor Holdsworth's team from passing on the real data to other scientific establishments around the world and the discovery that they had used violent criminal means in the attempt had led to the fall of the government and jail sentences for their minions who had been unlucky enough to be given the job.

Russell Voss had suffered more than any for his pains. The bullet that had shattered a vertebra might have been intended for an inanimate target, but it had left him seriously and permanently injured: He was paralyzed, with no control of his legs and only slight movement in his left arm.

His had been the major contribution to deciphering the Cepheans' message. All pre-Cephean predictions about alien signals had been shown to be hopelessly naive. Everyone had expected such a signal to use universal physical objects such as the hydrogen atom and concepts such as "distance" and "time" as its language and to be fairly simple to understand as a result. They had all expected the aliens to be mostly concerned with divulging the nature of themselves and their world. All of Earth's attempts at interstellar communication had been of the kind that said: "Here we are, this is what we look like, this is where we live, this is what our world is like.'' It had been taken for granted that any alien would want to say the same sorts of things.

No one had expected the enigmatic and almost impenetrable message that was received between July 1994 and May 1995. Russell Voss had been the first to fully unravel its true meaning. Some said that he was still the only one to understand it properly.

The signal had indeed been divided into two parts, as had been suspected when the qualitative changes had been detected in the messages received after December 1994. The first blocks of Part I had been expected to contain the definitions of the symbols in which the rest were encoded. That had turned out to be true, but in a way it was true of Part I as a whole. Voss had attempted to explain it to the public in his first book on the Cepheans:

''The first half of their signal is a superbly elegant, and un-nervingly brief, symbolic description of the universe: its cause, its beginning, its evolution, and its future. It has no introduction, no commentary, and no explanation. It is in fact cryptic.

''But we must not assume that the Cepheans were deliberately obscuring its meaning or being secretive. It is cryptic to us like an unfamiliar foreign language is. If we were given a document in a foreign language, we might be able to break its code, so to speak, once we knew what the contents were about. We could make guesses about certain words and try to find patterns that made sense. The Cepheans' is such a document.

''It might seem strange to send a message that cannot be understood until the recipient knows beforehand what it's about! But we know that we share the same galaxy as they do: When they look up at the galaxies outside the Milky Way, they see the Andromeda galaxy and all the others that we see, in almost exactly the same configuration. Always assuming they have eyes. And a sky. And an up.

''They see these galaxies in the same way that we do, so it is to be expected that they will have similar explanations for them. Their explanations may differ in sophistication from ours, but they must produce results that match the visible universe if they are explanations at all. In other words, the behavior of the universe, being identical in the Cepheans' eyes as it is in our own, is the common ground, the 'language' in which their letter is expressed.

''Of course, it is a letter composed of symbols, for without a means of directly communicating concepts between minds, what other way is there? They have used five hundred or so different symbols, which may not seem a lot to describe the whole universe with, but compare it with the thirty or so that English speakers use for their description of the universe, such as it is. These symbols, in Part I of the message, form a complete and beautifully symmetrical 'Grand Theory' that explains and predicts the existence of the universe. In form, it ascends from the specific to the general, from the particular to the cosmic. But it can be equally appreciated and followed in the reverse sense, just by reading the messages, and the internals of each message, in the reverse order.

"Now, I know that will sound far-fetched to anyone who has studied the history of natural philosophy, but I have to say that that's my understanding of it. The search for such a complete and symmetrical theory was popular in myths and legends, and in less enlightened times all sorts of fanciful and worthless fantasies were concocted to explain the existence of, and to find a purpose for, the world and the individual mind. All of these suffered from the same fault that the dogma of creationism, now deceased, suffered from. They were all circular, closed flights of fancy that could not in principle be disproved. Their originators saw the fact that they could not be disproved as proof in itself.

"The Cepheans' Grand Theory seems to me as close to a perfect answer to the ultimate questions as we humans are ever likely to need or have. While it does not suffer from being closed to refutation, I must stress, however, that it is still just a theory. It is merely a long string of inert, lifeless symbols to which the mind can attach meaning. The meaning we can attach to it is a description of how the universe around us is constructed, how it must be perceived by any mind within it, and how we may predict and to some extent control it.

"Part II of the signal is a development of the theory depicted so wonderfully in Part I, in more direct terms. Its full meaning has not yet been extracted, but it seems to be a detailed account of how the implications of the Grand Theory can be tested and put to use.

"It is a remarkable fact that while the expression of their theory is advanced beyond our capabilities, most of its contents are not. Not only can we understand what is being said, but we actually recognize a lot of it from our own theories. What the Cepheans have done is to bind together many of our great ideas of physics that have had independent origins into a new and solid

structure. Not only have they unified the forces of nature, but
they have unified all our most important theories.

"It may be inevitable that the Cepheans' Grand Theory must
remain beyond the abilities of all but the few who have the necessary specialized educations and skills. That is a great pity, for
the theory is very beautiful. Perhaps this Grand Theory represents the final chapter in the physicist's book, the ultimate goal
of complete unification of all previous laws. Certainly one would
expect a race with millions or even *billions* of years more history
than us, orbiting their very ancient star as they do, to have had
time to come close to such a state of knowledge.

"But if that is so, is it not very remarkable that just a few
years before the Cepheans were ever heard of, we ourselves,
with only a few hundred years of civilization behind us, were
starting to formulate the first tentative equations that are entailed
in the Grand Theory? Either there is an almighty coincidence
in the developmental state our two races or the Grand Theory
is indeed ultimate. If the latter is the case and there is no more
fundamental physics to discover, then a question raises itself in
my mind: What have the Cepheans been doing over the last
millions of years?"

Pegasus's engines shut down. Suddenly Sheilagh felt the entire vehicle falling. Her arms lifted from her lap, and her hair
rose about her head. She felt her stomach rising against her
diaphragm. The vehicle had seemed to be standing on its tail,
and now that it had abruptly lost its support, it was falling back
toward the Earth three hundred kilometers below. Despite this
being her third flight, she still found it impossible at first to
shake off the feeling that in a few seconds the atmosphere would
start tearing at the wings. The absence of an outside view with
a horizon had helped increase her disorientation.

The spaceplane pitched forward gradually under the command of the autopilot, and all motion seemed to stop. As the
pilots went through the orbit-entry checklist, Sheilagh gazed
past them at the view of Earth. She could see the curved, azure
horizon capped with solid capes of clouds standing out above
their darker shadows. Her disorientation vanished, and she felt
again the exhilaration of being a space traveler.

Pegasus had placed itself in an orbit that in twenty minutes
would catch up with Mars Terminus, twelve kilometers ahead
of them. Its occupants could already see their destination through
the forward window, an intensely colorful patch standing above

the deepening blue of the atmosphere, a collection of angular and curved white, gold, silver, and red shapes. It looked about as big as the Moon as seen from Earth.

They drifted tail-first under the space station toward the docking ports at the farther end. Attached to the Earthside of Terminus was the long vehicle that was to become their entire world for the next twelve months. It was composed of seven segments in a line. The nearest was an angular, slightly wider section about ten meters long. The nearer end of it possessed two rocket exhaust nozzles that peered out of holes in the center of a large, brown heat shield that curved slightly as it reached out beyond the edges. Next to the propulsion unit was a ten-meter-long silver cylinder with a long, flexible docking tunnel connecting it to the space station. It was a special version of the Mars Transfer Vehicles that had originally been designed to carry five astronauts to Mars. This one was destined for an even greater adventure.

At the farther end was a separate structure composed of five segments, four similar cylindrical ones with a central segment separating them into two pairs, smaller and rectangular. It bore the initials of the All Nations Interstellar Communications Enterprise.

The other end of the docking tunnel was attached to one of a pair of larger cylinders, the space station's America and Asia modules. Their sides touched, and their interiors were joined by a broad tube. A rectangular framework of girders enclosed them, and at one end were two pairs of long solar panels that spread 100 meters across the sky above them. Beyond the twin cylinders was another identical one, the Europe module, lying across their ends. Protruding from one end of the third cylinder was the docking structure. At a port on the other side from *Pegasus* was another Marscom Trans-Atmospheric Vehicle, *Tsiolkovsky*, its slender white dart shape illuminated by the bright Earthglow.

In another two minutes *Pegasus* was at a standstill fifty meters away. The pilot manually turned the craft so that the hatch, above the passengers' heads, faced the Mars Terminus. An electric motor sounded as the external hatch cover was drawn aside to expose the docking port. The gap between the spacecraft slowly closed, and with a light bump the two joined. *Pegasus* was gently pulled around as the docking clamps on the space station captured it.

CHAPTER 14

VOSS'S RECOVERY LASTED MANY MONTHS, DURING which time Sheilagh gently forced her presence upon him, hoping to salvage something of their original relationship out of his tragedy. But in that she completely failed. If his injuries had had any effect on him, it was to snuff out any tenderness that remained. Since that one spark of mutual feeling had been kindled and abruptly extinguished six years before, she had had to slowly forget about the pain it caused her.

During the two years following Voss's convalescence, he had worked on developing and disseminating the Cepheans' Grand Theory; she had used the time to gain her Ph.D. but had rarely spoken with him. Each time they had met, the barrier had grown. Voss had rejected her because the secrets of the universe beckoned him away, allowing no competitors for his time. How could she argue with that?

She had chosen to work on the Grand Theory because it had suddenly opened up a vast unexplored tract of research opportunities, and there she was at the very center of things, a personal friend of the first man to discover it. But she knew later, years later, when she had understood more about herself, that she had been helplessly bound to Voss, wanting desperately to nurture back to life the love that she knew was dying in the desert he had spread about him.

Voss had been the obvious choice for the position of chief scientist on the ANICE project, whose British base was at

Abingdon in Oxfordshire. Sheilagh had herself been immediately caught up in a fantastic series of developments culminating with her selection as mission specialist for the ANICE flight. Her life was filled to overflowing with demands on her time, with research, training, and designing the experiment and the laboratory systems. She was also based at Abingdon and frequently worked with Voss, but their relationship reverted to being purely professional.

Meanwhile, Voss's personal goal, for which he had sacrificed everything, was essentially achieved.

The Cepheans' Grand Theory explained mass, gravitation, and all the forces of nature in terms of the geometry of space. To Voss's amazement it turned out to be the clear expression of his own geonics theory for which he had been vainly searching. For decades people had been working on so-called Caluza-Klein theories, extending the fundamental equations of Einstein's general relativity, which were expressed in the four dimensions of space and time, to no less than eleven dimensions. Time was the manifestation of the fourth dimension, with the velocity of light acting as the multiplier; mass was the equivalent of the fifth dimension, with the gravitational constant G acting as the multiplier. The increase in the dimensionality of the equations greatly increased their complexity, of course, and it was that complexity which Voss had come closest to unraveling.

One prediction of Voss's geonics theories was the existence of an ultimately fundamental particle, which he called the "preon." It was a multidimensional black hole in which the seven spatial dimensions, beyond the four seen in the contemporary universe, were bound up. The binding up of space, the extra dimensions, inside preons was the source of the preons' materiality. Matter and space were therefore seen as two facets of the same thing.

The binding up of dimensions in the preons had occurred in the earliest moments of the universe's history. The event that had started the evolution of the universe had been the collapse of one of those ten dimensions. That had resulted in a rapid succession of further collapses for a total of seven dimensions. Once that process had started, the time dimension had become part of the universe and had taken part in all the processes; the universe had started to evolve. The collapsed dimensions appeared as a great condensation of preons in the 4-D spacetime, and to compensate for loss of "volume," the remaining spacetime expanded rapidly. The expansion was simply an increase in the distances separating the preons as time increased.

The early universe was a region of spacetime, three spatial dimensions and one temporal dimension, that contained large numbers of preons with seven internal dimensions in addition to the four they moved in. The subsequent evolution of the universe was described by the Cepheans in a way that paralleled Voss's geonics theory but used a new kind of mathematics to express it, so that the impenetrable equations did not arise.

But the single most startling result of the Grand Theory, which was the essence of the second part of the message, was that *instantaneous* communication between distant points in the galaxy, without contravening the laws of relativity, was possible using the extra dimensions bound up in the preons.

The implication was, of course, that the Cepheans were expecting a call.

Near-global agreement had eventually been reached on a decision to construct the fantastic machine suggested by the second part of the Cepheans' message—the geonic communications device, or "gecom," as it came to be known. All the scientists involved, including Voss, had recommended that the experiment take place aboard a spacecraft very far away from the Earth. That was because the conditions created by the experiment were difficult to control, so that an accident could result in the spontaneous creation of enough energy to devastate an entire continent and obliterate all life on Earth. Once the experiment in space had been perfected and proved safe, the Earth-based one being built in southern England would be turned on.

The scandal that had developed in late 1995 had resulted in the formation of the Mars Commission from the wreck of the Multinational Mars Mission. It was an example of the age-old trick of removing any blemish of disrepute from an organization by renaming it. Konstantin Lebovsky rematerialized as the chief executive officer of the mission to Mars. When ANICE was formed and the decision to build the machine in space was made, Marscom was in the best position to provide the necessary space capability in the shortest time. Marscom had the resources and international infrastructure to manage the new ANICE project, and they were duly given the new commission.

Two Mars Transfer Vehicles and three Mars Lander Vehicles were being built as part of the original plan for the Mars Mission. The first craft, consisting of one MTV and two landers, would be launched in early 2001, taking advantage of a favorable alignment of the two planets. Three months later, the second craft would be launched out of Earth orbit and follow a longer path to reach the red planet seven months after the first. Both craft were to follow paths that would take them past Mars in hyperbolic, that is, open, orbits such that they would use the Martian gravitational well to swing them around onto a return trajectory to Earth. The first craft would dispatch its two landers, one unmanned and the other with five people on board, and return unmanned to Earth after a round-trip flight of twenty-four months. The returning MTV would use aerobraking in the Earth's atmosphere to slow it to an orbital velocity, as would the landers in their approach to the Martian surface.

When the second mission arrived at Mars, its five occupants would land at the same site, while the first crew would blast off to catch up with the second Mars Transfer Vehicle on its way back to Earth, powered by fuel extracted from the Martian permafrost. The second crew was to spend three years on Mars in the facilities constructed and tested by the first mission.

When the ANICE project started in 1996, the Mars plans were modified. The construction of Mars Terminus was brought forward, and an extra Mars Transfer Vehicle was assembled there to be ready for the ANICE project launch date, April 6, 2000. MTV 1 and 2 would then be assembled to be ready for their March and June 2001 launch dates. A space laboratory was constructed out of four MTV hulls and a smaller, entirely new control module sandwiched between them. The whole laboratory took the place of the Mars landers attached to the MTV. The combined vehicle was to be sent into an elliptical orbit around the sun, initially behind the Earth and then diving down toward the sun to meet up with Earth exactly one year later. If everything went according to plan, it would arrive just a few days after the first Mars mission was under way.

Marscom regarded the ANICE project as a great opportunity for rehearsing its Mars missions and for giving their MTV systems the best kind of testing possible. There was a good spirit of cooperation between the two organizations. It was also, of course, the best way of undoing the damage done by the 1995 scandal.

In mid-March Sheilagh and her fellow astronauts on the ANICE program had been given twelve days' leave. On the 23rd she was guest of honor at a dinner party held by Professor

Holdsworth and Doreen. Bill Tomlinson, Cindy, Walter Feinberg, and his wife, Linda, were there. They had not seen Sheilagh for nearly a year, and they were struck by the change in her. She was so much more self-assured, no longer the student searching for a path down which to travel.

The evening began as a kind of repeat celebration of their exploits six years previously. Feinberg treated them to another very colorful, wildly exaggerated description of his kidnapping by the CIA outside that very house, paying especial attention to the right hook he had landed with immense satisfaction on the chin of one of his captors.

"I expected Dr. Voss to be here, Professor," Feinberg said.

"He was invited, of course," the professor replied. "He's based in Abingdon now, at the ANICE center. It's a little too far for him to travel, I think. Besides, he's hardly ever seen these days. I doubt if he would have come, anyway. He spends every waking minute working on the Grand Theory's millions of implications and ramifications. It really has become an obsession with him, I'm afraid. Have you heard from him, Sheilagh?"

"Not much," she replied. "He was closely involved in the design of the gecom for the space laboratory, of course, but for the last year I've heard practically nothing from him."

Once the meal was over and the caterers had cleaned up and left, the conversation turned to the immediate future and the dark journey that lay before Sheilagh. They all felt a sense of foreboding, as if they might never see her again.

"But the experiment," Feinberg's wife, Linda, said. "Isn't it dangerous? Everyone has been saying it is."

"Yes, it is," Sheilagh said quietly. "That's why we're taking the final stages of it out into space. The point is that while the probability of an accident is very small, the risks are substantial. An accident might be very devastating."

"And if something does go wrong," Bill said, "the spacecraft crew would know nothing about it. Instant vaporization. Gone to join the dust clouds of the galaxy a few million years sooner than the rest of us. I'd prefer that to most ways of going."

"Bill," the professor said, adopting a schoolmasterly voice, "please remember that there are people present who are closer to the dust than you are. Have a thought for their feelings!"

"Sorry," Bill said, slipping farther down into his chair and draining his glass.

"And do you really think you might communicate with the Cepheans while you're out there?" Linda asked.

"We might," Sheilagh answered. "Nobody really knows. The second part of the Cepheans' message didn't actually tell us what kind of device to make; it just elaborated on the theoretical idea of faster-than-light communications. We're making the assumption that they are waiting for civilizations who read the message to try to communicate. To be honest, the gecom— that's what we call the device—is very primitive. We can't actually direct a signal toward Cepheus. We're just going to try to make some kind of a noise with it, so to speak."

"What do you think they'll say if you do make contact?" Linda asked.

"Well, it's my guess," Sheilagh said, "that, if by some miracle we do make contact, we'll be able to start a dialogue with them. We could talk to them almost like using a telephone or a videophone."

"Has anyone any idea what they will look like?" Cindy asked.

"How can we have any idea?" Feinberg said. "We've got absolutely nothing to go on."

"But assuming they are physical beings and not just the classic sci-fi free-energy things," the professor said, "there could be some strong similarities between us and them."

"You mean they may be humanoid?" Bill asked incredulously.

"No, not necessarily *that* strong," the professor said, "although nature would be hard done by to come up with a better design for an intelligent, highly adaptable creature living in Earthlike conditions. But even if the conditions are different, the whole universe is made of the same atoms. Chemistry is the same everywhere, and we know stars and planets are very similar. I don't think an alien biology can be greatly different from Earth's, not unrecognizably so, anyway."

"I wonder what they are really like," Doreen said. "I don't mean their appearance, I mean what they are like inside, how they think. What makes them want to communicate with us?"

Doreen's words, by some ineffable mechanism, summoned up an old memory in Sheilagh's mind that was so poignant that for a few moments the room and her friends disappeared behind a screen of faded images. It was a memory of a strange encounter with an alien life that had prompted her youthful mind to wonder at its own existence, to ponder the deepest question a conscious mind was able to ask.

She had been sixteen and scrambling alone among the glistening wet rocks on the shore of a remote sea loch on the Isle of Skye in the Hebrides of Scotland. The rest of her school party had refused to set foot out of doors, daunted by the low, gray overcast and cold drizzle that had blotted out the black crags of the glen. After slipping unnoticed out of the hostel, she had walked alone down the rocky track that made for the deserted beach at the head of the loch. The wet beach had been scattered with a few clumps of dark-brown seaweed left stranded by the morning tide. A muddy track on the left led toward the fantastically tortured basalt ledges and crevices at the base of the mountains that formed the eastern side of the loch. About two miles down that track, sitting with her back to a rock, just above the shoreline, she had gazed out over the silver water that rippled gently out of a uniform, horizonless mist. The silent drizzle had soaked her hair and fallen in drops from her nose, ears, and chin. A distant rush of swelling streams had echoed softly around the cliffs.

All along the shore she had noticed no animate life, no movement or activity that showed the presence of any fellow creature. Then, after an unknown length of time, a small, mottled bird, a juvenile dunlin, had arrived and perched on a rock just three feet to her right. It had called once in a thin, pleading voice and then stood in silent communion with Sheilagh and the cold wet world around them. When she had turned her head to look at the bird, with its plump body and thin horizontal bill, it had just returned her glance with a slight turn of its head. She had realized suddenly that it had known all along that she was there and not just mistaken her for a rock. It had deliberately sought her company. For hours they had remained together, hardly moving, watching the truculent wavelets slapping against the barnacle-encrusted rocks. The rain had run gently and continuously their faces, heedless of the geological ages that separated their forms. They were two alien creatures brought together by the infinitely more alien, inanimate universe around them.

To Sheilagh, that spontaneous act of sharing, like a mutual confession of need, had arisen from the same motivations that had to lie behind the Cepheans' transmissions. She had always thought of the aliens as real creatures, made of their own equivalents of flesh and blood, but had never really needed to visualize any particular form for them. The emotional force that urged them to communicate was more easy to understand.

"What puzzles me," Bill was saying as Sheilagh's thoughts returned to the present, "is if the Cepheans are really millions of years ahead of us, as they surely are, then why isn't their presence more obvious?'' He lifted up his hand as if to indicate the world beyond the room. ''I mean, if they can send signals through eleven-D spacetime, surely they can do some pretty impressive things with normal matter, like engineering a few stars, for instance. And they must find interstellar travel a real cinch by now.''

''There are lots of possibilities, Bill,'' the professor said. ''One is that the transmitter of the radio signals is a machine made to last for millions of years, and the Cepheans themselves have long since destroyed themselves. Just like we are threatening to do. Another is that maybe their physical nature prevents them from making such exploits.''

''But they could send machines,'' Bill objected.

''Yes, they could send machines,'' the professor went on patiently. ''But it may be that the Cepheans have evolved to such a state that they no longer desire to travel between the stars. They may have no 'outward urge,' as it was once called.''

''I still think that if they could do such things,'' Bill said, ''then they would. It seems inevitable to me.''

''That's an anthropocentric attitude,'' the professor said. ''But you said 'if they could.' That may be the real answer to your question. Their Grand Theory does not overturn basic relativity. There is absolutely no way that interstellar travel could be made at faster-than-light speeds, even if communications may be.''

''What if the aliens' time scale is very slow?'' Bill suggested. ''If they live at a rate where what seems like a second to them is thousands of years to us, then the speed of light would be almost infinite to them. They wouldn't mind the boring journeys.''

''Atoms vibrate at the same frequencies everywhere, Bill,'' the professor said. ''There may be a small difference in time scales, but not more than a factor of ten.''

''But there may be life-forms made of very cold matter, near absolute zero,'' Bill persisted. ''They might use very slow moving matter.''

''Then they would not have had time to evolve.'' The professor waited for Bill to continue the discussion, but Bill conceded. One could not give the aliens an extremely slow subjective time *and* give them enough time to evolve a civilization.

''It may be,'' the professor continued, ''that advanced civilizations do travel routinely between nearby stars, but across the galaxy? I doubt it very much.''

"So you really think you are going to talk face to face with an alien, like on a videophone?" Linda asked Sheilagh.

"No, I'm afraid that's not possible. The bandwidth of the equipment we're using is much too small for that. We might manage something like Morse code."

"Oh, what a shame. But you'll be the very first person to communicate with them?" Linda said with an expression of complete wonderment on her face.

"I hope so."

"Wow. Any room for one more in that thing?"

"All tickets are sold, I'm afraid," Sheilagh said with a laugh. "Sorry."

"You will be in constant contact with the Earth, though?" Doreen asked. She then looked surprised at what she had said, putting a hand up to her mouth. "Goodness! I never thought I'd live to ask that of anyone. Here I am talking about interplanetary travel as if you did it every day. 'You won't forget to phone?' That's just what I said when our eldest went off to Australia."

Everyone laughed.

"I promise I'll phone," Sheilagh said. "But the distances are going to be a problem. The ship will be as far as 150 million kilometers away—over eight light-minutes—so we won't be able to converse normally. We'll be as far away from Earth as it is from the sun, only we'll be sort of lagging behind it. We will reach that far out in late November, then we'll start to close in again."

Cindy's chin dropped, and she gaped at Sheilagh.

"You're going to be *that* far away? I had no idea. I thought you were just going out by the Moon for a year and then coming back."

"The whole idea is to get far away from Earth, Cindy," Sheilagh said, "and the Moon and any other planet, for that matter. We're not taking any risks with property that doesn't belong to us yet."

"But that means that you won't be able to get back anytime you need to," Doreen said.

Sheilagh was quite unperturbed at the idea. "That's right." She sat up so that she could demonstrate with her hands. "We are going to be in our own, different orbit around the sun. We're going to go out away from the sun and lag behind the Earth. We'll go out two-thirds of the way to Mars's orbit. Then late next November we'll start to fall back toward the sun, and we'll go straight past the Earth's orbit—"

Doreen was horrified and gasped as Sheilagh moved her hands in front of her to depict the gravitational dance she was describing.

"—the Earth being ahead of us, you remember, then dip down toward Venus's orbit, gaining a lot of speed, until we meet up with the Earth from the sunward side exactly a year after we left. The whole idea of the orbit is that if something happens to our engines, we'll get back near to Earth anyway."

"What about when you do get back?" Linda asked.

"We're going to use aerobraking in the atmosphere," Sheilagh replied. "The Mars vehicle we're using was built to make just one major burn to get to Mars; the return was to be like ours, automatic, once the flight was started."

"Just think of it," Bill said with awe, "a tiny little craft out there in the empty blackness, floating along hundreds of millions of miles from home, and our little Sheilagh on board."

Sheilagh sighed and looked down at her hands for a moment. "It's certainly going to be lonely," she said. "I've tried to imagine what it will be like when the Earth is just a faint light in the sky, no bigger than a star. There'll be no up and no down. No sky or land, just empty blackness that we'll be falling through."

"Are there any windows?" Cindy asked.

"Only very small ones. You have to make a special effort to look outside. It will be like being in a submarine or something; people do that for months on end, don't they?"

"Who are the people you're going with?" Linda asked.

"Well, there are two pilots. One is Gene Wong, who's the mission commander, which means he makes all the decisions about the well-being of the vehicle and crew. He has an uncanny feel for astronavigation, computing orbits and things. He doesn't seem to need a computer! Then there's Nina Yazdovsky who's a Russian and second in command. She's a pilot and a medical doctor as well. They are both from Marscom. Then Dilip Salwi is the senior specialist, my boss if you like, from ANICE. He's from Delhi. Apart from a few billion bacteria I'll be the lowest form of life on board."

"What are they like?" Linda asked.

"Well," Bill interjected, "they're very small, unicellular in fact, not fussy about what they eat—"

Sheilagh and Linda both threw things at him.

"They're all great," Sheilagh said to Linda, pointedly ignoring Bill. "We've been training together for over a year now, and we all get along very well. Gene's in his middle fifties and a father of four, all grown up now. He's normally very reserved and modest, but he can be a really strong leader in a crisis. Nina, unlike Bill, is very witty. She's prettier as well!''

Bill threw a missile back and pouted. ''I'll scratch 'er eyes out!''

''She's extremely well educated,'' Sheilagh went on. ''She can speak dozens of languages and is always showing up my meager knowledge of English literature. She's about thirty-five, and her husband's a professor in Leningrad. Dilip is forty-odd. He got a physics degree at Cambridge, so he must be good. Before my time, of course.''

They talked lightheartedly for another hour and a half, then it was time for the guests to leave. They said their farewells to Sheilagh. It was a strange experience for all of them. They felt they were the first humans ever to say farewell to someone who was to travel to the stars.

Sheilagh went to the professor and gave him a hug.

CHAPTER 15

AT 11:31:03 COORDINATED UNIVERSAL TIME, APRIL 6,
2001, the largest single orbital structure ever assembled by man
ceased to exist. At that precise moment, the ANICE spacecraft
separated from Mars Terminus and began its momentous voyage, donning at the same time the formal and slightly optimistic
mission call sign of *Unity*.

For two hours the world watched them pull apart as the scenes
were relayed from inside and outside both craft. *Unity* maneuvered
to a position above and ahead of Mars Terminus, where it hung
like a huge, white segmented insect floating in the blackness.

Professor Holdsworth and Doreen sat together on the couch
in their Somerset home and watched the spectacle on their large
screen. The countdown for the firing of *Unity*'s engines that
would send men and women out of the Earth–Moon system's
gravitational well for the first time was being announced by the
Marscom flight communicator. Thirty seconds remained.

Doreen reached to her right and picked up her husband's hand.
"I can't remember being frightened like this before," she said.
"How brave they all are."

Professor Holdsworth squeezed his wife's hand. He felt the
hard, slender bones beneath her old skin. They watched in silence as the moment of no return approached.

Sheilagh was strapped into her seat not for her safety but to
prevent the abrupt impulses of loose weights hitting walls from

overtaxing the directional control systems. The acceleration produced by the engines would be one-tenth of Earth gravity, not enough to cause injury to loose occupants. The slightest error in the duration or direction of the burn, however, could result in an error of thousands of kilometers at the end of the trip, one year and a complete orbit of the sun later. It was essential that all the matter in *Unity* receive the same acceleration at the same time.

She began to wish she had some task to perform to occupy her mind and drive out the rising fear. Twice she allowed herself to contemplate the terrible depths of space that awaited them. The precarious nature of the journey and their utter dependence on their craft and each other overwhelmed her. All the months of training and preparation could not help when the moment arrived. In truth, though, she did not want anything to diminish the feeling. Salwi, sitting at her right, turned and looked at her, and she could see the effects of similar thoughts in his nervous smile.

In front of them Wong and Yazdovsky calmly watched the display screens as the computers controlled the countdown functions. They showed two schematic views of the Earth and their orbit around it in cross section from above and to the side. A small white square moving along a green arc depicted *Unity*. Ahead of it, a second, red arc diverged from the green and, with a decreasing curvature, moved off to the screen's edge. Numbers at the top of the screen showed the time left until the burn at $-00:00:10.00$, and two coordinates of velocity increment both showed zero. Below each were two numbers representing the target velocities. They read -2459.8 and 5064.3 meters per second.

The white square glided along its arc.

"Engines start," Wong announced calmly.

There was a sound of turbopumps rapidly spooling up.

For two seconds Sheilagh's heart stopped. Nothing else had happened!

Then, to her relief, she felt the gentle push and a distant noise like rushing water.

Yazdovsky recited the engine thrust conditions. On the screen the white square had changed to yellow and was moving along the red arc, almost imperceptibly gaining speed. The velocity readings on the screen wound upward steadily.

With a dim blue glow just visible in its rocket exhausts, *Unity*'s image moved slowly across the TV screens of the watching world and gradually diminished until the whole vehicle became a single white dot in the darkness. Then even that disappeared.

After nine minutes of burn, *Unity* passed into the shadow of the Earth. After twenty-two minutes, its engines shut down, the velocity increments showing perfect agreement with their targets. Nothing could now deflect *Unity* from its yearlong solitary quest among the sun's planets, in search of the mysterious Cepheans.

The distance from Earth was increasing by 659,000 kilometers each day. The crew spent the first few days setting up the vehicle for its long silent journey. Solar panels were unfolded from the sides of *Unity*'s main module. Solar storm monitors that would warn them of any flare activity on the sun that would produce a dangerous flux of x-rays and high-energy particles were activated and tested. Because they were going to be as far from the Earth as the Earth was from the sun, they could not rely on Mission Control to warn them in sufficient time. When such radiation was at dangerous levels, they would confine themselves to the "storm shelter." That was the fifth and largest of the cabins, closest to the "front" of the craft where the space laboratory was coupled. It was well shielded by the water tanks and recycling equipment and the food stores as well as by steel plates.

The whole vehicle was oriented so that the engine exhaust nozzles faced the sun, and the space laboratory therefore faced away.

During the second day, while Wong and Sheilagh were performing tests on the space laboratory's power systems, he questioned her about the physics of the experiment.

"It's a faster-than-light communications system," she said matter-of-factly.

"Yes, but how does it work?"

"It's like a radio beacon and receiver combined," Sheilagh replied, trying to keep it simple, "except that instead of using radio waves, that is, photons of electromagnetic energy, it uses the equivalent carriers of the geonic force, the geons."

"And they are eleven-dimensional field quanta," Wong said. "I have a little difficulty imagining these things." He smiled wryly and scratched his bald head.

"Yes," Sheilagh said, "everybody does. The best way is to not attempt to imagine or visualize them. We can't experience more than the four space and time dimensions, so our imaginations have nothing to go on when asked to conjure up eleven. Just don't try.''

"Then how am I to understand?"

"Imagine you're looking at the surface of a sphere—"

"Okay."

"—on which there are two points. Call them A and B."

"Okay."

"Now, imagine the surface is a two-D analog of our three-D universe."

"That one again. Okay, no problem."

"Well, a geon is like a photon of light traveling *through* the sphere from A to B."

Wong thought for a few moments. "You mean the signal can pass between A and B using a dimension which is outside the universe?" he asked.

"In a way, yes. Except that the geon travels through not one but seven dimensions. They're not actually 'outside' our universe. More like 'inside' it, wrapped up in the particles that make up matter."

Wong did not look any less bemused. "But your sphere is only an analogy. How in the three-D universe can a shorter path exist between two points than that taken by a light pulse?"

"Well, the universe was very much smaller when the preons condensed than it is now. The eleven-D distance between two preons is tiny compared with the three-D distance."

"These preons, as you call them, are little knots of extra dimensions that condensed like a mist after the Big Bang?"

"That's right."

"Then are they all connected through these extra dimensions?"

"Not physically, but geons can travel between them and cause interactions."

"What kind of interactions?"

"They can change their internal orientations, change them from one type of preon to another, and they can exert a force between them. We are going to try and detect the force."

Wong's smile vanished, and Sheilagh immediately knew that he had understood. After months of training together, she knew that he reacted in exactly the opposite way to most people when confronted with a problem. He would smile broadly until the insight occurred, and then he would adopt a slight frown. Sheilagh believed he was always trying to defeat the other person's argument regardless of how valid it might be. The smile was rarely absent for long.

She continued her explanation. "To the eleven-D universe, the preons are intensely curved pieces of spacetime. In other words, they carry enormous geonic charges. They are in fact geonic black holes. Trying to transmit signals by applying ordinary forces to the preons won't work because all you'd effectively be doing is sending gravitational or electromagnetic signals, and they travel at light-speed in our universe. What we've got to do is somehow unravel the eleven-D spacetime of the preons so that a little region of less-curved eleven-D spacetime exists through which we can send our geons."

"How do we know where to send them?"

"We don't. In fact, that is the great uncertainty about this whole business. By unraveling a preon just for a moment, we effectively generate an eleven-D spacetime wavefront, a ten-D sphere traveling outward in all directions. The current eleven-D universe contains a huge amount of geonic mass and is therefore very tightly curved. It is a completely closed universe of very small size. When we unravel a preon, we send out a very loud signal to all nearby parts of that universe. We are relying on the Cepheans to pick it up and somehow home in on our location."

Wong was smiling again. He felt sure that this time he would defeat her. "Now, explain to me how we can just go ahead and defy relativity."

"Oh, that's no problem," Sheilagh said, and proceeded to explain.

Any signal that could travel faster than light could be used in principle to send messages back into the past. A machine could be constructed that sent a message to itself at a previous time, telling it to turn itself off before it sent the message. That kind of violation of causality arose immediately when supralight signals were postulated. However, in order to achieve the transmission of information into the past, the machine would need to communicate, using its supralight signals, with another similar machine that was traveling at a relativistic speed with respect to it. Special relativity, the theory that had been put forward by Einstein nearly 100 years previously, had explained how not all observers would agree on what constitutes the present. That would depend on how fast they were moving with respect to each other. Two events that were simultaneous to one observer were not to another. An observer moving very fast with respect to a second would see events happening in his present that the second would believe had happened in the past. Thus if the first was equipped with a faster-than-light communications machine, he could send a signal back into the second's past. The second one, then, with a similar machine, could use the first as a kind of relay station to send messages to himself in his own past. That was clearly paradoxical and therefore impossible.

The transmission of information through 11-D spacetime by unraveling preons was possible only *when the source and receiver were at rest, or nearly so, with respect to each other.* When they were at rest, the communication was indeed instantaneous. As the relative velocity between source and receiver increased, so did the propagation delay, together with the relativistic effects of time dilation, while at the same time the geon interaction strength decreased, reducing the amount of information that could be communicated.

The usual argument against that was that a chain of transceivers each moving very slowly with respect to its neighbor could be used to transmit nearly instantaneously between any velocities if enough were used. However, that was not possible, because the effects of finite propagation delay, time dilation, and degraded interaction levels were compounded at each link.

That did not totally prevent causality violations, which could occur at extremely microscopic levels. Indeed, that effect was happening all the time even in normal quantum-mechanical particle interactions. It was that, the Cepheans' theory said, which was the true reason for nature's fundamental uncertainties and fuzziness at extremely small scales, as described by quantum mechanics.

Three days after the departure of *Unity*, Professor Holdsworth and Doreen were invited to the ANICE Center in Abingdon. It was housed in the buildings vacated years before by the Joint European Torus project that had demonstrated the feasibility of economical power generation from nuclear fusion. The main laboratory that had once contained the enormous reaction chamber of JET was home to the second of the geon communication experiments, or gecoms, as they had become known. The first gecom had been built there and packaged into eight containers, four of which had been flown to Cape Canaveral, where they had been sent into orbit by American shuttles, and the other four smaller ones had been sent to Guyana and launched in TAVs. The second gecom was bigger and potentially more powerful than the first. It was essentially unrestricted by power and space constraints.

Professor Holdsworth was a distinguished visitor to the center, and he and Doreen had been shown around the laboratories by the ANICE director, Manfred Schopf, a tall, energetic man with a strong reputation for leading large scientific projects to success.

They were standing on a balcony that overlooked the cavernous interior of the laboratory. Doreen stood between the two men, hanging on to an arm of each. The height made her feel a little dizzy.

A thirty-meter diameter ring of steel pipe with a cross section of about ten centimeters occupied the center of the floor. It was not perfectly circular, having two straight sections beneath and across from them. On the far side, the straight section passed through a series of about a hundred small rings, all connected by thick cables. Around the curves, the pipe was followed above and below by flat plates. Immediately below the onlookers it entered a large cubic chamber whose interior was hidden from view. Also entering the chamber from the center of the ring was another similar steel pipe, which led from a large rectangular structure stretching almost completely across the interior of the ring. On either side of it, two identical smaller structures pointed directly at the cubic chamber.

"We send a pulse of electrons around the ring," Schopf explained, speaking normally, as there was no obtrusive noise in the laboratory. His strong German accent echoed faintly from the walls. He pointed to the far side of the ring. "The purpose of those little rings over on the far side is to cool the electrons, make them stick together more. The idea is to produce as short a pulse of electrons as we can. The rings are electromagnets, controlled very accurately by electronics so that they give the electrons just the right kind of push not only to speed them up but also to keep them close together."

He gestured with his hands in a counterclockwise direction around the ring. "The electrons are sent this way, and a similar bunch of positrons are sent the other way." He made the same gesture in the opposite direction.

"Positrons, being the antiparticles of electrons, have the opposite charge, so we can store both types in the ring simultaneously if we send them in opposite directions. When we have made bunches of electrons and positrons that are small enough, we make them collide head-on, there in that square box below us. Normally, when you collide electrons and positrons like that, you get great showers of all sorts of other particles. In fact, that is exactly why physicists do it, to see what other particles there are. But here we do something different. That thing over there is a powerful laser. With it we produce pulses of laser light that for a very short time are as powerful as a thousand Niagara Falls.''

Schopf looked at the professor, whose eyebrows were rising. ''We should get the Niagara Falls adopted as a standard unit of power, eh, Professor?''

The professor chuckled politely.

Schopf continued. ''All this power is concentrated in the tiny region in which the electron and positron bunches are meeting. The way we do this is quite clever, though I say so myself.'' He pointed at the two structures on either side of the laser. ''Those are also lasers, but of lower power, and they are used to make what we call a phase-conjugate mirror.''

Doreen looked at him with a grimace. ''Steady on, young fellow. I was still reeling from the thought of a thousand Niagara Falls. It's a good thing I'm holding on to both of you.''

''It's quite simple, really, believe me, Mrs. Holdsworth.''

''I hope so,'' she replied with a challenging look at the tall German.

''It is a special kind of mirror that instead of reflecting the light as in an ordinary glass surface, with angle of incidence equal to angle of reflection and so on, exactly reverses the light back the way it came. They have been known for years now. In fact, the Americans and Russians use them in their strategic defenses to track orbiting weapons.'' He looked down at Doreen as he went on. ''Imagine a box into which we send a short pulse of light. When the pulse of light is all inside the box, we turn on our lasers, which make the gas inside the box absorb all the photons of light and reemit them in exactly the opposite direction to which they came in. Out comes the pulse of light, an exact reverse copy of the one that went in. In fact, the mathematics describes the returning pulse as being the first one *reversed in time.*''

''That's an interesting kind of mirror,'' Doreen said. ''I wonder what it would look like if one stood in front of it?''

''That is a very good question, Mrs. Holdsworth. If you think carefully about it, all you would see is the light that comes from your own pupils to the mirror and back again. The mirror would appear dark all over, like the inside of your pupils.''

Doreen laughed. "Oh! That's not very useful. You mean it wouldn't let me see myself when I was younger? Make me feel better?"

The three laughed at her joke.

"To us," Schopf continued, "they are very useful. What we do is to send out two identical pulses from the big laser and reverse the first one so that it meets the second one head-on. That's one thousand Niagaras meeting one thousand Niagaras. Quite a splash, I can tell you!"

"And what happens when they meet?" Doreen asked.

"Well, because the two pulses are the exact inverse of each other, we can arrange for them to exactly cancel in a tiny volume in the chamber, just for a brief moment. Now, we arrange for the electrons and positrons to meet at exactly the same moment and in the same place that the laser pulses meet."

"Sounds difficult," Doreen said, impressed.

"It requires very careful timing and alignments, yes. Now, you are aware that positrons and electrons are mutual antiparticles. Well, antiparticles are exactly like their counterparts *reversed in time*. So, what we have done is to bring together two beams of particles, the electrons and the laser pulses, such that they meet their antibeams coming the other way in time. There is a perfect time symmetry about this that does not normally appear in our world."

"But you said earlier that other researchers have been colliding positrons and electrons for years," Doreen said.

"Ah, yes, but they always do it inside bubble chambers and the like, which have strong magnetic fields in them to make the particles produced in the collisions travel in curved paths that distinguish them. The magnetic fields break the time symmetry. We are doing it under conditions which will, we hope, be totally time symmetrical. The laser pulses produce standing electromagnetic waves oscillating between zero and, well, a rather enormous value. The electric field produced is about ten thousand volts across a distance the same as the width of an atom."

The professor was clearly impressed.

"That is enough, according to the theory," Schopf went on, "to cause the electron-positron collisions to produce small numbers of the elusive preons. The free preons exist for a very short time, but long enough for some of them to still be around when the electric field reduces momentarily to zero. This is where the time symmetry is exact and we get our sought-after unraveling of the preon's inner dimensions."

"What's dangerous about it, Dr. Schopf?" Doreen asked. "Why does Sheilagh have to go off into the depths of space to try it out?"

"We don't really think it *is* dangerous," Schopf said quietly. "But we are moving into unknown territory, and while the chances of an accident are very small, the consequences are very serious. In risk analysis, Mrs. Holdsworth, you have to multiply the probability of failure by the cost of the consequences. In this case the consequences could be the destruction of all life on the planet."

"Yes, I'd heard that. I suppose that would be a problem." She looked up at her husband with a teasing look of pride. "And to think that it all started with Adrian's little project in Somerset years ago!"

"Dear, don't encourage people to think that I started all this," the professor said. "Dr. Schopf," he continued, wanting to change the subject, "the preons that you say are created in the collisions—are they the preons that make up the electrons themselves?"

"Yes, that's right. The preon pair that make up an electron get close to their counterparts in the positron, and with the huge electric field present, it is possible for two of them, the two with exactly opposite symmetry, to interact. Once the interaction has started, the electric field reduces to zero, and the exact balance of symmetries causes them to unravel each other. It's as if they want to return to the original conditions in which they were made, in the early universe. The unraveling is only momentary. In our instruments we detect that as a scattering of the returning light pulse that comes back toward the laser. It is in the scattering of the laser pulses that we hope to receive the Cepheans' new messages. This time they'll be coming through the unraveled dimensions of the preons and in theory can be received almost immediately after they've been transmitted, even from ten thousand light-years away."

"How do you think the Cepheans can do that, though?" Doreen asked.

"Their radio messages imply they are capable of sending geon beams, not just a burst going in all directions, like we are trying to achieve. Geons are the carriers of the geonic force that the preons feel. When a geon arrives at our detector, it will cause some sort of push on the preons. Their momentum will be different when their dimensions collapse again. We measure the momentum changes by the way the re-formed preons spread the laser pulses.''

Doreen probed further: ''Where does the danger of an explosion come from?''

''The biggest danger, though unlikely in the extreme, is that we have misinterpreted some of the Cepheans' equations.'' Schopf was showing signs of discomfort at the question.

''Yes, but what would be the result if it did occur?'' Doreen insisted.

Schopf answered reluctantly. ''The worst that could happen is that we cause some of the eleven-D spacetime's energy to appear in the reaction vessel. If that happened, it would probably make this project a lot more international than it now is. It would be spread all around the solar system in hours, together with large pieces of the European continent!'' He looked down with a straight face at Doreen.

''Oh, dear, that's not very funny, is it?'' she said.

''No. But that's not all,'' Schopf said. ''There is also a possibility that very energetic gravitational waves could be generated. These would rock the Earth–Moon system enough to tear it apart. This is why we are not planning to send the space laboratory into a near-Earth, or lunar, orbit. Out where the space laboratory is going, it would merely cause a few minor earthquakes. We hope.''

''Are you saying that this energy will just appear, as if from nowhere?'' Doreen said.

''No,'' Schopf replied with a frown. ''From the classical relativistic point of view, the energy is produced by conversion of mass in the vicinity of the reaction—the space laboratory itself, in fact. If there were no matter near the reaction, there would be no energy produced, but of course the matter that comprises the laboratory itself is of necessity near the reaction. If we were to perform the experiment in Earth orbit, then in the eventuality of such a catastrophe, much of the atmosphere and possibly of the Earth itself would be annihilated.''

Doreen stared up at him. ''You really mean that what Sheilagh will be doing is that dangerous? All that power could be released?''

''It is not dangerous at all, in my opinion. These things are not going to happen. The odds are extremely remote. The reason we are doing it out in space is simply that the consequences of an accident are so catastrophic that they outweigh the remoteness of its occurrence. The odds are billions to one against it happening, I should say. But destroying the Earth is a bit too high a stake even at those odds.''

''But you imply,'' Doreen said, ''that our misinterpreting the theory is the only fear. Isn't there some talk that the Cepheans might do something nasty once they know where to find us?''

''I think only some very crazy people believe that nonsense. An intelligent race that has reached such a high level of knowledge is hardly likely to go around setting expensive booby traps for others.''

Doreen looked out across the vast chamber.

Little boys playing with fire, she thought. So what's new?

Sheilagh and Salwi began the long process of testing the gecom's component systems. They were in constant contact with Mission Control at the Guyana Space Terminal, from where their messages were relayed to Abingdon. The space laboratory was of course too small for a large cyclic accelerator like the one in Abingdon. Instead, two very special and very expensive twenty-meter linear accelerators, whose design was derived from the space-based particle accelerators used in the American strategic defenses, provided the electrons and positrons. They faced each other across the laboratory, each taking up most of the two segments at either end. Mounted parallel to the electron accelerator in segment two was the high-power laser, which was a scaled-down and lower-power version of the one in Abingdon. Its beam was reflected through right angles by diamond prisms in the central segment so as to pass through the reaction vessel. The control computers were contained in the central segment. In the equivalent position in segment four, farther from *Unity*'s main module, was the phase-conjugate mirror system, also scaled down from the Abingdon machine. One great advantage they had in space was that the vacuum in the reaction vessels could be made very much greater than any possible on Earth simply by opening the chamber to the outside. The near perfection of the vacuum in interplanetary space compensated for the reduction in capability caused by the overall scaling down of the gecom.

The strategic defence technology of the nineties had also provided the extremely compact nuclear power generator situated at the very end of the forward MTV module, segment five. Its external cooling vanes broke up the large external wall of the laboratory that faced away from the sun.

On the fifth day, when *Unity* was approaching four million kilometers from Earth, Salwi and Sheilagh started the sequence of test firings of the gecom subsystems. The main laser was of very advanced design, thanks to the French, who had been the only nation willing to make public its designs for compact space-borne lasers, but it was very difficult to fine-tune to produce maximum power.

Finally, on day thirty-two, at 23 million kilometers, all systems were ready for the first attempts at lighting the geon beacon that, they hoped, the Cepheans could detect.

The human race was about to signal its presence.

CHAPTER 16

SHEILAGH AND SALWI, WEARING PRESSURE SUITS BUT carrying their helmets, entered the space laboratory and sealed the hatch behind them. They pushed along with them a square container that held provisions for three days. They floated down the long tunnel beside the electron accelerator and entered the control module at the very center of the laboratory.

On the other side of the coupling tunnel the hatch was also closed. *Unity* undocked and slowly turned through ninety degrees. Wong and Yazdovsky used *Unity*'s main engines for seven seconds to generate a twenty-six-meters-per-second separation speed, which, four hours after undocking, they canceled. They were 360 kilometers away from the space laboratory.

That was an arbitrary distance that had taken an inordinate number of man-hours to agree upon back at Mars Terminus. The Marscom people had wanted *Unity* as far away from the space laboratory as possible in case of mishaps with the gecom. On the other hand, they also wanted it close by in case an urgent rescue was necessary for the laboratory's occupants. *Unity* needed to be within eight minutes' flight time of the laboratory to be of use in a survivable accident. But that meant that the main engines could not be used because they pointed in one direction only, and *Unity* would have to be turned through 180 degrees at the halfway point to allow deceleration over the second half of the rescue flight. The main engines would have to be shut down for that turn and started up again immediately afterward. That was not possible to accomplish in a hurry.

Using the only other means of propulsion, the maneuvering thrusters, a distance of twenty-two kilometers could be covered in an eight-minute flight. That distance was deemed insufficient, but in the absence of better ideas, the decision was made to go ahead with it.

Then Wong had suggested a daring answer to the problem. His plan called for a seemingly wild and impossible maneuver using the main engines. In order to cover the gap in the shortest time, he suggested that the main engines be kept running for the entire maneuver, including during the turn. Using the main engines on the end stops of their gimbals, a turning moment would result that could be used to rotate the ship. That would require some high-speed directional control of the rockets, but it was just within the capability of the hardware. The resulting sideways velocity produced by the engines firing across the direct line of flight could be canceled by following a complicated curved path across the gap. Navigating the curve had to take into account the steady reduction of *Unity*'s mass as it used up fuel.

After many days simulating the possibilities, a curved flight was found that was within the capabilities of the guidance systems, so *Unity* could be a safe distance away and still be able to make the rescue if needed. Once on station, *Unity*'s main engines remained ready for immediate use, with the guidance parameters for the rescue maneuver loaded into the computers. The radio signal from the laboratory was used to keep accurate track of its position, which was continuously fed into the guidance programs.

The space laboratory was visible under extreme magnification, using *Unity*'s optical telescope, which had been designed as a combined navigational aid and scientific instrument for the Mars missions. The laboratory's slightly blurred image, at the limit of the telescope's performance, appeared on one of *Unity*'s screens. Two views of the interior of the laboratory were shown on other screens.

To Wong and Yazdovsky, with the rescue maneuver foremost in their minds, the distance separating them from their friends seemed immense. But Sheilagh and Salwi, occupied with their delicate and difficult tasks and unable to see out of the laboratory, remained unaffected by their unique isolation, alone and propulsionless, with only short-range communications to *Unity*.

Wong and Yazdovsky were waiting for the final "go" from the controllers on Earth to reach their main receiving antenna, which had been realigned with Earth. After eighty seconds of light-speed travel the clearance arrived and was relayed to the laboratory. Wong and Yazdovsky, seated in the maneuver control station, gazed at the screens and said a few words, wishing luck to their friends. Sheilagh and Salwi donned helmets, both slightly annoyed at the inconvenience they caused. They were stationed at a console containing several screens and two keyboards, with their backs to the actual reaction chamber. They were "standing," holding their feet under bars beneath the console. One screen contained a colored schematic of the gecom's systems. Another contained a set of oblongs with brief textual labels over which Salwi moved a triangular cursor, working a small, red rollerball control with his right thumb. By pressing one of the three buttons beneath his fingertips, Salwi started the automatic sequence.

"Okay," he said. "Gecom preliminary testing started at 13:12:10 Coordinated Universal Time. Preon interaction experiment."

Sheilagh interpreted the changes appearing on the screen.

"Starting main laser priming." Her gentle Scots accent, together with the TV pictures, beamed across the gulf to *Unity* and from there to the ground stations eighty light-seconds away. Retransmitted by the large antennas at the space terminal to a communications satellite, they reached most television screens on Earth. Most TV stations chose to carry the pictures despite ANICE's insistence that it would probably require many hours of trial before a successful preon interaction was stimulated.

"Mirror is ready. Accelerator charging under way." Sheilagh spoke as if the proceedings were everyday occurrences. "Positron generation started. Electrical loads are normal. Main laser is primed. Okay, we're ready for the calibration pulses." She turned to Salwi on her left.

"Okay, laser calibration pulses," he said, and with a light touch pressed one of the rollerball buttons. There was a heavy buzzing *crack* as the laser fired. Three green lines, each rising to a square pulse, appeared on the central screen. Six immense pulses of laser energy had been generated, reflected, and collided head-on in the titanium and steel reaction vessel behind them. For the calibration, the three electron pulses that had burst down one of the accelerator tubes had not met any positrons. The calibration pulses allowed the computers to calculate the expected broadening of the laser pulses when the positrons were included. Any broadening beyond the expected level would indicate that preon interactions were happening.

"One hundred and two percent nominal power," Sheilagh announced quietly. "Pulse widths captured okay. There's a fifteen-picosecond error in the laser timing." She typed in a command on her keyboard.

"That should correct it. Okay, laser is recharged. Shall we calibrate once more?"

"Yes," Salwi answered. He repeated the procedure.

"Okay, this time we're better," Sheilagh announced. "Pulse widths are fine." She typed in another command. The three lines on the center screen were replaced by one.

"That's a good clean control pulse. Right. Ready for the first try."

She turned to Salwi, her face almost hidden by the reflections of the screens in her helmet's faceplate. Salwi used the rollerball to move the cursor over the PREON INT panel on his screen. Selecting it with a push of the central button, he then moved the cursor to the EXECUTE panel and pressed again. The laser cracked once more. On the central screen the green line showing the average of the three calibration pulses was overlaid with a red one. The two matched almost perfectly.

Sheilagh looked at a set of numbers that appeared on the right-hand screen. "Missed by a mile! The positron accelerator is out of spec, as always on the first shot."

"Okay, let's ignore that one," Salwi said. "Ready again?"

"Yes."

Crack. The red line was replaced by another. Again it matched the green one.

"Accelerators are fine on that one. The interaction was positioned exactly in X and Y, and just a little off in Z, but the reverse laser pulse was a hundred nanometers out."

She typed in another command.

"Right. Compensated. Ready again."

Salwi pressed the button again. This time, after another loud *crack* from the main laser, the red line appeared, with the central pulse being perceptibly broader at the base than the green one. Both Salwi and Sheilagh noticed it, but their first comments were about the tiny jolt that had shaken the laboratory at the precise instant of the firing.

"Did you feel that?" Sheilagh asked with some alarm in her voice.

"Yes, I did. What did it feel like to you?"

"Like something hit the lab from outside."

They both looked around the lab for anything unusual. Sheilagh freed her feet and guided herself up and over the reaction area.

"Maybe it was the power supply," Salwi said. "If there was a momentary short somewhere, it could cause the main conductors to jump with all that magnetic field collapsing suddenly." He pushed himself back to the console and typed in a command. A screenful of numbers appeared.

"*Hmm*, nothing unusual with the power."

"What's up, guys?" Wong asked over the radio.

"Sheilagh and I just felt a kind of jolt. Just as if we were hit by something. Do you think it could have been a meteorite?"

"A jolt?" Wong asked, as if Salwi were joking.

"That's right," Salwi responded. "A bit hard to describe. We didn't hear anything, just felt a small, sudden movement just as we fired the accelerators."

"It's possible it was a meteorite," Wong said, "but that's a helluva coincidence, it arriving just then, isn't it?"

"I suppose it is," Salwi replied. His voice trailed off as he tried to find an explanation.

"A helluva coincidence at any time, in fact," Wong said. "Being in the same place at the same time as a meteorite, I mean. It must be something you guys are doing."

Sheilagh was back at the console. "A nine percent probability of preon interaction," she read from a screen.

Salwi came over to her and looked at the display. They both stared at the red pulse on the screen and the short column of figures next to it.

"Definite broadening there," Salwi said slowly. He thought in silence for a while, then made his decision. "We'll shut down," he said finally. "There's something going on in the interaction that we don't understand. We'll get Abingdon to look into it."

He and Sheilagh released the catches on their helmets and removed them.

"Gene," Salwi called, "we're shutting down for investigations."

"Okay," Gene's voice answered. "We'll be over in four hours."

Over four hours later they joined Wong and Yazdovsky in *Unity*'s living quarters. They discussed the situation and composed messages to be read to Mission Control. The eighty-two-second delay was growing by two seconds each day, and conversing with Earth was a slow affair.

The Abingdon scientists, led by Russell Voss, recommended that the reaction vessel be instrumented and an attempt be made to repeat the effect. The instruments would enable the location and nature of the jolt to be deduced. Maybe then they would be able to understand its cause.

Two days later Sheilagh and Salwi were back in the laboratory preparing for another attempt at producing preon interaction. *Unity* was once more on station 360 kilometers away.

An ingenious way of detecting small movements in the shiny metal reaction vessel had been concocted by Salwi. The laser that was intended as a spare for the two mirror energizers was mounted close by the reaction vessel. Its beam was split into two, and each half was put through a small, short-focus lens. Two broad cones of laser light then illuminated the side of the vessel, producing a minute pattern of stripes as the two beams interfered with each other. An electronic camera was mounted next to the laser and was used to capture the interference pattern every few microseconds both before and after the gecom firing. The movement of the fringes, analyzed by a computer program that Sheilagh quickly produced, betrayed the smallest movement of the metal.

Sheilagh and Salwi again went through the calibration process. All the time the world watched from 25 million kilometers away.

"Ready for the first try, then," Sheilagh called, gazing at the central screen with its green line defining the control pulse shape. They both tensed for the expected jolt.

Salwi pressed the button, and again the laser cracked. A red line appeared that showed a clear broadening over the control.

"No jolt!" Sheilagh announced, rather surprised.

"What about the camera?"

On the rightmost screen an amber depiction of the fringes of the reaction vessel appeared. There was no movement apparent.

"Nothing," Sheilagh said flatly. "No movement at all. But there definitely was an interaction. Shall we try some tuning to get a stronger one?"

Salwi thought for a while. "Control, this is space laboratory. We've got indications of a weak interaction but no movement of the reaction vessel. I propose we try for stronger interactions. Do you agree?''

All four astronauts waited patiently, listening to the communications hiss as Salwi's message sped back to Earth.

Over three minutes later, a period during which no one had spoken, Mission Control replied with a recommendation to go ahead. Salwi looked across to Sheilagh, who typed in a couple of commands that would adjust the laser and accelerator timing to bring them into better alignment.

"Ready," she called calmly.

Salwi pressed the EXECUTE button once more.

At that instant the whole craft shook with a terrible violence, and the center of the reaction vessel burst open, flinging jagged fragments of metal around the interior. The screens on the console shattered, as did all but the strongest objects around them. A great blue arc of electricity shot out of the electron accelerator as it burst open. Sheilagh was hit by several fragments that went straight through her suit, but she felt nothing. A rending shock of compression extinguished her consciousness in an instant, before the fragments had reached her.

Salwi was also hit. A large, jagged piece of the shattered reaction vessel crashed into the back of his helmet and went straight through.

Moments later the laboratory was in darkness except for an eerie blue sparking light coming from the accelerator as the shorted power supply spilled out its energy. Sheilagh and Salwi, their feet still under the bar beneath the console, swayed gently in the flickering light, their bent arms floating up in front of them. Droplets of blood were scattered over the remains of the console.

"Jesus!" Wong gasped, staring disbelievingly at the telescope picture.

He and Yazdovsky had seen the interior TV pictures disappear into storms of color, while on the telescope screen several white fragments of varying sizes suddenly appeared spinning from the sides of the laboratory's control module in a silent concussion. They heard only static on the intercraft comms link.

Wong hit the button that started the desperate rescue maneuver. His right hand closed loosely around the control stick mounted on the panel before him. His face was pale and frozen. Yazdovsky tersely called out the main engines' propulsion figures as they started to push the craft along. Then, grim-faced, she began attempting to contact the two people inside the crippled laboratory.

It was spinning slowly on its long axis as the air that escaped obliquely from a jagged rent in the control module side pushed it around.

Yazdovsky cursed. "We'll never dock with it spinning like that."

Unity picked up speed gradually. Wong and Yazdovsky were strapped into their seats because of the substantial centripetal forces that were expected during the rapid turn a few minutes later.

Mission Control, agonizingly aware of the emergency a minute and a half later, kept silent. There was nothing they could do. As *Unity* began to turn, the large antenna no longer pointed at Earth and the signals stopped. The world waited in a terrified blind and deaf silence.

Wong and Yazdovsky remained grimly silent as they fought to stay ahead of their craft's attitude as it raced along its curved flight path.

Unity's rate of turn accelerated sharply as it went through the halfway point of the flight. Just at that moment a red warning panel lit up in front of them. It spelled out the words ROLL GYRO FAILURE. Yazdovsky cursed explosively and spit out the word "Manual!"

Wong's right hand gripped the control stick while his left rested on the two coupled throttle sliders at his side. His face could have been carved from marble. Only his eyes showed movement as they jumped between his central screen showing the rapidly changing geometry of the two vehicles' relative positions and peripheral displays showing accelerations and angular rates.

His left hand pushed the throttle levers to maximum.

"We're overshooting," Yazdovsky said calmly.

The split-second loss of control as the gyro had suddenly failed caused a small error in the spacecraft's attitude. With the main engines firing at nearly full thrust, that caused a large deviation from their expected course. The guidance computers were disconnected and were useless anyway without the failed gyro's information. The success of the hair-raising maneuver was solely dependent on Wong's innate skill as a pilot.

As *Unity* careered toward the space laboratory, the remaining minutes of flight seemed like hours to the crew. Wong was using the computer systems' indications of where the other vehicle was at the time of the accident. He hoped it had not moved.

Unity's position was a best guess. Without the angular rate information from the failed gyro, the computer could not be precise.

"Roll gyros back on line!" Yazdovsky called out.

"Forget it," Wong said tersely. "Get me fore and aft visuals."

Yazdovsky cursed again, this time at herself for not thinking of that before Wong had asked for it. The two screens of static from the laboratory cameras were quickly replaced with scenes from the fixed wide-angle cameras on *Unity*'s exterior.

"Okay, that's good, that's good," Wong said more slowly.

As *Unity* sped past the laboratory, its engines firing at full force to slow it, the laboratory moved from the rear-view to the forward-view screen. It grew smaller steadily. Yazdovsky, who had already been suited up, donned her helmet and prepared herself for the dangerous space walk that seemed inevitable with the laboratory spinning as it was.

The view of the space laboratory steadied as *Unity* finally canceled its motion away from it. Wong shut down the main engines and stabbed a button that switched his control stick over to the maneuver thrusters only.

"Get the Earth antenna aligned," he called out. "We're gonna need their help with this. I'll try to keep the attitude steady. Get it as close as you can."

Yazdovsky floated over to the communications console and started working to point the antenna at Earth.

Wong let out an astonished cry. He was staring at the picture of the space laboratory, now five hundred meters away.

About a hundred meters to the right of the laboratory on their screen, a tiny blue light appeared for a second. It then disappeared and reappeared about fifty meters closer. For a couple of seconds nothing happened. Then, in a small region in the center of the laboratory's image, its white surface faded until it was completely black. The whole image was moving, turning out on itself as if it were being deliberately distorted by a visual-effects processor. The dark patch expanded and pushed the laboratory's image out with it. The laboratory looked as if it were being squeezed from within into a thin circular band. After a few seconds, all that could be seen of the laboratory was a thin, bright, irregular ring, like pale Bailey's beads in a total solar eclipse. Inside the ring was featureless darkness.

As that was happening, *Unity*'s crew became aware of a force on their bodies that tugged at their chests, making them involuntarily inhale. Loose objects flew about in random directions. They could hear ominous creaks and groans coming from their craft. There was one loud bang and a jolt. A whole set of warning lights appeared on a panel in front of Yazdovsky.

"Hydrogen leak!" she called loudly. "What the hell is happening?"

Wong, without reasoning why, fired the thrusters to move *Unity* away from the strange object ahead of them. He was confused further by his craft's behavior, because its initial response to the thrusters was very sluggish. Then, after a few seconds, the motion accelerated much more rapidly than could be accounted for by the thrusters alone. Eventually he had to reverse the thrusters strongly to bring *Unity* to a standstill two kilometers from where the space laboratory had been.

They tried desperately to assess *Unity*'s condition. It was soon obvious that things were very bad.

"Oxygen *and* hydrogen leaks," Yazdovsky called out, gazing around the panel displays in front of her. "Interior pressurization dropping. Helmets, Gene!"

"We've got to find those fuel leaks," he said. "If they're close enough together to mix, we'll need wings, not helmets."

The liquid hydrogen and oxygen fuel tanks were contained in the propulsion unit at the rear of the craft. Wong stared at the status display showing the pressure dropping in both fuel tanks.

"Must be tank ruptures," he said with a slight tremor in his voice. Even his calm was being overtaxed by the events of the last few minutes. "There are no rates in the fuel pipes. Gotta be." A feeling came over him that he had experienced few times before, once when making his first night landing on a carrier and another time when scuba diving with his young son. His bottle had contained air contaminated by the compressor's exhaust fumes, and they'd had to make an emergency ascent from thirty meters, sharing the other bottle. It was as if he had taken out a loan on time. His mind raced calmly at a speed dozens of times faster than normal.

Without hesitation he turned to his control panel, reached up, and lifted the black cover from a small red lever mounted above his head. He pulled firmly on the lever.

Explosive bolts severed the connection between *Unity*'s main module and the propulsion unit. Wong commanded a burst from the thrusters to take *Unity* farther away from the uncontrolled and dangerous object.

They worked feverishly on their other problem of loss of cabin pressure. They reduced the pressure setting to a barely breathable level to slow the leak and ease the demand on the air supplies. While scouring the interior for sight or sound of the leak, they were distracted by the sound of several objects striking the exterior. The propulsion unit had exploded as the hydrogen and oxygen had mixed. Some small pieces of debris had impacted *Unity* without causing any real damage except a few scratches. The larger pieces had been sent spinning off in all directions.

They eventually traced the leak to the main hatch set into the long side of the main module. For some reason it had unseated its seal. After Wong had suited up, they evacuated the interior and opened and reclosed the hatch with the seal properly made.

Once the cabin was back to pressure and they were out of their helmets, the state of tension that the life-threatening crisis had put them in gradually subsided. The communications controller at the space terminal had shown heroic restraint and was calmly and infrequently attempting to make contact. While Yazdovsky brought the telescope to bear on the space laboratory, Wong described their condition. His first statement was that the space laboratory was effectively destroyed and that he could see no hope for Sheilagh and Salwi.

The minutes that followed were filled only by the hiss of electrons dancing in the vacuum.

The image of the space laboratory filled their screens. From the greater distance the circular band of white was broader.

"Roger, *Unity*, we saw the visual effects on video. No ideas down here, I'm afraid." The calm female voice continued over the Earth link. "Mission controller recommends staying well clear and no action to stop any further separation. The thrusters are going to be critical systems now."

That was a gentle way of reminding Wong and Yazdovsky of the predicament they were in. Without the main engines they were incapable of making any of the adjustments to their course that would be required to ensure a safe return to Earth. They would most likely miss it by tens of thousands of kilometers and continue on another yearlong solar orbit.

But worse still, if they *were* on course, they were destined for a fiery reentry without their heat shield.

CHAPTER 17

UNITY DRIFTED SLOWLY AWAY FROM WHATEVER IT WAS the space laboratory had turned into. Wong and Yazdovsky kept it under close scrutiny, using the telescope camera. They were both frightened by the terrible unknown power it represented. No reflection was received by the docking radar.

Hours dragged by without the slightest visible change in the ring's appearance. The video signals from *Unity* that showed the transformation of the space laboratory were replayed over and over again on the Earth's TV channels. Wong and Yazdovsky were asked to repeat their descriptions of *Unity*'s odd behavior during and after the ring's appearance.

After five hours of intermittent communication from Mission Control, *Unity* finally received a message, originating from Abingdon, that contained an explanation of some of what had happened. The trouble was, it took a lot of believing.

" '*Unity*'s response to the thrusters when you were backing off,' " read the controller, " 'and the stresses on its structure suggest a strong tidal force. In other words, *Unity* was in a strong gravitational gradient generated by the ring. We know this sounds crazy, but it's a working hypothesis. The subsequent motion suggests that *Unity* was straddling a region where gravitational attraction gave way to gravitational repulsion, repeat, gravitational repulsion. The resultant stretching of the vehicle caused the fuel tank problems and may have caused others.' "

That idea sounded less crazy to *Unity*'s occupants, faced with the reality of the ring within three kilometers of them, than it did to its originators in Abingdon.

" 'When you backed away, you pulled yourself off the gravitational barrel and were repelled as you moved away. This supports the recommendation to stay clear.' "

Wong remained expressionless.

" 'The ring may be an optical effect caused by gravitational lensing, but we've no firm theory there. The masses involved would have to be immense. One configuration being looked at is a very strong attractive mass surrounded by a shell of repulsive mass. At large distances the effects would cancel. However, no configuration that reproduces the effects has been found. This sounds crazy, we know, but we've got some crazy observations to explain. There have been no observable effects reported on Earth or from any of the interplanetary probes.'

" 'As to the original problem with the explosion in the space laboratory, we have no theory as yet. We're looking into it. Some are speculating that a strong gravitational wavefront was created. This would have the effect of a compressional pulse, but to cause any physical damage, it would have to be of staggering strength.' Message ends there. Mission controller wants to repeat his praises to both of you for your great skill and presence of mind. We're beginning to realize how quickly you moved out there. Well done, you guys. Over."

Wong and Yazdovsky decided that the ring should be kept under constant surveillance, and so they started a rota of six-hour watches. Wong was the first to attempt sleep.

Nina Yazdovsky settled back to watch the ring's unchanging appearance. She contemplated their situation. Sheilagh and Salwi dead, *Unity* crippled and getting 34,000 kilometers farther away from Earth every hour. There could well be much undiscovered damage to *Unity*'s structure and systems that would make itself known in the coming weeks. The thought of ten months more of the flight after the last few hours' events was crushing.

Her attention returned to the screen. It took a second or two for her to realize that the scene had changed. The space laboratory was back, looking like nothing had happened.

She spoke to Mission Control and went to rouse Wong. He was back in front of the screen before Mission Control answered, alert again after only fifteen minutes' rest.

"Yes, we see it," the calm controller's voice said. "Mission controller is advising no action except to try raising the space laboratory on the ICC.''

The last transmission started in the middle of Wong's message to Mission Control saying that he was going to maneuver *Unity* in closer for a docking. Such communications clashes were quite frequent and were expected because of the long propagation delays. To help overcome the difficulty, the communications equipment had large solid-state storage devices that recorded the last hour of voice communications and could be quickly commanded to replay any portion that was missed while continuing to record the ongoing communications.

Wong was of course fully aware of it but chose on that occasion not to take advantage of the feature.

Unity began to edge closer to the space laboratory while Wong kept talking.

"It's not spinning anymore," he said slowly, peering at the screen. "There appears to be no damage at all. Except . . . Yeah, there are some pieces of the exterior missing. Must be the pieces that flew off in the explosion.'' He turned off his microphone. "Nina, can you raise them?''

Nina shook her head. "Nothing.''

Turning his microphone back on, he continued to talk to Mission Control, again clashing with one of the messages urging him to hold back. "No sound from space lab. Five hundred meters. Nothing unusual about *Unity*'s motion.''

The space laboratory grew larger. *Unity* was on the sunward side of it, and the gaps in the outer skin of the central control module were clearly visible. The curved surface of the pressure vessel underneath was intact.

"Suit, Nina,'' he called without taking his eyes off the screen. Yazdovsky was already suiting up.

"*Unity*, back away from the laboratory,'' the controller's anxious voice came through. "Repeat, mission controller wants you to back away.''

Wong turned to Yazdovsky, who was fastening her pressure suit, and indicated the communications console with a motion of his head. Yazdovsky reached over and flicked a switch. Mission Control's messages could no longer be heard.

"Go ahead, fire me,'' Wong murmured to himself.

"Three hundred meters,'' he recited. "We should get enough reflected sunlight off *Unity* to see by, but just in case we don't, let's have lights.''

Two brilliant beams of white light illuminated the surface of the laboratory. Very slowly the smaller vessel edged around the larger. As it did so, it turned its forward docking port to face the port on segment one of the other vehicle. The sun appeared in the TV picture, and it became impossible to see. Wong slowed the approach a little and waited until the sun's glare slipped slowly behind the dark shape ahead.

At last, the TV image's contrast improved and he could see the docking port on the laboratory brightly lit by one of *Unity*'s lights. A minute later the two craft were safely linked. He rushed to suit up.

Yazdovsky helped him into his suit, then went to the forward hatch, opened it, and entered the short tunnel that separated the two vehicles, closing the hatch behind her.

Unexpectedly, she returned almost immediately.

The screw lock on the laboratory's hatch was impossible for her to release by hand. Wong also tried and failed. Somehow it had been closed extremely tightly. Squeezing together in the tunnel, by a combined effort they managed to open the hatch and push themselves through.

The tunnel alongside the electron accelerator was utterly dark, but with their flashlights they noticed no signs of damage. They rushed toward the central chamber.

Anxiously they swung the beams of their flashlights around the space. To Wong the interior looked no different from the way it had before, but Yazdovsky noticed that the reaction vessel had changed. The central interaction area had a large spherical enclosure where before it had been a simple square box.

Sheilagh was hanging on to a bar that separated the console area from the cover of the main laser aperture. Salwi was under the console clutching the foot rail, floating face upward. His helmet had been broken open by some terrible impact, and they could plainly see that he was dead.

Yazdovsky went swiftly up to Sheilagh and peered into her faceplate. "She's alive!" Then a moment later, "Doesn't look too good. She's in shock, I think. We'd better get her back to *Unity* fast."

She then shone her flashlight at Salwi. She let out a choked cry, and her face instantly turned white.

"God, what a mess!"

They both knew they could do nothing for him. Most of his head had been removed. The shock made them both feel faint. It was as if those were not the remains of their friend but of someone else.

While manhandling the unprotesting Sheilagh along the tunnel and through he connecting hatches, Wong and Yazdovsky became more and more concerned about her condition. She was conscious, but she seemed oblivious to what was happening.

Back in *Unity* she was removed from her pressure suit and examined closely. Her face was pale, but she was warm and her eyes moved to follow the others' motions. After a few minutes she put her hands up to her head and moaned.

Sheilagh's condition improved slowly the next day, although for a long time she remembered nothing at all and was conscious only of acute headaches and pains over most of her body. Severe bruises appeared all over her. She could offer no clues as to what had happened in the laboratory. Salwi pressing the button to fire the gecom was the last memory she had before coming around in her cabin in *Unity*. There was no recollection of an explosion, just an abrupt halt to her memory. The pictures of the accident and the subsequent events left her speechless with amazement.

Salwi's body was still in the laboratory's control module, frozen in the extreme low temperature vacuum that prevailed in there without power or air. Nobody for the moment had the strength of heart to return. Sheilagh especially felt the anguish of his death. He had been her close colleague for two years.

When she was feeling better, Wong told her about their predicament. "We're not in good shape, I'm afraid, Sheilagh," Wong said, smiling incongruously. "We had to jettison the whole propulsion unit because the fuel tanks were venting badly." He made no attempt to tell her that his quick thinking had, for the time being, anyway, saved their lives. "We're basically adrift." He shrugged as if he were telling his wife that the drains were blocked.

"We won't be able to make any course corrections to ensure a close approach to Earth, and we're gonna be incapable of aerobraking. The ground boys are trying to get an accurate fix on us. Also, we don't have good reserves of oxygen."

"How much?"

"About three hundred days' worth. Just about enough to get us back to Earth if we don't breath too much. We lost all pressure in one of the tanks during the accident."

"What can we do?"

"Not much." Wong maintained his sardonic smile. "All we can do is stay alive so that a rescue attempt can be made."

Sheilagh looked away from him and fought off the drowsiness brought on by the painkillers.

"What kind of a rescue? If we've lost our heat shield, then the rescue vehicle would have to have its own way of getting back to Earth orbit."

"Yes, it would," Wong said. He was relieved to be spared having to spell it out. "They need to put together a special rescue vehicle to get out to us and then make a return somehow. It would require a big delta-V, a lot of fuel. But they've got ten months to come up with something."

Ten months! Sheilagh had of course been prepared for a twelve-month mission, but most of that time was to have been filled with the challenge and excitement of the gecom experiment. Ten months of hanging around waiting for a rescue would be unbearable.

"Another possibility," Wong went on, "is that they could get some kind of vehicle out to us as we pass the Earth, one with an aerobraking ability, then both vehicles would do another twelve-month orbit before we reenter. Technically easier 'cause of the reduced delta-V."

Sheilagh looked around the interior of *Unity*. "We can't spend another two years out here," she said. "Ten months is going to be hard enough. There must be another way."

Wong shrugged. "I'm afraid there isn't, Sheilagh.. There just isn't a vehicle with the specific impulses required. In ten months' time they will at least have the next MTV ready. They probably will have some rescue vehicle based on an MTV or even the TAVs."

Sheilagh closed her eyes to think more clearly. She felt like she used to when she had had two hours too much sleep in the morning. A dull, drowsy ache filled her head. Looking up at Wong, she asked, "What kind of velocities would be needed to send some vehicle out to us now? Say, to get here in a month?"

Wong shook his head, again forcing a smile. "That's impossible, Sheilagh. Look, I'll show you."

He moved over to a computer terminal next to the maneuver station and beckoned her to join him. In response to a few typed commands a diagram depicting *Unity*'s orbit around the sun appeared. The Earth, the sun, Venus, and Mars were included in the display. He made the program move the tiny symbols representing each body slowly along their orbits.

"This is where we will be in about thirty days—we have to give them that long to come up with a vehicle."

Sheilagh studied the screen. The blue circle of the Earth was advancing counterclockwise along its orbit. Trailing behind it, farther from the sun, was a slower-moving gray oblong representing *Unity*.

"But a rescue would have to be attempted no later than thirty-three days from today. After that we're too far away from Earth." He indicated the Earth with a cursor controlled by a rollerball. "If a rescue started then, it would have to leave Earth on an outward path that would reach the position we're going to be at in, say, thirty days after that." He traced the imaginary rescue trajectory out to meet *Unity*'s oblong. "They'd need a substantial change of velocity to achieve that position."

Sheilagh looked at Wong. "The problem being that there's no vehicle around capable of such performance, I take it."

Wong nodded. "Then there's the problem of getting back. They might be able to get to us with some kind of vehicle, but getting back on a shorter trajectory than the one we're already on is asking too much." He sighed and looked apologetically at Sheilagh. "We have just got to make it through the next ten months."

"Are they looking into the options?" Sheilagh asked.

"They have already and concluded that there's no possible way to do it."

Sheilagh was shocked. "You mean they've given up trying?" She frowned deeply and shook her head. "There's got to be a way. What about a TAV? Their engines have got the biggest specific impulse. Can't they be used?"

"The TAVs are designed for atmospheric and low-orbit work, not interplanetary flight. Once in orbit, they carry only enough fuel for reentry."

"But a TAV can be refueled once it's in orbit. Then it can go anywhere it likes! Have they thought about putting extra fuel tanks in the cargo bay? Or using external tanks?"

"I'm sure they have, yes," Wong replied, raising his eyebrows. "What I meant was that all this was looked at over and over again before we left the ground. We knew all along that any rescue was going to be impossible. You knew it, too."

Sheilagh sighed and looked about desperately for inspiration. But none came. She dragged herself into her cabin and slept.

While she was sleeping, Wong reentered the dark laboratory and moved Salwi's body along the tunnel to the fifth segment at the far end of the laboratory. It was frozen solid. The slow drop of pressure and rapid freezing had preserved the physical integrity of what remained. He wrapped it in an aluminized plastic sheet from *Unity*'s medical supplies. There was a space between two equipment lockers beside the positron accelerator. Wong placed the body in the gap and strapped it in.

The job of handling his friend's frozen body made him feel sick. To stop himself from actually being sick, which would have been extremely dangerous for him in his pressure suit, he moved away and set about inspecting the interior of the laboratory. He moved farther down toward the end of the segment where the power supply was mounted externally. He looked for signs of damage in the accelerator coils and in the electrical cabling but found none. A red light shone on the power supply control panel, showing that the inexhaustible power it still generated was being dumped uselessly into the thermal radiators.

Traveling back toward *Unity*, he entered the fourth segment, which contained the phase-conjugate mirror equipment. Again he could see no signs of damage. It was still on standby power.

In the central control module the consoles were silent and dark, but in the beam of his flashlight they appeared normal. A small red light shone from between them, showing that power was available. He could not see any evidence of the explosion, although the reaction chamber looked somehow different in the dark. He was at a loss to explain what had hit Salwi so hard.

The rest of the equipment in segments one and two was also in perfect condition as far as he could see.

Sheilagh woke after six hours of deep sleep, feeling much better. She got out of her cabin and heated a tray of food.

"Sheilagh," Wong called from the navigation computer terminal.

She pushed herself over to him.

"I've been looking at the details of possible rescues." He punched a few keys, and a moving display appeared on the screen that showed a curving arc between the orbits of the Earth and *Unity*. "That's the best outward trajectory. The total delta-V required is twenty-three kilometers per second, which with a TAV, or an MTV for that matter, would require it to carry 172 times its own empty weight in fuel. That's equivalent to forty-two shuttle loads, just of fuel!" He turned to look at Sheilagh. His expression said: "Too bad, but it was worth a try."

Sheilagh conceded the argument. "And that's just to get to us," she said gloomily.

"Yeh, getting back again . . . well, the numbers just get sillier squared."

He tapped the screen with the pen in his right hand. "That figure might not be the lowest possible, but it'll be close enough." He sighed. "No, I'm afraid we've got to stick it out. But aren't you forgetting the mission's purpose? You've still got a job to do, you know."

"I wish I had. At least then I'd have something to occupy my mind for the next ten months."

"But you have," Wong said.

Sheilagh was confused. "The laboratory has been damaged, and the reaction vessel exploded, didn't it? And all the electronics will have been frozen. They can't withstand cold that extreme. And that weird effect—I shouldn't think there's a lot left of it."

"It looked okay to me a couple of hours ago when I went in to move Salwi's body. Everything's on standby power."

"What? But there was an explosion in there. Dilip was killed by it! And you've seen the video. There were bits flying off the outside!"

"I know," he said. "But inside it looked like new. Somehow the inside was not affected as much. You want to go take a look? It's time we got in there and powered it up."

"What did you do with . . . with his body?"

"I stowed him behind the mirror equipment, in segment five."

Yazdovsky glided over to join them. Wong moved over to the right-hand seat of the maneuver control station, where the status displays of the spacecraft systems could be summoned.

"There is a problem, though," he said. "There's a half-meter split in one of the lab's seams, so any activity in there will have to be done in suits."

"Gene," Yazdovsky asked, "where exactly was the open seam?"

"I can't remember exactly," he replied. "Rerun the video of the approach to the lab after the accident."

Yazdovsky slipped agilely into the communications console seat and called up the video record on all the TV monitors. Before the pictures reached the point where the optical effects started, and when the spinning lab's image was in the correct orientation, she froze the replay. Part of the large angular wall of the laboratory's control module was missing, revealing the dark curved surface of the pressure vessel beneath. Where that met the cylindrical perimeter pressure wall there was a narrow crack next to the bolted flange.

"There"—Wong pointed with his pen—"just above the 'N' of ANICE. There's no way we could repair that kind of hole."

"We could get a closer look from the docking rerun," Yazdovsky said.

Wong nodded, and Yazdovsky typed in a few commands. The forward view from *Unity*'s camera as it moved along the length of the space laboratory prior to docking appeared on one of the screens. Yazdovsky halted the replay when the central control module was fully in view. It was illuminated from behind the camera. On the upper left was the dark trapezoidal patch where the external covering had been jarred away. The joint where the two curves of the pressure walls met at the flange looked flawless.

Wong stared blankly at the new picture. "Huh?" He stuck his head, closer to the screens and compared the two contradictory pictures. All three were speechless for a few moments.

Sheilagh was the first to speak. "It's been fixed!"

Wong raised a hand to his forehead and continued to stare at the screens. "It must be a trick of the shadows," he suggested without conviction.

Yazdovsky said, "I knew there was something odd about it. I had this feeling as we approached for the docking that something had changed, apart from the rotation."

"Do the lab's internal cameras still work?" Sheilagh asked.

Yazdovsky shook her head. "No, they got smashed by the explosion." As she spoke, without looking at the screens, she stabbed twice at a couple of buttons on the panel to demonstrate her point.

Wong and Sheilagh looked at each other.

"Do that again, Nina," Wong said.

Yazdovsky pressed the buttons again to activate the lab's internal cameras.

They could see a very dim reflection of the red lamp on the console power indicator reflecting from the steel accelerator tubes leading to the reaction chamber.

"They're working!" Yazdovsky cried.

Sheilagh moved closer to the screen and scrutinized the picture through narrowed eyes. Sensing that Yazdovsky was about to change the picture again, she suddenly held up her right hand.

"Leave it!"

After two tense seconds she backed away and spoke very slowly. "What the hell is that? Who put that thing there?"

"What? What thing?" Wong asked anxiously.

"The reaction chamber! It's been—" She fought for an explanation. "It must have been blown out like a bubble by the accident. How amazing!"

"It used to be a square thing, right?" Yazdovsky said.

"That's right. And what are those two tubes sticking out of it?"

Dimly illuminated by the red light, the screen looked extremely eerie.

"We've got to get in there," Sheilagh demanded. She lifted a hand to her temples and grimaced as pain shot through her head. "We've got to get in there!"

CHAPTER 18

SHEILAGH AND YAZDOVSKY SHUT THE LABORATORY hatch behind them and, using flashlights, worked their way past the huge coils of the electron accelerator into segment two. Sheilagh's pulse increased as she maneuvered herself down the narrow space between the main laser and the accelerator. She glided into the open space of the control module, shining her flashlight at the reaction chamber. It stared back at her, hard, shiny, and alien.

Yazdovsky moved over to the nearer of the two TV cameras mounted on the wall. She removed it from its mount and fixed it to the front of her suit.

"Okay, Nina," Wong said from *Unity*. "I'm getting a good picture. Try some of the lights. The switch is on the left of the port you've just come through—no, sorry, the right from where you are." Yazdovsky's arm loomed darkly in his picture and suddenly turned bright red as the laboratory's lighting came on.

"Let Gene see the reaction vessel, Nina," Sheilagh called. Her head throbbed.

Yazdovsky maneuvered herself toward the center of the room. As she came to the reaction chamber, the picture from her camera steadied. Where the two circular accelerator channels met the one coming from the main laser there was a half-meter-diameter sphere constructed in two halves. The two pieces were bonded invisibly together along encircling flanges. Two narrow tubes emanated from one of them at points opposite the laser. The surface of the metal sphere was smooth and shiny.

Sheilagh shook her head.

"Nina, can you see any signs of the fracture in the hull?"

The TV picture wobbled as Yazdovsky scanned the walls. "No, Gene, it looks sound. There aren't any signs of damage at all."

"Why don't you try a little pressurization," Wong suggested. "Maybe a few millibars to see if it holds. I'll turn on the stabilizer in case a leak causes any rotation."

"Okay."

Yazdovsky moved to the pressurization control panel a meter from the tunnel port. She turned it on with a hopeful stab of her gloved hand. It came to life, and she punched in a command to introduce a small volume of nitrogen.

"That's ten millibars." Her voice crackled in the intercom. "Seems to be holding okay."

"Leave it at that for a while, Nina."

In front of Sheila the bright metal surface of the reaction chamber reflected the lights. She moved closer to it and touched it. "It's as smooth as a mirror," she called to Yazdovsky, who was gathering the camera cable in her hands. "There are no signs of machining or anything. In fact, it's almost as if it's been plated. There's no doubt about it. How and why I couldn't tell you, but this reaction chamber has been deliberately made to fit our equipment."

"You're sure it's not just some kind of deformation of the original one, caused by the accident?" Wong's words carried no conviction. He could see the chamber perfectly well on his TV monitor.

"Let's try powering up the console," Sheilagh suggested. She was beginning to feel nauseous from the throbbing pain in her head.

"Gene?" Yazdovsky asked, wanting confirmation from the commander.

"Go ahead."

Sheilagh moved across to the console. "But they were all on when the accident happened. Did either of you turn them off?"

"No, we didn't touch them," Wong said.

Sheilagh pressed the switch next to the power indicator light. The screens remained blank, but several colored lights appeared above them. Then she pressed the RETURN key on the center console. She grimaced as the pain in her head pounded. The console screens came to life.

"They're working!" she cried. On the right-hand screen was a kind of schematic diagram containing some moving symbols. On the left was a page of text:

To: Matthews From: Cepheans

Make errors. More control. I damaged. ANICE OPM 343 Voss/efp I have copied and corrected. Term three of field propagation energy is real infinite. Can not normalize. Beacon message is always correct. Not contradiction. I repair damage and injury.

"Nina! Bring the camera!" Sheilagh's pulse was pounding painfully in her head as the realization swept through her. Yazdovsky came up beside her and pointed the camera at the screen.

"We've done it! We've bloody well done it!"

"Keep the camera steady," Wong called. "There's a world watching."

Yazdovsky frowned and looked closely at the message.

"But it's in English," she said incredulously, "and it calls itself Cepheans! Someone's playing a joke on us, I think."

Sheilagh calmed herself and looked soberly at the screen for a few seconds, as if afraid that Yazdovsky might be right. She then shook her head and grinned through the pain.

"Look, it mentions one of Russell's reports. They must have been able to read the computer's memory. All the composed messages for the Cepheans and all the project documentation are stored in the memories. They have been able to go through them all and learn all about us, including the English language. The name 'Cepheans' is all over the place in the reports. They've even copied the style of a memorandum." She laughed out loud at the bizarre conjunction of the mundane and the momentous.

"What's on the other screen?" Wong asked calmly when he could get a word in.

Sheilagh leaned toward it. "It looks like the top-level schematic of the gecom. But it's been altered. Let me see . . . There are two extra components in the chamber. They seem to be controlled by the same timing circuit as the laser. I can't tell what they do, though."

"Let's get a closer look, Nina," Wong said.

The picture on Wong's screen closed in unsteadily on the right-hand screen.

"Do you think I could try the next level of schematic in case there's more?" Sheilagh asked.

"Hold on," Wong commanded. "We should get a full record of everything on the screen first."

"I'll get a hard copy printed," Sheilagh said, and without waiting for a response, she pressed two keys on the keyboard. A second later two exact duplicates of the screens' contents appeared in a slot under the console.

"Slow down, Sheilagh," Wong said commandingly. Then more gently, "This is a big moment. Let's savor it."

Sheilagh laughed at Wong's coolness and at the excitement that was bubbling through her. "Sorry, Commander Wong," she replied. "Awaiting orders."

"That's better," Wong replied with a slight chuckle. "Now, let's see what the differences are between that schematic and the original."

"That would mean overwriting the current screen," Sheilagh objected. "Let's try the schematic hierarchy first, eh?"

"Okay, okay," Wong conceded.

Sheilagh used the rollerball to the right of the keyboard and positioned the cursor over one of the two orange rectangles that were depicted inside the reaction chamber. The image zoomed in rapidly on the object, which expanded into a new full-screen schematic at a greater level of detail.

"There's more, all right," Sheilagh said, and peered intently at the screen.

"Hmm," she said. "It's not clear to me what this is intended for. There is a set of concentric rings, each with a small gap right across it. They are each connected to oscillators. Some impedances are marked that imply the rings are superconductors."

The totally unfamiliar details in their schematics produced a chilling sense of awe in Sheilagh. Somehow they were even more significant than the text message. She moved the rollerball and selected a fixed menu item that was marked DESCRIPTION. A small window appeared on the screen, bearing the words NO DESCRIPTION AVAILABLE.

"Oh, well, it was worth a try." She sighed. "The coils are set very close to the actual interaction volume, and there's another set on the other side. The separation is less than a hundred microns. I really couldn't tell you what they do."

"Sheilagh?" Wong called. "Is it possible to get a full dump of the machine's memory so we can transmit it to ground?"

"A full dump would take years to transmit, Gene," Sheilagh answered. "There's over a hundred terabytes of memory in this thing."

"Well, the schematics and the report mentioned in the message, then?"

"Yes, I can put them onto a lode, and they could be read by the comms computer."

"Okay, do it, please."

Sheilagh reached below the console and picked out a flat silver rectangle a few centimeters long. It was a layered optical data-encoding cartridge, commonly called a lode. They held several hundred times the amount of data that an optical disk was capable of holding. Inserting it into a small slot on the console she typed in a command on the keyboard. The small, central screen echoed a line of characters and then issued the message COPY COMPLETE AND VERIFIED, 5120763304 BYTES."

Sheilagh browsed through the schematics of the strangely modified gecom. Some of the changes she could understand, such as an alteration in the laser's cooling system that looked impossibly intricate but doubled its average power output capability. The laser priming and trigger circuits had been altered to increase the pulse rate by a factor of 100 and to decrease the pulse length to a tenth of its original duration.

"This is fantastic," Sheilagh breathed when Yazdovsky looked over her shoulder. "All the things we wanted to do but didn't know how. It's mostly just superior technique, better fabrication. Some of it is really beautiful."

"Have you any idea of the purpose of the changes?" Yazdovsky asked.

Sheilagh held herself away from the console with straight arms. "The message indicates that we were doing several things wrong and in fact were unwittingly creating a great danger—for them as well as for us, which is puzzling. But the mods are intended to make it safe. They want us to try again, I think."

"The first person singular is a language error, you suppose?" Yazdovsky inquired.

"Probably. The documentation in the computer probably contains a preponderance of *I*s over *we*s. The message suggests that they didn't have much time to learn because they were too busy repairing and fixing the lab."

"And fixing you as well," Yazdovsky added, looking through

the corner of her eye at Sheilagh. "It says 'injury' as well as 'damage.' "

With a reluctant nod of her head Sheilagh acknowledged Yazdovsky's point. She must have been injured, but not as badly as Salwi. So the Cepheans did not have unlimited capabilities despite the fantastic things they had done to the gecom.

But there were hundreds of questions that begged to be answered. How had the Cepheans gotten to the laboratory? Why had they not stayed? What was it that had caused the accident, and how could it have harmed the Cepheans, as the message stated? The tone of the message was an odd mixture of authoritative, contemptuous, and apologetic. She was certain that it was a false impression created by the Cepheans' language difficulties. To be able to achieve all they had done in just a few hours was utterly amazing by human standards, and it was surely asking too much that they could also have picked up the delicate subtleties of the English language at the same time.

For nearly three hours data from the space laboratory's computer streamed back to Earth. At Abingdon, Russell Voss's team began their analyses of the technically dazzling changes that had been made to their schematics while others studied the consequences of the dramatic events on board *Unity* and the space laboratory.

Early the next morning a meeting of all senior ANICE staff was held in the main conference room at Abingdon. The windowless room with its padded, fabric-lined walls and thick carpets deadened their voices. The long wooden table was equipped down its center with flat, flush-fitting nonreflective computer screens that had the visual appearance and tactile feel of high-quality paper. Only a few of the attendees brought actual papers with them.

Seated at one of the semicircular ends of the table, Manfred Schopf called the meeting to order. Voss, as chief scientist, was seated in his wheelchair to his right, and Bill Tomlinson, in charge of the gecoms technical team, leaned back in his seat near the other end of the table. Apart from Voss and Tomlinson, there was Professor Oyama, in charge of the space laboratory mission management team, Stewart Fletcher, who was ANICE's PR man at Abingdon, Dr. Jaime Perera, chief of the laser physics group, Dr. Tanya Page, the policy-group leader, and seven other senior staff members and managers.

Schopf's strong voice and sibilant Bavarian accent brought immediate attention from all those present.

"Good morning, ladies and gentlemen. I must say that recent events seem to have caught us a little off balance. While no one could possibly have predicted what has happened on *Unity*, we must, repeat must, get our act together again immediately. I remind you all that three lives may depend upon us performing to the very peak of our abilities in the coming days and weeks." He paused to acknowledge the unspoken agreement with those words from the others.

"Now, let us first hear from Professor Oyama, who will provide an overview of events." Schopf looked expectantly at the elderly, spectacled Oriental at the left center of the table. Professor Oyama cleared his throat, leaned forward over the table, and spoke with a clear high voice, looking right and left at his colleagues.

"The situation is as follows. We have every reason to believe that the aliens have made a detailed study of all the space laboratory's systems, including the computer and its data banks. They almost certainly have obtained a complete readout of its optical memories." A few murmured comments were heard around the table. "You don't need me to spell out what this means: They have obtained access to all of our stored messages. The thousands of diagrammatic and holographic images painstakingly created by Dr. Page's team have been disclosed in their entirety to the aliens. These detailed descriptions of the Earth and our view of the universe altogether amount to a total disclosure of the human race's condition—a large proportion of its accumulated knowledge. The aliens modified the computer's start-up programs to cause their message and the schematic processor to be loaded on power-up. The message, incidentally, was a display-memory file, in other words, exactly like our own messages. A detailed search of the computer's storage has revealed just one modified item—the report that the message refers to. Now, the other thing that we can deduce is that they also have read our entire project documentation that was stored with the messages in the computer's memory. This was definitely not intended to be disclosed. It contains many of our discussions on the possibility of Cephean hostility and other rather delicate matters. The most immediate and surprising result of this disclosure is that the aliens have learned the English language!"

"But their message was hardly textbook English grammar,"

put in the dark-skinned, rotund man sitting opposite him. "Even I can see that." He looked around for appreciation of his joke.

"No, Dr. Perera," Oyama replied, his gray eyebrows showing clearly above his glasses, "but it *was* English, and surely by now they will have reached as high a standard as our examples allow."

"They'll be as confused as hell," Fletcher said with a grin.

"They may well have a little difficulty with the rather variable standard of English we have used, I admit," Oyama agreed. "And in fact, it creates problems for us, as I shall explain in a moment. The remarkable fact is that the Cepheans learned enough of the language in five hours, solely from our reports and memoranda, to leave us that brief, historic communication. In fact, the Cepheans showed a number of very remarkable capabilities. I understand that Dr. Voss's calculations show that the damage seen on the space laboratory's exterior must have meant that the interior was almost destroyed by the gravitational shock wave that passed through it. So we must believe the Cepheans' claim to have undone the damage. The manner in which they did so is a complete enigma. We are all, I'm sure, deeply shocked and saddened by Dr. Salwi's tragic death. Dr. Matthews seems, mercifully, to have recovered. Why he should be left for dead while Dr. Matthews was cured only deepens the mystery of what happened during that strange metamorphosis of the laboratory. We can maybe infer that the aliens are not infallible."

"Or maybe that they are unconcerned about the astronauts' well-being," Page suggested from the other end of the table.

"Yes," Oyama admitted, "that could also be the explanation. We can only speculate. Dr. Matthews should of course be hospitalized as soon as possible, but as we all know, *Unity*'s trajectory cannot be altered and we are forced to wait another ten months. Even then we face a very serious difficulty getting to and returning from *Unity* as it flies past the Earth."

"Any progress with that, Professor Oyama?" Schopf asked.

"Dr. Yanchinski's team in Guyana is working on a way to use two TAVs with external fuel tanks, Dr. Schopf. I'm afraid that even so, they have not been able to come up with any workable rescue trajectories. To get to *Unity* before it reaches Earth, equip it with a heat shield, and direct it into an aerobraking maneuver is not possible because of the huge velocity changes required to get out there and rendezvous. To get to them after they pass the Earth is easier, but then returning becomes impossible. We simply don't have vehicles capable of such performance. The very best scenario is to send up the TAVs with provisions for another year and to use their engines to bring them back in an aerobraking maneuver eleven months later.'' He looked over his glasses at Schopf.

"That's not good," Schopf commented gruffly. "We have to get them back this orbit. The TAVs are not built for lengthy occupation, and *Unity* is damaged. Who can say how long its life-support systems will last? There is too much danger on such a long flight." He looked up sharply at Oyama. "I presume that any vehicle currently available, from any country, is being used in their studies."

"That is correct, Dr. Schopf," Oyama said.

"What is the miss distance on their return?"

"Forty-six thousand kilometers," Oyama read from his screen. "With a relative velocity of fourteen kilometers per second. To match their speed and then return would require a multistage vehicle of great size."

Schopf sighed heavily. Marscom was responsible for the safety of the astronauts and the vehicles, leaving Schopf powerless to do anything—a position he was unaccustomed to being in.

"We will get them back," he said sternly. He had no idea at the time how it was to be done, but he was not going to accept a negative response from Guyana. As a top-class physicist he was fully aware of the technicalities of astronautics and therefore of the seriousness of the rescue problem. But having spearheaded three of the largest scientific enterprises in history, he did not shirk at the prospect of putting together a completely new high-speed space vehicle in nine months. He made a mental note to put the problem at the top of his list of priorities. Then he looked up again at Oyama, and his expression lightened. That subject was closed.

"Please continue."

"Let me return to the language problems," Oyama said. "The fact that the Cepheans appear to have taught themselves our language and have read all our messages is perhaps to be regarded as a great stroke of luck. It means that we can probably dispense with all those tedious preliminaries that we have been taking for granted would be necessary. We can reply to them directly using whatever vocabulary and grammar have been used in the project documentation."

"Can you really make up a message using the existing words?" Bill asked.

"Ah, well, Dr. Tomlinson," Page said, "that depends on whether we follow the instructions of our political masters. Apparently they want the first messages to have a certain—well— a certain dignified formality and think that poor grammar would rather preclude that."

Bill snorted with contempt. "Oh, save us! Do they really think that 'dignified formality' is going to be recognized by the Cepheans? They could just as well take it as hostility."

Bill placed his palms over his eyes and shook his head.

Page was anxious to allay Bill's fears. "The message will be composed by us, not by the politicians. They will have to approve what we produce, but most of them recognize that there are differences between human diplomacy and alien. For example, we're not going to use some dumb sentence about wanting 'peace and friendship.' " She made quotation marks in the air.

Perera looked startled. "Why ever not? That is what we want, isn't it?"

"Dr. Perera, you must understand that conversing with an alien intelligence is not a simple matter. We must be careful to avoid any unintentional connotations. We know that the first messages are going to be scrutinized very closely by the aliens, or at least we must expect that. If we talk about wanting peace and friendship and that kind of thing, they could well infer that we considered the opposite a possibility. We have to keep to plain and simple statements that as far as possible don't allow any secondary interpretations."

Perera arched his eyebrows and rocked his head from side to side. Page's explanation was plausible.

"Anyway," Oyama said, "we are currently working on several new messages in English that at least try to recoup some of our dignity after these unforeseen events. They are in the general vein of mutual cooperation and are expressive of a desire to share knowledge. Pretty much the usual stuff. Now, the other important area is Dr. Voss's; he has been analyzing the changes to the schematics of the gecom. Perhaps Dr. Voss would like to explain his results himself."

"Yes, of course, thank you, Professor Oyama," Voss said. "First, however, I should talk about the error that I am very greatly ashamed to admit has been made in interpreting the Cepheans' radio messages. The report that is mentioned in the latest message does indeed contain a correction to one of the equations of preon interaction. One of the operators in the

Grand Theory formulation appeared to have a close analogy with a parallel one in my geonics theories. This misled me into assuming the wrong interpretation for it. Basically, when there is a perfect alignment of the interaction beams, then the energy release we all feared becomes inevitable. It was this that caused the damage to the laboratory and the injuries to Sheilagh and Dr. Salwi. Preon interactions don't occur, but instead the preons constituting nearby matter annihilate, releasing their mass energy. What we need is close alignment but not exact alignment. The analogy was false, and I confess to being responsible for the crisis we are now in.''

"Dr. Voss, we will not allow that statement to pass," Schopf objected. "You have done more to make this enterprise possible than any other person alive, and you can't conceivably be blamed for any problems we have now. There are dozens of other physicists who made exactly the same miscalculation. One may say that that was because of your strong leadership in the field, which I'm sure may be true, but that is the last reason for you to accept all the blame.''

"Hear, hear," Bill said, and several others expressed their agreement with Schopf's words.

"That's very kind of you, but it was really unforgivable in my eyes. But anyway, the effect was just as described in the message. One of the terms in the interaction equations does really have infinite values in certain circumstances. It's a new kind of mathematical approach I wasn't aware of before.''

"What is your assessment of the Cepheans' changes to the gecom?" Schopf asked.

"The overall effect is to greatly widen the bandwidth of the system, basically by increasing the rate at which it can be fired by a factor of about eleven. Then there is the addition of the monopole detectors. During the interactions, when the time symmetry is putting great stress on the geonic field, it is possible, when the symmetry is nearly perfect, to get pairs of particles called magnetic monopoles instead of the preon unraveling that we want. These are very rare and very heavy particles; they are in fact true eleven-D particles. Their momentary existence is a problem because if they are allowed to persist, even for very short times, then they provide a sort of connection between eleven-D and normal spacetime. The preons are like coiled springs, tightly wound. We're trying to unwind them, open them up a little without breaking them. But the monopoles have the same eleven-D dimensionality as the preons and can interact strongly with them. In a sense they are like wire cutters that just cut right through the coils. The violent unwinding is the source of the gravitational energy."

"Would the Cepheans notice this release of energy?" asked a man sitting next to Perera.

"Yes, they would if they were looking for the geon pulses at the same location, I think. We don't know, of course, how their receivers work, so it is not possible to answer your question definitively. But it would seem that they did suffer some damage to whatever devices they use. I'm afraid that we'll have to do a lot more work before we understand all this, though."

"How do those monopole detectors help, then?" the man asked.

"The Cepheans' detectors are rather ingenious devices that can detect monopoles as soon as they are created. They do this by maintaining tiny, symmetrical quantized currents in their superconductor loops that will jump to higher quantum states, and thus destroy the time symmetry, whenever a monopole comes near. This in turn removes the conditions that the monopoles need for their existence, and they annihilate each other, releasing their energy as other particles—a minor puff instead of a destructive jolt. The beauty of them is that they are failsafe. They are simple solid-state passive devices. If there are any faults with them or they are not energized, then the time symmetry is automatically broken."

"Are these effects potential sources of artificial gravity?" Oyama inquired.

"Certainly, Professor Oyama," Voss answered. "That is one very promising prospect which we'll be following up as soon as we've got more time. If we could control the unwinding so that it happened more slowly, we could generate symmetrical gravity fields, in theory."

"That leads us to the strange visual effects, Dr. Voss," Schopf said. "Have you any more ideas about them?"

Voss paused for a while. "The only explanation I can suggest is that they were caused by a spherical shell of strongly attracting gravitational mass surrounded by one of gravitationally *repelling* mass. Now, I'm the first one to point out that repulsive mass is not possible in the Grand Theory, so this so-called explanation is really no such thing."

"We'll have to get that one from the Cepheans themselves, perhaps," Schopf suggested.

"We are similarly at a loss," Voss continued, "to explain the mechanism by which they modified the space laboratory's equipment and cured Sheilagh's injuries. They clearly had some powerful control over the matter in the lab, both at the microscopic and macroscopic scale. We have no idea at all about that. One small clue is that they introduced no extra matter. Nothing was transmuted, and nothing introduced; they just *rearranged*.''

"That," Oyama suggested, "would tell us that their actions were done at a distance. That makes much more sense than making them appear and disappear in person in the space laboratory."

Bill Tomlinson had been thoughtful for some minutes. He looked up at that point in a way that attracted the room's attention. "Something else has occurred to me," he said slowly. "They have all our messages and therefore know not only what we are but *where* we are. If they can do such amazing things from great distances, why haven't they shown up on Earth? They've got all the info they need about the sun and the Earth and about *Unity*'s mission. They should be able to work out the Earth's location from that. If they really are interested in communicating, why aren't they here now?"

"It might not be possible for them," Voss answered. "They located the space laboratory by its gecom. Remember those strange blue objects that appeared briefly before the effect started? Well, they were presumably scouts—test probings to find out the real location of the gecom after the approximate one had been ascertained by the gecom firing."

"Ah!" Fletcher cried. "They wanted to find the offending source of gravitational energy before it did them any more harm!"

"Right," Voss said. "But it took them a little while to do it. Remember that several minutes elapsed after the last firing before they eventually found it. I think, then, that their powers are limited in that respect. They need a signaling gecom to home in on."

"If you think about it," Schopf said, "if the Cepheans were able to do these things wherever they want to, then we would have seen evidence of it years ago." He shook his head. "It is easy for us to get carried away with ideas of supreme power when thinking about aliens. But there are fundamental barriers even with Grand Theory science."

Bill slumped back into his chair. "Well, I like my aliens omnipotent," he muttered grumpily, causing several chuckles around the room. "Millions of years of technological development? Surely omnipotence is not too much to expect?"

But he wasn't sharing the amusement around him. He had not intended his comments as a joke. He was thinking of his friend and her colleagues on board the tiny, fragile vessel 40 million kilometers away from home.

CHAPTER 19

THE PRELIMINARY TEST FIRINGS OF THE MODIFIED gecom had been concluded successfully without any trace of the damaging gravitational waves being detected, and everything was ready for the first attempt at communications. *Unity* was attached to the space laboratory.

The scene on board the space laboratory was relayed to Earth from its two cameras, one mounted on the wall overlooking the entire laboratory and the other mounted above and behind Wong and Sheilagh as they stood before the console. A third picture, showing the contents of the console screen, was also transmitted back to Earth. Yazdovsky manned the maneuver control station.

Sheilagh, Wong, and Yazdovsky had had several days to prepare themselves mentally for the upcoming events. Wong developed the same outlook he always did when about to embark on a dangerous or important task, such as the first test launch of the Big Lifter Shuttle he had piloted three years before: he closed his mind to any characteristic of his mission that was likely to affect his composure. That meant that he lost the immediate thrill of the moment, but, he reasoned, if the thrill of the moment is going to affect your abilities and maybe kill you, who needs it? He could turn on to the excitement at his leisure after the event.

Unlike Wong, Sheilagh was determined that the exhilaration of actually being part of the (hopefully, not literally) earthshaking events was not going to escape her. What it needed was sufficient mental control and discipline, and to give herself confidence and inspiration, she thought of how Russell Voss would approach the task. Standing in front of the console with the communications channel to Mission Control hissing faintly in her headset and the bright screens waiting patiently for her hands to type in the commands, she felt calm and prepared.

With his characteristic aplomb, Wong announced: "All systems up and running. We're about to start the gecom."

Sheilagh's fingers moved quickly and delicately over the keyboard. With a small flourish, like a concert pianist, she touched the final key that set the gecom's control programs running. "The gecom is running," she announced after a few seconds.

The modified laser no longer made the sharp sounds it had before. Instead, it hummed with a gentle power.

"Strong preon interactions indicated. We are ready for the first message."

The first action was to send the greeting message repeated three times, wait five minutes for a reply, then repeat the process until one was eventually received. Sheilagh looked at Wong for the signal to go ahead. That, along with the ability to command a halt if the safety of the crew or the spacecraft was threatened, was the only authority Wong wanted over the process. Authority, according to his definition, was conferred by appropriate experience, knowledge, and expertise. That was why he was the commander of the mission and why Sheilagh Matthews was going to be Earth's representative during any discourse with the aliens. He nodded his head.

"Sending message A," Sheilagh announced.

On the screen the first message from Earth to an alien civilization appeared slowly from the top of the screen. The upper half of the screen showed a simple picture of the crescent Earth, the dark side showing city lights, deliberately exaggerated. Below that stood a man and a woman; between them were a boy and a girl, about six years and eight years old, respectively. Their pictures were as realistic in coloring and shading as could be managed on the computer screen. They wore no clothes and had no features that would identify them with any particular race. A subtle background shading produced a parallax effect that indicated, at least to human eyes, that the four individuals came from the surface of the large starlit planet behind them. Such graphic effects would have made no sense, of course, in a very first exchange, but the composers were relying on the already extensive knowledge of Earth and its inhabitants that the Cepheans had gained from the computer's memory.

Below the pictures was the brief text of the message, composed for the politicians with dignified formality in mind but attempting to steer clear of obfuscation:

> WE ARE THE PEOPLE OF EARTH. WE GREET OUR GALACTIC NEIGHBORS. WE WISH THAT THIS HISTORIC COMMUNICATION MARKS THE BEGINNING OF LASTING COOPERATION AND FRIENDSHIP THAT BRINGS UNDERSTANDING AND MUTUAL BENEFIT.

Page's group in Abingdon had wanted the message to stop after the second sentence but had succumbed to political pressure to add more ceremony to it. The odd phrasing of the additional sentence, which had originally started 'May this historic moment . . .' was the result of Page's editing.

Sheilagh's attention rested on the smaller central screen that monitored the gecom's output. Nothing was apparent.

Then a sudden change on the right-hand screen attracted her attention. Its plain white background broke up into multicolored snow. She immediately thought with dismay that by unbelievable coincidence the video circuits had chosen that moment to fail. Before that thought had time to fully register, the snow was replaced by a burst of colored images that changed too quickly for her eyes to follow. It was like a fast scan through the contents of a videolode.

"How the hell—" Sheilagh was aghast. "There's no way that lot is coming through the gecom. There are sixty-seven megabits of data in a video frame!"

It was impossible to catch an individual frame of the information that was streaming at a mind-numbing pace onto the screen, but the impression she got was of a mixture of line drawings or schematic-type images with others that looked like noise.

"Are we recording this?" Wong asked, as if he were watching a TV program.

"Yes, yes," Sheilagh told him without taking her eyes off the screen. "We can get an hour of video on a lode." She let out a sharp sigh of exasperation. "We should have expected something like this. I don't think we could have been more stupid, expecting them to talk to us in English, indeed!"

"What do you think it is?" Wong said.

Sheilagh shrugged. "I have no idea."

"Any idea, then, how they're doing it?"

She drew in a deep breath and slowly let it out again. "They must be controlling the video circuits in the computer. But if they can do that, they can probably control anything else in the lab." She looked at Wong with wide eyes as the realization hit her. "Even us!"

Wong remained impassive. "Nina, can you detect anything abnormal with the systems in the lab?" he asked calmly. "Or with *Unity*, for that matter?"

There was a brief pause while Yazdovsky scanned the status displays. "Nothing showing here," she called.

"I don't think there's any cause for concern," Wong announced. "Let's just see how long this lasts."

"But it could be years," Sheilagh exclaimed. "There's no way of telling what's going to happen now!"

It was, in fact, just forty-five minutes later that the fantastic flow of images stopped. In the minutes that followed, with everyone stunned by the unexpected flood of information, no one thought until it was too late to send a response indicating that the message had been received. Ten minutes later the same message started appearing again. After the second time Sheilagh sent a reply consisting of the words "We have received your messages" replacing the original message of greeting below the picture of Earth and the four figures. The Cepheans' message did not repeat after that, and in the dazed aftermath no more attempts at communication were made. The decision came from Mission Control and Abingdon to shut down the gecom.

Another three days passed before the contents of the new message were understood by the people at Abingdon.

To Sheilagh's great surprise, it was Russell Voss who sent the message.

"It's rather devastating news, I'm afraid," his image said from the video terminal in the "storm shelter" cabin. He was using the video terminal in his office that was mounted low down on his desk. Deep in shadows, hiding his larger-than-life face, his dark eyes looked fathomless. "It's another stage in the boot-strapping process that you suggested years ago, Sheilagh. But this time we're getting out of our depth. The Cepheans want us to build a kind of interface to the brain. We presume the idea is to perform some sort of direct mental link; they don't go into

the details about what they would use it for. It's possible they
have a cognitive network and want us to plug ourselves into it."

Voss continued to talk steadily. There was no way for Sheilagh to interject any responses because they were more than five
minutes apart in communications turnaround time. "The real
problem is that the design is bioelectronic. The current estimate
is that it will take us fifteen years to develop the capabilities
required to make such circuits, even with their messages to help
us. Like the radio message, the new one is in two parts; one
theory, the other practice. I must say that both parts are quite
mind-boggling. From what I can gather, the theory discusses
biological circuits—made of biological molecules. Then it talks
about genetic engineering in rather a general way, as if they are
familiar with many different natural genetic mechanisms. There's
a little bit near the end about DNA and specifically human or,
I should say, Earth-type genetics. They even go into consciousness with equations and numbers—just as if they were hard scientific disciplines."

Sheilagh's mind was spiraling unsteadily. She wanted time to
think, but Voss's voice continued at its constant pace.

"But that is nothing compared to the second part. They quite
nonchalantly expect us to genetically engineer a human being
with the necessary bioelectronic circuitry to take part in this
mental communication—or whatever it is they can do with it.
How far away we are from that sort of capability is anyone's
guess. Fifty years is the only figure I've heard anyone suggest.
We're all beginning to feel a bit small."

"Anyway," he went on, "that's the position so far. No doubt
you could use a little time to think. It took me a long time to
appreciate the significance of all this, but now there seems to
be something inevitable about it. It fits in perfectly with your
theory and Professor Holdsworth's. The Cepheans are providing
a succession of ever more sophisticated science based upon
demonstrated abilities. If we can unwrap preons, then, they reason, we must be close to genetically engineering bioelectronic
circuits. The fact that we are fifty years away from it is neither
here nor there to them."

He stopped talking, but his image remained on the screen.

"That's amazing, Russell. Absolutely amazing." She adjusted her position in front of the screen, knowing how discon-
certing it was to hold a conversation with a talking head that
slowly drifted away from the vertical. "What exactly does the
brain interface look like? How does it work? How can they

produce such incredible effects at a distance? And if they can, why can't they just directly tap into someone's normal brain patterns, so to speak? Why do we have to build a special interface? Do they say? And how's the Abingdon gecom coming? Is the monopole detector working yet? And, most important of all, how're the rescue plans coming?''

Five minutes later Voss's response arrived.

''About the rescue: I'm afraid they haven't got a firm plan yet, but there is a possible mission being worked out. It requires a lot more hard work by the Marscom engineers, but they've put together a vehicle design that we think might get you back home next April. They've come up with a mission using two TAVs linked together as a sort of two-stage vehicle. They're going to put two of the Big Lifter external tanks into orbit and connect it up to the TAVs' engines. So don't worry.

''About the gecom here, it's scheduled to be ready in three days. I'm supervising the project myself. The loops are constructed; we've just got to install them. They give no hint as to how they did it, no. But I think the gecom is used as an accurate position marker; they couldn't produce the effect just anywhere, only close to a working gecom. It might be that the preon interactions have other properties that we don't know about, something that is either not in the Grand Theory or is deeply buried in it. But whatever technique they used, it can't be sophisticated enough to manipulate brain cells individually, and in any case they don't know all the details of brain function. That is left to us to provide. There is another point, though: This brain interface is very nonspecific to humans. The front end of it contains circuits that transmit different senses. Apart from visual, aural, olfactory, and orientational, there are senses for position, speed, and acceleration included—just as if we had specific organs that detect these things! It's as if we had full three-axis inertial navigation systems in our heads. On top of that, there are circuits for x-rays, infrared, and radio waves. Then there are detection senses for charged particles, macroscopic pressure, magnetic fields, electric fields, and thermal and electric conductivity. How about that for a set of senses?

''The other side to it is the transmission of thoughts. There's something completely new here and really exciting. Most of the senses are *two-way*, so one could think of a smell or a sight, or a place for that matter, and the idea is encoded in the Cepheans' format and placed on the transmission antennas. At first I thought that for us humans it wouldn't work too well, because if we think of a sound, for example, then the actual aural centers of the brain don't respond in any noticeable way; the concept is formed in other, less specific regions of the cortex. However, one of the people here has pointed out some research done in the Soviet Union where they show that the sensory regions of the brain can indeed be stimulated by effort of will. Apparently, if we just close our eyes and imagine a scene, nothing happens in the sensory cells. But if the cells are stimulated artificially, with the eyes closed, it is possible to *modify* the cells' activity just by willing it. Imagine it. You have a scene, say, a table and some chairs, being fed artificially into your visual cortex. You could imagine one of the chairs rising up and putting itself on the table. Or you could make the tablecloth change color. We can't do this in normal circumstances, because the incoming real signal overrides the attempts at modification that we make. But if the internally generated perturbation is sensed and fed back into the incoming synthesized signal, as they did in the Soviet experiments, then the subject can completely control what he sees—by pure willpower! You could create any scene, any experience entirely from your own imagination. Presumably the Cepheans would detect the currents in the antennas directly and then put them into the cognitive system they have, to be eventually fed back to the brain interface as changes to the sensory inputs."

The thought occurred to Sheilagh just then that the bodily senses, like touch and body position, were not included in his list. But Voss was talking about that very thing.

"There are no circuits for purely human senses, like touch. They would require specific details about an individual and his or her body and nervous system. No, the Cepheans' design is for a sort of generic sensory node in a cognitive network. The idea is indescribably appealing. Think what such an interface would mean! Complete freedom from the prison of the body. All of the basic senses being fully and accurately stimulated by the interface, and the reverse senses allowing us to move about in and interact with a truly synthetic world. If we wanted to move, we'd just conceive of the motion and it would appear in the motion and position circuits. If we wanted to alter something, push it or turn it, say, we'd just visualize the process and the visual information would be transmitted through the interface. And all the time the actual cognitive experience would be happening within our real brains, but without us suffering the dangers and difficulties of actual reality! It's quite literally mind-boggling.''

Sheilagh realized at that moment why he had personally sent the message. He needed to tell her, because she was the only one who would really understand what it meant to him, cruelly and unjustly imprisoned in his broken body.

All the recent years of pragmatic indifference melted in her heart, and a wave of tenderness for him overcame her. She longed to be back on Earth, to touch him again.

"Most odd," Professor Holdsworth confessed. "So the Cepheans are not telling us everything?"

He and Bill Tomlinson were walking with Voss along the bank of the Thames, just south of the ANICE buildings. Bill was pushing Voss's wheelchair. A fresh wind stirred the overhanging branches noisily and cleared away the exhaust fumes of the river craft.

They had just learned of Voss's latest theoretical results, namely, that the Grand Theory provided no mechanisms for the Cepheans to perform their tricks with the space laboratory and its computer.

"No, they're not," Voss replied. "And there's another thing. That microwave transmitter of theirs must have a continuous power of at least a hundred gigawatts if we assume even the best possible efficiency for it. The microwave scattering is much higher along the line of sight than we at first believed, and we can't accept that it would be beamed right at the sun from that distance. Now, I don't know about you, Bill, but that figure impresses me. It's equivalent to a hundred good-sized nuclear power stations all working together. We couldn't possibly put together a transmitter on that scale. It would need all kinds of new technologies, not to mention the economic resources.''

"Yeah," Bill said, "but there's nothing unknown about the theory for that. We understand all the principles. With this new trick of theirs, they're showing us something beyond our current theories—even the ones we borrowed from them.''

"Yes, that's right.''

"Still no response to your gecom?" the professor asked.

"None at all," Voss replied. "It's as if they don't want to talk to us anymore.''

"I take it you've tried making contact through the space lab's gecom?" the professor asked.

"Yes, and still no response," Voss said. "I think they're paying no attention until we get this cognitive interface working, which is going to take years and years. We haven't even started to approach the problem. The ANICE top brass are even talking about dissolving the organization at the end of the year. It's a depressing thought that all our efforts might come to this. And we've still not found a way to rescue *Unity*'s crew.''

"Incidentally," the professor said rather gravely, "I spoke to Lebovsky yesterday. He's not giving the rescue mission more than a ten percent chance of being ready in time." The pain of having to report that news was apparent on his face.

Voss hesitated before replying. "Yes, I'd heard as much. I'm afraid it may be worse than that."

"But the full effect of Schopf's management is yet to be felt," Bill said. "He's been there a month now, and from what I saw of him here, there'll be some action soon."

"I'm sure you're right," the professor said, trying to echo Bill's optimism.

"It's appropriate he should at last be on a project *making* rockets," Bill suggested with a grin. "He's used up quite a few in his career giving motivational boosts to people."

"They must be thinking of their own survival now," Voss said quietly, thinking of Sheilagh and her companions. "I'm starting a new project to attempt communication between their gecom and ours, mainly to give them something to work on. Neither device is built for such a purpose, but it might help their spirits a little."

They approached a bench, and Voss expressed a desire to rest. "It's uncomfortable being bounced around by the rough path. Let's sit for a while."

Bill apologized for his thoughtlessness and positioned Voss's wheelchair in front of the bench. They all looked out across the dark water.

"You're not giving up the attempts to communicate with the Cepheans again?" the professor asked.

"We'll be monitoring for modulations whenever we run the gecoms," Voss replied simply. There was a tone in his voice that hinted at some unspoken thought.

"You don't sound too hopeful," the professor said.

"I don't think we'll hear from them until we've got a cognitive interface working, but I'm not going to wait that long."

The others were baffled.

"There's a simpler way to achieve this cognitive interface," Voss told them bluntly.

Bill realized what his friend was suggesting. "You're going to try that yourself?"

"Yes."

"But it's dangerous," Bill said.

"As I see it," Voss said, "I am the one person in the world with the experience and the ability to do it. I have been using EE controls for years, and I have the mental control and the willpower that will be needed."

"You've been considering this for some time, then?" Bill asked.

"Yes," Voss said. Then his voice took on strength and zeal. "Just think what we stand to gain. If I can somehow link up to the Cepheans, there's no knowing what I might discover. The potential is limitless."

"What exactly is this idea you have in mind?" the professor asked plainly.

"To construct the interface as specified, but using conventional electronics," Voss replied. "To the Cepheans it would look electrically the same. But as we can't make a real input-output port to the brain, we could do our best with the kinds of implants that are being developed for people who have lost their vision. There's a company in California that has made a matrix of electrodes that can be safely attached to the surface of the brain. It's some sort of organic membrane with conductors embedded in it. My idea is to equip myself with three of these for the visual and aural regions of my brain. But, and this is the big question, can it be modified to not only stimulate the cells but do the reverse—to detect the cells' spontaneous activity? That's what we must attempt. We could also use conventional EE, of course. With some more research, I think I could build an EE that would encode the notions of basic movement. Our own sense of movement is almost entirely visual, so we'd have to invent a motion sense in any case."

The professor was stunned by his nerve and resolve, while Bill was a little puzzled.

"Explain to me again why we can't just use conventional electronics for the whole thing," he asked, "without using brain implants, that is."

"It wouldn't be very useful, that's all. We could, I suppose, put the incoming visual signals onto TV screens in front of each eye, then use some very sophisticated video processors to manipulate the image in real time. But the whole purpose of the cognitive link is a direct high-speed connection between sense and action. We can't hope to achieve that with just knobs and buttons. It may even turn out to be technically easier this way, as well as being much more rewarding.''

Professor Holdsworth was touched by the strength of purpose in Voss's words. He knew that Voss was reaching for his own freedom, a temporary release from his subjection to incapacity. Who could blame him for wanting to rediscover the freedom of spirit that only unimpaired health could foster? The Cepheans' cognitive network was out there waiting for him. His freedom was within reach, but the professor could see the risks.

''There is a very great danger here,'' the professor said. ''If I understand you correctly, you're going to connect yourself directly into the Cepheans' cognitive network without knowing what to expect. It could be very damaging to your mind, let alone the physical dangers.''

''The risk is quite high, I'm afraid,'' Voss said, ''especially of damaging the areas of the brain involved. Of course, any kind of surgery on the brain is risky.''

''You don't have to do this,'' the professor said.

''I feel compelled to do it. I haven't mentioned the real reason. You see, I don't think the rescue mission is going to succeed. Sheilagh's not going to be coming back.''

They were both struck by the certainty in his voice. They knew that he and Sheilagh had once been very close, but now they saw for the first time that Voss loved her. He would accept any risk in order to bring her home.

''If I can communicate with the Cepheans,'' Voss went on, ''then I might learn from them how to get her back. They may help. I've got to try.''

CHAPTER 20

SHEILAGH WAS ALONE IN THE STORM-SHELTER CABIN.
A personal message from Russell Voss was on its way across
the decreasing gap between *Unity* and Earth. Their ship was
falling at ever-increasing speed toward the tiny blue drop of
fragile life that was their true home. In just over 160 days they
would race past it, the most beautiful sight an Earthborne mind
could possibly experience, and it would tear their souls from
their bodies.

The deadline for the rescue mission was long past. The hope-
less, despairing efforts of their rescuers to defeat the laws of
dynamics and send a ship to deliver them safely back had failed.
It had never been possible.

Unity's crew had performed their duty. Their sacrifice had
built a bridge to another age for the people of Earth. They had
to leave to others the journey that had begun on the far side.

But such thoughts did not comfort them. Their inevitable death
was an unbearably bitter prospect, and they sank deeper into
despair as the days passed.

The screen came to life. Sheilagh at first did not recognize
the face that appeared. It was Voss, but his head was bald.

"Sheilagh, I'm going to try to get the Cepheans to help. I'm
going to try to contact them through their cognitive network."

He explained his idea, describing the delicate membrane that
sat against his cerebral cortex.

"The implant seems to have worked. I can definitely generate

199

some feedback on the visual circuit. It just needs more practice.''

There was a long pause. Sheilagh's spirits suddenly revived, rising up from the depths. Russell was doing it for her! He had risked his life to make a crazy attempt to save her and her friends.

He spoke again. His voice was tender and shaken by the pain in his heart. ''Sheilagh, I'm sorry. I'm sorry about the years we lost, the chance I threw away. I understand now. I've been a fool, chasing a mirage. It isn't as important as you are to me. It's too late now to recover everything we might have had, but I'm going to try to make amends. You're the only thing that matters to me now, and I'm going to get you back.''

Tears spilled down Sheilagh's cheeks. He could not hear her, but the words forced themselves out. ''It isn't too late, Russell, it isn't too late.''

''The Cepheans have a lot more capabilities than they tell us about, and they must be able to do something. It's the only chance we have left. We'll make the first attempt in six days' time. We're going to need both gecoms, so you'll have to get back to work straightaway. I'm sending the details of the program after this message.''

Her heart pounded in her chest. All along she had never known for sure why he had rejected her. Had there been no room in his mind for the demands of friendship, of caring for someone else? Had his quest for the cosmic mysteries consumed him utterly? Or had he simply rejected her?

But now there was hope. Suddenly, out of the darkness flared a brilliant flame of hope, sparked by Russell Voss's courage and love for her, love that he had after all been hiding from her and even from himself. There was a chance of escaping death, and the greatest of all possible reasons for wanting to.

And there was a bridge that could be reached and crossed.

Voss asked the nurse to put the soft velvet covers over his eyes. His vision went completely dark. Since the matrix of electrodes that lay against his visual cortex had been implanted, his own vision was affected once the external drive circuitry was activated, and it interfered with the artificial signals. Similarly, his ears had to be covered by the soft acoustic ear pads. His head was securely but gently held against the supports of the dome enclosing it. Microwave circuits transmitted their signals to two electronic controllers attached to the inside of his skull. From there, the signals were decoded and sent to the millions of individual electrodes on the delicate membranes that were in electrical contact with the surface cells of his brain.

The sensory void he was in was unnerving, but he had gotten used to it over the last ten weeks. He asked the technician to gently bring in the aural channel.

"Can you hear me? Dr. Voss, can you hear me?" The familiar voice of the nurse filtered into his hearing. He concentrated his will to adjust the amplitude of her voice through the EE controls in the headset.

"Okay," he said, "now the vision, please."

Gently, the nurse's smiling face brightened in his vision as he mentally controlled the strength of the circuitry's signals.

Her face moved rapidly counterclockwise around a circle as he exercised the EE control of the twin TV cameras mounted in the headset.

The signals from the TV cameras entered electronic circuitry that converted them for the Cepheans' cognitive interface. From there they were converted into radio signals interpretable by the implanted microcontrollers. The same microcontrollers received the signals from the membrane that sensed the brain cells' activities generated from within the brain itself by Voss's deliberate will.

In the bank of electronics beside Voss was a modified video processor. Instead of receiving its image-processing commands by computer link, it was connected directly to the visual outputs of the interface to Voss's brain. In the previous weeks Voss had trained himself to use the very simplified cognitive loop. A purely electronic scene produced by the video processor would be presented on his visual cortex, and by carefully willing it, Voss could manipulate the image any way he desired. The tiny modifications would be sensed by the membrane and sent back to the video processor to be incorporated into the scene. Eventually he had learned how to construct crude scenes from a blank image. He was greatly pleased to find that the system was quite stable; fears that wild fluctuations would produce random and mind-damaging signals that would overpower his ability to control them had been proved to be unfounded. In fact, the response of the system was sluggish; it was quite difficult to make the changes to the images he wanted.

After three weeks of self-training Voss had succeeded in making the world's first cognitive loop. On the high-resolution TV monitors attached to the processor, the image in his vision had been displayed in stereo, and he had demonstrated the power of the cognitive loop to his skeptical colleagues. It looked just like a very fancy computer-art tool, and it was difficult then to see that it was the biggest leap in Earth's evolution since the first primitive glimmer of consciousness had arisen 280 million years previously.

On the two hundredth day of *Unity's* mission they were ready to attempt Voss's bold linkup with the Cepheans' mysterious cognitive system that had been so tantalizingly hinted at in their gecom message. The video processor was removed from the loop and replaced by the inactive antennas.

On his right side a white-coated technician sat before the console of the gecom computer that had been constructed as an exact duplicate of the one in the space laboratory. Behind Voss was the large cube containing the Abingdon gecom's reaction chamber.

"Dr. Voss," came the console operator's voice, "we're ready to start the experiment. Mission Control reports *Unity* is standing by."

"Okay, Bob," Voss said calmly. "I'm set."

The Abingdon controller informed Mission Control, and in thirty seconds a request that *Unity's* gecom be fired up was starting its 150 million kilometer sprint to a very special point in the depths of interplanetary space. At the same time, the Abingdon gecom was started. After six minutes the TV cameras and microphones were switched out of the circuit, and Voss was returned to an eerie, blank silence.

With careful synchronization of the clocks at Guyana and on board *Unity*, the message describing Voss's invention was broadcast first from the space laboratory's gecom and then more slowly from Abingdon's.

A tiny bleep informed him that the first message had been sent. It was followed in a few seconds by two more.

He was ready. The moment approached that he had never before dreamed would be possible in his lifetime. In the abysmal darkness he waited.

A tiny, silvery circle appeared and slowly grew, taking on an elongated and angular appearance. Soon it filled the view and was backed at infinite depth by bright unvarying stars. It was *Unity* and the space laboratory.

For minutes it stood out of the void, motionless and unchanging. To the right, the visible side of *Unity's* cylinder showed black streaks and shallow, irregular indentations, evidence of the propulsion unit's fiery demise. On the left, the white segments of the space laboratory shone in the intense light. Two triangular pieces were missing from the smaller central segment to reveal a black and reflective curved surface.

The intense contrasts and awesome 3-D depth of the image were almost overwhelming. He was free, disembodied, floating in space at an unimaginable distance from his own frail body. But he was still aware of the gravity in the laboratory holding him into his chair, and that helped him remain calm in the vertiginous depths of space around him.

There were no sounds to be heard.

Where was the image coming from? Was he generating the image, or was it coming from outside? Was there really cognitive feedback?

To see if any feedback was present, he decided to try experimenting with the image.

"I'm going to try to move around *Unity* to the right."

Coupling the idea of circling about an object to the visual parallactic changes it would produce was a very difficult mental task. Simultaneously using the EE device to generate motion signals made it almost impossible. The image of *Unity* suddenly collapsed inward from left and right, and its colors went crazy. In the background, the stars blinked in and out.

"Whoa, steady now—that's too difficult." The image restabilized. "I'll try just the visual change."

With great concentration he visualized motion around the object before him.

"That's it! It's moving!"

The image of *Unity* slowly rotated in front of him, but he saw that there were several mistakes in the image. Closer parts of *Unity* disappeared behind farther ones, and pieces of it stretched and distorted fantastically.

"Not very good, I'm afraid, and look, the stars aren't moving. I'm not moving; it's *Unity* that's rotating!"

At that point the image collapsed again. Voss had realized the significance of what was happening.

"My God! You realize what this means!" His voice wavered violently as he spoke. "The Cepheans are definitely doing this. I'm in their network! They must be processing my visual signals directly. The sensitivity is fantastic—I can hardly control it."

"Calm down, Dr. Voss," the nurse's voice intruded. "Your heart rate is 180. You must slow it."

"Okay. Sorry. This is hard to handle. I'll fade it out for a while."

The image grayed, darkened, and then disappeared.

"That's right," the nurse breathed softly. "It's coming down. Take your time; there's no hurry."

After a few minutes he was ready again. He brought the gain on the implant circuits back to normal. But this time there was no image of *Unity*, just a featureless blackness. Then, slowly, a faint structure appeared all over the image: a few broad, wavy, barely detectable streaks of less deep blackness.

"Ha! I don't believe it!" Voss exclaimed. He was speaking quickly as the excitement grew again. "This is amazing! The thing I was visualizing just then, while trying to calm myself, was a black velvet curtain—a mental trick I've used for years to help clear my mind. Well, *voilà*, a black velvet curtain!"

The image developed quickly into exactly what Voss had described. His viewpoint moved backward to reveal a large, gently undulating velvet curtain hanging from big wooden loops a great height above. A light gray wall appeared at the left and right.

"That's exactly what I visualized!"

"Stay calm, Dr. Voss," the nurse commanded.

"The curtains in the school assembly hall," Voss announced very slowly, stressing each word as if he did not believe what was happening. "Just exactly as I imagine them."

"Dr. Voss, you're overexcited. Please stop." The nurse was quite agitated herself.

Voss turned the image off completely. "Okay, let's think about this carefully."

He calmed himself again. "Whatever the signal is, it's powerful enough to amplify even the slightest signals coming from the visual cortex. It seems that it will faithfully reproduce any image I want it to. The sensitivity is quite incredible. Are there any clues as to how the signals are being sent and received, Bob?"

"Yes, Dr. Voss," the white-coated technician answered into his microphone. "The voltages are just appearing in the receiving antennas, and there is a small impedance change in the transmitting ones. Just as the signal is being tapped by a very high impedance drain."

"Just as we expected," Voss said. "The question arises now: If it will produce any image I want it to, then how are we to learn anything about the Cepheans themselves?"

"Russell? This is Bill Tomlinson. I'm in the control room."

"Yes, Bill," Voss replied. "You've got an idea?"

"What if you visualize the Cepheus 8 transmitter? Try putting yourself near the Cepheans' star?"

"That's an idea. But I've no idea what to visualize—there's nothing to start with."

"Well, try making a slow approach to the star. Start from *Unity* if you like and turn to look in the direction of Cepheus 8, if you can visualize the star patterns. Then make a movement toward the position of Cepheus 8. See what happens."

"Slow, you say?" Voss said.

"Just a few hundred thousand times *c*, yeah."

"I only have a vague idea of the star patterns," Voss said. "I couldn't visualize the details."

"You might not need to," Bill suggested.

"Okay, I'll give it a try. But I'll not do it from *Unity*. I'll do it from near the Earth to get the orientation of the polar axis."

"That's a great idea. Good luck!"

Voss began to concentrate on an image of the Earth from several thousand kilometers, spinning slowly but much faster than in real time. He commanded the gain to increase, and as expected, the image appeared in his vision and on the TV monitors.

"What a beautiful sight," Voss said, as if he had had nothing to do with its creation. He left the spectacular scene unchanged for a while. "I'll look up to the polestar now. I can remember the shape of Ursa Major, of course." The familiar Big Dipper shape appeared high above the Earth's image, which slowly slipped down out of vision. "Now I take the two pointer stars at the right of the dipper shape . . . and up to the polestar. Now Ursa Minor is down and to the left . . . and Cassiopeia up way across the other side. So far, so good. Now Cepheus is up to the left of the polestar. There! Hey, I'm not doing that! Those details are not mine. The Cepheans must be helping."

In the center of Voss's vision, at the junction of the constellations Cepheus, Lacerta, and Cygnus, the stars and nebulas gleamed with crystal clearness. A bright swath of light crossed the scene behind the star images.

"That is way beyond my knowledge of the sky," Voss said with awe. "It's beautiful. Is anyone watching in stereo?"

"Yes, we are," Bill responded from the distant control room where he and four companions were viewing the stereo image. "It's quite a show. As far as I can tell, it's perfectly accurate. Either you've got a much better visual memory than you think or the Cepheans really are helping you. By the way, don't worry, all this is being recorded okay.''

"Good. There might be some valuable information in this if it really is a Cephean signal. I'm going to suggest the motion now. Can someone describe to me just where Cepheus 8 is?''

"Okay, Russell," Bill offered. "From Polaris, go straight out at about half past nine toward that bright diffuse nebula—*wow*! That's certainly not from a star atlas. It's like a space telescope shot!''

"Now," Bill continued, "you see the two bright stars to the right of the nebula?''

"I've got an idea," Voss declared suddenly. "I can put up a cross hair or something so that you can guide me.''

Two fine white lines appeared to the right of the nebula, twisted and broken. But in a few seconds Voss was able to straighten them and form a cross.

"This is fascinating," he said. "The way to do it is to think of the cross as an actual solid object. It then becomes rigid in the image.''

He moved the cross to sit over the upper of the two stars Bill had mentioned.

"They pointed to a little triangle that points up and slightly right?'' Bill asked.

"Got it.''

"That's it. The lower left star of the triangle . . . right . . . has a dimmer companion just below and to the left? . . .''

"Yes.''

"You've got it. Well, Cepheus 8 is just over twice as far below and a little more left than the companion . . . that's it . . . right a little . . . Bang on.''

"Okay, thanks, Bill.''

The cross hairs disappeared. Voss left the indescribably beautiful scene steady for a minute.

"I'm going to suggest a little movement now.'' Voss strained his mind to generate the motion signal through the EE device. Nothing in the image changed.

"A bit more . . .'' he said with effort. Still nothing happened to the scene.

"You've accelerated at twelve kilometers per second squared," the technician said.

"Ha! That's probably all I can manage.''

"Try visualizing the motion," Bill suggested.

"But I don't know the distances to the stars. I couldn't possibly visualize motion through them, at least not accurately. We might get apparent motion, but it wouldn't be real. Anyway, maybe such impossible superrelativistic motions are not allowed in the Cepheans' network.''

Despite his own protests, Voss tried visualizing motion toward the Cepheus 8 radio beacon. All he could achieve was a zooming effect, the magnification of the view, like using higher telescopic powers.

"It's no good. There's nothing happening," Voss said. "I think perhaps your first idea is right, Bill. This is constructed from my memory of the space telescope shots. The cognitive feedback is incredibly powerful; it must cause the slightest suggestion to be amplified, even ones I'm not consciously aware of. There's a whole universe in this thing, millions of them, in fact, but all of them seem to be mine. I could go exploring through them all, but I'd not find the Cepheans unless they showed themselves.''

"But the Cepheans are directing the interface," Bill said, "so they are aware of you. You've got to let them know you want to communicate.''

"Maybe if I visualize something coming from them," Voss suggested. "Perhaps they're waiting to be invited.''

"It's worth a try.''

Voss moved his viewpoint backward so that the Earth was included in the lower left of the image. Then he concentrated on visualizing an object appearing from the direction of Cepheus 8. The object, he decided, should be a simple sphere. Any suggestion of shape or form could be misleading. He would leave that as a way for the Cepheans to signal their involvement.

A tiny point of light appeared at the position of Cepheus 8. Gradually it grew brighter under Voss's guidance. He was imagining a sphere glowing with its own light racing toward the Earth at supralight speed. The moment it had grown large enough to have a noticeable disk, it was abruptly extinguished.

"Sorry," Voss said. "I'll try again.''

The point of light reappeared and grew until its disk was seen, and then it vanished again.

"What's the problem?" Bill asked.

"It's strange," Voss replied. "It fades out just as it's getting close. I don't believe I'm doing it.''

Once more Voss's imaginary sphere appeared, grew, and then disappeared.

"I'm sure I'm not doing it," he said with conviction. "Hey,

it's coming again, but I'm not doing it this time. Look. This is
it, this is it!''

From the same point in the sky, a tiny white circle appeared
and approached with the same impossible swiftness as Voss's
spheres. It grew into a distinct ring of pale light that slowed to
a stop in front of him. In Voss's 3-D vision it appeared quite
close, maybe fifty meters or so, which would have made it ten
meters in diameter. In the center of the ring was complete darkness. It immediately reminded Voss of the strange ring effect
that had transformed *Unity*.

Everyone else was speechless with awe. After two full minutes, and with superhuman strength of will, Voss spoke.

"I'm going to move toward it. I think they accepted the invitation. Perhaps they're inviting me in return. Here goes . . ."

Gently he moved toward the ring. It grew and expanded
around him. Suddenly he was inside and was surrounded by
total darkness.

CHAPTER 21

AT THE EXTREME TOP RIGHT OF HIS VISION, A BRIGHT disk slowly appeared and continued to brighten until it became dazzling. In the center, a large white crescent emerged from the darkness, and at first he thought it was a planet illuminated by the star. The dark side was completely black, as black as the spaces between the stars, and its presence was apparent only from the lack of stars within its extent. Subconsciously Voss reasoned that there were no bright objects on the dark side of the sphere; otherwise, it would have been glowing dimly by their reflected light. Suddenly, in response to that thought, the dark hemisphere was bathed in a soft white glow and the fine lines joining the mixture of hexagons and pentagons that made up its surface were visible. That immediate reaction to such a subliminal thought came as a shock, and in his amazement the glow was extinguished and the shadow returned.

Immediately he began to move forward and down in a steep curve around to the starlit side. That was also made up of the pure white shapes joined by barely perceptible black lines. He got the impression that the object was less than planet-sized, but at the same time he realized that there was no way to be certain of it. The perception of depth was completely dependent on the visual signals being generated in the interface; the originators of the image could give him as much depth perception as they wished. The object could be microns or kilometers across.

He hung before its bright surface and wondered what purpose

it had and why he was being shown it. In his mind he began to strip the surface away to discover what was inside, and he chastised himself for being surprised when the image obeyed his thoughts. The covering hexagons and pentagons faded away, leaving hundreds of plain gray balls of many sizes packed together underneath. His viewpoint moved again toward the right until he could see well into the dark side, where again the dim glow appeared and revealed that the gray balls continued all around the object. However, just before him, at the boundary of the dark and light hemispheres, the balls formed a noticeable pattern, like lines of latitude stretching part of the way around the sphere. They were set in alternating lines of larger- and smaller-sized spheres that created a wavelike formation. The pattern extended from pole to pole and about one-tenth of the way around the circumference. He became intrigued by the sight and cautiously willed his viewpoint to approach the object.

With a frightening lurch, he dropped toward the sphere. As the gray balls came closer, he could see that each of them was also composed of hundreds of smaller spheres. The wavelike pattern continued at that smaller scale.

His plunge continued until it halted abruptly above one of the gray balls. He could plainly see that the smallest balls did not break down into yet smaller ones but were smooth-surfaced and mounted on a jet-black nonreflecting background. Or maybe, he thought, there was nothing but darkness behind them.

With a start, he realized what he was looking at.

"It's their transmitter!" he called out. "They are showing me their beacon! That wavy pattern is the area that creates the fan-shaped beam for the lighthouse beacon." The viewpoint shot out again at great speed to the point above the terminator. The hexagons and pentagons magically rematerialized.

He mentally calculated the size of the object, assuming that the smallest spheres were separated by the radio beacon's wavelength. "That would mean this whole thing is about ten kilometers in diameter," he said.

"That makes sense," came Bill's response. "If those gray things could absorb energy as well as transmit microwaves, then they'd get all the power they need from the sunlight—I mean starlight. Always assuming it's as far from that star as we calculated and that the star is the same one we thought it was."

The technician's voice broke in. "The microwave channel is off the scale. It's their beacon, all right."

Voss's voice trembled with excitement. "There's no sign of

life—whatever it may look like!'' He felt like a little boy again. ''I wonder what they're going to do next.''

As he spoke, the beacon began to slide away to the left. Suddenly he became aware of unfamiliar fields of stars moving across his vision. The motion stopped; centered in his view was a bright yellow disk of barely discernible size.

''A planet?'' Bill theorized.

His guess was proved correct within seconds as the disk rapidly grew and became covered with swirling oranges and yellows. Its appearance was very reminiscent of Jupiter's, with great eddies curling across its face, except that it seemed smaller. The texture of its atmosphere was coarser, the vortices of color larger relative to the disk. Voss could not see any obvious bands of color, except perhaps near the poles, which were lighter compared with the overall tone of the rest. The large, open, and interconnecting swirls in the atmosphere were each composed of many colors so that there was no obvious background. He also noted no visible flattening of the planet caused by rotation, as was easily detected on Jupiter. Nor was there any sign of a surface below the clouds. The image was bright, but judging by the stars in the background, it was nowhere near as bright as Earth's appearance from low orbit.

His viewpoint began to drop toward the equatorial regions. The approaching surface soon covered the entire field of view. Then the viewpoint rotated upward so that the horizon was visible, flattening rapidly. It continued to flatten until it was perfectly straight, and it remained so as the foreground parallax showed that the heart-stopping drop was continuing.

''It's big,'' Voss exclaimed rather breathlessly as the plummeting motion became more apparent near the tops of the clouds. ''Much bigger than Jupiter, I would say. I can see individual clouds now . . .''

The scene below him was astonishing in its color and depth. It was made more so by its unfamiliarity; nothing like it had ever been witnessed by the eyes or imagination of any human. Towering yellowish clouds bigger than mountain ranges loomed tall and majestic, overhanging unimaginable depths of orange and brown. The clouds were streaked with sinuous whorls of darker on light and lighter on dark intermixed in a bewildering profusion, each cloud having a unique hue and pattern. Above and in between the clouds, hanging above the immense canyons, were dark, flat cirrus clouds like trails of smoke.

This vast panorama of clouds filled the view to the level horizon, but it also had some large-scale structure. The clouds differed greatly in their individual heights and also rose and fell in massive waves as if they spiraled around a center away to the right.

With the light illuminating the clouds obliquely from the right, Voss concentrated on the depths below, in which he could see fantastic multihued shadows and deep orange glows appearing through the slightly translucent clouds. A yellow haze, fading into blackness, was apparent above the tops. Striations began to appear in it. One or two flashes of darkness told of his passage through some of the thin upper cirrus. Suddenly the horizon disappeared behind a titanic sulfur-yellow expanse of cloud that reached out toward him for what looked like hundreds of kilometers, revealing a stupendous golden cavern beneath. Its walls were so distant that no cloudlike billows could be discerned, just the great expanses of swirling colors.

In a bright flash, he glimpsed the illuminated side of a canyon as he dropped dizzyingly past the cavern's mountainous floor. For several seconds he fell down the wall of colors until suddenly the scene was extinguished in a featureless brown haze. Three times the haze opened to reveal a darker, deeper cloudscape; then the light dimmed until he could see nothing at all.

Downward motion seemed to continue for a long time; then slowly he came to rest.

The impenetrable darkness remained for about a minute, mercifully giving Voss time to recover his composure.

"They're moving into the infrared," the technician's voice told him. "They're matching the visual channel to the infrared signal. We should get a view soon."

Total darkness gradually gave way to a deep-blue featureless glow that slowly changed through green to yellow. As it did, a few vague features appeared. Voss was thankful that they were stationary ones.

In a few seconds the astonishing scene cleared. It was composed entirely of yellows, oranges, reds, and browns. The sky was a deep red, almost maroon, and showed very faint regions of shade. It looked like a cloud base. Below him was a brighter yellow mist, devoid of features. But before him, seemingly floating without support, was a large, irregular structure of intricately connected shapes, some rounded, others filamentary and fan-shaped. The shapes were of many different colors and textures, some of which glowed with their own light and illuminated their neighbors, while others were simply lit from below by the yellow light. Voss noticed two other similar structures in the distance. He could see that the atmosphere, whatever its nature, was hazy, causing contrast and brightness to decrease in the distance. That gave the structure the appearance of being very large and distant. Voss guessed that it was several kilometers across.

"Pressure is over seventy atmospheres," the technician remarked tensely, "and temperature 180 Celsius. Carbon dioxide, methane, higher hydrocarbons."

Movement near the structure caught Voss's attention, and he tried tentatively to edge closer. As the strange structure approached, he could see thousands of shapes, with a great range of sizes, floating around and among the labyrinthine webs and networks. The scene reminded him of pictures of a coral reef with its fantastic and colorful menagerie of animals and plants. As he drew closer, the similarity grew stronger. He could see what were clearly animals, thin, bright blue diamond shapes floating on edge and moving with rapid fishlike wriggles. Other tube-shaped animals were moving around with a variety of methods. Some were wriggling like fish; others formed their bodies into spirals and rotated, corkscrewing themselves along. Other, fatter ones had bulging waves encircling them that moved rapidly down their bodies, apparently pushing them along. The waves showed iridescent colors.

The reef was composed of the great branches of a plant or many different kinds of plants that grew together in a great tangle of shapes and that moved gently in the currents of air. They grew on what looked like the gray, nonliving remains of other creatures. Between them, many thousands of animals swam, dazzling the eye with shapes and colors and drawing involuntary gasps of wonder from all those watching the scene on the TV monitors.

With the predominant illumination coming from below, the feeling of being upside down was disorienting.

"Where is the light coming from?" Voss queried.

"Don't forget it's infrared," Bill told him in a whisper. "There's some source of heat lower down in the atmosphere."

"This all seems to be natural," Voss declared. "There's nothing artificial here."

That observation brought no response. Why the Cepheans should choose to show that particular place to them could not be guessed at.

The tour of the reef continued. Voss spotted a strange creature whose method of motion was intriguing. It was covered with long, stiff hairs, and its skin appeared to emerge out of an orifice at its large head, pass back along its body, with the hairs pointing backward, and disappear into a similar orifice at the much smaller tail. The hairs met and formed a tubular tail just before disappearing.

Another one had two spiral patterns of deep red blades on its white surface, one at either end of its ovoid body. It moved by contrarotating the spirals. There were two white spots at its head that did not move.

On the lower surfaces of the reef, the plants were gray and pressed flat against the reef as if they were dead. Few animals inhabited those regions. On the upper surfaces the plants were growing vigorously. Voss began to imagine the whole reef growing skyward through the atmosphere, perhaps buoyed by the old, dead growth. As he did so, the tour came abruptly to an end and the scene faded once more into darkness.

Throughout the previous ten minutes of the amazing experience, the voice channel had been filled with excited exchanges between Voss and the operators and scientists. The channel was silent again as the visions of the breathtaking journey through the atmosphere back into space sped past on the TV monitors. All were wondering what was to come next.

"People of Earth, this is the planet Arrea. You are welcome to it."

The accidental juxtaposition of the momentous and the banal was later to become a source of amusement, but at the moment the words were spoken, no one noticed it.

The voice that made the announcement was quiet and sounded like a perfect blend of all the voices that had been using the sound channel, more male than female and with an odd accent that no one could identify.

It was met by a stunned silence as the planet's image swirled hugely below.

"I have tried to adopt your own acoustic means of communication. You will understand if I make errors." The voice was impassive and almost monotonous.

"If you wish to communicate, then I suggest that you help me with my attempts to speak your language."

Voss was the first to recover from the shock. "You speak our language very well. My name is Voss. Can you tell us who you are?" He spoke very slowly and deliberately.

For a while there was no answer, and Voss became worried that whoever or whatever it was had gone away.

"Your speech changes much. You have many different ways of speaking. Help me with my speech. Modify my speech as you hear it."

Voss suddenly realized what he was being asked to do. Instead of speaking in a deliberate way, which was bound to confuse the Cepheans, who had only heard him speaking excitedly, he should mentally correct the Cephean's speech as he heard it. He spoke again in a normal voice. "I understand. I will try to help. My name is Voss. Can you tell me what your name is?"

The reply came quickly, and as he heard it, Voss mentally corrected the Cephean's speech. It was surprisingly easy, although it was not possible for him to catch every one of the many pronunciation errors. "Voss. That is good. You are helping. My name is the Cepheans."

Voss was momentarily perplexed by that response, and before he could speak, the strange voice continued.

"I have understood the messages you had stored in the machines in *Unity*. They are very interesting. You want information in return. Let me explain to you about me."

The voice paused. Voss said, "Please go ahead," in a wavering voice.

"I will go ahead. I understand that human beings are individual corporeal entities. The Cepheans are different. You will understand with difficulty. To explain about me, I will describe the evolution of life on this planet you see which you can call Arrea."

It was all very different from the pomp and ceremony that everyone had been building up to. The Cepheans seemed unconcerned about such things, as if the first meeting between alien races separated by ten thousand light years of impassable galactic space was commonplace to them. Perhaps it was.

"Unlike Earth life," the voice continued, "Arrean life developed in the atmosphere. The atmosphere is much deeper and with higher pressures than Earth. The upper levels are lit by the sun and are turbulent, but the planet's rotation is slower. There are less winds than your own neighbor planet Jupiter which you speak of. Beneath it is more stable. The heat coming from the planet's gravitational shrinkage produces no lower limit to the atmosphere for very large distance.

"Life-forms developed one billion years ago in the very dense lower levels. A carbon-based chemistry was dominant. No metals or heavy minerals were available, so the biochemistry is unfamiliar to you. The upper regions were colonized to take advantage of the lower temperatures and densities. After 250 million years sentient life-forms appeared. One hundred million years later self-adaption. This is a stage of evolution of life that you have not known. But you will soon know with my help."

Voss was beginning to reel under the weight of the events he was witnessing. Despite all his preparations and careful mental training, he found himself unable to cope with the flood of new information.

"Your process is slow," the voice said impassively. "I will wait."

The Cepheans' description had contained several large jumps of logic that he was unable to follow, and that was the main cause of his confusion. Why should the release of gravitational heat mean "no lower limit to the atmosphere"? And what did they mean by "self-adaption"?

"I will try to help more," the voice announced after a few seconds' pause. "You will be affected strongly by this . . . meeting. You are the twenty-oneth separate primitive to contact. You will receive a large amount of knowledge and benefit."

Voss collected his thoughts and tried to get some control of the situation. After all, his performance was going to be re-played and analyzed for the rest of history.

"Did you say we were the twenty-first race to make contact with you?" he asked.

"No, that is what I meant. Yes, there have been twenty previous contacts. The first occurred two million seven hundred nineteen thousand six hundred forty-four years ago. The most recent was sixty-seven thousand two hundred zero one years ago."

Voss was too nonplussed to reply.

"Five contacts have been from the Andromeda galaxy."

Two seconds after that staggering news, the image of the planet abruptly disappeared.

"Hell!" the technician snapped into his microphone. "The damned laser's gone down! Overheated."

The sudden disconnection from the fantastic alien world left them all numb. No one moved or spoke. The mundane surroundings of the laboratory slowly diffused into their minds.

"Sorry, guys," the technician said nervously.

"Did—did that really happen?" Bill asked, rubbing his eyes. "Or have I just woken up? Tell me, someone. Tell me!"

CHAPTER 22

"WE MUST SEEM LIKE SOMETHING THEY FOUND under a stone," Bill said dismally.

The difficulty with the laser was more serious than simple overheating and was going to require several hours to fix, and so an unofficial meeting had formed in the coffee bar next to the laboratory.

Dr. Page had provoked Bill's comment by mentioning the Cepheans' statement about their evolution having reached a stage unfamiliar to humans. "But what kind of evolution can they mean?" she asked.

"We have yet to find out," Voss replied, "but we can make some guesses. You remember how they described us as 'individual corporeal entities'? Well, that suggests that they are not individual, or not corporeal, or not either. In which case we've got a lot of work to do. We've never seriously considered communicating with such beings."

"But what are they?" Perera asked. "If they are not individuals and don't have bodies, that doesn't leave much more than free energy."

"Don't forget their cognitive network," Voss said. "They may be entities that exist purely within that, without having bodies at all. The lack of individuality could mean that there is only one such entity or that there are many that have the ability to . . . share or merge."

"Whatever they are," Bill said, leaning forward over the table with his hands cupped around his mug, "they must have been trying to make contact for over two million years for the radio beacon to reach the Andromeda galaxy. That's about a thousand times as long as our civilization and about forty thousand times longer than we have had radio telescopes."

"They must have evolved during that time," Page suggested.

"Not necessarily," Voss replied. "We humans have not evolved a great deal over the last two million years, only relatively minor changes to our genes. Our technical abilities have evolved, of course, but maybe the Cepheans' technological evolution reached a plateau long ago. I'd like to know what they meant by 'self-adaption.' "

"Their biological evolution was very fast," Page said. "Only one billion years to get where they are now, while we've taken three already."

"Do you think we'll be able to contact the Andromedan races as well, Dr. Voss?" Oyama asked.

"That would be rather exciting," Voss replied. "But as you said yourself, we're only speculating. My guess is that we will be able to contact all twenty of the other races. Perhaps we have already done so."

"What on Earth do you mean?" Page asked with an incredulous laugh.

Voss was silent for a few seconds. "I'm not sure. Just an idea I had."

Everyone waited for him to explain.

"Look at our own evolution," he said eventually. "We have only just reached the stage where we possess true technology. Imagine what we might become if we had another thousand years of continued development."

Bill looked up abruptly. "You mean before making contact with extraterrestrials?"

"That's exactly what I mean. If we try and extrapolate our technological capabilities a thousand years in the future, we might find the Cepheans a little less strange."

"We'd have much more powerful computers by then," Perera suggested. "We could probably create artificial intelligences as powerful as our own."

"And if we had them, we would use them directly in this cognitive network of the Cepheans," Voss said, drawing the conclusion that he knew they all had seen. "In one thousand years we could create artificial minds that could outstrip us quite easily in all respects: faster reasoning, bigger and more efficient memories, even the ability to combine or merge with others.''

He let the others think about that. "So instead of being presented with a dim-witted natural mind, numb to most senses, the Cepheans would see an artificial mind as powerful as their own. And one with a similar nature, one that could divide and merge with other such entities.''

"Wait a minute," Oyama said. "Are you suggesting that the Cephean we heard was just a machine intelligence and not a natural being at all?''

"I'm suggesting more than that, Professor Oyama," Voss answered, "I'm saying that such artificially created minds will become the natural minds of the future. It is the next logical stage of evolution. It is nature evolving past the stage where the conscious creatures it has produced create their own artificial worlds of concrete and steel and electronics, to the point where they can take over the role of biology and artificially create minds like their own.''

"That's too far-fetched for me," Oyama grumbled.

"But Russell's right," Bill declared. "One thousand years is a long time by our standards. By then we will have genetic engineering and bioelectronics down to a T. We could create whatever conscious beings we wanted to.''

"Create consciousness?" Oyama scoffed. "That's going too far. How can you possibly predict that? We don't even know what consciousness is.''

"But in a thousand years we will," Bill said. "We already have machines that are almost indistinguishable from humans in their behavior. We think they're not conscious only because we created them ourselves, because we understand how they work.''

"Think about how we would regard those machines if they were made of organic molecules," Voss suggested. "In the future we will make them from organic circuits, possibly created by genetic engineering. We could grow a machine that spoke to us and existed independently as an individual.''

"That's terrifying," Page exclaimed.

"It might be to some people," Voss said, "and it would create a lot of moral debate, I know, but we can't encumber ourselves with such problems here. The Cepheans, or any other aliens, might not have any qualms about creating artificial people. What we've got to do is try to imagine what a world might be like where this happened.''

"Sheer hell!" Page cried with a grimace. "There'd be no order, no society. Every individual would be unique. There'd be no common ideals or feelings with which to create a civilization. Such a world couldn't last."

Perera nodded his bald head vigorously. "Dr. Page is right. It would be impossible to allow the creation of any artificial beings with whatever characteristics the creators chose."

That was something Voss had already thought about. "I think the problem we have," he said, "is that the possibilities are so many and varied. We find it hard to think clearly when there are so many ways for things to develop. Imagine some observer on Earth just as life was beginning. If he had seen what was about to happen, with the infinite possibilities of genetics based on DNA molecules, he would have thought the same way. He would have seen the astronomical number of possibilities, of potential organisms, far too many for any stable equilibrium to be established. He might imagine that every organism would be a unique individual so different from all others that evolution would rapidly get nowhere, just a random walk about the place it started from. But instead, what happened? Evolution followed a directed path. The biological mechanism working in conjunction with the environment produced its own direction to go in, its own motivation. We got unique individuals, all right, but they were grouped into species. From that came civilization, eventually. And all these organisms working selfishly toward their own independent ends constituted a balanced and relatively stable whole. The variety produced stability, not chaos."

"You are suggesting, then," Perera said, "that the ability of biologically evolved intelligent creatures to create others artificially is the next logical stage of evolution?"

"That's right," Voss replied. "We call it artificial, but to an outside observer it would appear like a natural progression, like the development of a backbone or of sight. It amounts to a mechanism for escaping the confinement of the DNA molecule. We humans are the first creatures on Earth to possess the means to transfer information between generations without using the chromosomes—books and computers, etc. It's only natural that this new external information should come to be used in a genetic way."

Perera nodded in a slower, more thoughtful way. "That is a very provocative idea." He stared into the distance as he spoke. "You are saying that evolution might continue on this new frontier it has just opened up." His eyes refocused on Voss, and his hands moved gracefully in front of his face. "Conscious minds direct the changes instead of environment and the whims of the DNA molecule itself."

"DNA's dominion would be over," Voss said solemnly. "The conscious mind determines the future."

"But hold on," Bill objected with a frown. "What you're talking about doesn't relate to the Cepheans. We were on the point of saying earlier that they don't possess bodies. That's different altogether, isn't it?"

"That could be the next stage," Voss said. "I think that after many generations of this new, non-DNA artificial evolution, which, by the way, may be what the Cepheans meant by 'self-adaption,' then this cognitive link between individuals would be possible. Eventually, new individuals would be created that could share a kind of mental unity."

"Like telepathy?" Page queried.

"In principle, yes," Voss answered, "but an engineered telepathy. Each individual would possess the bioelectronic equipment to receive and transmit sensory information just like in the Cepheans' network. Eventually the association of any one particular consciousness with any one particular body would be broken. All members of the network would be able to move their conscious viewpoints around a huge system of cognitive nodes, to enter any body they wished to and merge with whatever consciousness is already there."

"I'm getting a bit bewildered by all this," Page confessed with a self-conscious laugh.

"But there would still be a need for the physical body, though," Perera said. "There would be no conscious entity free of the physical—the circuitry, if you like."

"Oh, no, of course not," Voss replied. "I'm not suggesting any kind of disembodied spirit. That idea is pure fantasy. No, in the real world any conscious mind has to be tied to matter. In this case, though, not tied to any particular piece of matter."

Professor Oyama put up his right hand to object. "Wait a second. You say 'not tied to any particular piece of matter,' but I don't see that. They might be able to move their conscious viewpoints, as you call them, between different bodies, but the actual seat of their consciousness would still be in one particular, uh, brain, I suppose you'd call it. You couldn't just transmit a mind from one receptacle to another. The sensory information, maybe, but not the actual source of consciousness."

Voss thought carefully about that. "That may be true, I agree, Professor Oyama."

Bill sat up and cleared his throat. "I can see another possibility."

Everyone looked at him expectantly.

"We have suggested a world where the inhabitants are capable of flitting about between different brains. But those images we received from the Cepheans were not from the viewpoint of any material object. They were synthetic—created as a piece of information processing."

They all looked at him as if to say "So?"

"So," he continued, "that suggests something different. Wouldn't it be likely that instead of moving between different individuals, they would simply synthesize whatever experiences they wanted? The experiences could be completely artificial or tied directly to something real going on elsewhere."

Perera opened his large dark eyes very wide. "Now you are talking not only about artificial minds but artificial universes for them as well?"

"Why not?" Bill argued. "Any race that has the ability to create artificial minds would certainly have the information-processing power to create artificial experiences for them."

"After consciousness partially disconnects itself from matter, it then disconnects itself from the real universe," Voss said. "It certainly sounds plausible."

Outbursts of amazement and disagreement were heard around the table.

"Now you really are going too far," Oyama objected.

"I don't think so," Voss said calmly. "We have ourselves the ability to create our own universes with our imaginations. In fact, many people say that that is all we ever do—that's what consciousness is. So there's nothing very far-fetched about this. I think Bill is right. The creation of artificial minds is bound to be paralleled by artificial universes. Of course, this isn't saying that the real world would be ignored. The artificial worlds would be used just like we use our imaginations, to predict or relive experiences or to explore new ones. The real world would still be the most important one."

"But all this is so speculative," Oyama said with a frown. "It can't possibly be of use to us in dealing with the Cepheans. The future has so many possible ways to turn out, we can't expect to predict it all as we sit here."

Voss answered his protest with great seriousness. "The time

has come when we have to try, Professor Oyama. We are in contact with an intelligence so far evolved beyond ours that we barely recognize it. The Cepheans are presenting us with a view into our own future, which we can either try to understand or ignore.''

"I wonder how the other twenty coped with it," Page asked.

"It may have been very different for each one," Voss replied.

"What Dr. Voss was driving at earlier on, if he will permit me," Bill said with a glance in Voss's direction, "was that in only one thousand years we may be capable of all these things ourselves. So it is quite possible that all the other twenty had reached the stage of so-called self-adaption before they met the Cepheans. We might be presenting them all with a problem. We're too primitive!"

"What's so special about the Cepheans?" asked a brown-coated technician sitting next to Page. "I mean, why do those guys have to play the central role?"

"There is nothing special about them," Voss said politely and patiently. "Think about it. Assume one race was the first to try contacting others. Every time another race joins them, they merge. Their cognitive networks are coupled together. So to any newcomer they look like just one race, at least at first."

The technician exhaled loudly and slowly. "Boy, are we getting out of our depth," he said, slowly shaking his head.

"That's why we're teaching ourselves to swim," Bill said.

"They may be special because of the radio beacon, though," Voss continued. "There is no way of knowing which ones would construct radio beacons. It might be that the one we have seen is the only one—a remnant from the planet Arrea's past. On the other hand, all twenty races may have constructed their own. In which case we'd be the odd ones out."

"That raises a good point," Perera said, replacing his coffee cup fastidiously on its saucer. "If these futuristic beings really do exist, with their artificial universes, then why should they be bothered with making contact with others? They can satisfy whatever urges they have just by inventing the right universe. Why should they bother with the real one?"

"A worthwhile point, Dr. Perera," Voss said. "We haven't begun to think about the psychology of such beings, if we can use that word. But I would expect that the real universe would remain the dominant force in their minds. No matter how advanced they became, they must always be tied somehow to matter and nature. Like us, they couldn't just ignore them. But that is less fruitful speculation. Let's wait to get the news from the horse's mouth.''

Professor Holdsworth swung his chair away from the desk, stood, walked slowly across the conservatory that years before had been his team's workroom, and adopted his customary pose, gazing rather absently through the window. A leafless branch noiselessly scuttled to and fro across the glass.

Bill had telephoned to recount the recently adjourned discussion at Abingdon, and the professor was carefully thinking about all the conjectures that had been raised. He had not watched the continuous television broadcasts from Abingdon because he found the uninformed speculations unbearable, but he joined in with Bill's great excitement over the amazing developments. His first thoughts were for Sheilagh and her comrades; they still had no indication whether the Cepheans could, or would, help with a rescue.

As he watched the wind shaking the rain off the branches in front of him, he felt a growing unease. Bill's conjecture about Earth life presenting a problem to the Cepheans by being too primitive stuck in his mind. Something did not seem right. Everybody seemed so caught up in the excitement. But then, perhaps he was just being old and stuffy. Voss had matured considerably since the events of six years before. He was a very sensible chap; he would think things through properly.

Twenty-one different cultures and civilizations, merged! That was certainly not what he had been expecting when he had started his project at Springley Castle, ages ago, it seemed. But then, he was not at all sure what he had been expecting.

Too primitive?

He involuntarily looked up at the gray sky above the trees, imagining the darkness beyond, filled with distant clouds of stars.

He had never really pondered the question of why an alien should *want* to establish contact with others across the galaxy. But he found himself pondering it now.

Just a few seconds after the gecom was restarted, the image of Arrea appeared in Voss's vision. The Cepheans' voice continued as if there had been no break in communications. It was just as well that Voss had replayed the entire recording of the previous session.

"You are in contact with all of these now. I speak as them all."

Voss unconsciously framed the words "for them all" in his mind.

"No, I do mean 'as them all,' Voss," the voice continued unsettlingly. "There are many things that you do not understand. I do not have form like humans. From knowledge of my own evolution which has taken place separately in twenty-one locations throughout our galaxy, its satellites, and also the Andromeda galaxy, I can deduce that your race has followed a unique developmental path. You are the only ones to achieve contact with others before self-adaption."

So Bill was right, we do present a problem to them, Voss thought. He also noticed that the Cepheans' had been practicing their English during the break.

"Can you please explain to us what self-adaption is?" he asked.

"Your process is more stable. I thought that you were understanding me."

Voss thought carefully about his next words. "We think we understand, but we know we have a great deal to learn from you. We would prefer to have everything explained. You have already had a chance to study our state of knowledge from our messages. We will understand more easily if you frame your explanations in those terms."

"I was doing that. Self-adaption is described in your own messages. It is from them that I learned the word. But I make the mistake of forgetting your primitive individuality. Perhaps Voss does not have access to all your knowledge. I will try once more."

Bill spoke for the first time. "Russell, self-adaption may be in some of our descriptions of artificial intelligence. It's a different context, but that might be where they got it from."

"The context is identical," the voice came. "The name refers to an intelligent entity modifying itself or its offspring to better suit its purpose. Do you understand?"

"Er, yes. That's how we understood the words," Voss responded.

"I will explain the evolution of one of my origins that is closest to Earth life. Pay close attention."

Arrea's image raced away at an incredible speed. In just three seconds it was a faint yellow disk reflecting the light of the dim orange star below it. The motion ceased, and the view swung up and around to the right across bright fields of stars and nebulas. It rested on a bright, hazy oval of light shining above the band of the Milky Way. Before Voss had time to recognize it as the Andromeda galaxy, the viewpoint raced forward toward it at a speed that must have been millions of times faster than light.

"This is purely synthetic vision, of course?" Voss inquired in wonder.

"It is created in what you have called my cognitive network. Whether that is synthetic or not depends on your viewpoint, not anything I might tell you."

Voss decided that such questions could wait.

The Andromeda galaxy spread out before his mind—an unimaginably large swirl of stars, gas, and dust with thousands of bright globular clusters scattered above and below its disk. Voss was familiar with photographic reproductions of that scene, but this was infinitely more beautiful. Photographs tried to depict all the variations in brightness, from the brightest cluster of stars to the blackest cloud of dust, in the range from paper-white to ink-black. Even projected slides had comparatively little more scope. But here, the full range of contrast that his visual cortex was capable of was being made use of. Millions of times more powerful than a photograph, the scene overwhelmed him. The others, viewing it on TV monitors, were not party to that staggering experience.

With his mind reeling, Voss was flown between the globular clusters and over the galaxy's central bulge and then was diving deep into the center of one of the arms of the spiral on its far side. After a race through colorful clouds of stars and dust, one star was singled out as the obvious destination. They came dizzyingly to rest above a blue-white planet that resembled Earth very strongly.

"This is Gon-Di, the first of my origins to manufacture an interstellar beacon. The life on its surface will resemble that of Earth externally, although its biology is quite different. I am creating an image for you of Gon-Di one hundred million years ago. There is no need to go further into the past. As the images have unsettled you, I will wait before proceeding."

Voss fought hard to steady his thoughts, if that was possible in the circumstances. "I'm ready now. Please proceed."

"At this time," the voice continued, "there was one landmass on Gon-Di."

The image of blue seas and white cloud tops was joined by another, overlaying one that showed the single dark-colored continent straddling the equator. By some strange trick, the Cepheans were making it possible for Voss to see either image or both just by willing them to appear. Somehow, both images were present in the same positions but without hiding or interfering with each other. It was rather like the effect seen when looking into a well-lit room through glass that was reflecting a bright exterior. The internal and external images could be alternately brought to the fore without anything changing outside the brain of the viewer.

"The mobile life-forms—I will call them animals, although they would not fall under your definition—were widely distributed over its extent. When the landmass separated into four continents"—As the voice spoke, the underlying image of the continent split into four roughly equal parts that slid across the ocean to widely separated positions—"the land-based animals began to diverge along separate evolutionary paths. On all four continents a dominant intelligent animal evolved from one common precursor . . ."

A third scene replaced one of the continents. It was a picture of a creature that resembled a large insect more than it did any mammal. Its black body was wide and shallow, held high and horizontal on six tubular, tapering legs. As it moved, the legs had no joints. They flexed along their entire length, but more so near the body. The creature displayed great agility and speed. The two forward legs were slenderer and possessed four digits, each of which could fully oppose the others. Occasionally the creature would move without using the front limbs for support. The creature possessed no obvious head, but two clear, lidless hemispherical eyes took up most of the body's front end. There was no mouth. The body remained high off the ground on the nearly vertical legs.

The three other creatures appeared over the images of the other continents. All four bore basic similarities—six limbs, four opposable digits, two eyes—but varied a lot in general shape. One was very large bodied and shorter-legged; another was even slenderer than the first. One had developed an upright body posture and used only two limbs for locomotion.

"Civilizations had developed on each continent before physical contact occurred."

Voss's viewpoint above the planet began a rapid descent down to the surface of one of the continents. Having expected it, he was a little less unnerved than he had been by previous experiences. He was soon looking down upon a scene that depicted something like a small town of large, low buildings with curving walls. Deep red vegetation in the form of very tall trees and a multitude of lower-lying shapes covered the open spaces. In the distance, large geometrical shapes varying from near black to orange were visible in all directions. Between the buildings there was activity among the inhabitants.

"When contact was made between the civilizations, unlike similar events in your own history, there were no wars, no attempts by one race to dominate the others. The four species shared their knowledge and resources to the benefit of them all."

The scene of the town faded into another, presumably moving forward chronologically. The changes were similar to those an Earth town would have gone through from the sixteenth to the nineteenth centuries, except that there was little physical expansion. Buildings became more varied in size and shape, and industrial areas arose, complete with chimney stacks. There was a sparse network of roads and streets over the entire scene.

"The technological development was very rapid, leading to an information-processing stage only two generations after integration of the four civilizations."

The scene changed again to one that looked remarkably similar to a modern town anywhere on Earth. Large glass buildings collected together in the center of the town. Wide, curving highways crossed the landscape, intersecting in elegant multilevel junctions outside the towns. Except for the foliage color, the scene resembled one on Earth very strongly.

"All of these developmental stages have been part of your own history. Atmospheric flight had become commonplace, but spaceflight was limited. There being no military needs and no moon to aim for, the activities in space remained purely scientific. By this stage Gon-Di had a global government and had reached the stage of holistic science, so the planet's other lifeforms were spared the ravages that you have inflicted on your planet's.

"The next major development was their bioelectronic technology, which enabled them to replace most electronic systems with self-regulating and self-repairing biological ones."

The scene changed before them. The large buildings disappeared, together with the major highways. The town dissolved into many small collections of low buildings that varied greatly in shape, and there was a large increase in plant life.

"Decentralization of the society followed. With all manufacturing and service industries operated by genetically engineered and bioelectronically equipped robots, the small Gon-Dian population turned to more inward pursuits. Within a few generations they had engineered the galaxy's first cognitive network.''

The view sank lower until it was at ground level. Voss felt like he was in a kind of open forest. Tall single-stemmed trees with broad canopies were surrounded at their bases by varied foliage. They were on a broad plaza whose surface was covered with a deep red mat of low-lying vegetation. On the edges of the plaza were the smooth, colorful walls of the houses. Forming many small groups around the space were several varieties of creatures; most of them, Voss noticed with amazement, were almost humanoid. They were behaving as if they were playing together. Some were standing in a rough formation, and above their heads a white disk was floating to and fro. He could hear noises like those in a tropical forest, but he could not tell where the sounds came from.

''These are the first generations of purely self-adapting animals,'' the voice continued. ''They are the creations of the Gon-Dians and have the ability to reproduce themselves by what you would call artificial means. They were created originally to maintain the Gon-Dians' industry; they designed, built, and operated the biological machines that produced everything needed by society. All heavy industry was replaced by bioindustry many generations ago. The need to process metals and other substances by brute-force temperatures and pressures had been superseded by the more direct approach of bioindustry. Molecular science could produce materials with any desired properties. The Gon-Dians, meanwhile, lived within their cognitive networks.''

Slowly, as if they were walking along, they moved toward a low, wide door in one of the buildings and passed through. Inside, apart from the unusual squashed proportions, it resembled a typical human habitation. The walls were colored and decorated with objects of art. Some were square frames, like pictures, that contained colorful three-dimensional scenes. They passed through another door, and before them was a Gon-Dian floating above the floor of a darkened room. Its six limbs were moving slowly, and its fingers flexed. It was rotating very slowly through the air. Around the center of its body was a wide belt from which a single narrow spike thrust out.

''Using this network, any individual could share the experiences of others elsewhere. For example, this individual is scaling a mountain peak on one of the other Gon-Dian continents. A Gon-Dian would spend one-third of its life in this empathic state.''

Voss struggled to remain calm under the tide of information coming at him. ''How does the cognitive network operate?'' he asked tentatively, trying to stem the flow a little.

''The small conical object over there is the local node in the network. It is converting the optical signal coming through the network of underground cables into the electrical form necessary for the Gon-Dians' central nervous system. The Gon-Dians' biology is quite different from Earth's. Their genetic information is carried only by the central nervous system.''

''Is the node a bioelectronic device?'' Voss asked.

''Yes. It uses molecular circuits. It is considerably more powerful than any Earth computer. To continue . . .''

The room faded and was replaced by the familiar aerial view of the Gon-Dian landscape.

''Within a few years of the cognitive network being established, the Gon-Dians began to generate conscious entities like themselves that existed only within the circuits of the nodes. They also constructed new nodes that generated synthetic experiences as well as relaying the real ones. The proportion of their lives spent within the network increased until few Gon-Dians were willing or able to produce real experiences. So synthetic experiences began to dominate. They relied more and more on the purely synthetic minds within the network.''

With his mind beginning to flounder, Voss vainly strove to accept all the things he was hearing. They were no surprise—indeed, they were almost exactly what they had been talking about a few hours earlier—but the rate at which the Cepheans presented the facts exceeded his ability to absorb them. Before he could frame another time-out question, the voice was continuing.

''The next development was to convert the bioelectronic nodes . . . you wish me to pause.''

Voss felt like a dog spared a beating. ''Er, yes. I'd like to ask another question.'' He struggled to remember what it was. ''You say the Gon-Dians created artificial consciousnesses that existed only within the network?''

''Yes. The theory is contained in the last message I transmitted to you.''

''Ah, yes. We haven't actually fully understood that yet. Does that mean that you are yourselves, er, artificial?'' Despite the voice's continued use of the first person singular, Voss had always gotten the impression that there were many minds behind it. He could not have explained that if anyone had asked.

"I was about to explain that. I was merely waiting for your process to become steadier."

"Oh, okay. Please carry on."

"The Gon-Dians next learned how to genetically engineer organisms that possessed the bioelectronic circuits of the nodes. These were small plantlike organisms that obtained energy and nutrients in a similar way to the native flora. They still exist today on Gon-Di, growing and reproducing like normal plants. They do not possess the mechanisms for variation and so do not evolve, but so far their carefully engineered design has survived the natural competition."

"The next obvious stage," the inexorable narrator continued, "was for the Gon-Dians to engineer the nodes into themselves. The first Gon-Dians with functioning cognitive links were created nearly two million years ago. This was the penultimate stage of their evolution."

"So by then," Voss interjected, anxious to keep the pace easier, "they had a planet containing large numbers of these cognitive nodes in plants, and they each possessed one themselves?"

"Yes," the voice replied evenly, displaying no impatience.

"And in the network with them were some artificial consciousnesses that shared both real and artificial sensory environments?"

"Yes."

"So the next step was for the original Gon-Dians to die out altogether?"

"That is correct."

Was it Voss's imagination or did the voice sound a little pleased, like a teacher pleasantly surprised by a dim-witted student?

"In the final stage," the voice continued, "the Gon-Dians' individual minds became disconnected from individual bodies. The distinction between the real and artificial consciousnesses in the network was lost completely. It was inevitable that the corporeal nodes came to be regarded as unnecessary, and so they eventually died out. This happened very rapidly—in a single generation."

"But that must have left just the nodes hosted by the plants. What was to stop a fire or volcano or the biorobots that must have got left behind from destroying the plants?"

"The biorobots," the voice said, unhesitatingly adopting Voss's newly coined word, "were, and remain, part of the network. They are equipped with simplified nodes that enable the Gon-Dians to control their behavior. There is no cruelty or thralldom involved here. There are no conscious minds among the biorobots. As to the possibility of natural disaster, most possibilities are covered. There are many million biologically maintained nodes in orbiting vessels. An automatic bioelectronic system guards the planet against damaging meteoritic impacts. There is very little chance of permanent and total destruction of the system. Even the total loss of Gon-Di would not greatly affect my network, which is extended over twenty-one locations in and around two galaxies. Most of these centers are also planet-based, but there are also several free-space locations. The transmitter near Arrea is one of them."

"Am I really talking to all your origins, then?" Voss was anxious to continue, but tiredness was creeping into his mind like a fog.

"Yes, you are. Unfortunately, your language does not contain any constructs that embody these ideas, so I find it difficult to explain."

For the first time Voss felt the voice was pausing to think. When it next spoke, it was more slowly than ever before.

"I am one mind as I speak to you. But I am also many billions of minds that have independent existences. Minds merge and diverge freely." A short pause followed those enigmatic words. "Once you have understood the message I have sent, all this will be clearer to you."

Voss was fading rapidly. There were hundreds of questions in his mind, but not one of them would frame itself clearly. He was far from surprised when the voice spoke about that.

"If your fatigue is distressing you, do not continue with this. I understand your dependence on a physical body. Rest now. I will be waiting when you return."

The image faded gently into darkness, and he asked the nurse to uncover his eyes. It took a full three minutes for the reality of the laboratory to meaningfully impinge on his mind. As it did so, a searing ache in his head rose to an unbearable crescendo.

He returned reluctantly to the solitary confinement of his body. Sleep, he needed sleep.

CHAPTER 23

TWIN WHIRLPOOLS OF BRILLIANT LIGHT LAY POISED
*beneath him, each escorted through the infinite depths by shoals
of lesser lights like pilot fish. He was one mind—one mind that
inhabited a hundred worlds, a trillion bodies. He felt all their
feelings, simultaneously experienced all their lives. His senses
encompassed two great galaxies. He was one mind having a
single point of attention that at the same time had billions. The
boundaries of his mind dissolved as if the bones of his skull had
dematerialized and released the pent-up pressure of his thoughts
to the open universe.*

*Was one mind greater than a multitude? Did it have the power
of all combined, or was it only as strong as one of its components? Was it all-powerful?*

*In the galaxies before his omnipresent vision, twenty-one tiny
spheres of penetrating radiance stood out and dimmed their
surroundings. Brilliant shafts of light stretched out from them
and formed a web like chromosomes in a galactic mitosis.*

*Then, with a nonchalant twist of impossible parallax made
effortless by dreams, he saw a tiny speck of light floating free
among the giant strands of the web. Disconnected and alone, it
drifted between the stars like a pollen grain on the surface of a
vast, dark ocean.*

*Unity! Of all the names to choose for that most isolated and
lonely speck of spindrift and its precious contents, insignificant*

*even next to the insignificant planet that it followed around its
insignificant star!*

Was there really a way to span the gulfs that separated minds?

*Sheilagh was in the bubble of air that fell endlessly around
the sun. Was she farther away than when she had lain next to
him, her head touching his own, their thoughts separated by a
few centimeters of fragile, watery cells, each composed of atoms
that were made of empty space?*

*He, who was almost never unaccompanied but always alone,
had been the closest that any human had ever been to true mental contact with another. But the other had been an alien! Or
billions of aliens all at once! Was there any difference between
an alien mind and a human one?*

*Then the strangest part of his dream: He dreamed that he
woke and turned his head on the pillow, something that he had
difficulty doing now. He looked into Sheilagh's sleeping face beside him. In his dream he moved closer until her head and his
merged into one.*

It was twenty-four hours before Voss had recuperated enough
to try the link once more. This time he was determined to find
answers to the questions that nagged them all. How had the
Cepheans repaired the space laboratory in defiance of their own
Grand Theory? How did they energize the antennas in the cognitive links? What did they intend to do with their primitive new
contacts? Could they save *Unity*?

Apart from those and others concerning the true nature of the
Cepheans, the team had questions arising from the previous
communication. It was Professor Oyama who raised the subject
when the team assembled in the laboratory control room prior
to the next attempt.

"Dr. Page has noticed something very intriguing in the
Cepheans' statements," he said, leaning against one of the consoles. "Several times they made comparisons between the Gon-
Dians' past and our own—for example, when describing the
unhumanlike lack of conflict between the four races when they
first contacted each other and their holistic science avoiding the
ecological destruction that we have caused."

"That's all valid, isn't it?" Bill asked from the chair beside
Oyama.

"Sure it is," Oyama replied. "But what's intriguing is that
we have never told the Cepheans about such things."

"Weren't they in our space lab messages?" Voss asked.

"No," Oyama replied. "Dr. Page's team generated thousands of messages, but all of them concerned our current knowledge of science. They said very little about our society or its past."

Everyone apart from Page and Oyama was shocked by the news. They each tried to find an explanation.

"TV and radio signals?" Bill suggested.

"What? From ten thousand light-years?" Oyama protested.

"Sorry, I mean perhaps they detected TV and radio signals in the laboratory while we were running the gecom. If they can detect our antenna transmissions, they can probably detect radio signals picked up by conductors in the lab. The cognet antennas are shielded, but other conductors might act as antennas."

"That's plausible," Voss said. "If they can remotely detect our electrical signals in the cognet antennas, who knows what else they're capable of."

"Hundreds of radio and TV stations all pushing out current Earth culture," Bill commented.

"Oh, dear," Page said dismally. "Whatever will they think of us?"

"Whatever they do think, they seem to be willing to continue the dialogue," Voss said hopefully. "Let's get on with it, shall we?"

The Cepheans' answers to their questions were freely given and devastating in their impact. To Voss's astonishment, the image presented to him when he resumed the cognitive link was that of his dream—the two galaxies of the Milky Way and Andromeda floating in an eternal gravitational dance through space.

"The Grand Theory is a fabrication."

That blunt statement was the response to Voss's first question.

"It is a convenient mathematical trick that predicts most of nature's behavior, but it is not a true description of the universe."

Voss reeled.

"Then you have a more fundamental theory?" he asked shakily. His astonishment was increased by the realization that he had not actually spoken his question, merely framed it in his mind.

"Why do you suppose that there is *any* truly fundamental theory?" asked the placid voice. It seemed to be produced from the galaxies in front of Voss and to reverberate around the dark spaces.

"Well." Voss fought for words. "Nature must have some underlying principles, some basic causes. It must make sense in the end. It must be possible to understand the universe by some process of reasoning."

"It has never been done."

"You—you mean that even you have not reached any true understanding of the universe?"

"I did not say that. I meant that no process of reasoning has ever predicted the properties of the entire universe. *I* understand the universe but am unable by pure reason to explain it entirely. It is possible to prove that no self-consistent explanation is possible."

For the first time Voss found himself doubting that the masterful voice he was hearing was telling the truth.

"But there must be an explanation for everything. How can anything have no cause?"

"Once you understand the theory of consciousness, you will see that the so-called real universe exists only within each conscious mind. I inhabit many universes, and each is apparently consistent within itself. Nevertheless, it is possible to prove that they cannot be so. The conscious mind unavoidably alters everything it perceives, and so inconsistencies in nature are undetected by it. Causality is a product of the mind, not of nature."

Voss struggled desperately with that terrifying idea. Calmly and confidently the alien voice sought to demolish the basis of all science. The one tenet that the mind had to cling to was that cause preceded effect. The Cepheans were sweeping that aside in one stroke. The immense inverted pyramid of mankind's knowledge teetered on its crumbling apex. How could he believe it?

"You should not be surprised," the voice announced. "Your science has come close several times. I quote Kurt Goedel: 'It is impossible to prove the non-contradictoriness of any logical mathematic system using only the means offered by the system itself.' He proved this long ago. Don't you believe it?"

Voss sought for words. "But—but that's a statement about logical mathematic systems, not the universe!"

"Exchange the word 'system' for the word 'universe' and you have a better statement of the truth than any I can produce in your language. The idea stems directly from an understanding of consciousness, which you will gain once you have studied my messages."

"But do you have a real explanation for consciousness? I suppose you must have if you can create new ones at will."

"Yes. As I have said, this is explained in my message. I can try to explain it now, but it requires careful concentration."

Did they mean they thought him incapable of understanding?

"Go ahead."

The voice paused, more for Voss's benefit, he felt, than for any need for the Cepheans to gather their thoughts.

"You have on Earth a great range of organisms, some of which are clearly conscious, others clearly not."

"Yes."

"If you consider the simplest forms of animal life, say, the protozoans, you can see that each organism is conscious only in the sense that it reacts with its surroundings."

In front of Voss a white shape like a nerve cell replaced the twin galaxies. A central lobe was surrounded by several projecting and branching processes.

"The amoeba can detect light and chemical gradients in the water and alters its behavior accordingly. This behavior stems from a model of its universe held in its single cell."

To symbolize activity, the fernlike ends of the processes lit up and their excitation traveled back toward the central lobe and then out along other processes.

"I'm not sure I follow you," Voss said.

"The amoeba's universe is comparatively simple, consisting of a small number of properties to which it reacts in simple ways. The amoeba sees only these stimuli. The real universe, to the amoeba, is a simple one. Similarly, a more complex organism, say, the earthworm, has a larger universe, one having more properties. But still, it has no perception of greater things. It cannot know of the Earth and the stars."

Several more nerve cells were added to the picture, and more complicated interactions began among them.

"All right."

"Each organism possesses a model of the universe according to its senses and uses the model to determine its behavior. If the earthworm's universe becomes too dry, it burrows down to find damper soil. But it can never know about atmospheres and rain."

Voss guessed that the image in front of him was a sort of schematic to represent the inner model hard-wired into a simple organism.

"I see. You mean there is a kind of simulation going on in the nervous system of every organism."

"That is approximately what I mean. Each organism has a different simulation, as you call it, a different model explaining the stimuli it receives. Most would completely disagree about what the universe is really like. But all must have simulations that adequately predict their own universes to provide them with a guide to the appropriate way of responding to them."

Voss suddenly began to realize what the Cepheans meant.

"Earthworms and amoebas are not self-aware creatures, of course," the voice continued in its didactic tone. "But self-awareness comes about as a result of the inner simulations becoming more sophisticated."

A great number of cells were added to the picture until it became a large mass of fantastic intricacy.

"A self-aware creature is one whose inner simulation of the universe *includes itself within it*."

Buried in the center of the white mass, a small region of red appeared as an overlaid image. It bore thousands of interconnections with its surrounding white cells.

Stunned, Voss could only stare mutely at the structure before him.

"That's beautiful," he declared quietly after a while. "I've never seen that concept before."

"It's only an approximation to the true theory, which is a formal, mathematical description of the interactions between inner models and outer universes. You will find, when you study it deeply, that it provides the only true description of any possible universe. You might call it a calculus of consciousness."

For the first time the voice laughed gently.

"I cannot use any of your own likely names for the theory because you have used them all for other, rather trivial things. Earth science has skirted the edge of this theory for centuries. Your so-called philosophers have worked away at their obscure, illogical, circular arguments for generations. They have disguised their emptiness with weird language. They fiddle with semantics."

Voss wondered whether they were speaking with unbiased disinterest or contempt.

"The theory cannot give you a description of the universe, but it will tell you how to interpret any one that you devise, like the Grand Theory."

"In order to do what you did on *Unity*, you must have had a good theory," Voss said, feeling with satisfaction that his question had reached the core of the problem.

"I did. It is a theory that produces a better description of the universe than the Grand Theory. You will discover it for yourselves one day."

So, Voss thought, they are not going to tell us.

"Are you not going to disclose it?"

"You will discover it on Gon-Di. Now that you are part of our cognitive network, all our knowledge is available to you. You do not need our help."

With that statement the Cepheans apparently made clear their intent.

"Okay, I understand. We are grateful to you."

"Did you expect me to cut you off from our network?"

"No, no. Of course not. I just wanted to say that we are very grateful."

The voice was silent.

"Can you tell us anything about the techniques you used on *Unity* and the ones you use to operate our link here on Earth?"

"The gecom produces pulses of geons that interact with nearby surrounding matter. There are monitoring stations around the galaxy that enable me to see the exact details of everything in your laboratory whenever your gecom is running. When your space laboratory was damaged, it caused the destruction of one of these monitoring stations. They are programmed to detect artificial geon sources and colocate with them. That is how the cognitive network is transmitted through the galaxy and to the Andromeda network. When the strong gravitational shock wave was produced, it did as much damage to the monitor as it did to your laboratory."

"But the Grand Theory predicts no interactions between normal matter and geons. How can it be so good at predicting everything else and not that?"

"When you combine the Grand Theory with the calculus, you will see the changes."

"I don't understand."

"In the universe in which I am communicating with you, the Grand Theory *does* predict an interaction. In yours, it does not."

"You mean you can modify the laws of physics at will?"

"I can create any universe necessary for any purpose whatsoever."

"But the Earth exists in the real universe, not one of your imaginary ones!"

"Real and imaginary universes are indistinguishable, providing all have the appearance of self-consistency. Causality is one of the things that connect physical theories with the calculus. Contrary to your current belief, it is not absolutely tied to nature itself, merely a concept of mind.''

A rather wild idea surfaced. ''Is something like that an explanation for the error I made in interpreting the Grand Theory?'' he asked.

''Yes. Your original interpretation of the Grand Theory was consistent, but things changed when the accident occurred. Large transfers of energy caused serious causality violations in both regions. The damage was a result of this. Yes, I know that you believe the damage was the result of a gravitational shock wave which you had failed to predict. That is the explanation now, and it is consistent. As I said, the conscious mind alters whatever it perceives to remove causality violations.''

That tangled and impossible logic left Voss feeling like a fly in a Klein bottle. Deciding that more probing might further endanger his hold on reality, he changed the subject. ''Okay, but you haven't explained how you actually did it.''

''The geon interactions provide a means of mapping the distribution of matter. By generating and focusing geons, I can also manipulate that matter. But in order to do this, the map has to be very accurately defined. In other words, the illumination of the surrounding matter by the geons must be maintained. For example, I now have a complete picture of your laboratory and of you, Voss, and your companions. In this way I was able to repair the damage in your space laboratory. With the gecom destroyed, I had to use the monitors to extrapolate an approximate location for the origin of the causality violations from the few geon pulses that had been produced. Those blue spheres that appeared on your videos were the focal points of geon beam probes that were attempting to localize the source. With no geon beam being produced to illuminate the laboratory, I needed to use a clamping technique to maintain a very accurate registration. Those optical effects that so puzzled you were the effects of the gravitational clamp that was needed to isolate such a large object. The effects are neutral, except at very close range, where there are some strong gravitational gradients. If you had created such problems on the Earth, I would have been powerless to help you.''

Voss was about to bring up the problem of the damage those gradients had inflicted on *Unity*, but the voice continued.

''I had a very short time to make sense of what I had found. The gecom itself was easy to understand, but the two humans were of an unfamiliar biology. There was obviously a great deal of mechanical damage to their tissues, but the biggest difficulty was that they clearly required an atmosphere of oxygen and had been denied that for several minutes. I made repairs to the tissues of Matthews, but Salwi was very badly damaged. Much of his tissues were scattered. I could not help him in time. Matthews's supply of air had been greatly diminished by venting through the broken seam of the pressure vessel, so I had to extract new supplies by molecular manipulation of other materials in the vehicle. It took many hours to find relevant information in your machines' data banks. Is Matthews recovered now?''

"Matthews is fine, but she and two others in another spacecraft will definitely die if you can't help us return the vehicle to Earth. We are powerless without your help.''

"I know that the space laboratory now has a smaller craft attached to it that must have been nearby at the time. But it seems to be undamaged.''

"The occupants had to jettison the vehicle's propulsion unit. They cannot make it back to Earth.''

"I will correct that. If the problem is urgent, it can be dealt with immediately.''

"What could you do?''

"I could make corrections to the vehicle's path. It would require very large amounts of energy to project momentum changes of such size over the galaxy, but it can be done.''

Relief flooded over Voss as if he had been holding his breath until that moment. Sheilagh! She's going to be saved!

It was dawning on Voss and all the people at Abingdon that a new era had started. The world had a new ally possessing powers beyond imagination. It was going to take a little getting used to.

Instead of having to be endured by the astronauts for another 164 days, the mission would be terminated in just 30. Two huge transfers of momentum were to be made, one as soon as the crew was ready and a second when *Unity* arrived near the Earth to put it in an orbit accessible to the TAVs.

Between those two times *Unity* would be traveling at a speed greater than any ever attained by a man-made object. With calm assurances, the Cepheans dispelled some nervous objections that should the second momentum transfer fail, the astronauts would be destined for the first interstellar voyage. The Cepheans expressed great concern for the well-being of all the astronauts.

Two seconds after the crew started the space laboratory's gecom, all communications between *Unity* and Earth blacked out for a few moments. When they returned, *Unity* was traveling at fifty kilometers per second toward Earth.

Throughout the thirty days *Unity*'s screens held a maximum-magnification image of the approaching Earth as seen through the big telescope. At first the tiny, blurred image accentuated the crew's feelings of isolation, but each day it was possible to see it grow a little as the distance decreased by another five million kilometers.

Every day the communications turnaround time decreased by about sixteen seconds, and the astronauts' involvement with Earth life increased proportionately. They felt their terrible isolation coming to an end.

Sheilagh spent hours in her cabin rerunning the sounds and images that daily poured directly into Voss's mind from across the galaxy. Never in her most fanciful imaginings had she expected such an amazing end to *Unity*'s voyage.

In her mind the Cepheans had always been real biological creatures, creatures that endured the same pains of life and death that humans did, a race that sought to share its experience of the rough, inanimate touch of the universe. To her that hard, physical interaction with the natural world was the real material of life. All her life she had not suffered anyone to argue the existence of spirits independent of the body. Each person, each mind was bound by unbreakable bonds to the intricate web of matter that made up the body. The revelation of the Cepheans' evolution into unbound, unlimited consciousnesses whose ultimate origin had been natural life, but which later became artifacts of bioelectronic circuits, and claimed to be able to inhabit synthesized universes indistinguishable from the real one, had thrown her ideas into turmoil.

Was that really the ultimate destiny of an intelligent race? Death, as the ultimate destiny of individuals, was just as certain as ever, but for the race to be taken over by its own immortal creations seemed wrong.

Sheilagh struggled with an unresolved potpourri of feelings. The human race was on the brink of ultimate discovery, the start of a new, possibly the last, epoch in its history. Starting very soon, future generations would be changing, getting farther and farther from their origins. Whatever the opinions of current generations, it was inevitable now that permanent contact with the Cepheans had been established.

Maybe she was sad at the impending end of the current ways of the world. But then, could anyone honestly regret its passing? The world still suffered from the squalid greed and stupidity that had evolved into mankind's minds over millions of years. Was not the future now a lot brighter than it had been? According to the Cepheans, the future of the human race was going to be anything that it wanted it to be—any and all possible futures coexisting.

No, it was not sadness that dampened her spirits. It was fear. Fear of the incomprehensibility of the future. Instead of finding an advanced race of intelligent beings that had successfully traveled the perilous path of evolution and arrived at a harmony of coexistence with their world, mankind had uncovered an opening in the fabric of reality into which it was forced to leap.

CHAPTER 24

UNITY HURTLED PAST THE MOON. SHEILAGH, ALONE IN the control module, started the gecom for the last time. She floated suitless near the reaction chamber.

The entire vehicle became cocooned in a scintillating bubble of light as the Cepheans prepared to slow its headlong fall to Earth.

Bill placed the dome over Voss's head and connected the antenna circuits. He placed his hand over his friend's, which rested on the arm of the chair. Then he stood and walked over to the computer console, where he powered up the gecom systems. When all was ready, he switched off the external signal feeds from the room. Voss was entirely alone. Bill started up the gecom and left.

A brilliantly colored coral reef appeared. The sunlight flickered in restless ripples over the fantastic fans and thousand-fingered hands of the coral. A tumult of iridescent life-forms flitted around him and scattered away as he swam effortlessly over the ridges and through the tunnels. He was in warm, almost intangible water, swimming. He breathed easily, as if he were in the air. He looked down at his naked body, which was perfect and strong, and he could control and sense every cell within it.

Around a corner, and there among a shoal of tiny blue fish that danced around her was Sheilagh, naked as he was, with her

hair swirling and waving. He knew she was really there, not just
an image, but she was there, sharing every moment of their
experience. As *Unity* plunged to Earth and the geons illuminated her body, they met in the Cepheans' network, their last
chance.

He swam up to her and looked into her beautiful eyes. They
touched and caressed, dancing around each other, getting closer
and closer until they seemed to merge in the sea of warm, bright
turquoise that filled their senses.

On Sunday, November 25, 2001, *Unity* abruptly appeared out
of a brief communications blackout into a circular orbit seven
hundred kilometers above the Earth.

Sheilagh's senses returned her to the familiar surroundings of
the control module. The hard edges and staring lights punctured
the beautiful waking dream that had come over her. She had
been with Russell in an impossible floating world. How had he
managed that? He must have arranged for the Cepheans to connect her into their network while they used their mysterious
techniques to slow down the ship. That meant they must have
complete knowledge of the structure of her brain. It had been
so real! All her senses taken over.

She lingered in front of the console, trying to recover the
feelings that were fading slowly into the shadow of memory.

Wong's excited voice stabbed out from the console speaker.
''Sheilagh! Hey, what're you up to in there? We're back. We're
in Earth orbit. Come on, take a look!''

Her eyes focused again, and she forced herself back to the
present, now hard, cold, and unfriendly. She stopped the gecom
and executed the shutdown procedures. The last time, she
thought. What joy that thought gave her! Soon they would be
back on Earth, out of that hateful dead world of metal and electrons. She would soon be with Russell again, only for real. She
wondered if his condition had changed in the year since they
had last seen each other. Maybe there really was some hope of
his injuries being at least partially repaired. But it did not really
matter to her what his physical state had become. People were
not bodies. They only lived in them.

She laughed aloud into the console microphone. ''Okay,
Gene, I'll be there in a couple of minutes. I'm just closing this
beast down.''

She watched the remaining command lines being echoed on
the screen as the main laser and accelerator systems were shut

down. Then she hit the main power switch. The console went dark.

That suddenly caused her to think of Salwi. Her friend and colleague was gone forever. Only in the memories of the people who knew him did his warmth and intelligence remain. That was still a kind of survival, infinitely better than the alternative of not having existed at all. She thought of the fact that his body was up in segment five, alone and forgotten. She had never seen how he had been injured. It had been very gruesome, and he must have died instantly, according to Wong and Yazdovsky's brief, reluctant descriptions. Poor Dilip.

All was quiet. She shook off the sadness that had wrapped itself around her. She turned and pushed away from the console, toward the tunnel entrance, through segment two, back toward *Unity* and her companions.

PART THREE

PART THREE

CHAPTER 25

DOREEN GREETED THE TWO VISITORS ON HER DOOR-
step with a huge smile. "Sheilagh! Russell! How wonderful."

"I hope we haven't caught you at an inconvenient time,"
Sheilagh said as she gave Doreen a hug. "We were in the area.
How are you both?"

"Oh, we're fine, thanks. I can see that you're both in fine
form. And little Stuart! How he's grown!"

Doreen reached out and took the infant from his father's arms.
A bright smile of recognition dispelled the drowsy look on his
chubby face.

"He's been asleep all the way," Sheilagh said.

"He's probably going to be hungry, then," Doreen said with
confidence, as if her own nursing days were a lot fewer than
fifty years in the past.

They went through into the Holdsworths' living room. The
patio doors were open to let in the fragrant June air.

"And how's Sir Adrian?" Voss inquired.

"The same as ever," Doreen answered brightly, returning
Stuart to his mother. "He's out in his usual spot, communing
with nature. I'll fetch him."

"No, we'll go to him, Doreen," Sheilagh said.

They made their way down the garden path, lined with fresh
colors and scented with spring fragrances. At the end of the
garden, behind an overgrown fence and overlooking the wooded
sides of a shallow dell, was a small patio. Professor Holdsworth

was sitting in the sunshine, apparently dozing. He looked up when he heard their voices and then, with a warm smile, rose stiffly and greeted his guests. He exchanged a kiss with Sheilagh and shook Russell's hand.

"How nice of you to visit. I must say it's good to see you both looking so well." He did not add, "Especially you, Russell," but it was there in his voice.

He looked at his young friend standing quite straight and steady on his thin legs. The change in Voss's condition over the last year seemed miraculous. His face had filled out and lost the shadow of pain that had disfigured it. His eyes were bright and held the animated glow of youth.

The professor motioned them to sit. "How are things at Abingdon?"

"Going much more slowly now," Voss replied as they seated themselves around the weathered wooden table. "It's been eighteen months now since the Cepheans' vocal responses ceased. We've been sort of taking stock of our discoveries, taking a closer look at them."

"There must be a heck of a lot to get through," the professor said. "In my opinion it's about time this helter-skelter scurrying after more and more cosmic confidences was tempered with a bit of restraint. What will they all do when there aren't any left?"

Voss laughed at the professor's taunt. He was glad to see that the mischievous twinkle was still sparkling in his gray eyes.

"Oh, I don't think it will ever come to that," he answered. "But there is a great deal to understand. Personally I believe the Cepheans have left us to explore the network on our own as a kind of intellectual fitness program. They realized that spoon-feeding us all the time was making us flabby. They can't have been used to dealing with primitives like us before."

The professor seemed to Sheilagh to be politely hiding skepticism about her husband's remarks.

"And what about you, Sheilagh?" the professor inquired. "Still enjoying motherhood?"

"Oh, yes, indeed." She turned Stuart around so that he could grasp the table edge and achieve his obvious goal of taking part in the conversation. "After all the excitement of the last few years, it's good to settle down to a more natural way of life."

"That's quite right," Doreen agreed. "All this network stuff leaves me cold. What's it got to do with plain, ordinary everyday living, that's what I'd like to know. We're all still flesh and blood and need feeding and washing and loving. Those are the experiences that make up real life, not all those unnatural fantasies piped into people's brains.''

"I don't think many people would disagree with you," Voss said. "We're a long way yet from reaching the Cepheans' level. Maybe Stuart's generation will be faced with the decision whether to go along the same path or not, but the end of that path is a hundred years or more away. We have got a great many very basic problems to solve before we can contemplate controlling our own evolution.''

"But there's already been so much progress as a result of the Cepheans," the professor said. "Our new skills in neural technology have made possible some quite miraculous medical feats.''

The professor spoke in a tone that slightly puzzled Sheilagh. It was almost as if he were being polite about the Cepheans for Voss's sake. Their knowledge had, after all, helped in the repair of his injuries and given him a normal life again.

"We can counteract some of the problems of evolution as well," Voss said. "Many of the solutions to serious genetic disorders, like sickle cell, are now within our sights.''

"That's what knowledge is ultimately for," the professor said. "The correction of nature's errors, not its vanquishment. And the prevention of our own errors, of course.''

"Well, maybe we can hope to achieve that level at least," Voss said. "There's a good chance, I would say. The network is turning into a sort of ultimate testing ground for ideas. We can simulate the results of any new theory or concept just by accurately depicting the right conditions in the cognet antennas. That's how we've been making progress since the Cepheans left us alone. The bioengineers have made some fantastic strides. That's where the greatest excitement is. With what we've learned so far, with basic particle physics pretty much sewn up, we can concentrate more resources on the purely Earth-related studies, particularly bioengineering and consciousness studies. There's no need for the big, expensive particle accelerators anymore. Even observational astronomy doesn't need its big telescopes now that the Cepheans' views of the universe are there to be explored.''

"You think we humans will begin to understand ourselves a bit better from now on, then?" Doreen asked.

"No question," Voss said. "We've been neglecting the study of man ever since the scientific revolution started. Now that we've found the answers to the so-called big questions about the universe and so on, we can finally get round to the really difficult ones about what it is to be human and alive.''

He took hold of Stuart as Sheilagh passed him over. Sheilagh stood up and went over to the wooden rail that marked the very edge of the patio. She looked out over the trees for a few seconds, then turned around and leaned against the rail. She was on the verge of saying that she hoped no answers were found but decided not to bother. She did not know for sure what such questions might be. Anyway, wasn't being human and alive enough of an answer?

Voss stood Stuart on the table and felt him bouncing himself up and down, pushing his feet against the rough wood. His son's discovery of having limbs that could be used in all sorts of exciting ways had coincided with his own recovery. As his muscles had gradually responded to the new nerve impulses arriving via the artificial spinal bridge in his back, his accustomed detachment from the physical world had slowly dissolved. He no longer bothered so much with the Cepheans' network. Simulated experience, no matter how wonderful or strange, could not compare with the exhilaration of real material living.

''What's on your agenda at the moment, Professor?'' Sheilagh asked, returning to her seat. ''Are you going to accept Russell's invitation and speak to the conference next month?''

She was referring to the First World Conference on Cephean Science to be held in Anaheim, California, the next month. Russell Voss was one of the organizers and had invited the professor to address the conference at its opening session. The reply had been noncommittal.

''Well, it's funny you should ask that.''

The others looked at his aged face.

''Knowing that you might peg out at any moment alters your outlook on life, you know.''

''Oh, nonsense, Professor, you've got years in you yet,'' Sheilagh said reproachfully.

''Maybe. Maybe not. That's the point, really.''

''You mean you're going to start spending more time down at the pub,'' Doreen said.

He shared the laughter, but then his face adopted a more serious expression. ''You know, I'm a bit disturbed by the way things have turned out. I think I will accept your kind offer to let me speak to the conference, Russell. There are many things that need to be said.''

"So," Doreen said with a playfully reproachful look, "you've got some scheme to personally alter the course of history, I suppose."

"Well, he's done it before," Sheilagh said.

Sheilagh, her legs stretched out in front of her and her fingers interlocked across her stomach, fixed her eyes firmly on the professor.

"This urge to look inward at oneself—that's not a natural way to be." The lines on the professor's brow deepened. "Yes, I admit there are many things we have to correct here on Earth. There's no denying that we've got to learn to make a better job of organizing and restricting our activities on a crowded planet. But there's still a whole universe out there waiting to be discovered. Because the Cepheans can conjure up any experience they want, they've lost interest in exploration. They have even lost the means to do it."

Sheilagh found that his words expressed her unspoken views perfectly. "There's no adventure," she said.

The professor brought his right hand down gently on the arm of his seat. "Exactly!" he said. "They have never physically left their own solar system after millions of years of civilization."

The professor's words stirred up a conflict in Voss's mind that he had struggled with over the last year as his body had returned to his control. The purely intellectual adventures that he had striven for and achieved during his adult life had seemed the ultimate goal of existence. Why should the mind restrict itself to the confines of the physical world with all its dangers and limitations? There were vast universes of logic and mathematics to probe that were infinitely more beautiful and rewarding to the explorer than anything the physical body could enter. But with his returning motor functions, Voss had felt a rekindling of the urge for physical adventure that he had smothered in his youth. It was the same feeling that made people risk their lives climbing mountains and racing cars and flying to Mars. It was the paradoxical notion that life felt more worthwhile the more it was risked. How true it was that the body was the ruler of the mind.

"It seems to me," the professor continued, "that we are on the verge of making a very big mistake. If we continue with this obsession with the cognitive network, we'll end up just like they are. There's already been talk of abandoning the Mars program soon. The plain fact is that the Cepheans, despite their apparently limitless mental abilities, have become static, nonevolving. That's why they *are* so old. They've lasted for millions of years in exactly the same state. Just like the shark, they long ago reached the end of their evolutionary road. There were no more pressures on them to change.''

''There has to be an end to evolution, surely?'' Voss said. ''We must eventually come to some stable condition that needn't and couldn't change.''

''We certainly will be going down that route,'' the professor said.

''And the Cepheans did construct that beacon,'' Voss said.

''Ah, yes,'' the professor said, leaning forward and looking from Sheilagh to Voss and back. ''But *why*?''

So, Sheilagh thought, that's what he's been up to. As she looked at her old professor, his long white hair moving in the gentle wind and reflecting brightly the yellow rays of the evening sun, she was suddenly overcome by intense emotion. She knew that she loved the old man in a way that she could not possibly love any other person in the world, even Russell or her son. She was certain that it was in some way reciprocated. She also knew that no direct expression of that mutual feeling would ever pass between them; it would just exist as a wordless bond joining their lives.

But the main force of her emotion was a heart-crushing sadness that soon he would be gone. Even though his life would soon leave him, he was still working on projects that would come to fruition decades after his death and whose fruits would very likely change the course of human history in ways he could never know.

The main auditorium at the newly rebuilt Anaheim Convention Center was filled to overflowing. Apart from the thousands of researchers active in the new sciences opened up by the Cepheans, there were representatives from many governments, thousands of engineers and managers from companies eager to utilize the new technologies, and hundreds of people from the media.

Russell Voss made the welcoming speech and declared the conference open.

''Before we begin, ladies and gentlemen, it is my pleasure to reintroduce you to Sir Adrian Holdsworth, who is going to speak to us this morning. It was his discovery of the lighthouse beacon that started the amazing series of events that has led us to where we are today: at the beginning of a new era in the history of the

Earth. Some of the things he is going to say today will surprise you and will, I think, disturb you. I believe we should all heed his warning.''

Voss turned to the professor, who stood and walked slowly to the podium. The hall was silent for several seconds, then applause broke out and quickly built to a crescendo. The professor waited, motionless. As he waited, he saw the thousands of faces staring and smiling in his direction, and the significance of the next few minutes bore down on him. For the first time in his long life he had the desire to change the direction in which the world was traveling. Here, now, with most of the world's leading minds gathered before him, ready to listen to his words, he had his one chance and his one remaining duty to fulfill. A movement must be started, there, among those people, before the momentum of Cephean science grew too large to be deflected.

When all was quiet, the professor began his speech. He spoke quietly into the microphone, his voice calm but displaying just a hint of the feebleness of age.

''Ladies and gentlemen. Just over a month ago my dear friend Dr. Voss asked me if I wanted to speak at this, the opening of the First World Conference on Cephean Science.'' He grinned. ''My immediate reaction was, 'You must be kidding,' based solely upon the terrifying thought of standing up before thousands of the brightest people in the world and being required to say something sensible.''

As he had hoped, there was a loud, amused reaction.

''After a few moments' thought, I was still tempted to decline his offer. I felt there was little left to be said, and nothing to be said by me, now that our voyage into the new era has begun.

''But after several days of indecision I eventually made up my mind. There *is* something to be said. Something of the utmost importance. And nobody else seems to be saying it.''

The hall was utterly silent.

''Ten years ago we won a famous victory. Its significance at the time was not widely appreciated, but when Sheilagh Matthews discovered that faint alien signal in the constellation Cepheus, we destroyed forever the last vestiges of the crumbling edifice of dogma that had stifled enlightenment and advancement for nearly two millennia. The Earth had been dragged from its throne at the center of the universe by Galileo. Now, the human race was removed from the center of its own universe by our discovery that elsewhere in the galaxy intelligent minds had evolved. No longer were we the unique, privileged creations of a supernatural being who had made us alone to appreciate his works.

"Very soon afterward we won a second victory. One equally great but, sadly, perhaps not so final. It was a victory over evil, a victory over selfishness and greed, over the individual's desire for power over others. If Russell Voss had failed, in those precious few seconds, to transmit to others the alien messages that had just yielded up their secrets, then we would know nothing of the Cephean science today. The small group of people who we were foolish enough to allow to govern us would still be in place, and their cynicism and contempt would have been perpetuated. Enlightenment and advancement would once more have been the price.

"But, my dear friends, there is a third victory that we must gain. It is the most important of all, and the most difficult, for most of us don't even see the danger. The price of losing this time will be the highest price it is possible for us to pay: extinction."

He waited for the murmurings that had sprung up to die down.

"It is my opinion that we are walking willingly into an evolutionary trap with our eyes closed. We are being stalked by a very cunning and stealthy predator and are in grave danger of becoming his next prey. The Cepheans are that predator. And the cognitive network is the trap."

That did not go down very well. There was a general commotion throughout the auditorium and a single cry of "Rubbish!" from near the front. Most, however, seemed to want to hear more. A few heads were nodding.

The professor grinned. He poured some water from the jug in front of him into a glass. "Sounds a bit far-fetched, doesn't it? Well, let me try to explain what I mean.

"What do we know of the Cepheans? We know only what they have told us, of course. They are the end products of twenty-one evolutionary processes that have all reached the same stage of bioengineered artificiality. Now we come along, and they tell us we're different. We're unusual." He looked around, imploring his audience to understand.

"Well, I don't believe it! As far as we know, we may be more typical of life in the galaxy than they are! What we discovered when Sheilagh picked up that beacon signal was just one kind of alien life. We didn't find a rich community of different civilizations that had each developed in their own way, we found a terribly clever but totally stagnant and uniform machine that has nowhere to go.''

There were a few more cries of derision, countered by several calls for silence and many heads nodding in agreement. The professor was relieved to find he had some followers. Perhaps Sheilagh and Russell had been working on his behalf in the last few weeks.

"Let us ask ourselves why the Cepheans constructed that transmitter. The transmitter is not, it seems clear to me, a relic from the Arreans' past, from before they formed the cognitive links to the whole network. Why should they bother seeking other civilizations if they have everything they could ever want inside their own artificial experiences? Why try to communicate with other civilizations?''

Again he looked appealingly at his audience, willing them to see for themselves what he feared.

"Because they are the product of a different kind of evolution,'' he prompted.

Someone in the front row gasped, "My God, he's right!''

The professor continued, more encouraged than he had expected to feel at that point.

"They are the end product of competition between artificial minds. If a cognitive network did develop as the Cepheans described, with its multitude of inhabitants, then it would almost certainly become a place of intense competition—just like a biological system. Such a system would have to have a limited capacity, a maximum to the number of entities it could accommodate. Just like any Earth environment has a limit to what it can support. That number might be very large, but it is obviously finite, and however big it is, the system would quickly fill up to capacity.''

He spelled out his fear slowly.

"So there would be competition for space. And as a result, only the dominant, most aggressive entities that were good at displacing the others would survive.''

The idea was catching on. The dissenters were silent.

"What kind of entity would dominate the others and survive? One that had a strong urge to oust any weaker ones from the network. And then what would happen when two independently evolved networks, with their separate bioelectronic circuits, came into contact? One of the races would completely take over the other, like a sort of cultural conquest, only on a grand scale. The urge to seek out and take over other networks would be part of their makeup, just like it is part of ours to compete for scarce resources in order to secure the continuance of our genes. Another inevitable evolutionary trait would be to encourage the development of other networks elsewhere so that they could be taken over at a later date.''

The professor grimly stepped through the logic that had become a conviction over the previous months.

''Not only does it fulfill their urge to create more of themselves by increasing the capacity of the network, it also ensures the spread and continuance of the dominant network in the event of localized natural catastrophes such as supernovas. If they really are millions of years old, then they would have seen lots of those. There may well have been other networks around the galaxy that didn't possess the urge to spread. They would have been at the mercy of natural destructive forces and probably died out. In any event they couldn't become the dominant ones.

''So, ladies and gentlemen, if you've followed me so far, you will perhaps share my view that we're being prepared for consumption. And the Cepheans are not the free, combined minds of twenty-one highly developed races, but are simply one selfish, usurping, destructive, artificial organism.''

The professor pronounced the final sentence with a force that left the hall chill with foreboding. After a short pause he continued in a lighter voice.

''Contacting developing, as opposed to developed, races and steering them in the right direction for conquest is easier and cheaper than actually going out into space and building your own network nodes around the galaxy. And it ensures a successful result. Rather like domesticating your own pigs instead of hunting wild boar that might bite back. This explains why the strength of their radio signals is so carefully chosen. Any stronger and they would be detected and deciphered by underdeveloped civilizations that are not ready for the knowledge and would be destroyed by it; any weaker and the recipients would be too sophisticated to be fooled.

''The conclusion, then, is that we can't be certain of anything the Cepheans have told us. They could have been feeding us lies, plausible lies, of course, embedded in large amounts of truth, but intended solely to speed our development of a cognitive network.

''Many of you might say, 'So what?' You may feel that we are so far from achieving our own cognitive network that such fears are premature. I think this conference will prove you wrong. In one generation I believe we will have a global cognitive network, and we will have genetically engineered humans born with the necessary interfaces to live with it and in it. Soon after that all humans on the planet will be the same. With all the physical and material problems of life resolved by the new science, there will be no barriers to this development. Then there will be just one step left to take: the final step of evolution, the end of our normal biological existence as individuals.

"All of this is inevitable, I believe, if we continue blindly toward total dependence on the Cepheans' network. It is inevitable that we will grow closer and closer to them in form, eventually to be absorbed into the conglomeration of the galactic network that we would have helped to extend."

He stopped and took a sip of water from the glass in front of him.

"How are we to stop this? How can we relieve our dependence? Well, there is a way, perhaps. If we open our eyes to the danger, now, at the very start of this process, then we have a chance.

"I think we should begin the next stage of SETI. The time is ripe. We've got the knowledge and the resources now. We've even got the organizational experience.

"I want today to resurrect an old idea. An idea that exemplifies the questing and questioning urges that are the essence of the human soul. I want us all here to encourage our governments to undertake a new joint project. We should start now the process of building a radio telescope on the lunar far side, away from the radio noise of Earth. It's an old idea whose time has come. I have spoken to Konstantin Lebovsky, the head of the Mars Commission, about this idea and he is very enthusiastic. The Marscom engineering centers are running out of work now that the Mars first stage is developed. This would be the ideal continuation."

Something in his voice told his audience that there was more to come.

"It would, of course," the professor continued, "be a symbol for the world to look upon that might stimulate the spirit of adventure and exploration in their minds. And to that same end I want to suggest another project that would certainly stretch the imaginations of future generations."

Everyone waited patiently for him to continue.

"We have the beginnings of a technology, started so catastrophically in the space laboratory, that can produce gravitational waves. We could, given a few more years of research, turn that into a very powerful drive for a spacecraft. Russell Voss knows this, and so do many others of you here. It has received little attention because of the current preoccupation with the Cepheans' network. No one sees the need for spacecraft drives anymore. Well, it is now within our power to construct a robot probe that could reach Alpha Centauri in just a few years of flight. And with gecom communications, once it gets there, we could explore a new solar system in real time: directly interact with what we find. If we start now, we could be remotely controlling a robot probe on the surface of another Earthlike planet within twenty years.

"You people gathered here are the only people on Earth who can make that possible. I humbly suggest that you have a duty to future generations to make the attempt."

EPILOGUE

A SLIGHT JOLT TOLD PAREKH SHE WAS ON THE
lander's systems and free to start the descent. The blue planet
appeared above her, laced with clouds, while the smooth surface
of *Namu* shone eerily in the reflected sunlight.

She fell smoothly away from the mother ship and decelerated
strongly to slow her orbital speed. In minutes the tenuous atmosphere was scorching her protective skins, and she could see
little of the scene through the bright orange glow. The buffeting
of the variable air tested her balancing skills, but she confidently
maintained total control. Superimposed upon the opaque sheets
of flame blocking her vision, a dark, curved line crossed by four
straight ones that emanated radially from a point directly in front
of her depicted the planet's horizon as she plummeted toward it.

Minutes later the flames dissipated, and she was airborne in
a smooth, clear stratosphere. From that height it was impossible
to see the surface, except directly ahead, where the sunlight
reflected patchily from the ocean. Gingerly, she increased the
angle of attack of her wings to slow her airspeed as the descent
continued. The static pressure on her sides increased as she
plumbed deeper into the ocean of air.

At ten thousand meters she opened her abdominal intake, and
the hard air rammed into her engines. Again she raised her nose
to bring her speed down, at the same time gently thrusting her
engines to maintain altitude. Soon the onrushing air had slowed
to subsonic speed.

On the image of the clouds stretching before her, but without hiding them, a solid picture of the Corvus mountain range appeared 100 kilometers ahead on the edge of Caledonia. She was planning to overfly them by 1,000 meters and descend rapidly to the Jian-Ching river that twisted through the dark forests beyond.

With unconscious ease she recreated the topography of the landscape before her from the immense volume of map data stored in *Namu*'s cells. The clouds that obstructed her view were a nuisance but nothing more.

She entered the moist, gray stratus. As she crossed the coastline and the rocky slopes raced up toward her through gaps in the clouds, she felt the gentle bubbling of the moist air pushed reluctantly out of its sluggish depths. Then, as she crossed the sharp ridges, powerful gusts tugged at her body. With a natural ease she flexed her wings to meet the air's playful buffeting.

For a few seconds, as she flashed in and out of the cloud base, disjointed images of the dark forest flickered in her vision. Then, suddenly, she was clear of the clouds and gliding in the cool, still air.

As she crossed the river at two thousand meters, she banked gracefully to the right and turned into a long glide along its silvery length. Brighter patches of yellow unevenly bordered the water, standing out strongly from the violets and purples of the forest. Infrared vision told her they were marshes and would not provide a suitable landing place. But she already knew where she was going to land, and when she reached a thousand meters she could see the place—a long narrow curve of red rock on the inside of a gentle curve in the river. There were about ten variously sized flat rock shelves that provided perfect touchdown spots.

A movement below her caught her eye. One of the larger animals they had seen from *Namu* had leapt into the water after food.

She fixed her attention on her landing place. One prominent table of rock that had been identified from orbit looked flat and clear of debris. It would do perfectly.

She slowed her flight by raising her nose and curving her wings downward. Flaps extended from her trailing edges, and she angled the rush of air from her engines down toward the ground. Her legs extended down behind her and opened out to provide more drag and lift. As she approached the shelf from over the water, she dipped down below its level slightly and then rose up into a perfect stall, legs extended forward. The air sucked strongly at her upper skin, and with one strong beat of her wings she landed softly on two feet.

As she settled into the payload-deployment stance, her engines spooled down quietly until only the natural sounds of the planet could be heard. The rock was warm and rough, and a soft rush of falling water echoed from the cliffs.

Her main task was completed, and it had been great fun. All that remained was to connect the automatic sensors that would monitor atmospheric conditions at the landing site; then she could take a rest.

"A great job, Parekh!" Stuart Voss called through the local channel. "A most exhilarating ride."

Parekh removed her arms and legs from the flexible sleeves of the cognet terminal and reached up to remove the head enclosure. The soft rings of the primary interface tickled as they disconnected themselves from the nerves beneath her bald, brown scalp. She unplugged the dense bundle of fibers from their connector in her suit and swung herself upright in the body-temperature water. With a push on the flat sides of the tank she was up onto the side. The technician waited with a large white robe as she unzipped and climbed out of the suit.

In the next chamber Stuart Voss concentrated on establishing the familiar test patterns before making the final connection to *Namu*.

Four light-years away, Earth's first interstellar probe orbited the only terrestrial-type planet to have been discovered at Alpha Centauri B. That K5-class sun orbited its slightly larger companion every eighty years. Both stars possessed planetary systems, but only one blue jewel had a sufficiently stable orbit in the close binary system to sustain long-term evolution. It more than made up for the lack elsewhere.

Stuart activated the cognet link and took stock of the infrared scene inside the lander's cramped external pod. All he could see, as expected, was the inside of the door.

He held on to the bars above his hands as the clamps holding his body retracted. The pod's door slid away and revealed the crystalline rock glinting in the light from the two suns. He put forward his right leg and let go of the bars. As the mission plan dictated, he knelt down and rested his hands on the surface. Any malfunction of the remote link or of his motor or balance systems could mean a damaging fall.

All was well. He switched out the infrared for the optical

channel, raised his head, and stood up. There was a gentle breeze on his mouthless face, and the conical purple treetops swayed. He turned and started to unload the containers of equipment from the racks in the pod.

When it was all neatly stacked on the surface, he decided, at the mission commander's recommendation, spoken through the local channel, to explore the surroundings a little. He walked away from the lander, standing tall and erect with its wings folded. Climbing up a shallow rocky bank, he came across the first plant, a clump of fine violet fibers that vibrated stiffly in the breeze.

After examining the plant, being careful not to touch it, he stood up on the highest part of the outcrop and looked around at the scene. Despite the strange coloring and the unrecognizable plant shapes, it was powerfully reminiscent of Earth. Of course, he had to remember that the gravity was nearly twice and the air pressure over four times that of Earth. The interface was compensating for those differences. But even so, it was a planet that any human being could understand, could appreciate. From orbit there had been plenty of signs of animal life on the surface but clearly no evidence of large-scale civilization. There were no telltale signs of artificial structures or of major alterations to the flora. But that did not mean it was uninhabited.

After the historic first panoramic survey had adequately documented man's first true experience of an alien planet, Stuart jumped down from the crag and walked back to the lander. He was careful to avoid the small, colorful plants that grew out of the cracks in the rock, fully aware that hundreds of excited and occasionally cantankerous exobiologists were watching through his eyes and impatiently waiting for their first remote samples. There was a lot of work ahead of him.

The first step was to open the other pod and activate the smaller locum that was specially equipped for biological surveys. As he walked around the lander's angled legs, an unusual movement at the edge of the forest caught his eye. Something had moved with a separate motion in front of the trees. He strained his vision to the limit but could not see anything. The mission commander suggested switching back to infrared.

The trees darkened and the rocks brightened as the infrared channel replaced the optical one once more. Standing rock-steady in front of the trees was a slim creature with a conical body and a round, snakelike head pointed at the sky. No limbs were visible.

Stuart switched back to optical, keeping his attention on the creature. He could see it now. Its skin was dark and shiny and reflected the tree trunks around him in a perfect camouflage. The two oval orange eyes on either side of the head had tiny white slit pupils that stared at him. Stuart suddenly realized that there was a third, central eye that was also staring unblinkingly back at him. He concentrated on remaining motionless, directed by the mission plans that had optimistically anticipated such encounters.

With an unconcerned air, the creature turned around and moved off with a slow, graceful flowing motion into the trees.

ABOUT THE AUTHOR

Ken Appleby was born in Dudley, England, in 1953. He received a bachelor's degree in physics in 1975 and started a Ph.D. course in cosmic-ray physics before quitting to start work as a software engineer in the aerospace industry. Relocating to California in 1980, he worked in software technical management until he became a freelance consultant in 1985. Since 1987 he has been living in Cambridge, England, where he runs a one-man company developing software products in the artificial intelligence field. His hobbies include classical and folk guitar and mountain climbing. He also computes his own orbits. *The Voice of Cepheus* is his first novel.